HOLOCAUST THEATER

Facts about the Holocaust are one way of learning about its devastating impact, but presenting personal manifestations of trauma can be more effective than citing statistics.

Holocaust Theater addresses a selection of contemporary plays about the Holocaust, examining how collective and individual trauma is represented in dramatic texts and considering the ways in which spectators might be swayed viscerally, intellectually, and emotionally by witnessing such representations onstage. Drawing on interviews with a number of the playwrights alongside psychoanalytic studies of survivor trauma, this volume seeks to foster understanding of the traumatic effects of the Holocaust on subsequent generations.

Holocaust Theater offers a vital account of theater's capacity to represent the effects of Holocaust trauma.

Gene A. Plunka is a professor in the English Department at the University of Memphis.

HOLOCAUST THEATER

Dramatizing Survivor Trauma
and Its Effects on the Second
Generation

Gene A. Plunka

Routledge
Taylor & Francis Group

LONDON AND NEW YORK

First published 2018
by Routledge
2 Park Square, Milton Park, Abingdon, Oxon, OX14 4RN

and by Routledge
711 Third Avenue, New York, NY 10017

Routledge is an imprint of the Taylor & Francis Group, an informa business

© 2018 Gene A. Plunka

British Library Cataloguing-in-Publication Data
A catalogue record for this book is available from the British Library

Library of Congress Cataloging-in-Publication Data
Names: Plunka, Gene A., 1949– author.
Title: Holocaust theater : dramatizing survivor trauma and its effects on the
    second generation / Gene A. Plunka.
Description: New York : Routledge, 2018. | Includes bibliographical
    references.
Identifiers: LCCN 2017036620 | ISBN 9781138685062 (hardback) |
    ISBN 9781138896246 (pbk) | ISBN 9781315103778 (ebook)
Subjects: LCSH: Holocaust, Jewish (1939-1945), in literature. |
    Drama—21st century—History and criticism. | Theater—History—
    21st century. | Holocaust survivors. | Children of Holocaust survivors. |
    Collective memory. | Memory in literature.
Classification: LCC PN1650.H64 P575 2018 | DDC 809.2/9358405318—dc23
LC record available at https://lccn.loc.gov/2017036620

ISBN: 9781138685062 (hbk)
ISBN: 9781138896246 (pbk)
ISBN: 9781315103778 (ebk)

Typeset in ApexBembo
by Apex CoVantage, LLC

MIX
Paper from
responsible sources
FSC
www.fsc.org
FSC™ C013985

Printed in the United Kingdom
by Henry Ling Limited

CONTENTS

ACKNOWLEDGMENTS

A 2016 University of Memphis Faculty Research Grant allowed me to finish writing the last two chapters of the manuscript.

I would like to thank these playwrights who kindly agreed to do interviews with me: Richard Atkins, Robert Caisley, Wendy Graf, Donald Margulies, Ari Roth, Diane Samuels, Marsha Lee Sheiness, Faye Sholiton, and Ronald John Vierling. Their contributions to this book were immensely valuable to my research.

I am grateful to Arnold Mittelman, president of the National Jewish Theater Foundation, for permission to cite from these plays photocopied from the Holocaust Theater Archive: Enzo Cormann's *The Never-ending Storm*, Wendy Graf's *Leipzig*, and Marsha Lee Sheiness's *Second Hand Smoke*. I also want to acknowledge the assistance from Dr. Joel Berkowitz, professor of Foreign Languages and Literature at the University of Wisconsin at Milwaukee, who provided information about Yiddish playwright Morris Freed.

I very much appreciate the diligent work of Ben Piggott, acquisitions editor in Theatre, Performance, and Dance Studies at Routledge, for moving the manuscript forward in the very early stages of review. I also want to thank Kate Edwards, editorial assistant at Routledge, for helping to prepare the contract and the production of the book.

Finally, I want to express my gratitude to Dr. Jackson R. Bryer, Dr. Stephen Tabachnick, Dr. Brad McAdon, Mark Lapidus, and Stanley Plunka and his wife, Rhona, for their encouragement and support. By inquiring about the status of my research, my friends, relatives, and colleagues made the book much easier for me to complete.

1

INTRODUCTION

When the Nazi plan for genocide went awry because of the end of World War II and the concomitant destruction of the Reich, the Germans inadvertently created the most fascinating experiment in history. Survivors of the Holocaust provide the answer to the question of what occurs when humans lose their humanity and when their culture has been removed from them. The Holocaust was perhaps the only period in history that allows us to determine the psychological effects of extreme trauma on human beings in a manner that no civilized experiment on mankind could ever duplicate. This book focuses on the psychopathology of survivors and the psychology of second-generation offspring of survivors as manifested to the public through dramatic literature.

The Nazis persecuted perceived threats to the Reich, including Jews, homosexuals, Gypsies (Sinti and Roma), Jehovah's Witnesses, criminals, political dissenters, pacifists, and people with mental health problems. Because the genocide against the Jews as *Untermenschen* (subhumans) was meant to eradicate them from European society, in contrast to some of the other asocials who were incarcerated by the Nazis to punish rather than annihilate them, the majority of this study focuses on the psychopathology of Jewish survivors.

Holocaust survivorship comes in myriad forms. Many survivors suffered trauma as a result of hiding from the Nazis; some were sheltered by Righteous Gentiles or by the clergy, while others fled in fear for the safety of the forests.[1]

Hiding itself was psychologically damaging since discovery often meant certain death, and thus living in daily fear over a prolonged period of time undoubtedly took its toll on the psyche. Many Jews were escapees wondering if the anti-Semitic local population would turn them in to the German authorities; fugitives were often living in cellars, barns, or attics and had to rely on the charity of others. They were typically separated from their families, had no access to medical care, suffered from unhygienic living conditions, and were constantly hungry, cold, and paranoid. Jews and various other "enemies of the Volk" were enlisted as slave laborers in 1,600 labor camps or ghettoes, 1,202 satellite camps (*Aussenlager*), and 52 concentration camps.[2] This horrendous level of daily starvation and deprivation, replete with constant beatings among the incarcerated prisoners for no apparent reason, produced its own type of mental illness among survivors. Moreover, the abysmal conditions in the Eastern European ghettoes that were to sequester Jews before their deportations led to ubiquitous anomie and apathy. Faced with daily poverty, degradation, starvation, overcrowding, German brutality, and even deaths of fellow family members due to deterioration of health, Jews were already becoming mentally unstable before they were to realize their eventual fate in Germany or Poland. Finally, those few who survived the Polish extermination camps (Treblinka, Belzec, Auschwitz-Birkenau, Sobibór, Majdanek, and Chelmno) suffered the most acute form of trauma recognizable in civilization.

Jews were persecuted in Germany even before the advent of the Holocaust and thus suffered a great deal of psychological damage prior to being sent to concentration camps or deported to their deaths-in-life in Polish extermination camps. Historians might argue that the start of the genocide was as early as Kristallnacht on 9 November 1938; others may insist that the bulk of the killings began with the June 1941 invasion of Russia but certainly was accelerated after Reinhard Heydrich solidified his plans for mass murder at the Wannsee Conference, held on 20 January 1942. Yet, in Germany, the persecution began when the Nazis gained governmental control in 1933. The propaganda machine, initiated by Josef Goebbels, characterized the Jew as a form of bacillus or parasite that infected the Nazi plans for an idealized racial state. Jews were excluded as participating citizens in Nazi society. Jewish businesses were boycotted, and many Jews lost their jobs as professionals working in Germany as physicians, lawyers, professors, or teachers. Anti-Semitic violence led to assaults on Jews and vandalism against Jewish property. Jews were banned from public education, libraries, cultural institutions, parks, and beaches. With regard to the outlawing of Jews in the early years of the Reich, German psychoanalyst Ulrich Venzlaff wrote, "Thus, a lot of people – especially older people of social position and discrimination – were literally broken down as a result of this prolonged rejection: to be marked as a leper overnight, to be torn from all social ties, to be expelled from vocational positions and to be victim to the lowest instincts of the rabble."[3] Years of such persecution before the Holocaust actually began only exacerbated the trauma they were about to experience in the death camps.

Although the sequelae of Holocaust survivors have been well documented, it would be remiss of any research scholar to pursue a full-length study of the psychopathology of survivorship without reviewing the causes of such traumata. Jews who were in hiding or had been in labor camps certainly are included as victims of the Nazi attempts at genocide, but typically the psychopathology of the Holocaust has been most prevalently studied in survivors of concentration and extermination camps. Furthermore, the effects of the psychological trauma as represented onstage have almost always, but not exclusively, been demonstrated via the personae of concentration camp survivors. Thus, it would be useful to reiterate what most of the victims encountered as they entered *l'univers concentrationnaire*.

After spending months or even years in ghettoes, Eastern European Jews, facing squalid conditions and starvation, accepted deportation orders with the promise of better living conditions in an unspecified labor camp. Western European Jews were confined to crowded, unsanitary detention centers as disembarkation points before boarding the trains to the East. Jews were then crammed like sardines into freight trains without access to food, water, or sanitation facilities and with little air to breathe. The journey often lasted for days of misery, punctuated by cries, screams, and shrieks of those suffering onboard; children were crying constantly, parents bemoaned their loss of power over their offspring, and many of the elderly died en route, precipitating the first disintegration of the extended family. In short, many who made it to the gates of the concentration camps were in a panic before the real trauma began. Transporting humans as cattle was the first step in transforming souls into commodities.

Upon arrival on the ramp of the extermination camp, families were torn apart, and those who were unable to work (children and the elderly) were gassed, then incinerated in the crematoria. This initial temporary feeling of alienation and isolation upon separation was exacerbated into full-blown depression when family members later learned that their parents, grandparents, children, or siblings were gone forever. All prisoners were soon bereft of their personal possessions, including their clothing and any money or jewelry that they carried with them. *Häftlinge* (inmates) were greeted by Kapos shouting orders, vicious dogs barking, the smell of burning corpses, and an environment that seemed completely alien to civilization – all resulting in deportees being confused and dazed, wondering if they were dreaming or perhaps going insane. Leo Eitinger describes the scene on the arrival ramp: "The SS men drove everyone out of the cattle cars, bellowing and beating the new prisoners blindly and indiscriminately. Their mission was to create a panic situation."[4] The inmates' heads, armpits, and pubic areas were shaved in public view; they were given showers in extreme temperatures; they were provided with ill-fitting, tattered tunics, and uncomfortable wooden clogs to wear; and their names had disappeared since they were now referred to only as the tattooed numbers on their arms. Individuality disappeared in the camps since inmates were bereft of all personal identity, as well as social identities, having lost their businesses, fortunes, homes, property, and jobs.

The daily life of the *Häftlinge* was filled with pain and suffering. Lawrence L. Langer notes, "The Nazi purpose was to obliterate the victim, not merely punish or defeat him: to nullify his spirit, grind up his bones, disperse his ashes, until he literally vanished from the face of the earth."[5] Prisoners were forced to sleep in overcrowded beds that were slats of wood covered with straw.[6] Sanitary facilities were limited-access open latrines with no toilet paper. Work details consisted of slave labor designed to demoralize the inmates physically while wearing down their souls; workplace accidents frequently resulted in injuries. Prisoners labored twelve to eighteen hours daily, soaked in their own urine and excrement while wearing thin tunics that did not protect them from harsh or freezing weather conditions. Roll calls were conducted twice daily and were usually dreaded because prisoners had to stand for hours in inclement weather and were at the whim of sadistic guards. When a roll call resulted in a discrepancy in the numbers, the whole procedure had to be repeated until an accurate count of prisoners could be verified. Rations consisted of a chicory liquid that substituted for coffee, a watery gruel the SS referred to as soup, and bread, sometimes topped with margarine. Since the intake of approximately 1,200 calories per day was insufficient, prisoners suffered from malnutrition, and hunger tormented them constantly, transforming humans into vicious beasts in their attempts to steal food from their colleagues. Lack of food, vitamin deficiencies, and unsanitary conditions, including tainted water, caused diseases,[7] the most common of which included diphtheria, scarlet fever, dysentery, pneumonia, edema, diarrhea, as well as tuberculosis and other respiratory ailments; typhus, carried by the lice in the blockhouses and on the prisoners themselves, was also widespread.[8] Extreme food deprivation increased fatigue, reduced brain capacities (memory), and kindled irritability. Thirst was also a major problem that could drive most inmates nearly insane to the point where they could barely think coherently. Charlotte Delbo, a survivor of Auschwitz and Ravensbrück, recalls being thirsty for days, her tongue reduced to a "piece of wood," so parched that she could not salivate, speak, or eat: "I couldn't hear anything, see anything. They even thought I had gone blind. It took me a long time later on to explain that, without being blind, I saw nothing. All my senses had been abolished by thirst."[9] Most prisoners suffered from gastrointestinal disorders, and frostbite was pervasive; scabies, a nonfatal skin disease, was a terrible annoyance. Prisoners were also subject to daily beatings for not following camp procedures or for seemingly inauspicious or capricious offenses judged unacceptable according to the Kafkaesque whims of the SS or Kapos. At times, prisoners were ridiculed by the SS after having performed repetitive or inane actions (deep-knee bends, hopping, dancing) to the point of fatigue. Living a regimented life without a moment of privacy, prisoners lost their individual identities as humans; they were soon reduced to the level of animals. Without a means to satisfy their sexual desires in a normal manner, *Häftlinge* became even more frustrated. Paul Chodoff, a physician who has written extensively about the concentration camp syndrome, summed up how debilitating the *lager* was for an inmate: "His entire environment was designed to impress upon him his utter protoplasmic worthlessness, a worthlessness which had no relationship to what he did, only to what he was."[10]

The first few weeks of life in the concentration camp separated the weak from the strong. For many, the initial nightmare of the indecipherable camp environment, which meant getting accustomed to the unreality of the reality of casual death, indifference to life, perpetual suffering, and the loss of one's dignity and value as a human being, was too much to bear. Inmates were often informed by senior prisoners or by camp guards that they had no chance for survival, and the only escape route was through the chimney of the crematorium. The weak degenerated into *Muselmänner*, the "moslems" who behaved as if they were in a stupor, unable to respond to the horror surrounding them; they typically died within a few weeks. Only those prisoners who were able to process the idea that their existence was a life in death condition of endless suffering were able to survive. As Primo Levi comments in *The Drowned and the Saved*, Jews, in particular, learned one valuable lesson if they were able to understand the illogical world of the concentration camps: "The 'enemy' must not only die, he must die in torment."[11] If prisoners could struggle beyond this initial stage of shock about the limited possibilities for their own mortality, they entered into a second stage of survival. Chodoff describes the next stage of evolution in the *lager*: "The fright reaction was generally followed by a period of apathy, and, in most cases, by a longer period of mourning and depression."[12] Thus, prisoners who survived through the first stage of bewilderment about an environment that was unlike the real world progressed if they accepted the hopelessness of their situation and the fact that their loved ones were now dead.

Insecurity about whether one would stay alive in the death camps caused just as much psychological damage as the constant degradation and dehumanization. Jews were slated for annihilation through slave labor, so selections for gassing, which occurred randomly, were obviously the most traumatic incidents, inculcating the prisoners with a sense of acute fear and stark disgust. The killing of Jews was a priority of the Nazis' racial policies. Norwegian psychiatrist Eitinger reports on the hopelessness of reprieve for the Jews interned in the extermination camps: "Nothing could change this sentence of death, no appeal to higher justice, no personal attitude, quality or qualification – nothing."[13] The selections for gassing also forced the inmates to come to grips with the notion that they would never again be able to see any of their relatives.

There were several predisposed factors that contributed to the longevity of life in the concentration camps. Understanding German was critical since not following an order that one did not understand was a death sentence; Jews who spoke Yiddish at home could navigate German, but those who had to learn the language were at a severe disadvantage in the camps. Age was relevant since youth made it easier to accommodate the hard labor the inmates had to endure. One's profession or trade was significant since the Nazis could use skilled workers and frowned upon intellectuals or middle-class professionals. Criminals, political prisoners, and some Jews who had been previously arrested could fare better than other inmates in the concentration camps since they had already been accustomed to incarceration. Elie A. Cohen, a survivor of Auschwitz and Mauthausen, argues that having a vestige of spiritual life offered prisoners some solace, for they were able to "escape into regions of the mind which the SS were unable to corrupt."[14]

To survive the abyss of the concentration camps, one had to develop coping mechanisms. Obviously, aggressive behavior had to be curtailed, so prisoners developed regressive behavior so that their attitudes toward the SS became more or less ambivalent rather than overtly hostile, understanding that the latter would result in beatings or a death sentence. Daydreams of revenge and the overwhelming need to bear witness to the crimes of the Nazis embellished perseverance. Joel E. Dimsdale, a physician who has written about coping strategies that were employed to combat stress in the camps, notes, "*Survival for some purpose* was an extremely powerful motivating strategy. The person who had to survive to help a relative, to bear witness and show the world what had happened, or to seek revenge – this person was using a strong coping style."[15] Another important defense mechanism against the SS was for the prisoner to affiliate with a political group or with citizens of the same nationality; by doing so, the individual could mitigate the omnipresent feeling of being represented as a number instead of as a human being and could receive valuable input and advice from others. Lone wolves in the camp almost always perished, yet individuals who banded together in groups could provide mutual emotional support, especially since they understood that they all suffered the same fate. Finally, adhering to a state of apathetic detachment allowed inmates to be inured from death that was endemic to the concentration camp experience. Paul Schmolling acknowledges, "Many survivors have reported that they developed a kind of psychic shell or armor in the camps which served the purpose of protecting the self from further damage."[16] Thus, prisoners learned that to ignore the punishment, beatings, and murders of fellow inmates was a viable option if they wanted to have any chance of survival.

Viktor E. Frankl, a Viennese psychiatrist who spent three years in various concentration camps, including a brief internment in Auschwitz, became one of the most influential advocates of the concept that Holocaust survival was a matter of free will. Frankl developed the concept of logotherapy, which is essentially an extension of the existential notion, postulated in the 1940s by Albert Camus and Jean-Paul Sartre, that human destiny is based upon actions, rather than a deterministic philosophy that contends that we are defined by class, heredity, or environment. Frankl's *Man's Search for Meaning*, written in 1945, argues that despite the shock, apathy, and degradation among the *Häftlinge*, prisoners could maintain a sense of dignity and spiritual freedom that makes life worth pursuing. He writes, "The experiences of camp life show that man does have a choice of action."[17] Frankl acknowledges the omnipresence of suffering and death in the camps but insists that one who believed in the meaning of life could find dignity in suffering. Frankl claims that despite the horrendous chances of survival, a sanguine outlook could overcome the trauma: "It became easy to overlook the opportunities to make something positive of camp life, opportunities which really did exist."[18] Frankl shares the view of many other Holocaust scholars who understood that inmates who lost faith in life were doomed to death in the camp, but he differs from the majority in his opinion that enduring suffering freed one from death. Frankl even quotes Nietzsche's famous aphorism "Was ihn nicht umbringt, macht ihn stärker" (That which does not kill me makes me stronger).[19] Logotherapy thus was designed to instill mankind with the belief that they must not lose hope no matter how much they despair since there is meaning in the struggle for life. Logotherapy focused on the quest for a meaningful life in the future, so prisoners, Frankl argues, had a reason to survive. Frankl contends that despite the confining reins of totalitarianism, humans have free will: "Logotherapy tries to make the patient fully aware of his own responsibleness; therefore, it must leave to him the option for what, to what, or to whom he understands himself to be responsible."[20] Frankl thus postulated that even in the concentration camps, suffering could be turned into human achievement, there was an opportunity to take responsible action, and even helpless victims could change themselves and their fates.

Logotherapy represents Frankl's attempt to find meaning among the horrors of civilization. Elie Wiesel, another Auschwitz survivor, disagrees with Frankl's existential search for some type of morality in the abyss. Wiesel states, "In truth, Auschwitz signifies not only the failure of two thousand years of Christian civilization, but also the defeat of the intellect that wants to find a Meaning – with a capital M – in history."[21] Of course, the will to live and the hope for a better life in the future were the vital incentives for the prisoners to endure endless torture and suffering. However, the will to live by *itself* did not guarantee survival. Instead, luck was the dominant factor in survival, and survivor testimony documents this fact again and again.[22] Those deported to extermination camps such as Belzec, Chelmno, Sobibór, and Treblinka had almost no chance of being saved; almost all were dead upon arrival.[23] Will to power was nonexistent in the camps since, unlike the heroes Frankl envisions, the deportees to the camps possessed neither power nor freedom of choice. Virtually every Jew rounded up by the *Einsatzgruppen* (killing squads) in Russia was executed without "benefit" of being able to exert "free will" in the camps.[24] Able-bodied deportees to Auschwitz had a chance to do slave labor; children, the invalids, and the elderly had no such luck. Those who were fortunate enough to be deported to the concentration camps later during the War had less time to spend there and thus had a better chance of surviving. Selections for gassing were based on the whims of the SS. Epidemics in the camps wiped out entire barracks; the will to survive such diseases was moot. The camp itself defied logic, so even prisoners who adhered to all the rules were subject to the caprices of the SS. Cohen explains that the concentration camp experience guaranteed that nothing was left to free will: ". . . nobody was certain of anything: one could be transported, or lose the function to which one owed a measure of security, or fall into disgrace, or be caught in an offense."[25] At the end of the War, survival in the camps was a matter of sheer luck; if the Russians, Americans, or British had liberated the concentration camps a few days later than they did, many other prisoners would have died in the interim.

Terrence Des Pres, a scholar who examined survivor testimonies, is a major proponent of the view that camaraderie and social support networks enhanced survival and helped to keep dignity and moral sense alive in the camps. Des Pres convincingly argues that nobody in the camps survived without help, and reports by survivors regularly include deeds of courage and resistance.[26] In the extermination camps, there was an elaborate system of bartering and a black market in food, shoes, blankets, spoons, bowls, and clothing. Individuals had to "organize" to obtain the bare necessities to survive since items could not be acquired without collective action. A fallen inmate was usually beaten or tortured by the SS, so his comrades would typically prop him up, especially during the arduous roll calls or when the daily toil made one too exhausted to stand. Des Pres asserts, "Through innumerable small acts of humanness, most of them covert but everywhere in evidence, survivors were able to maintain societal structures workable enough to keep themselves alive and morally sane."[27] Bruno Bettelheim, a survivor of Dachau and Buchenwald, concurs with Des Pres about the value of camaraderie. Bettelheim observed that his fellow prisoners rekindled their "will to live" when a helping gesture of kindness was offered by one's colleagues in the camp.[28] Furthermore, several psychoanalysts shared the view that prisoners in contact with helpful peers or colleagues were believed to be better able to resist degradation in the sense that misery loves company.[29]

Despite these survivor reminiscences of sporadic camaraderie in the camps, the majority of the time spent during incarceration was largely about selfish survival without regard for others. In this atmosphere where humans were reduced to animals, compassion was absent. Lawrence L. Langer describes this horrendous aspect of this legacy of the Shoah: "Perhaps the grimmest bequest of the Holocaust experience was that men were driven to choose survival at the expense of their humanity, creating a kind of solipsistic animality as the supreme value."[30] The instinct for self-preservation was much stronger than any other and always trumped empathy for others. Auschwitz survivor Ella Lingens-Reiner explains this ruthless camp environment that always involved tough moral choices:

> It was simply like this: will you be cold, or shall I be cold? will you risk falling ill on entering the camp, or shall I? will you survive, or shall I? As soon as one sensed that this was at stake everyone turned egotist. But, then, one was also quite alone, with nobody to help; in camp hardly a day passed when one's survival was not at stake. This principle, this enforced necessity of glaring egotism, dominated all of the inmates of the concentration camp, the best and the worst.[31]

Instead of compassion, prisoners became ruthless, hardened, callous, inured to the suffering of others. Prisoners learned to look out for themselves first and foremost, even if it meant sacrificing the life of someone else. In a civilized society, conscience, ethical principles, compassion for others, and altruism often determine our behavior patterns, but in the uncivilized, degrading world of the camps, egotistical needs came first. Eugen Kogon, who has written extensively about the psychology of prisoners in the camps, concludes that inmates regressed to primitive states in which values were abrogated: "the soul had to grow calluses," and "there were many dead martyrs in the camps, but few living saints."[32] Starvation forced prisoners to behave like animals, for the hunger drive must be satisfied, even if that meant stealing food from fellow inmates. Primo Levi, a survivor of Auschwitz, recalls the lack of compassion and pity for others endemic to the camp atmosphere:

> Furthermore, all of us had stolen: in the kitchen, the factory, the camp, in short 'from the others,' from the opposing side, but it was theft nevertheless. Some (few) had fallen so low as to steal bread from their own companions. We had not only forgotten our country and our culture, but also our family, our past, the future we had imagined for ourselves, because, like animals, we were confined to the present moment.[33]

In short, survival meant that human virtues disappeared and humanity faltered. Elie A. Cohen suggests that the possibility of comradeship occurred only when veteran prisoners were fully adapted to their level of misery or when prisoners were resigned to their deaths. Either way, he concludes, "Though not denying the existence of comradeship in the camps, I am convinced that it did not reveal itself until individual danger of life had ceased to be prevalent."[34] Strangely enough, the major advocate for comradeship as a vital support system in the camps, Des Pres, when one reads him quite carefully, begins to contradict himself. At one point, after writing about help and mutual care recalled by survivors, he then states, ". . . but in the larger picture, the image of viciousness and death grows to such enormous intensity that all else – any sign of elementary humanness – pales to significance."[35] Des Pres also admitted, "Compassion was seldom possible, self-pity never. Emotion not only blurred judgment and undermined decisiveness, it jeopardized the life of everyone in the underground," and in the next sentence, he remarked, "survivors had to choose life at the cost of moral injury."[36]

Adding to the insanity was the fact that the concentration camp was an absurd place that defied logic. Most people who are incarcerated in any institution are there because they are being punished for some crime or offense. Jews, however, had committed no crime except for being born and therefore were bewildered about why such excruciating terror had been singled out for them. With death in the *lager* being treated so casually and without the proper civilized burial rites, prisoners understood that they were in an environment unlike anywhere else in history. The underlying principle of the concentration camps was based on the notion that prisoners were to be kept off balance through a lack of reason and rationale; nothing was logical, so inmates could never get comfortable with the system. The classic tale of Primo Levi reaching for an icicle to quench his thirst and then being denied to do so becomes a metonym for the absurdity and unreal atmosphere of Auschwitz. When Levi asked the Kapo "Warum?" (Why?) when he could not snatch the icicle, he was told, "Hier ist kein Warum" (Here there is no why). Prisoners were asked to do slave labor that was meaningless, such as moving one pile of dirt from one spot to another, only to be told to move it back again to its original location. Much of the drudgery had no purpose except to keep a young work force occupied daily. Prisoners were beaten at random for innocuous offenses; the seasoned prisoners were so accustomed to daily beatings that they took them for granted. Inmates were sent to the gas chambers for having swollen legs or scratches on their bodies – inevitable results of a life of hard labor. At times, *Häftlinge* were transferred to other concentration or labor camps at random, often to prevent what the SS perceived were groups of like-minded people or nationalities bonding together for moral or religious support. Intelligent, rational minds were useless in unraveling this mayhem. Thus, prisoners in the concentration camps not only had their bodies eroded, but also lost their minds as well in attempting to apply logic to an absurd universe.

When most of the camps were liberated in 1945, the cutting of the barbed wire was only the beginning of another round of agony for the survivors. Primo Levi recalls, "In the majority of cases, the hour of liberation was neither joyful nor lighthearted. For most it occurred against a tragic background of destruction, slaughter, and suffering."[37] Survivors now felt the full agony of the deaths of friends and relatives, their own pain and exhaustion, and the *angoisse* of having lost their humanity. Understandably, most survivors in their testimonies about the Holocaust were reluctant to relate liberation to closure; Langer recalls that one surviving victim declared that at the time of liberation, "Then I knew my troubles were *really* about to begin."[38] Once these skeletons were able to be nursed back to health, a process that took approximately six weeks, they returned to their native communities to seek information about their relatives. They typically found their homes destroyed and frequently occupied by strangers, their communities wiped out, and they were informed that their family members perished during the War. Many Jews returned to anti-Semitic environments and were treated with indifference, disdain, or hostilities by the local populations who had their own communities devastated by the Nazis and had little empathy for others. Chodoff mentions that their idealistic fantasies about life after their suffering deteriorated instead into more bitterness, resentment, depression, and "temporary flare-ups of antisocial or paranoid behavior."[39] After having been exhausted from the Holocaust experience, survivors had to find the energy to begin a new life amid the rubble and to do it without money, social support systems, or a profession to rely upon. As their abilities to feel and think returned, survivors also now had the unfortunate chance, even the obligation, to ponder what had happened to them in the camps. Wiesel claims that this burden now weighed heavily on survivors during post-liberation: "At Auschwitz, not only man died, but also the idea of man. To live in a world where there is nothing anymore, where the executioner acts as god, as judge – many wanted no part of it."[40]

After liberation, as Wiesel suggests, survivors had to learn how to live a new life – essentially to remake themselves both physically and culturally. Charlotte Delbo wrote about two selves – her persona in Auschwitz and her post-Holocaust self. She compares herself to a snake that must shed its skin, but unlike the reptile whose old skin disappears, her skin of painful Auschwitz memory does not renew itself and is an unalterable, persistent accompaniment. Delbo recalls that during her period of recovery from the trauma, she had to learn basic things, such as how to walk, speak, smile, answer questions (in the *lager*, the SS gave orders and never asked questions), think intelligently, recognize colors, and identify common smells.[41] The loss of culture was particularly profound, as survivors found it difficult to relearn simple things, such as brushing one's teeth, cooking, or using soap, toilet paper, a handkerchief, forks, and knives. Others had to regain the ability to read. Moreover, most of the selfish coping strategies that were necessary for survival in the camps (e.g., "organizing" to obtain food, stealing from others, avoiding punishment, etc.) were completely useless, and even detrimental, for social life in the civilized world. Survivor morale faltered because the victims were now forced to assimilate the past, which drained their energies from focusing on coping with a new environment in the present. Delbo insisted that this remaking of one's life was virtually impossible: "I'm not alive. I died in Auschwitz but no one knows it."[42]

Prior to the Holocaust, there were 8,861,000 Jews in Europe, but only 400,000– 500,000 survived.[43] Many of these lost souls immediately emigrated to other less hostile locales worldwide, particularly the United States, Canada, and Palestine. By the end of 1946, there were approximately 250,000 Jews who had no place to go and thus ended up in displaced persons camps that had been created by the United Nations, the Joint Distribution Committee, and the International Refugee Organization in Germany, Austria, and Italy.[44] Again, as in the concentration camps, individuality was decimated as the Jews were crammed together for years in small spaces surrounded by barbed wire. Psychological and psychosomatic illnesses, particularly cases of typhoid and tuberculosis, that had been dormant in the concentration camps because the body was at that time fighting just for survival, were now taking their toll in the displaced persons camps.[45] Sanitary conditions in these camps were poor, while housing and medical facilities were inadequate. Many displaced persons did not have proper clothing and thus were confined to wearing their old concentration camp tunics. In truth, the Allied occupying forces were unable to cope with the physical and mental illnesses they had to manage in the displaced persons camps.

Displaced persons camps waned when the state of Israel was established in 1948, as Jews began to emigrate there en masse. In 1953, the last displaced persons camp in Germany was disbanded. All ex-prisoners who wished to emigrate to foreign lands were now required to appear before review boards that judged whether the survivors were worthy to be received by the host countries. Once they were accepted into their new homelands, they had to adjust to learning a new language, adapting to new customs, finding employment, and rebuilding families. Without the proper education or training for certain types of jobs, many survivors became more depressed as they were confined to low socioeconomic levels.[46] Immigrants who had survived the Holocaust were often viewed in these host countries as strange or awkward individuals devoid of the proper social skills.

In September 1953, the Federal Republic of Germany enacted the Bundesentschädigungsgesetz (Federal Compensation Law) that allowed survivors restitution if they could prove that their trauma had been aggravated by Nazi mistreatment to the extent that they were unable to work to their full capacities. However, if the trauma was determined to be the result of a predisposition of the individual (*Anlage*), the claim was dismissed. To receive compensation, survivors had to be examined by German psychiatrists to assess their physical health and to ensure that previous persecution was the actual cause of their deteriorating health. Many survivors feared the examination, which they equated to another type of German interrogation; some determined that it was not worth the aggravation, so they decided to forgo the possibility of restitution. The victims were required to bring documentation and foreign health certificates as evidence of their previous injuries – all of which exacerbated their bitterness, hindered the healing process, and brought back remembrances of German persecution and "selection."[47] Even more demeaning to these traumatized victims was the notion that the *Vertrauensärzt* (confidential physician) would grant no compensation unless he adjudicated the claimant to be more than twenty-five percent disabled.[48] German psychiatrists at the time focused on physical injuries or neurological organic brain damage for suitable compensation but ignored depressive or mental illnesses. At the time, relatively very little was known about daily psychological life in the camps, so simply being a survivor did not constitute enough mental illness for the psychiatrist to conclude that one's ability to work was severely impaired. Joost A.M. Meerloo reported that a neurological examination was believed to be sufficient, but no psychiatric interview was considered necessary; consequently, many patients were sent home with the disclaimer, "I'm sorry, I cannot diagnose any bad result from your concentration camp sojourn."[49] Even so, psychiatrists adhered to the assumption that even extreme trauma, unless there are traces of physical damage, does not affect behavior of a previously healthy individual. As the number of claims increased, the German government realized the enormous amount of money that had to be expended and exhorted psychiatrists to be even more discriminatory with regard to the indemnification laws.[50]

Since virtually all of the German psychiatrists were Freudian trained, many of the early diagnoses of ex-prisoners were based upon Freud's principles of psychotherapy. Freud died in 1939 shortly before the advent of the Holocaust, so he had no opportunity to restructure his psychoanalytical theories to adjust to the trauma experienced by Shoah survivors. Freud's theories were derived from his experiences in a civilized society, where the sustained torture and brutality of the Holocaust had not previously existed. Thus, Freud's view of trauma did not coincide with the previously nonexistent condition of human torture over an extended period of time. However, since the German psychiatrists based their theories about trauma on Freud's writings, many of which turned out to be misleading, we must examine in detail how Freud influenced their opinions.

In its Greek derivation, "trauma" referred to a "wound" or bodily injury. In the early 1880s, traumatic neurosis (*Schreck Neurose*) was seen in the German literature as resulting from physical injuries, such as blows to the head.[51] In 1885, Freud studied with French neurologist Jean-Martin Charcot, the prominent psychiatrist who introduced the notion that severe emotional reactions to accidents (traumatic hysteria) were psychological in origin. When Freud returned to Vienna, he began working with his colleague Josef Breuer on the etiologies of hysteria that Charcot suggested were based upon traumatic emotional experiences that were manifested into physical symptoms.

Freud's early training as a neurologist led him to explore mental phenomena in physiological and chemical terms. In essays leading to *Studies in Hysteria* (1895), Freud agreed that what provokes traumatic hysteria is some type of accident but concluded, "Quite frequently it is some event in childhood that sets up a more or less severe symptom which persists during the years that follow."[52] Freud discovered that through memory and abreaction, the patient's hysterical symptoms of the pathology could be ameliorated. This was a difficult point for Freud to make since recall of traumatic events conflicted with his view that humans gravitate toward the pleasure principle as gratification and logically demand that painful situations be avoided. He also postulated that repression was an unconscious defense in response to the original trauma. Freud insisted that the determining cause for "the *acquisition* of neuroses" was to be found in "*sexual* factors."[53] Freud maintained that "anxiety neurosis," which arises from an accumulation of physical tension, is "once more of sexual origin."[54] In the 1890s, Freud focused on the sexual abuse of patients during childhood and wrote about its origins in hysteria in his 1896 essay, "Zur Aetiologie der Hysterie." His focal point was on the sexual and aggressive wishes of the child rather than on a traumatic experience as the point of departure. Freud thus contended that trauma occurred because of this repressed memory of childhood that assumed a form of prolonged latency that resurfaces years later with an appropriate precipitating condition – "an accretion of excitation." Neil J. Smelser summarizes the significance of Freud's psychoanalytic theories on trauma at the turn of the century: "To put the point blankly, Freud was beginning a journey that would lead to the conclusion that a trauma is not a thing in itself but becomes a thing by virtue of the context in which it is implanted."[55]

After World War I, however, when soldiers returning from the battlefields of Europe began shaking in the streets and manifested symptoms of what we now refer to as "shell shock," Freud was compelled to reassess his theories on trauma. Rather than revising the underpinnings of his theories on the psyche, Freud instead began altering his definition of trauma to mesh with those theories, particularly his previously established views on instinct, libido, and the sexual origins of neuroses. Freud was still arguing that, because trauma had been suffered for a brief period, one could eventually return to a healthy state through psychotherapy; thus, German psychiatrists post-World War II had difficulty understanding Holocaust trauma that was accrued through months or years of daily torture and suffering.

At first, Freud associated war neuroses with internal narcissistic conflict, claiming that the libido during wartime was directed not at some one but instead at the self. This notion moved Freud to rationalize that during war, the self moves away from instinctive sexual drives compatible with self-preservation and toward Thanatos or death instincts. Freud stated that war leads the human psyche to seek gratification, which is a normal part of the pleasure principle, but also to return to the quiet of nonexistence, which is the death instinct. The death instinct provided Freud with a means to make sense of World War I, which he viewed as the human tendency toward self-destruction. Freud reasoned that the repetition-compulsion of traumatic events was less related to the libido's efforts to expend its sexual energy and more related to one's desire to realize and concomitantly accept the death wish. This compulsion to repeat appeared to Freud to be more instinctual than the pleasure principle and thus could override it. Freud was therefore able to retain his theoretical perspectives on libido theory and simultaneously comes to grips with wartime neuroses.

In "Jenseits des Lustprinzips" (1920), Freud formulated the concept of the protective shield (*Reizschutz*), which functions against stimuli or excitations from the external world. The protective shield consists mainly of preparatory anxiety that acts as a hyper-cathexis to diffuse the external excitations that otherwise would overwhelm the ego or self. In *Beyond the Pleasure Principle* (1920), Freud revised his definition of trauma, writing, "We describe as 'traumatic' any excitations from outside which are powerful enough to break through the protective shield."[56] In other words, Freud then defined traumatic neurosis as a consequence of "an extensive breach being made in the protective shield against stimuli."[57] By 1926, Freud had reconfigured his definition of trauma as an experience of helplessness on the part of the ego when faced with an accumulation of internal or external excitation.[58] The key word here seems to be "external," which now allows him to move away from the theory that trauma is lodged primarily in childhood sexual molestation. Also, helplessness can now include both physical helplessness, as in war, and his traditional concept of psychical helplessness.

Although many of Freud's ideas have since been discounted, Freud cannot be easily dismissed because his theories influenced the thinking of German psychiatrists after the War. Aside from Frankl, no postwar German psychiatrist has been referred to and cited as an authority on the psychology of survivors more than Bruno Bettelheim. Bettelheim thus serves as an effective example of the pervasive influence of Freudian psychology on the study of Holocaust survivorship, as well as an example of how ingrained thinking about trauma went awry once World War II had ended.

Trained in Freudian thought, Bettelheim also had credence as a survivor of two concentration camps during 1938–1939. Relying on Freud's explanation of human actions in a civilized society where there has never been a precedent for turning humans into vermin, Bettelheim tried to make sense of an absurd, illogical system that was designed to reduce humans to mental illness before destroying them. In short, Bettelheim tried to bring the Holocaust into line with what he was intimately familiar with (Freudian psychology) – a system in which he had been trained to believe unlocked the motives for human behavior. Bettelheim, like most of Freud's acolytes writing about the effects of the Holocaust on survivors, thus resorts to an established coherent body of thought to explain how humans should have responded *theoretically* in a microcosm that has no precedent in civilized society.

Bettelheim placed the Holocaust itself in terms of Freudian psychology: the Nazis allowed the death drive to overpower their life instincts, while the Jews who went to the slaughter were unable to keep their death drive in bounds.[59] Bettelheim believed that the Nazis turned the death instinct against others while the Jews turned it inward. He observed that in the concentration camps, inmates regressed to a childlike state. Instead of the common sense notion that inmates understood that any violation of SS orders would have meant punishment or death, he argued that prisoners regressed to a childlike dependence on the guards. Like children, the *Häftlinge* found satisfaction in daydreaming, lived only in the immediate present, fought constantly with their peers, and boasted about their prowess.[60] Bettelheim contended that the wishful thinking of inmates in a world devoid of hope and the concomitant disregard for the possibility of death were nothing more than infantile behavior. Moreover, adults typically punish children to correct their behavior, but in the camps, Bettelheim asserted, inmates who were punished had their normal frame of reference as adults destroyed and thus regressed to children. Like children, they swore they were going to "get even" with their oppressors. Given menial tasks to perform forced these adults to accept their fate as obedient children. Bettelheim even claimed that the more seasoned veterans of the camps, in their childlike dependency on authority figures, had positive feelings for the SS as father figures.[61]

Probably the most controversial aspect of Bettelheim's Freudian notion of adult prisoners regressing to childlike behavior was his insistence on their passage through the oral and anal stages that Freud acknowledged were universal for all children. The oral stage of infant development was based on Freud's idea that since the child's ego was yet to be developed, the id seeks immediate gratification through pleasure, i.e., weaning and placing objects in the mouth. In the anal stage, the id competes with the developing ego. The focus is on the competing drives of immediate gratification during toilet training versus parental demands on the ego that delay the child's gratification in eliminating bodily wastes. Bettelheim argued that the prisoners' preoccupation with food and with their bowels was a regression to the oral and anal stages of childhood. As evidence, he mentions that the inmates were infatuated with food and talked about it incessantly. Furthermore, the SS cursed at prisoners, punctuating their commands in the "anal sphere" with words such as "shit" and "asshole." Prisoners, in turn, soiled and wet their clothing. Bettelheim concludes, "It was as if every effort were being made to reduce prisoners to the level they were at before toilet training was achieved."[62] What is so strange and alarming is that Bettelheim, himself a survivor, chooses to ignore the realities of the concentration camp to ensure that his psychological diagnosis complies with Freud's theory that stress results in regression to earlier stages of fixation. Bettelheim fails to mention that in the extreme conditions of the camp where *Häftlinge* were faced with starvation and malnutrition, common sense would indicate that hunger would preoccupy their thoughts and overwhelm all other bodily desires. Prisoners soiled themselves, not because they regressed to the anal stage of childhood, but because there were severe restrictions on latrine usage.

The problem is that Bettelheim's adherence to Freudian psychology is endemic of what is reiterated in the literature during the first wave of psychiatric analyses of Holocaust survivors conducted from the late 1940s to the 1960s. For example, writing in 1953, Elie A. Cohen contends that inmates, disregarding the laws of personal anal cleanliness and passing gas in public, regressed to the infantile phase of their lives. With regard to the cause of this regression, Cohen states, "The dependence of the prisoner on the SS, which may be compared to the dependence of children on their parents, caused regression."[63] Chodoff, the well-known and respected psychiatrist of this early period, also supported the Freudian model of coping: "Regressive behavior, of a greater or lesser degree, was almost universal, resulting from the overwhelming infantilizing pressures to which prisoners were subjected and their need to stifle aggressive impulses."[64] William G. Niederland, a pioneer in psychopathology studies of Holocaust victims, even suggested that the inmates became narcissists by turning their egos into love objects since self-preservation is, in the Freudian sense, narcissistic: "Under the impact of continued traumatization and with the constant threat of annihilation, the regression had to go to narcissistic levels; frequently it could not stop at the level of childlike, infantile-dependent, automatized behavior alone."[65]

In 1952, a group of Danish researchers concluded the first major study of Holocaust survivors. They examined nearly 1,300 Danes who had been interned in concentration camps and discovered that approximately seventy-five percent suffered from neurotic symptoms.[66] These Danish physicians designated the mental changes as "Repatriation Neurosis," which initially appeared to be a benign term that suggested a problem that survivors had in accommodating to changes of environment. As a follow-up to this study, an international convention was held in Copenhagen in 1954, where the term "concentration camp syndrome" was coined. In the 1950s, numerous investigations in Poland, Russia, France, and Norway confirmed that survivors suffered from neurasthenia,[67] but there was no proof that the cause of their fatigue, irritability, and anxiety was related to the consequences of being imprisoned. Like most Freudian-trained physicians, these early researchers maintained that only organic brain damage constituted the basis of the concentration camp syndrome. Eitinger explains the discrepancies of their early misdiagnoses: "These physicians must be excused on the grounds that doctors in our normal, well-behaved and well-organized society never have had the opportunity to see and to examine resurrected corpses."[68]

More data were gathered in the late 1950s and early 1960s, typically through interviews with concentration camp survivors who had completed the indemnification procedures. Paul Matussek, a distinguished German psychiatrist, gathered data from 245 such persons between 1958 and 1962. He narrowed down the psychological disturbances to three basic factors: resignation and despair (the survivor is depressed and no longer views life as meaningful), apathy and indignation (feelings of personal failure and worthlessness), and aggressive-irritable moodiness (one is unable to manage uncontrolled hostility).[69] In the early 1960s, Wolfgang Lederer examined fifty restitution claimants and diagnosed that they suffered from anxiety, chronic depression, insomnia, an inability to forget, social isolation, and a variety of psychosomatic symptoms that affected all of the organs.[70] Chodoff spent seven years interviewing 107 claimants (65 females and 42 males) who had completed the Restitution Examinations. He found that depression was a significant complaint of almost all of the survivors, as well as guilt manifested by a preoccupation with the past.[71] Chodoff also noted that his patients manifested the typical concentration camp syndromes that included chronic anxiety, irritability, hyper-apprehensiveness, and psychosomatic symptoms. Psychiatrist Guenther Emil Winkler studied thirty-two Jewish patients from Poland, the majority of whom immigrated to the United States after spending time in displaced persons camps. Although most of these survivors showed no indication of psychosis, they did display symptoms of chronic depression (mainly due to guilt feelings), irritability, phobias, nightmares, and a variety of physical ailments.[72] Eitinger's early study of one hundred Scandinavian survivors revealed similar psychological disturbances, with more than fifty percent complaining of fatigue, irritability, anxiety, memory impairment, insomnia, dysphoric mood, and loss of initiative.[73] Finally, W. Grobin's diagnoses of seventy persons applying for compensation under the restitution laws concluded that the majority of the victims suffered from anxiety and depression, while nightmares, vertigo, headaches, insomnia, and rheumatic aches and pains were present in all of the individuals.[74]

An important breakthrough in Holocaust survivor studies occurred in 1961, when American psychoanalyst and former refugee from Nazi Germany William G. Niederland coined the term "Survivor Syndrome." Niederland went beyond previous studies that characterized the concentration camp syndrome as consisting of depression, apathy, and insecurity. In his seminal 1961 essay, "The Problem of the Survivor," Niederland also included as part of the Survivor Syndrome a guilt complex; a full range of somatization (including headaches, fatigue, tremors, neuralgic pains, ulcers, and respiratory ailments); anxiety due to fear of persecution, resulting in insomnia, nightmares, hallucinations, and frequently paranoia; personality changes; and delusional symptomatology that often produced morbid brooding and inertia.[75] In a 1968 essay, Niederland added disturbances of cognition and memory, including a feeling of being lost and bewildered, to the diagnoses; he also noted that the most prevalent manifestation of the symptomatology was a chronic state of anxiety and bland depression.[76] In particular, Niederland did much to dispel the prevailing opinion that a diagnosis of traumatic neurosis (a childhood predisposition or *Anlage*) was sufficient to characterize the multitude of clinical manifestations he observed in survivors. Furthermore, he introduced the idea that the psychological traumata that he evaluated in Holocaust survivors rarely heal.[77]

In the 1960s and 1970s, psychologists and psychotherapists who conducted their own studies came up with results that coincided with Niederland's findings.[78] Edgar Trautman, publishing his results of a clinical study of sixty survivors in the same year as did Niederland, derived similar conclusions. He narrowed down the disturbances to anxiety manifestations (obsessive thoughts, hallucinations, panic attacks, and fantasies), depression, and somatic debilities.[79] Chodoff, who conducted psychiatric evaluations of twenty-three patients seeking reparations from the German government, concluded that the patients' symptoms could be broken into four categories: manifestations of direct anxiety (irritability, apprehensiveness, startled reactions to ordinary stimuli, insomnia, and nightmares), bodily effects of anxiety (physical ailments including gastrointestinal problems, headaches, joint pain, and diarrhea), depression, and "characterological changes" (feelings of inadequacy, helplessness, apathy, and seclusiveness).[80] Perhaps the most important findings of the period derived from Eitinger's study of 328 Norwegian and 262 Israeli concentration camp survivors. Eitinger, one of the foremost psychiatrists studying persecution effects, originally adopted the Freudian view that prisoners must have demonstrated organic brain disease to be diagnosed as having any sort of chronic symptoms. After years of examining the psychological symptoms of survivors, Eitinger changed his opinion to corroborate most of Niederland's conclusions. Eitinger discovered that symptoms occurring in more than fifty percent of patients that he examined included "poor memory and inability to concentrate, nervousness, irritability, restlessness, increased fatigue, sleep disturbances, loss of initiative, anxiety phenomena, emotional liability, dysphoric moodiness, vertigo, nightmares."[81] In 1968, psychiatrist Henry Krystal published the results of a workshop he held with other psychiatrists, including Dr. Niederland, to discuss the Survivor Syndrome. He stated that ninety-seven percent of his patients who survived the concentration camps suffered from anxiety and confirmed Niederland's findings that they also were plagued with sleep disorders, disturbances of memory and cognition, psychosomatic disease, and chronic depression; Krystal added that survivor guilt typically resulted in masochism.[82]

Research that was conducted on long-term traumatic effects on Holocaust survivors after the 1970s employed different methodologies than did earlier studies. Research after the 1970s was primarily conducted by psychologists who employed control groups, community surveys, questionnaires, and achievement scales/instruments rather than by psychiatrists who had interviewed patients shortly after the War.[83] Netta Kohn Dor-Shav investigated long-term effects on Israeli survivors ranging in age from forty-two to sixty-seven and concluded that twenty-five years after incarceration, they had difficulties in being accessible to others, suffered from a constricted, impoverished inner life, and appeared to be more labile, i.e., emotionally unstable, than the control group.[84] In a 1982 study of 135 Holocaust survivors in Montreal, Eaton, Sigal, and Weinfeld demonstrated that thirty-three years after the Holocaust, survivors still had stressful consequences, but the ongoing physical illnesses had somewhat abated.[85] Although one would expect that time heals all wounds, the research suggests otherwise. Arie Nadler and Dan Ben-Shushan conducted a study of Holocaust survivors in Israel forty years after the Shoah and found that most still complained about insomnia and nightmares and reported frequent psychosomatic symptoms, anxieties, fears, and bouts of depression.[86] Similar research done on eighty-six elderly (over sixty years old) Holocaust survivors in a nonclinical population in Israel determined that seventy-five percent suffered from survivor symptoms, the most common of which were anhedonia, hypermnesia, fatigue, nightmares, insomnia, and nervousness.[87] Finally, Jules Rosen and his team of investigators found that even forty-five years after the Holocaust, impaired sleep and sleep disturbances were found to be significant problems for two-thirds of those surveyed.[88]

During the last twenty years of the twentieth century, data had been accrued with regard to survivors' adaptability of social skills and success at economic achievement. In a 1978 study of 657 Jewish heads of households in Montreal who had formerly been imprisoned by, or fleeing/hiding from, the Nazis, Weinfeld, Sigal, and Eaton found that despite their neuroses, survivors compared well to the control group. The researchers concluded that their findings "focus attention on the magnificent ability of human beings to rebuild shattered lives, careers, and families, even as they wrestle with the bitterest of memories."[89] In 1988, Harel, Kahana, and Kahana conducted a study of 1,980 Israeli Holocaust survivors and compared them with a control group of Eastern European immigrants who came to Israel prior to the War. They reported that survivors, employing the coping skills that enabled them to survive during the Shoah, were adapting no differently than the control group. Good health, spousal support, and income adequacy were found to be the most important factors in allowing survivors to adapt to life in Israel.[90] In 1996, William B. Helmreich published his findings of 170 in-depth interviews conducted with survivors who immigrated to the United States. Helmreich certainly acknowledged the depression, anxiety, and paranoia expressed by survivors, but his findings justified the notion of successful achievement of survivors in America. He concluded that many have stable families, rich and varied social lives, successful work experiences, and have contributed greatly to the American Jewish community.[91] Thus, when we examine the lives of survivors in Canada, Israel, and the United States – three countries with the largest numbers of Holocaust immigrants – we may erroneously conclude that trauma was insignificant in their abilities to adapt, prosper, and become productive citizens.

However, the more likely conclusion is that Holocaust survivors, even though they were traumatized and could not be healed psychologically, were able to cope in their new environments. All Holocaust survivors were required to cope in the camps through behavior that forced them to repress their aggressive tendencies and comply with figures of authority. Because they were the hardiest individuals, they endured unimaginable strain and stress under fear of constant death. Prisoners who were forced to "harden" themselves to severe brutality and persecution in order to survive in the camps were thus enamored with a quality that allowed them to adapt to different environments after the Holocaust. (One must keep in mind that many survivors who were liberated died shortly after their freedom while many others, most notably Jean Améry and Primo Levi, committed suicide years later.) In a study conducted of female survivors in Israel twenty-five years after the Shoah, researchers A. Antonovsky et al. noted that camp trauma "hardened" inmates, which was psychologically devastating, although years later, it did "seem relevant to the capacity to resist new stress and to maintain a meaningful, and even satisfying, level of adequate functioning."[92] Survivors were able to adapt to foreign environments because they had reasons to be successful and to give meaning to their new lives: they were alive while their relatives were dead, they were going to make up for time lost during the Holocaust, and success would give them a renewed sense of confidence and feelings of self-worth that had been taken from them in the camps. Moreover, survivors often endured in the camps in order to bear witness; once liberated, they felt that they owed their lost relatives a duty to fulfill their expectations through hard work, responsibility to their wives and children, and adaptation to a new way of life so as to persevere in order to say prayers for the dead. Adapting and coping to a new way of life also diverted their minds from their traumata – during the day, they were preoccupied with running successful businesses (and hard work was not foreign to them), while in the evening, they turned their attentions to family issues.[93] Many survivors became so engrossed in their work that they refused to take vacations. In an effort to rebuild their lives, survivors understood that they were consciously turning their backs on death, making an overt attempt to reject the nihilism of the Holocaust. Becoming financially independent meant controlling one's identity instead of following orders given out by authority figures. Adaptability in a new environment meant success, which ensured security – the opposite of what was felt by the victims in the camps. In his interviews with American survivors, Helmreich heard them reiterate that work became a privilege as much as a necessity because this new lease on life now gave them the chances that the Holocaust never provided, such as payment for work, the right to quit a job, fixed hours of employment, training opportunities, and paid leave time.[94] Helmreich's research also coincides with the findings of the Transcending Trauma Project, a team of researchers who sought to identify the coping strategies of Holocaust survivors. After interviewing 275 Holocaust survivors and their family members, researchers Jennifer Goldenberg, Nancy Isserman, and Bea Hollander-Goldfein found that positive emotions and devotion to family members motivated survivors to function at a high level, adapt to their traumatic experiences, and create productive lives for themselves.[95] In summary, Holocaust survivors had many personal reasons to adapt, despite the fact that they still suffered psychologically from scars that would never heal.

In 1980, the American Psychiatric Association coined the term post-traumatic stress disorder and indicated that trauma would be a diagnosed psychological disorder. The definition of trauma conformed to what previously had been referred to as shell shock, war neurosis, and even Freud's term, traumatic neurosis. In 1987, a revised edition of the *Diagnostic and Statistical Manual of Mental Disorders* (DSM-III-R) included five diagnostic criteria for post-traumatic stress disorder, which was designated as an anxiety disorder. Directly linked to extraordinary stressors outside the typical range of human experience, post-traumatic stress disorder was associated with disasters, wars, and accidents by the DSM-III-R. The trauma was characterized by distressing recollections or dreams of the event; persistent avoidance of stimuli associated with the trauma and coinciding with efforts to avoid thoughts, feelings, or situations that arouse recollections of the trauma, thus often resulting in feelings of detachment or estrangement from others; and persistent symptoms of increased arousal that led to irritability, insomnia, hypervigilance, exaggerated startle response, or outbursts of anger.[96] In 1994, the DSM-IV redefined the category of post-traumatic stress disorder to state that the trauma "involves actual or threatened death or serious injury" or witnessing an event that pertains to death or injury to another person.[97] The response to the trauma must have involved intense fear, helplessness, or horror. In addition, the traumatic event must be re-experienced in either recurrent or distressing recollections, dreams, hallucinations, or flashbacks that induce psychological distress. Again, as in the DSM-III-R, persistent avoidance of stimuli associated with the trauma and symptoms of increased arousal were designated as criteria for the diagnosis of the "anxiety disorder" or trauma.[98] Also, painful guilt feelings about surviving, as well as feelings of shame, despair, and paranoia about constant threats, were now considered to be associated with the trauma. This edition of the DSM was the first instance when incarceration in a concentration camp was officially included as one of the stressors.[99] The significance of inclusion of post-traumatic stress disorder in the DSM was that now psychologists who conducted studies of survivors were able to relate Holocaust trauma to criteria that were well defined and accepted by a worldwide community of psychoanalysts.[100]

One major voice who has been recognized internationally for his work on genocide and survivor studies is American psychiatrist Robert Jay Lifton. Lifton lobbied to have post-traumatic stress disorder included in the DSM. Lifton developed expertise in trauma narratives through his work with survivors of Hiroshima and the Vietnam War, as well as survivors of the Buffalo Creek flood disaster. He argued that survivors' traumatic sequelae were neither pathological nor normal but instead were adaptive. Like most psychiatrists whose goal it is to heal patients, Lifton believed that the search for meaning among survivors is part of the post-traumatic impact.

Lifton defines survivors as those who have come into contact with death in bodily or psychic form and have remained alive.[101] He notes five characteristic themes that mark their traumata: the death imprint, death guilt, psychic numbing, conflicts around nurturing and contagion, and struggles for meaning. The death imprint involves an indelible image or feelings of threats of termination of life as an internal need to master or assimilate the threat. The survivor was confronted with images of death during the Holocaust that have become indelible. The death imprint, which produces anxiety (the fear of death), is coupled with death guilt. For survivors, grief and loss that have been overwhelming in their suddenness cannot be resolved.[102] Lifton states that the survivor feels responsible for what one has not done, what one has not felt, and most importantly, for what one was unable to do; since the guilt is unresolved, it keeps reappearing in dreams and in waking life. Most importantly, the survivor blames himself rather than the Nazis, which becomes what has been referred to as paradoxical guilt.[103]

Lifton designates psychological numbness, or "psychic closing off," as the inability to experience emotions. This mental anesthesia functions as a defense against the emotions associated with the horrendous conditions in the camps and is typically manifested in apathy, depression, and withdrawal from human contact.[104] The disruption of civilized values in the camps therefore has forced the survivor to "close off" emotionally, thus making it nearly impossible to return to normality.[105] When a person has been treated as a subhuman, the victim tends to internalize self-worthlessness. This leads to conflicts over nurturing. The victim requires nurturing to regain self-esteem as a vital human being, yet the survivor almost intuitively acknowledges that any such help is a reminder of weakness and was formerly unreliable; the survivor thus reacts negatively to such assistance.[106] Instead, the survivor, as an alternative to living in the realm of the annihilated, resorts to anger and violence. Lifton writes, "Many have noted that anger is relatively more comfortable than guilt or other forms of severe anxiety; it can also be a way of holding onto a psychic lifeline when surrounded by images of death."[107]

The last characteristic of the trauma common to all survivors, according to Lifton, involves reformulation, which is the task of finding meaning in the trauma so that the remainder of one's life need not be devoid of significance. The trauma of the Holocaust disrupted the normal order in the world, so the survivor seeks to understand why the secure world became disjointed. To overcome the death anxiety, death guilt, immobilizing anger, and, especially, psychic numbing, one must develop new psychic means to emancipate oneself from bondage to the deceased and to images of death. Unable to define the inexplicable, many Holocaust survivors tended to reassert themselves through strong ties with Israel and through the process of getting married and having children.

In recent years, psychoanalysts have noted that traumata are typically associated with loss, which, over time, produces anxiety and depression.[108] Traumatized individuals are plagued by conflicting desires to relive and deny the losses. Reliving the trauma, referred to as intrusive responses, often consists of explosive aggressive outbursts, startle responses, and nightmares or flashbacks.[109] Denying the trauma (warding off intrusive recollections), which is similar to Lifton's numbing response, consists of emotional constriction, social isolation, anhedonia, and estrangement from friends or family.

Cathy Caruth, a professor of comparative literature who specializes in trauma theory, has added another important voice to the conversation about survivor trauma. Caruth characterizes trauma as a wound that was not understood or fully assimilated when it happened initially but always exists to haunt the survivor to what remains unknown in one's actions and language. Caruth builds her theory around Freud's dilemma in explaining why the traumatic dream keeps returning against the will of the World War I survivor to avoid the painful memories, as would typically occur in trauma that was based upon a serious accident. Working through Freud's *Beyond the Pleasure Principle* and *Moses and Monotheism*, Caruth attempts to decode what mystified Freud about why traumatic neuroses ("shell shock") could not be treated as other traumata, which Freud believed stemmed from a serious disruption of the ego in childhood. Caruth argues that what returns to haunt the victims is not the violence of the initial traumatic event, but the way the violence was never fully initially comprehended and thus has never been given psychic meaning.[110] Bessel van der Kolk also agrees that trauma is about disassociation: how the experience is registered but cannot be integrated into the brain; the result is that the fragmented experiences become overwhelming.[111] In essence, the thalamus, the integrative function of the brain, fails to function normally because the trauma disallows the brain to integrate properly, thus fragmenting the original traumatic experience. The repetitive nature of the trauma keeps the survivor a victim of the fragmented, incomplete experience. In essence, the imprinting of trauma thus derives from a breakdown of the mind's integrative processes. This concept is in contrast to recent diagnoses of post-traumatic stress disorders that are perceived as events that overwhelm the mind because they return as the horrors they were originally thought to be. Trauma, associated with loss and close encounters with death, recently has also become more connected with the ongoing experience of having survived death or loss through an insistent return that is absolutely *true* to the originally incomprehensible event.[112]

Caruth, without being explicit about the Holocaust experience, implies that at the time of the trauma, inmates were bombarded with abrupt stimuli that became too much for the mind to absorb at the moment. Although the trauma of losing one's relatives and facing the fear of death daily were omnipresent, the victim was primarily concerned with survival, which dominated his or her consciousness. The trauma, as Freud acknowledged, thus appears in a latency phase rather than immediately, as would be true of most accidents that Freud believed triggered unconscious earlier effects of childhood. Caruth interprets the fact that because the survivor's trauma is indirect (i.e., not conscious), it becomes the basis for the repetitive nightmare – an attempt to master what was never fully grasped in the first place, rather than a simple memory of past events.[113] The conflict between the need to remember and the impossibility of grasping the threat to one's life exacerbates the trauma. Caruth contends, "It is because the mind cannot confront the possibility of its death directly that survival becomes for the human being, paradoxically, an endless testimony to the impossibility of living."[114] In other words, the trauma becomes even more enigmatic because it consists not only of having confronted death, but also of having survived without understanding why. By reinterpreting Freud, Caruth suggests that trauma should be viewed through a process of temporal delay followed by repetition and return through dreams and nightmares, rather than as a concept that has repression as its foundation.

Caruth mentions that repetitions of the traumatic experiences in the flashbacks, as neurobiologists have suggested, can lead to deterioration since the chemical structure of the brain is adversely affected. Much of the recent literature on the perplexing subject of survivorability has focused on coping mechanisms or methods of adaptation. Factors affecting the duration of the trauma include the severity of the initial stress, the age of the person at the original time of the terror (children later had more difficulty in coping), genetic predispositions, and the level of support systems later available to the survivor.[115] Psychotherapists are in the business of healing patients and thus continue to support the notion that survivors are curable. For example, Kahana, Harel, and Kahana underscore the significance of survivors sharing experiences with willing listeners, family members, and friends to assuage their trauma. With regard to these measures to increase empathy, Kahana, Harel, and Kahana write, "These results are congruent with observations in the mental health literature about the self-healing value of sharing stressful life experiences with others."[116] Caruth's research thus adds a critical element to the study of Holocaust survivors: contrary to what many psychologists and psychiatrists believe, survivor traumata are not healable (which is similar to what Freud discovered about shell-shocked soldiers after World War I).[117]

Despite the necessary homage to psychological studies and to psychoanalytic theory, my book is essentially about how trauma is represented in modern dramatic literature. For many theater practitioners and critics, the unusual approach of mixing a clinical approach employed by scientists and social scientists with dramatic criticism is foreign to them. Theater practitioners are trained to analyze productions as having a life of their own in which set design, costumes, movement, acting, sound, and lighting form the essence of a play. My approach is less involved with the life of the production and more involved with the content of the play, i.e., drama criticism. A major portion of this book focuses on clinical studies conducted by psychologists and psychiatrists because these professionals have the trained expertise to discuss the symptoms of survivors of traumata. Playwrights, who may typically be relatives or friends of Holocaust survivors, can write about the Holocaust survivor experience, but we must rely on the clinicians to explicate the nature of the psychopathology based upon experimental studies of Holocaust survivors in comparison to valid control groups.

Nevertheless, facts about the Holocaust are one means of learning about the devastation, but personal manifestations of the trauma, as represented in the theater, can be more effective than citing statistics, which are typically impersonal. Reporting the results of studies of survivors when compared to control groups may be valid to psychologists, but theater can induce empathetic responses among the masses that clinical studies fail to achieve. The theater, which possesses a powerful immediacy effect that no other art form can match, can be an effective medium to represent the visible effects of Holocaust trauma. The theater thus can become a viable means of understanding the traumatic effects of the Holocaust on *individuals*, for as audiences watch poignant plays about the Shoah, spectators can be swayed viscerally, intellectually, and, above all, emotionally.

Although there are several plays that tangentially focus on Holocaust survivorship, I tried to limit my selection of plays to those that best demonstrate the psychological effects of the traumata. My research is a comparative drama study of plays written about the subject in the United States, England, Scotland, France, Israel, and Australia. Chapter 2 focuses on psychological sequelae of the Survivor Syndrome as demonstrated in Gilles Ségal's *The Puppetmaster of Lodz*, Peter Flannery's *Singer*, and Richard Atkins's *DelikateSSen*. However, before delving into extensive explorations of the sequelae of the psychopathology of survivors, I explore how the spectre of the Holocaust is omnipresent in all survivors' lives. To do so, I examine three early Holocaust plays: *Coupled by Fate* and *Sparks*, both written in Yiddish by American playwright Morris Freed, and *Bells and Trains* by Israeli dramatist Yehuda Amichai. Chapter 3 portrays the manifestations of survivor guilt, typically demonstrated by the guilt survivors had about their inability to save family members from death, their self-reproach for having survived while more worthy relatives or friends perished, and their culpability for the lack of empathy for others and loss of morality that inured them to survive the horrendous conditions of the concentration and extermination camps. Such survivor guilt is well represented in Ron Elisha's *Two*, Gabriel Dagan's *The Reunion*, Enzo Cormann's *Toujours L'Orage*, Robert Caisley's *Letters to an Alien*, and Ben-Zion Tomer's *Children of the Shadows*. Chapter 4 is concerned with the traumatic effects faced by survivors who were children during the Holocaust. Child survivors faced the same traumata as adults, but their separation from their parents, coupled with their lack of adult coping skills and the loss of parental guidance during these "formative years," made their psychopathology more acute. The two plays examined in this chapter are Diane Samuels's *Kindertransport* and Wendy Graf's *Leipzig*. Chapter 5 examines the psychopathology of children of Holocaust survivors who are born into their roles as "memorial candles" that are raised to be surrogates for lost family members. The children become living symbols to counter Hitler's genocide and mitigate the past, and as such, they are reared to overachieve, mistrust outside authority, and preserve the memory of lost relatives. In this pathogenic environment where the parents have lost empathy, their offspring become overprotected so as to "parent" the parents, thus healing them. The plays discussed in this chapter are Faye Sholiton's *The Interview*, Ronald John Vierling's *Adam's Daughter*, and Ari Roth's *Andy and the Shadows*. At times, the offspring rebel against such demands from the parents that make it difficult to establish identities of their own. Chapter 6 examines what occurs when the violence expressed by the offspring is internalized (Donald Margulies's *The Model Apartment*) or externalized toward the Nazis (Marsha Lee Sheiness's *Second Hand Smoke*). Again, I want to stress that other plays would possibly fit into the parameters selected for inclusion in each chapter, but decisions had to be made about limiting the number of plays that I could discuss without duplicating major ideas. In short, the selection of the plays is not meant to be an exhaustive survey.

Notes

1 For more information on rescue of Jews by Christians and the clergy, see Gene A. Plunka, *Staging Holocaust Resistance* (New York: Palgrave Macmillan, 2012), especially 1–23, 63–87, 103–134.

2 Daniel Jonah Goldhagen, *Hitler's Willing Executioners: Ordinary Germans and the Holocaust* (New York: Alfred A. Knopf, 1996), 167.

3 Ulrich Venzlaff, "Mental Disorders Resulting From Racial Persecution Outside of Concentration Camps," *International Journal of Social Psychiatry* 10, no. 3 (1964): 179.

4 Leo Eitinger, "Auschwitz – A Psychological Perspective," in *Anatomy of the Auschwitz Death Camp*, eds. Yisrael Gutman and Michael Berenbaum (Bloomington and Indianapolis: Indiana University Press, 1994), 470.

5 Lawrence L. Langer, *Versions of Survival: The Holocaust and the Human Spirit* (Albany: State University of New York Press, 1982), 10.

6 For more information about the daily life of concentration camp inmates, see, for example, Sheryl Robbin, "Life in the Camps: The Psychological Dimension," in *Genocide: Critical Issues of the Holocaust*, eds. Alex Grobman and Daniel Landes (Los Angeles: Simon Wiesenthal Center, 1983), 236–242.

7 For a detailed inventory of the diseases prevalent in the concentration camps, see Elie Cohen, *Human Behavior in the Concentration Camp*, trans. M.H. Braaksma (New York: W.W. Norton, 1953), 65–70.

8 Ella Lingens-Reiner, a German physician who was imprisoned in Auschwitz and, in the latter stages of the Holocaust, was sent to Dachau, wrote one of the earliest accounts of disease in the concentration camps. She referred to typhus as the epidemic that claimed the greatest number of victims and became the "camp disease": "In Auschwitz there were only two classes of women: those who had got over typhus and those who had this prospect still before them." See Lingens-Reiner, *Prisoners of Fear* (London: Victor Gollancz, 1948), 62.

9 Charlotte Delbo, *Auschwitz and After*, trans. Rosette C. Lamont (New Haven and London: Yale University Press, 1995), 142.

10 Paul Chodoff, "The German Concentration Camp as a Psychological Stress," *Archives of General Psychiatry* 22, no. 1 (1970): 79.

11 Primo Levi, *The Drowned and the Saved*, trans. Raymond Rosenthal (New York: Summit Books, 1986), 120.

12 Paul Chodoff, "Psychiatric Aspects of Nazi Persecution," in *American Handbook of Psychiatry, New Psychiatric Frontiers*, 2nd ed., vol. 6, eds. David A. Hamburg and H. Keith Brodie (New York: Basic Books, 1975), 937.

13 Leo Eitinger, "Jewish Concentration Camp Survivors in the Post-war World," *Danish Medical Bulletin* 27 (1980): 232.

14 Cohen, *Human Behavior in the Concentration Camp*, 149.

15 Joel E. Dimsdale, "The Coping Behavior of Nazi Concentration Camp Survivors," *American Journal of Psychiatry* 131, no. 7 (1974): 794.

16 Paul Schmolling, "Human Reactions to the Nazi Concentration Camps: A Summing Up," *Journal of Human Stress* 10 (1984): 112.

17 Viktor E. Frankl, *Man's Search for Meaning* (New York: Simon & Schuster, 1984), 86.

18 Ibid., 93.

19 Ibid., 103.

20 Ibid., 132.

21 Elie Wiesel, *Legends of Our Time* (New York: Holt, Rinehart and Winston, 1968), 183.

22 One could adopt a cynical attitude toward the luck associated with Frankl's fate. He had been unlucky enough to be deported to Auschwitz in October 1944 but lucky enough to have remained there for only a short period of time. His transfer to a satellite camp of Dachau, although not a benign place but also not an extermination camp, probably saved his life. Had he been earlier deported to Treblinka, he would have been gassed.

23 For evidence that survivors attributed their fates to external factors, such as God, fate, chance, or miracles, see Jennifer Goldenberg, "The Hows and Whys of Survival: Causal Attributions and the Search for Meaning," in *Transcending Trauma: Survival, Resilience, and Clinical Implications in Survivor Families*, eds. Bea Hollander-Goldfein, Nancy Isserman, and Jennifer Goldenberg (New York and London: Routledge, 2012), 88.

24 Henry Friedlander and Sybil Milton, "Surviving," in *Genocide: Critical Issues of the Holocaust*, eds. Alex Grobman and Daniel Landes (Los Angeles: Simon Wiesenthal Center, 1983), 233.

25 Cohen, *Human Behavior in the Concentration Camp*, 125.

26 Terrence Des Pres, *The Survivor: An Anatomy of Life in the Death Camps* (New York: Oxford University Press, 1976), 99.

27 Ibid., 142.

28 Bruno Bettelheim, *Surviving and Other Essays* (New York: Alfred A. Knopf, 1979), 107.

29 For example, see Leo Eitinger, "Denial in Concentration Camps: Some Personal Observations on the Positive and Negative Functions of Denial in Extreme Life Situations," in *The Denial of Stress*, ed. Shlomo Breznitz (New York: International Universities Press, 1983), 208. Also, see Elmer Luchterhand, "Prisoner Behavior and Social System in the Nazi Concentration Camps," *International Journal of Social Psychiatry* 13, no. 4 (1967): 245–264. Luchterhand's research is based on interviews with fifty-two survivors who emigrated to the United States. He concludes that in the camps, there were identifiable prisoner social systems and that "a substantial part of the prisoner population developed a sharing relationship with one or more prisoners" (254). He even goes so far as to infer, "much of the strength for survival – psychic and physical – seems to have come from 'stable' pairing" (259).

30 Lawrence L. Langer, *The Holocaust and the Literary Imagination* (New Haven and London: Yale University Press, 1975), 6.

31 Lingens-Reiner, *Prisoners of Fear*, 23.

32 Eugen Kogon, *The Theory and Practice of Hell: The German Concentration Camps and the System Behind Them*, trans. Heinz Norden (New York: Farrar, Straus and Giroux, 2006), 304.

33 Levi, *The Drowned and the Saved*, 75.

34 Cohen, *Human Behavior in the Concentration Camp*, 183.

35 Des Pres, *The Survivor: An Anatomy of Life in the Death Camps*, 99.

36 Ibid., 131.

37 Levi, *The Drowned and the Saved*, 70.

38 Lawrence L. Langer, *Holocaust Testimonies: The Ruins of Memory* (New Haven and London: Yale University Press, 1991), 67.

39 Chodoff, "Psychiatric Aspects of Nazi Persecution," 939.

40 Wiesel, *Legends of Our Time*, 190.

41 Delbo, *Auschwitz and After*, 236, 238.

42 Ibid., 267.

43 See Yael Danieli, "The Treatment and Prevention of Long-term Effects and Intergenerational Transmission of Victimization: A Lesson From Holocaust Survivors and Their Children," in *Trauma and Its Wake: The Study and Treatment of Post-Traumatic Stress Disorder*, ed. Charles R. Figley (New York: Brunner/Mazel, 1985), 296.

44 Hagit Lavsky, "Displaced Persons, Jewish," in *Encyclopedia of the Holocaust*, vol. 1, ed. Israel Gutman (New York: Macmillan, 1990), 377.
45 Wolfgang Lederer, "Persecution and Compensation," *Archives of General Psychiatry* 12, no. 5 (1965): 469.
46 Venzlaff, "Mental Disorders Resulting From Racial Persecution Outside of Concentration Camps," 182.
47 For a thorough discussion of the German Indemnification Law, see Milton Kestenberg, "Discriminatory Aspects of the German Indemnification Policy: A Continuation of Persecution," in *Generations of the Holocaust*, eds. Martin S. Bergmann and Milton E. Jucovy (New York: Basic Books, 1982), 62–79.
48 Ibid., 64.
49 Joost A.M. Meerloo, "Neurologism and Denial of Psychic Trauma in Extermination Camp Survivors," *American Journal of Psychiatry* 120, no. 1 (1963): 65.
50 By the end of 1956, there were 165,000 claims filed. The number jumped to 260,000 by the end of 1957, with 95,000 applications for restitution filed within the first three months of 1957 alone. See Hans Strauss, "Neuropsychiatric Disturbances After National-Socialist Persecution," *Proceedings: Virchow Medical Society* 16 (1957): 96.
51 Rolf J. Kleber and Danny Brom, *Coping With Trauma: Theory, Prevention and Treatment* (Amsterdam: Swets & Zeitlinger, 1992), 13.
52 Sigmund Freud, *The Standard Edition of the Complete Psychological Works of Sigmund Freud*, vol. 2, ed. and trans. James Strachey (London: Hogarth Press, 1955), 4.
53 Ibid., 257.
54 Ibid., 258.
55 Neil J. Smelser, "Psychological Trauma and Cultural Trauma," in *Cultural Trauma and Collective Identity*, eds. Jeffrey C. Alexander, Ron Eyerman, Bernhard Giesen, Neil J. Smelser, and Piotr Sztompka (Berkeley: University of California Press, 2004), 34.
56 Sigmund Freud, *The Standard Edition of the Complete Psychological Works of Sigmund Freud*, vol. 18, ed. and trans. James Strachey (London: Hogarth Press, 1955), 29.
57 Ibid., 31.
58 Sigmund Freud, *The Standard Edition of the Complete Psychological Works of Sigmund Freud*, vol. 20, ed. and trans. James Strachey (London: Hogarth Press, 1959), 81.
59 Bettelheim, *Surviving and Other Essays*, 100–101.
60 Ibid., 76–77.
61 Bruno Bettelheim, *The Informed Heart* (Glencoe: Free Press, 1960), 172.
62 Ibid., 132.
63 Cohen, *Human Behavior in the Concentration Camp*, 174.
64 Chodoff, "Psychiatric Aspects of Nazi Persecution," 937.
65 William G. Niederland, "Psychiatric Disorders Among Persecution Victims," *Journal of Nervous and Mental Disease* 139, no. 5 (1964): 464. For a detailed report on the 1947 investigation of concentration camp survivors in Scandinavia, see Paul Thygesen, "The Concentration Camp Syndrome," *Danish Medical Bulletin* 27, no. 5 (1980): 224–228.
66 Leo Eitinger, "Pathology of the Concentration Camp Syndrome," *Archives of General Psychiatry* 5, no. 4 (1961): 79.
67 For example, the first report from a physician who had diagnosed the mental health problems of survivors was written by Paul Friedman in 1949. Friedman surveyed 172 survivors on Cyprus (84 children and 88 adults) and found a consistent behavior pattern of "affective anesthesia" that he concluded resulted from repression of fears and anxieties that made it possible for survivors to withstand repeated traumata. See Paul Friedman, "Some Aspects of Concentration Camp Psychology," *American Journal of Psychiatry* 105, no. 8 (1949): 601–605.
68 Leo Eitinger, "Concentration Camp Survivors in the Postwar World," *American Journal of Orthopsychiatry* 32, no. 3 (1962): 371.
69 Paul Matussek, *Internment in Concentration Camps and Its Consequences* (New York: Springer-Verlag, 1975), 246.

70 Wolfgang Lederer, "Persecution and Compensation: Theoretical and Practical Implications of the 'Persecution Syndrome'," *Archives of General Psychiatry* 12, no. 5 (1965): 464.

71 Paul Chodoff, "Depression and Guilt Among Concentration Camp Survivors," *International Forum for Existential Psychiatry* 7 (1970): 19–26.

72 Guenther Emil Winkler, "Neuropsychiatric Symptoms in Survivors of Concentration Camps," *Journal of Social Therapy* 5, no. 4 (1959): 285, 287.

73 Eitinger, "Pathology of the Concentration Camp Syndrome," 375.

74 W. Grobin, "Medical Assessment of Late Effects of National Socialist Persecution," *Canadian Medical Association Journal* 92, no. 17 (1965): 913.

75 William Niederland, "The Problem of the Survivor," *Journal of the Hillside Hospital* 10 (1961): 237. Niederland also expanded on the Survivor Syndrome in several later articles. For example, see "Psychiatric Disorders Among Persecution Victims," 458–474; William G. Niederland, "Clinical Observations on the 'Survivor Syndrome'," *International Journal of Psycho-analysis* 49, pts. 2 and 3 (1968): 313–315; William G. Niederland, "The Clinical Aftereffects of the Holocaust in Survivors and Their Offspring," in *The Psychological Perspectives of the Holocaust and of Its Aftermath*, ed. Randolph L. Braham (New York: Columbia University Press, 1978), 45–52; and William G. Niederland, "The Survivor Syndrome: Further Observations and Dimensions," *Journal of the American Psychoanalytic Association* 29 (1981): 413–425.

76 Niederland, "Clinical Observations on the 'Survivor Syndrome'," 313–314.

77 Other psychiatrists attending symposia on Holocaust survivorship or writing essays about the subject began repeating Niederland's suggestion that the "Survivor Syndrome" extends far beyond the initial diagnosis of traumatic neurosis and becomes difficult to heal in psychotherapy. For example, Ernest A. Rappaport reiterates, "The camp experience is so far outside normal experience and so far from the usual categories of thinking and feeling that it not only has no prototype as a derivative from childhood in the unconscious; it can also never be deleted from memory." See Rappaport, "Beyond Traumatic Neurosis: A Psychoanalytic Study of Late Reactions to the Concentration Camp Trauma," *International Journal of Psycho-Analysis* 49, pt. 4 (1968): 730. Hilel Klein and his team of psychiatrists also noted that the Freudian concept of traumatic neurosis was typically based upon a sudden, single traumatic experience, but the Holocaust was a long series of traumatic experiences. See Hilel Klein, Julius Zellermayer, and Joel Shanan, "Former Concentration Camp Inmates on a Psychiatric Ward," *Archives of General Psychiatry* 8, no. 4 (1963): 341. (In the literature, Klein's name is frequently spelled "Hillel" instead of "Hilel.")

78 For a thorough investigation of the literature of the 1960s that discusses the psychological consequences of Nazi persecution, see Klaus D. Hoppe, "The Aftermath of Nazi Persecution in Recent Psychiatric Literature," *International Psychiatry Clinics* 8, no. 1 (1971): 169–204. Also see Erwin K. Koranyi, "Psychodynamic Theories of the 'Survivor Syndrome'," *Canadian Psychiatric Journal* 14 (1969): 165–174.

79 Edgar Trautman, "Psychiatric and Sociological Effects of Nazi Atrocities on Survivors of Extermination Camps," *Journal of the American Association for Social Psychiatry* (September–December 1961): 119–122.

80 Paul Chodoff, "Late Effects of the Concentration Camp Syndrome," *Archives of General Psychiatry* 8, no. 4 (1963): 324–325. Also, see Chodoff, "Psychiatric Aspects of Nazi Persecution," 940–941.

81 Leo Eitinger, "The Concentration Camp and Its Late Sequelae," in *Survivors, Victims and Perpetrators: Essays on the Nazi Holocaust*, ed. Joel E. Dimsdale (Washington, DC: Hemisphere, 1980), 137. Also see Eitinger, "The Concentration Camp Syndrome: An Organic Brain Syndrome?" *Integrative Psychiatry* 3 (1985): 115–119, and L. Eitinger, *Concentration Camp Survivors in Norway and Israel* (London: Allen & Unwin, 1964).

82 Henry Krystal, *Massive Psychic Trauma* (New York: International Universities Press, 1969), 327–348.

83 One notable exception was a study conducted on 157 hospitalized Holocaust survivor patients that used as a control group 120 similar patients who spent most of World War II under extreme conditions in Soviet Russia. The scientists found a clinical picture of the Holocaust survivors that was similar to what had been suggested by previous literature published by Eitinger and Niederland. See T.S. Nathan, L. Eitinger, and H.Z. Winnick, "A Psychiatric Study of Survivors of the Nazi Holocaust: A Study of Hospitalized Patients," *Israel Annals of Psychiatry and Related Disciplines* 2, no. 1 (1964): 47–80.

84 Netta Kohn Dor-Shav, "On the Long-Range Effects of Concentration Camp Internment on Nazi Victims: 25 Years Later," *Journal of Counseling and Clinical Psychology* 46, no. 1 (1978): 1–11.

85 William W. Eaton, John J. Sigal, and Morton Weinfeld, "Impairment in Holocaust Survivors After 33 Years: Data From an Unbiased Community Sample," *American Journal of Psychiatry* 139, no. 6 (1982): 773–777.

86 Arie Nadler and Dan Ben-Shushan, "Forty Years Later: Long-term Consequences of Massive Traumatization as Manifested by Holocaust Survivors From the City and the Kibbutz," *Journal of Counseling and Clinical Psychology* 57, no. 2 (1989): 287–293.

87 S. Robinson et al., "The Late Effects of Nazi Persecution Among Elderly Holocaust Survivors," *Acta Psychiatrica Scandinavica* 82 (1991): 311–315.

88 Jules Rosen et al., "Sleep Disturbances in Survivors of the Nazi Holocaust," *American Journal of Psychiatry* 148, no. 1 (1991): 62–66.

89 Morton Weinfeld, John J. Sigal, and William W. Eaton, "Long-term Effects of the Holocaust on Selected Social Attitudes and Behaviors of Survivors: A Cautionary Note," *Social Forces* 60, no. 1 (1981): 14.

90 Zev Harel, Boaz Kahana, and Eva Kahana, "Psychological Well-Being Among Holocaust Survivors and Immigrants in Israel," *Journal of Traumatic Stress* 1, no. 4 (1988): 413–429.

91 William B. Helmreich, *Against All Odds: Holocaust Survivors and the Successful Lives They Made in America* (New Brunswick: Transaction Publishers, 1996), 14.

92 A. Antonovsky et al., "Twenty-five Years Later: A Limited Study of the Sequelae of the Concentration Camp Experience," *Social Psychiatry* 6, no. 4 (1971): 191.

93 Psychotherapists realized that these diversions were certainly no cures for trauma. Whereas employment and family matters worked to divert the mind from psychological disturbances, survivors were virtually all plagued by nightmares. Since approximately one-third of our lives is spent sleeping, survivors had no chance for egress.

94 Helmreich, *Against All Odds: Holocaust Survivors and the Successful Lives They Made in America*, 87.

95 Jennifer Goldenberg, Nancy Isserman, and Bea Hollander-Goldfein, "Introduction: The Transcending Trauma Project," in *Transcending Trauma: Survival, Resilience, and Clinical Implications in Survivor Families*, eds. Bea Hollander-Goldfein, Nancy Isserman, and Jennifer Goldenberg (New York and London: Routledge, 2012), 3–12.

96 Kleber and Brom, *Coping With Trauma: Theory, Prevention and Treatment*, 25–26.

97 American Psychiatric Association, *Diagnostic and Statistical Manual of Mental Disorders*, DSM-IV, 4th ed. (Washington, DC: American Psychiatric Association, 1994), 424.

98 Ibid., 428–429.

99 Ibid., 425.

100 For examples of such studies, see Klaus Kuch and Brian J. Cox, "Symptoms of PTSD in 124 Survivors of the Holocaust," *American Journal of Psychiatry* 149, no. 3 (1992): 337–340; Rachel Yehuda et al., "Depressive Features in Holocaust Survivors With Post-Traumatic Stress Disorder," *Journal of Traumatic Stress* 7, no. 4 (1994): 699–704; and Rachel Yehuda et al., "Individual Differences in Posttraumatic Stress Disorder Symptom Profiles in Holocaust Survivors in Concentration Camps or in Hiding," *Journal of Traumatic Stress* 10, no. 3 (1997): 453–463.

101 Robert Jay Lifton, *The Broken Connection: On Death and the Continuity of Life* (New York: Simon and Schuster, 1979), 169.

102 Robert J. Lifton, "Understanding the Traumatized Self: Imagery, Symbolization, and Transformation," in *Human Adaptation to Extreme Stress: From the Holocaust to Vietnam*, eds. John P. Wilson, Zev Harel, and Boaz Kahana (New York and London: Plenum Press, 1988), 19.

103 Kleber and Brom, *Coping With Trauma: Theory, Prevention and Treatment*, 98.

104 Aaron Hass believes that this psychic numbness or "closing off" mentality carried over from the attitudes that inmates adopted in the camps. To overcome overwhelming losses, stresses, and fears, *Häftlinge* blocked all capacities for emotions. Emotional awareness of the unimaginable brutality would have incurred demoralization. The psychic numbness defense was valuable at the time but proved to be maladaptive after liberation. See Hass, *The Aftermath: Living With the Holocaust* (Cambridge: Cambridge University Press, 1995), 4.

105 Dori Laub and Nanette C. Auerhahn corroborate Lifton's view of psychic numbing. See Laub and Auerhahn, "Failed Empathy – A Central Theme in the Survivor's Holocaust Experience," *Psychoanalytic Psychology* 6, no. 4 (1989): 377–400. Laub and Auerhahn mention that during the Holocaust, when fellow citizens, Allied nations, and obviously the Nazis proved unresponsive and malignant on a massive scale to the plight of the victims, faith in communication with others died. The victims, especially Jews, who were treated as a race of an unwanted, different species, later felt as if there was no longer anyone to rely upon. The sense of being treated by others as a nonhuman or subspecies with no links to humanity has tainted the typical human relationships that provide a foundation for civilized society. Laub and Auerhahn write, "The survivor's on-going experience of empathetic bankruptcy leads to a dread of getting close; closeness is expected inevitably to entail injury, loss, and abandonment" (385). The trauma precludes survivors from getting close to anyone, forcing the victim to confront his or her alienation.

106 Lifton, "Understanding the Traumatized Self: Imagery, Symbolization, and Transformation," 25.

107 Ibid., 26.

108 For example, see John H. Harvey, *Perspectives on Loss and Trauma: Assaults on the Self* (Thousand Oaks: Sage Publications, 2002).

109 Bessel A. van der Kolk, "The Psychological Consequences of Overwhelming Life Experiences," in *Psychological Trauma*, ed. Bessel A. van der Kolk (Washington, DC: American Psychiatric Press, 1987), 3.

110 Cathy Caruth, *Unclaimed Experience: Trauma, Narrative, History* (Baltimore and London: Johns Hopkins University Press, 1996), 6.

111 See Cathy Caruth, *Listening to Trauma: Conversations With Leaders in the Theory and Treatment of Catastrophic Experience* (Baltimore: Johns Hopkins University Press, 2014), 154. Other psychotherapists agree with Bessel van der Kolk. For example, Arthur S. Blank, Jr., claims that post-traumatic stress disorder is essentially a "processing deficiency disorder" that interferes with the ability to "integrate, digest, narrate, understand, comprehend" the original trauma. See Caruth, *Listening to Trauma*, 288, 291.

112 Cathy Caruth, "Introduction," in *Trauma: Explorations in Memory*, ed. Cathy Caruth (Baltimore and London: Johns Hopkins University Press, 1995), 5.

113 Caruth, *Unclaimed Experience: Trauma, Narrative, History*, 62.

114 Ibid.

115 For example, see van der Kolk, "The Psychological Consequences of Overwhelming Life Experiences," 10–12.

116 Boaz Kahana, Zev Harel, and Eva Kahana, "Predictors of Psychological Well-Being Among Survivors of the Holocaust," in *Human Adaptation to Extreme Stress: From the Holocaust to Vietnam*, eds. John P. Wilson, Zev Harel, and Boaz Kahana (New York and London: Plenum Press, 1988), 189.

117 For example, historian Dominick LaCapra, who has written extensively on trauma theory in relationship to Holocaust studies, notes, "Trauma is a disruptive experience that disarticulates the self and creates holes in existence; it has belated effects that are controlled only with difficulty and perhaps never fully mastered." See LaCapra, *Writing History, Writing Trauma* (Baltimore and London: Johns Hopkins University Press, 2001), 41.

2

THE SPECTRE OF THE HOLOCAUST AMONG SURVIVORS

As we have seen from the Survivor Syndrome, from the criteria for post-traumatic stress disorder listed in DSM-III-R and DSM-IV, as well as from Lifton's list of characteristics of survivor traumata, anxiety disorder defined in these major models includes analogous symptoms. Depression, irritability, nightmares, insomnia, recurrent distressing recollections in the form of hallucinations, and psychosomatic disorders were the most common manifestations of the psychopathology of survivors.[1] Most Holocaust playwrights who focus on survivor psychopathology demonstrate these symptoms sporadically, typically without exploring them in depth. In Chapter 3, I examine in detail several plays that explore the nature of survival guilt, which is related to the death guilt that Lifton and the DSM-IV mention as characteristic of survivor traumata.[2] Chapter 2 investigates plays that portray other notable characteristics of survivor psychopathology, including paranoia and apathy (Lifton's psychological numbness) that lead the survivor to view the world with hostility, suspicion, and mistrust (Gilles Ségal's *The Puppetmaster of Lodz*); lack of empathy toward others that degrades survivors to become ruthless aggressors (Peter Flannery's *Singer*); and hypervigilance and anger endemic to many survivors as a means to assuage constant anxiety and depression (Richard Atkins's *DelikateSSen*).

However, before delving into extensive explorations of the sequelae of the psychopathology of survivors, I want to explore how the spectre of the Holocaust is omnipresent in all survivors' lives. To do so, I will examine three early Holocaust plays: *Coupled by Fate* and *Sparks*, both written in Yiddish by American playwright Morris Freed, and *Bells and Trains* by Israeli dramatist Yehuda Amichai.

Moyshe (Morris) Freed was born in Lodz, Poland, on 17 October 1893 and immigrated to the United States in 1912, where he settled in Paterson, New Jersey.[3] His first novel, *On a Bord (Without a Beard)*, was published in 1919 in a weekly publication, *Der Shtern*. He wrote several novels, plays, and short stories; his most famous accolade was winning first prize in a short-story contest run by *Forverts* in

1916. Although his plays have been translated into English, there is no record of any productions in the United States.

Coupled by Fate and its companion piece *Sparks* are probably the two earliest plays written about trauma as a never-ending wound that is ubiquitous among Holocaust survivors. These two one-act plays are meant to be performed in succession; both occur in a displaced persons camp in the American Zone of occupied West Germany in spring 1946 – one year after the liberation of the camps. Khavele, a young Jewish woman in her early twenties, and David, a slightly older Jewish male, have survived Treblinka. Khavele and David have lost everything during the Holocaust, and now, since their lives are filled with loss, they hope to get married and share their *angoisse* together. These plays demonstrate that the liberation was nothing more than a Pyrrhic victory for the Jews, for the spectre of the Holocaust cannot be eviscerated.

In *Coupled by Fate*, Khavele is pessimistic about the marriage because, suffering from anxiety, despair, and depression, she is not in the proper mental state to enjoy a festive occasion that a wedding would provide. Khavele is plagued with nightmares about the deaths of her parents, aunt, uncle, grandparents, sisters, and brothers; she is the only survivor in a family of seventy. Her nightmares always find her back in Treblinka, the place that defines her life after the Shoah. Freed's play provides us with a portrait of the deeply rooted, ingrained vision of the angst-ridden survivor who can never heal from the trauma. Khavele describes herself as "wretched, friendless and alone," an alienated, isolated individual whose guilt about being the only survivor in her family precludes any chance of future happiness in her life.[4] She laments to David, "I am sick, broken, and of a melancholy mood always" (49). Freed depicts the state of mind of survivors whose experiences in the camps have been so debilitating that their souls have been lost and their culture obliterated to such an extent that they have, as Delbo suggested, degenerated into a different skin or persona. Khavele recognizes the dilemma of developing a new persona after the trauma:

> No, Khavele. A new life is not for you. Who and what are you to give your hand in marriage? You came out so sick and broken from the Treblinka Hell, you are no more than the flicker of a candle about to go out. Bliss is not for you. The memory of Treblinka will forever haunt you; will forever be a barrier to a new start.
>
> *(44)*

David persists in convincing Khavele to marry him, but she is adamant that beginning life anew after the Shoah is impossible, despite the temptations to do so. She insists to David, "I must reject you. No, I cannot think of marriage. I am too sick, too broken in spirit. The fires of Treblinka are still before me, and my desire to continue, to go on, is all but extinguished" (45). David argues that he is also bound by the harrowing experiences, but the bond of the trauma that they share means that the two survivors are ideal for each other. The turning point in their relationship is a dream about Treblinka that Khavele shares with David in which her dead family members exhort her to marry. Khavele interprets the dream, not as another nightmare, but as a sign that the marriage will be the seed for preservation of the family. She thus assumes that her marriage will pay homage to the dead she could not save in Treblinka and tells David, "Now, I am afraid to reject you – afraid to offend the wishes of the dead; my dead parents . . ." (48). Whether love is involved becomes a moot point for both of them. Instead, David explains that both of them are uprooted, without family, home, or country, but the Holocaust is their common denominator: "That's our common lot; the numbers branded on our arms is our common emblem of the pain, suffering, and torture we endured, the memory of which we will carry always in our being" (49).

Sparks further enhances the dichotomy between Khavele's two distinct selves on her wedding day, only now the survivor is encouraged to forget the past by a host of supporters in the displaced persons camp that includes ushers and Reb Bainish, a jester and songster. The dead of Treblinka are the ghosts that haunt Khavele, and Khavele herself feels at one with the loss; she is nothing but a subhuman who has been degraded and turned into vermin. She has lost any empathy for anyone and feels ashamed about her loss of humanity. She admits before the wedding ceremony occurs, "I guess the make-up around my eyes, the bit of rouge on my lips gives me some allure; but my heart remains dead; it has the stillness of the grave."[5] Khavele wants to call off the wedding because she feels as if she does not deserve to be happy while her relatives are dead; the Holocaust has destroyed the self-esteem that she had before the Shoah, turning her into a ghost of her former self. In short, as the title of the play sarcastically implies, she cannot rekindle the sparks of life. She remarks, "I am no more than a spark from a dying fire, that once was a flame with a lust for life. Only a spark, the fire is almost out" (58). Furthermore, Khavele suffers the debilitating psychosomatic effects of the Holocaust. Upon liberation,[6] Khavele, weighing only sixty pounds and racked by disease, had to be nursed back to life; before the wedding ceremony is about to take place, she faints from weakness.

Khavele's colleagues in the displaced persons camp encourage her to summon her strength and to remember that they too are sparks from what was once a bright flame. Khavele is recalcitrant about being able to shirk off the spectre of the Holocaust and admits, "I am weak, I am ill, how can I feel this happiness, when the heart is overwhelmed with sorrow, when sorrow is dearer to me than bliss" (60). She cannot reconcile the festive occasion, a time of rejoicing, with a wound that cannot be healed. She laments, "My spirit is encased in a web of sorrow. I cannot be liberated. For me the greatest bliss can only last a moment. The sorrow will be eternal" (61). However, in a melodramatic denouement that is incongruent with Holocaust drama, Khavele experiences an epiphany when Reb Bainish calls it a miracle that she escaped death only to be brought to the canopy. The happy ending is contrived rather than realistic, but the audience is still left with the prevailing notion that this bliss is temporary and can never be permanent.

Yehuda Amichai, long considered one of Israel's greatest poets, was born in Würzburg, Germany, in 1924. In 1936, his parents, who were Orthodox Jews, immigrated to Palestine to support the Zionist Movement. At age eighteen, he joined the

Jewish Brigade, allied with the British Army, and served in World War II. After the War, he became a member of the Palmach, a secret commando force of the Jewish underground army (Haganah) that helped smuggle immigrants into Palestine by circumventing the British blockade. In 1948, he participated in the Arab-Israeli War that led to the independence of the state of Israel. While attending the Hebrew University after the War of Independence, he began submitting poetry to various journals. He eventually developed into one of Israel's most prolific poets, but also wrote two novels, several plays, and a collection of short stories. Although he was nominated for the Nobel Prize in Literature several times, he never won. However, in Israel, he was awarded the Shlonsky Prize (1957), the Brenner Prize (1969), the Bialik Prize for Literature (1976), and the Israel Prize for Hebrew Poetry (1982). Other countries, such as Germany, France, the United States, Macedonia, Egypt, and Norway, have presented him with literary awards as well. His poetry, having been translated into forty languages and widely anthologized, provided him with an international reputation. Amichai passed away from cancer in 2000.[7]

Amichai's one-act radio play, *Bells and Trains*, first broadcast in Israel in 1963, occurs in a Jewish nursing home in the fictional small town of Singburg, Germany, in an unspecified year after the Holocaust.[8] All of the residents are Holocaust survivors recuperating from their losses. Henrietta, an elderly woman who serves as the protagonist of the play, is visited there by her cousin, Hans, who lives in Israel with his wife and children. According to Henrietta, the German government provides financial support for the nursing home because of "a guilty feeling."[9]

Bells and Trains depicts the spectre of the Holocaust haunting all of the residents of this nursing home. Like Khavele in *Sparks*, the denizens of Singburg's hospice facility are ghosts of their former selves. Each is a doppelganger without life or "spark" because they cannot escape the horrors of the traumata they encountered during the War. Henrietta provides for Hans a litany of the residual effects that the Holocaust has had on the memories of these survivors. Doctor Rieger, a dentist, is the lone survivor in his family of ten. Mrs. Gruenfeld's three brothers were burned in the camps. Herr Levin, a tailor who made Hans a suit when he entered school, is forced to live with the memory that his sons were shot on that same day by the Germans. Yoram's son was murdered because he dated a German girl. Herr Cahn, who operated a pharmacy in Kaiserstrasse, had his shop destroyed during Kristallnacht. Herr Rosenberg remembers that his daughter Lore, who played with Hans as a child, had seven of her sons killed one at a time and died of typhoid that she contracted while incarcerated. Henrietta herself recounts a brief marriage to a sixty-year-old man named Rudolf in Theresienstadt. Rudolf accompanied the coffin of old Rabbi Rothschild to the cemetery, but because he did not have a permit to return to the city, he disappeared and was never seen again. Henrietta describes the environment as "A paradise of ghosts" (57), and even Hans, a visitor, acknowledges, "This is a world of ghosts" (59). Hans also notices that the patrons sit in silence, spectres of their former selves, seemingly distraught as they wait for death. When Hans asks the nun Theresa why the atmosphere is permeated with morbid silence, Theresa responds, "What shall they talk about? They came here from the camps after the war" (59).

Bells and Trains depicts the omnipresence of the Holocaust in the lives of survivors. The nursing home becomes a microcosm for life in the concentration camp, where various stimuli induced terror among the inmates. In her book on trauma, Judith Lewis Herman writes, "To the chronically traumatized person, any action has potentially dire consequences."[10] Henry Krystal mentions that the persecutory complex is typically manifested in terms of constant fear, vigilance, and paranoia.[11] In his clinical studies of survivors, Krystal noted how outside stimuli, such as whistles, sirens, knocks on the door, late-night telephone calls, the sight of an authority figure (e.g., police officers) in uniform, or barking dogs, can reintroduce the paranoia: "Another classical symptom of this traumatic neurosis is the hypersensitivity to various noises and stimuli which, along with the pattern of conditioned reflex, brings back to the patient's memory some of the horror he had experienced."[12] As we have already seen, psychiatrists such as Chodoff, Niederland, and Eitinger, as well as the DSM-III-R, have acknowledged the need for survivors to avoid external stimuli associated with the original trauma.[13] Instead, in *Bells and Trains*, Amichai forces the survivors to experience a constant barrage of stimuli associated with the Shoah, thus solidifying the impression that the spectre of the Holocaust is forever enduring.

Throughout the play, the haunted that inhabit this nursing home are plagued by external stimuli associated with the traumata of the Holocaust. These stimuli are particularly reinforced through the genre of radio drama that Amichai so cleverly employs. Church bells, handbells, and dinner bells that are constantly chiming remind the survivors of the threat of sirens in the camps. Even the name of the town, Singburg, is synonymous with the constant cacophony of bells singing in the distance. The sounds of dogs barking in the town recall the German Shepherds that accompanied the Nazis on the arrival ramps. In the course of this brief one-act play, six trains pass by, some of them freight trains; the sound of the train on the tracks is, of course, a metonym for the Holocaust, and one that is never lost on the victims. Henrietta explains to Hans the significance of the passing trains: "Can you hear it? A freight train . . . They sent all of us away in a train like that" (65). Furthermore, as Alvin Goldfarb has mentioned, the regimentation in the nursing home parallels the Nazi system of organization and order in the camps, where daily activity was based upon routine and life was prescriptive.[14] Henrietta can tell the time of day when she hears the bells ringing and the trains clanging on the rails. For example, when she hears the Milan-Cologne-Amsterdam express, she knows that the time is 1:47. The punctuality of the noises of everyday routines in the nursing home combined with the punctual sounds of the bells and trains subliminally reinforce for the survivors the impression that they can never escape the Nazi regimentation that exacerbated their suffering.

Hans is determined to take Henrietta out of her misery by bringing her to Jerusalem, where she can obtain some solace from the diurnal stimuli that reinforce the trauma. Theresa tells Hans that there is no cure for the neurosis, implying that there is no afterlife for these ghosts, no panacea for their misery: "Do you think she will feel at home among people who have not been in the camps? Leave her here Hans. She is living in the past. She came from the past, and will return there" (64). Henrietta concurs with the nun; she must endure the trauma for the rest of her life. She says to Hans, "I must stay here. Because I know exactly when all the trains leave. I must stay" (65). Hans vows to return that evening for more persuasion, but Henrietta, in the last lines of the play, entreats him to leave the memories of the dead to the ghosts: "Hans, Hans! At 3:20 there is an express from Singburg . . . At 3:20 . . . Hans . . . Hans . . ." (66). Henrietta urges Hans to take the next train out of Singburg, but for the denizens of this nursing home, trains signify closure, not escape. Hans is a free man who has never been exposed to the Holocaust while Henrietta's doppelganger is a ghost of a person who died in the camps.

French playwright Gilles Ségal's *Le Marionnettiste de Lodz* (*The Puppetmaster of Lodz*), a long one-act play, is a poignant portrayal of the paranoia that forces Holocaust survivors to embrace life with apprehension and mistrust. Ségal was born in Romania on 13 January 1929, but he spent virtually all of his life in France after his family immigrated there in 1932. Ségal remembers the Holocaust vividly, for in 1942, his parents were arrested by the Nazis and deported to Auschwitz. Thirteen-year-old Gilles was sheltered in safe houses until the French Resistance could find him passage into Switzerland.

After the War, Ségal began studying philosophy at the Sorbonne and then met mime Marcel Marceau and director Jean-Louis Barrault, who became his mentors in the theater. Subsequently, Ségal had a long and successful career acting in television roles, on stage, and in the movies. Since 1954, he had appeared in more than sixty films, such as *The Madwoman of Chaillot* (1969), *The Confession* (1970), *Mon premier amour* (1978), and *Black Light* (1994). His most memorable film was Jules Dassin's *Topkapi* (1964), for which he wrote the screenplay and in which he played the role of Giorgio. From 1967 to 2003, he acted in thirty-five French television programs and was also active in the French theater, taking roles in plays by Molière, Shakespeare, Brecht, Weiss, Beckett, and Chekhov. Although he is not primarily known as a playwright, he has written one other Holocaust drama, *Le Temps des muets* (*All the Tricks but One*), which premiered on 17 January 1992 in a production directed by Kenneth Albers at the Milwaukee Repertory Theater. Ségal passed away in France on 11 June 2014.

Le Marionnettiste de Lodz, written in 1980, had its first production in France in 1983, with Ségal assuming the role of Samuel Finkelbaum, the puppetmaster. The following year, in 1984, Jean-Paul Roussillon staged the play at the Théâtre de la Commune in Aubervilliers. The first production of the play in English was at the Milwaukee Repertory Theater in 1988 in a version translated from the original French by the managing director of the theater, Sara O'Connor. *The Puppetmaster of Lodz* has been particularly popular in the United States, with productions at the Empty Theater in Seattle (1988/1989), Blackfriars Theatre in San Diego (1992), Theater Three in Long Island (1993), Marin Theater in Mill Valley near San Francisco (1999), Performance Workshop Theatre in Baltimore (2002), Mum Puppettheater in Philadelphia (2004), ArcLight Theater in New York City (2007), Writers' Theatre in Glencoe near Chicago (2007), and Unicorn Theatre of the Berkshire Theatre Festival in Stockbridge, Massachusetts (2012).

The Puppetmaster of Lodz is set in the outskirts of Berlin in 1950, five years after the end of World War II. Samuel Finkelbaum, a recluse who adamantly insists that the War is not over, refuses to leave his apartment for fear of being arrested by German authorities. His concierge keeps him alive by providing him with groceries and other necessities, but she cannot coax him out of hiding behind closed doors that he carefully locks from intruders. Once a renowned puppeteer from Lodz, Finkelbaum is a ghost of his former self. He was deported with his pregnant wife Ruchele to Birkenau, where his life was spared by working in the ignominious position as a *Sonderkommando*, whose task it was to burn the bodies of the gassed victims. Although Finkelbaum feels guilty about stealing bread from his fellow *Häftlinge* – an act of survival at the expense of his friend Schwartzkopf – and of succumbing to Nazi pressure to perform puppetry with corpses for a Nazi aficionado of Bunraku, the most horrendous burden he had to endure was the burning of his own wife's corpse. Finkelbaum is thus traumatized not only with his wife's death, but also with the knowledge that he lost his child as well. The guilt deepens because Finkelbaum stole bread from Schwartzkopf, who, in turn, robbed prisoners of *their* rations to provide sustenance for Finkelbaum so as to give him the opportunity to see his child upon birth. In short, as Edward R. Isser has remarked, "Finkelbaum is hounded by the guilt of his own survival and by his actions in the death camp."[15]

Finkelbaum suffers from symptoms associated with the paranoia plaguing many Holocaust survivors. In *The Aftermath: Living With the Holocaust*, Aaron Hass writes, "One striking characteristic of many survivors is their enhanced sense of vulnerability."[16] In her book on trauma, Herman corroborates the notion that the chronically traumatized person can never be at ease: "The sense that the perpetrator is still present, even after liberation, signifies a major alteration in the victim's relational world."[17] Chodoff, also mentioning similar conclusions about paranoia by Trautman and Matussek that were referred to in Chapter 1, states that one of the major characteristics of the Concentration Camp Syndrome was "depressive manifestations" signified by feelings of seclusiveness, apathy, hostility, and mistrust of others.[18] Having experienced the worst savage attack imaginable against the human spirit, Holocaust survivors thus typically understand – emotionally, viscerally, and intellectually – how vicious humans can be and subsequently learn to mistrust and fear others. Therefore, survivors who have low self-esteem because of the way they were dehumanized in the camps may try to close themselves off from the external world or from any emotions that might remind them of the traumata. This psychological numbness that Lifton referred to becomes the survivors' defense mechanism, but as Hass maintains, it proved to be maladaptive after the War.[19]

Realizing that five years of withdrawal and seclusion have been enough, the Concierge tries to coax Finkelbaum out of his apartment. Finklebaum refuses to comply, reacting with distrust and hostility, saying to her, "Aha! There it is! There's what you want. For me to go out and get myself arrested! That's why you charge me less, because they'll pay you a fortune to see that I get picked up!"[20] When the Concierge offers to provide Finkelbaum with a newspaper as proof of current events, he balks, stating, "A fake newspaper that you have expressly printed up? No thank you!" (9). The Concierge brings a member of the Russian infantry stationed in Berlin to persuade Finkelbaum that Germany is now occupied and the War is over. Yet even after producing stamped documents, Russian cigarettes, and photo identification, Popov fails to convince Finkelbaum, who resorts to his survivor mentality: "It's hard to survive when you trust people" (20). Finkelbaum believes that even his confidante, the Concierge, would betray him, explaining to Popov that he thinks the Russian's presence is a trick to lure him out for compensation: "Just because up to now she's resisted the temptation to turn me in doesn't mean she'll resist forever! Imagine if they double . . . if they triple the reward . . ." (22).

Other attempts to bring Finkelbaum out of seclusion fail as well. Visited by Popov disguised as Sergeant James W. Spencer, an American stationed in Berlin who urges Finkelbaum to testify against Nazis for their war crimes, Finkelbaum questions how an American could speak German so fluently.

Finkelbaum says that the idea that the Russians and the Americans are in Berlin could be nothing but a ruse to lure him out of hiding. The next visitor, Hyman Weissfeld, is visible proof that Jews can walk the streets of Berlin after the War, but Finkelbaum dismisses him as nothing more than a salesman. Weissfeld transforms into a doctor, but Finkelbaum recognizes the disguise. Finkelbaum, who distrusts German deceit, compares the doctor to Mengele, the Auschwitz physician who performed experiments on inmates without their consent. Finkelbaum remains stubborn and steadfast in his attempt to psychically numb himself from what he perceives to be malicious humanity.

Ségal's play adeptly captures the survivor mentality in which Finkelbaum's consciousness is firmly grounded in the Holocaust experience that shaped his life. When he prepares breakfast for himself, he weighs the ingredients as if they were precious rations that sustained him in Birkenau. He rationalizes that since God let all of his people be murdered, he has "a sacred duty to survive" (10). He also reenacts fleeing with his wife from the Nazis with their hastily packed garments, assuring her that the danger has subsided.

However, the most perverse aspect of Finkelbaum's paranoia is not his seclusion from the outside world, but his refashioning of the Holocaust experience by himself, in silence, without the Other and without God. Believing that God deserted the Jews during the Shoah, Finkelbaum has retreated to his puppets to recreate the Holocaust: the puppetmaster as Creator. Finkelbaum rationalizes what he is doing in seclusion: "Finkelbaum, the rival of God, since he too creates beings to whom he gives life, and from whom he can withdraw it at will, and, since God does not exist, the sole Creator of Creation!" (22). In his macabre fantasy world, Finkelbaum has created a second Holocaust replete with reminiscences of the traumata reenacted through puppet shows that he performs. Finkelbaum restages trauma through puppets dressed in camp tunics, a stage performance that is not therapeutic but instead serves to reinforce his hostility to the outside world. For example, one scenario is a reenactment of the Nazis tearing children from their mothers' arms and smashing the babies' heads against the wall. The most nerve-wracking performance piece includes the puppet of Finkelbaum's own likeness talking with his wife Ruchele, also played by a full-size puppet; at one point, Finkelbaum tries to exorcise his grief by having Ruchele hand him a knife so he can commit hara-kiri. In essence, Ségal, trained in mime himself, has presented audiences with a visual effect that viscerally conveys to spectators the survivor mentality: there is something pathologically wrong with a man who talks only to himself through puppets! Finkelbaum is not living life in the present; he is merely the ghost of a man whose body and soul perished in Auschwitz.

Finkelbaum's seclusion, his silence, is typical of many Holocaust survivors. Aharon Appelfeld states that survivor tales were thought to sound like something imaginary, so silence was preferred.[21] Charlotte Delbo adds that years after the incarceration, she could not speak about the trauma even to her own husband. Delbo writes, "I can do nothing to help him imagine what it was like. It's impossible, even if it took us a whole lifetime to talk about it. So I simply don't speak about it."[22] Moreover, Appelfeld contends there was a desire to bury the bitter memories rather than invigorating them in public. The Holocaust produced such shame and guilt in the ghosts who survived that they preferred to remain anonymous. Saul Friedlander notes, "The silence did not exist within the survivor community. It was maintained in relation to the outside world and was often imposed by shame, the shame of telling a story that must appear unbelievable and was, in any case, entirely out of tune with surrounding society."[23] The fact that the trauma produced by the Holocaust could not be understood by those who had not experienced it, coupled with the survivors' feelings of guilt and shame, all bred silence. Furthermore, the tension between the need to bear witness and the fear of betraying the sanctity of the dead often became unbearable. Finkelbaum's self-imposed five-year silence meant that he kept his emotions bottled up, which did nothing to ease the burden of his trauma.

At the end of the play, Schwarzkopf, Finkelbaum's comrade and fellow escapee from Auschwitz, enters the apartment. The stage directions indicate, *"The two men look at one another for a long moment and, immobile, weep without sound. Then they hug fiercely, brothers"* (48). William B. Helmreich, who has interviewed many former victims of the Holocaust, explains the silence among such meetings of survivors: "Because of their common history, there exists, among most of the survivors, a very strong bond, rooted in the events of the past, that ties them to one another in ways that only they can fully appreciate."[24] However, the encounter between the two men does not alleviate Finkelbaum's madness, for he refers to the puppet as his wife Ruchele and tells Schwartzkopf, "I believe the baby is due soon" (48). As they get drunk drinking brandy together, Finkelbaum gets up enough courage to agree to flee to Anvers with his colleague, whom he trusts, and leave the illusory world of distrust behind in an attempt to face the real world; after all, they have escaped from worse horrors before. Thinking twice about taking the puppets with him, Finkelbaum deposits them in the oven. He is thus back in Auschwitz as the *Sonderkommando* burning bodies again. After burning the puppets of the *Häftlinge*, he faces the dilemma of what to do about the Ruchele puppet. He cannot burn her again; instead, he cradles the puppet, as if his wife were still alive. When the Concierge asks Finkelbaum to confirm that the war is over, Schwartzkopf has the last words of the play: "So they say, so they say . . ." (53). For those who have suffered from such post-traumatic stress disorder, the ongoing trauma is proof that the Holocaust is never over.

Peter Flannery was born 12 October 1951 in Jarrow, Tyne and Wear, and grew up in northeast England. After obtaining a degree in drama from Manchester University in 1973, where he met his wife Liz, Flannery wrote his first play, *Heartbreak Hotel*, staged at the Contact Theatre in Manchester in 1975. During the late 1970s and early 1980s, he was the resident playwright for the Royal Shakespeare Company, where he wrote some of his best-known plays: *Savage Amusement* (1978); *The Adventures of Awful Knawful*, with Mick Ford (1978); and *Our Friends in the North* (1982), which won the John Whiting Award. After years of wrangling with the production details, the British Broadcasting Company produced *Our Friends in the North* in nine episodes in 1996 as a television adaptation of the play. Since 1983, Flannery has written mainly for television. In 1988, he wrote five screenplays for the television mini-series *Blind Justice*, and he has since written for television programs such as *Rose and Maloney* (2004–2005), *The Devil's Whore* (2008), *Inspector George Gently* (2010), and *New Worlds* (2014). During the British Academy Television Awards ceremony in 1997, Flannery received the Dennis Potter Award for outstanding achievement in television writing. Flannery has also worked in the film industry, writing screenplays for such films as *Funny Bones* (1995) and *The One and the Only* (2002).[25]

Under direction by Terry Hands, *Singer* premiered at the Royal Shakespeare Company's Swan Theatre in Stratford-upon-Avon, England, on 27 September 1989. The following year, the production transferred to the Barbican Theatre in London. Although the critical reception among the British reviewers was mixed, with several of them misconstruing the play as Thatcherism and fascism coexisting symbiotically, while others accused Flannery of anti-Semitism, most critics praised Anthony Sher's protean, electric performance as Singer. With the play's running time of nearly three hours and its large cast of seventy-five roles that must be doubled and even tripled, *Singer* has not had many productions worldwide. The next notable staging of the play was by the Oxford Stage Company at the Tricycle Theatre in London, premiering there on 15 March 2005. Sean Holmes directed Edward Peel (Manik), John Light (Stefan), and Ron Cook, whose performance as Singer was spellbinding.

Singer, written in five acts with a prologue and epilogue, spans forty years from Auschwitz to the Margaret Thatcher administration. The play's tone has much in common with Jacobean revenge tragedy, with the protagonist, Singer, assuming the persona of the witty, erudite tragicomic figure ranting against an unjust world. The play also has an epic theater quality about it, replete with the Chorus as a Brechtian-type-narrator, as we follow Singer's attempts to remake his life through forty years of trial and error.

Flannery used Primo Levi's *If This Is a Man* as source material for the Prologue of the play, set in Auschwitz. Pyotr Zinger and Stefan Gutman, two Jews from Lvov, Poland, have befriended a German gentile political prisoner named Manik. The first words of the play, "Cold. Cold. Cold," recited by Singer, set the stage for the refrain, repeated by the protagonist throughout the play, that indicates that the Holocaust never leaves one's consciousness.²⁶ The wily Singer is busy "organizing" during the camp's black market exchange program, trading his shirt for a bowl of soup. Singer is near death, but his fifteen-year-old nephew Stefan, Blockchief of the Children's Camp, urges him to bolster enough energy to remain alive temporarily. Stefan has given Mirchuk, a sadistic Ukrainian guard, two virgins from the children's camp so that Singer would have time to organize his coupons. Stefan and Singer have both witnessed the deaths of their family members and are on the verge of losing their minds. Stefan has lost all morality and recognizes the immense burden that weighs heavily on his conscience: he has calculated that he has sent 2,681 children from his Block to their deaths in the gas chambers. While exchanging coupons with the Kapos, Singer, the shrewd capitalistic businessman, learns an important lesson in survival that will color his future outlook on life: "Make a deal today and live until tomorrow. That's the important thing" (5). Mirchuk punishes Manik, who traded his shirt in the black market as Singer obliged him to do, by beating him. When Singer tries to intervene, Mirchuk forces Singer to pummel Manik with blow after blow to the head. Mirchuk, who has stepped in excrement, forces Singer to eat it, calling Singer a "piece of Jewish shit" (7). Singer, as the audience later in the play learns, is an educated person who had aspirations to be a dentist and had cultivated tastes in music, art, and theater; in Auschwitz, however, he is degraded as a subhuman that Mirchuk states is "worth less than this piece of shit on my boot" (7).

Act one, scene one of *Singer* introduces the motif that Flannery explores throughout the play: whether survivors who have been traumatized in the camps can ever adjust psychologically to civilized society. After liberation, Singer, Stefan, and Manik are met by a British immigration official who provides advice to ease their transition from refugees to citizens: "Forget: forget the past. You've had terrible experiences. But there is nothing to be gained by dwelling on the past. The future's what counts; you must make up your minds who and what you want to be" (11). The remainder of the play is about the impossibility of forgetting a process that demeaned humans and removed them from their cultural identity, disallowing them to determine whether their future lives could be fruitful. Manik has severe brain damage from the beatings he took in Auschwitz. Stefan, at the disembarkation dock, tells Singer, "I don't want to be told: forget. Nobody should forget; we should all sit down now and write down everything that has happened" (12). Singer, however, makes the decision at the dock to become an Anglican, changing his name immediately from Pyotr Zinger to Peter Singer and eagerly obliging to assimilate into British society: "We'll forget. We all want to be English. God save the Kink!" (11). Unfortunately, Singer, the focal point of the play, goes on an impossible quest to provide meaning for his life after the Holocaust.

Manik, who learned about the black market through Singer, helplessly clings to his mentor after the War. Brain dead from the beatings in the camp, Manik becomes the body that complements Singer's mind. Manik functions as the strong man, the muscle, that Singer needs to force refugees to comply with the demands he makes as a slum landlord. When Manik develops a conscience about removing immigrants from Singer's apartments, Singer consoles him by urging him to put the mind behind him and become the muscle he has degenerated into: "Don't *think* Manik. It's suicidal for you" (31). Manik has headaches from his camp experiences and has to take medication to calm him down. He is particularly attuned to outside stimuli that reinforce memories of the *lager*, and although he learns broken English, he regresses to the guttural German of Auschwitz when he hears references to "prisons" or "whipping" (55). Manik's fate is that he is never divested from his memories of the Holocaust. For example, when Stefan asks Manik if he would like to be photographed, Manik replies, "What I want, you cannot give. A picture of Manik before. Remember what I was before. Maybe you have a magic camera, yah?" (42–3). When Manik degenerates to a drunken homeless man later in the play and is rescued by Stefan and Singer, who offer him food, he thinks he is back in the black market of the *lager*: he "trades" his shirt for rations. In the last scene of the play, Manik appears to have lost his sanity. He refers to enterprising capitalists as "comrades," wonders if they are from the "Women's Block," and reverts back to his identity as political prisoner Otto Vanselow, once a citizen from Düsseldorf, who will forever be reduced to nothing more than a product of the camps. In his final remarks in the play, Manik, still subliminally trading in the camp's black market, laments to Singer, "I'm not Manik, comrade. I have a coupon somewhere. I gave my spoon for it yesterday. I was cheated. I need a friend, comrade" (95).

Stefan never was able to adapt to life after the Holocaust. In England, he worked as a photographer but also turned to painting as his hobby. He withdrew from society and became a loner devoid of friends or family. Stefan is completing a gigantic mural of children, running in fear and trembling in horror, as they are being led to the gas chambers. Moreover, the only subjects of his paintings are the visions of children suffering at Birkenau. During the soirée that Singer prepares for the elite of British society, Stefan brings a gift to his friend – a soup bowl from the camp; in other words, while Singer tries to forget the Holocaust, Stefan becomes his shadowy reminder of it. When asked why he would not alter the subject of his artwork and paint landscapes to improve his career fortunes, Stefan replies, "Career? You misunderstand. Everything must be recorded that can be recorded. Nothing must be forgotten" (80). Although he wishes that humans could erase memories because it would be soothing to forget, he sees it as his moral duty to keep the reality of the Holocaust alive, especially since Holocaust denial has become an industry. Stefan confesses, "The past must be confronted so that it will never return" (82). The faces of the children who were gassed appear to Stefan in his nightmares. Stefan tells Singer that his goal is to keep the children's images alive in his artwork:

> This girl's face came to me clearly in a dream last night. She came in a consignment from the East. She only lived long enough to be undressed and shaved. But suddenly I remembered – just at the end of the painting. Look here. There was a tiny thread hanging from the back of her coat. Just there. You see? No detail will be forgotten, Peter.

(82–3)

Stefan, who tried to remake himself through his art, could not, as Delbo suggests, wrinkle out of his skin as might a snake. At the end of the play, he commits suicide by slitting his wrists. His life parallels the path of another Auschwitz survivor, Primo Levi, whose books *The Drowned and the Saved* and *Survival in Auschwitz* were written as Holocaust remembrance; Levi committed suicide in April 1987. Elie Wiesel later commented that Levi had died in Auschwitz forty years earlier. Stefan and Levi could not transcend their pasts.

Although Manik and Stefan clearly depict through their personae the spectre of the Holocaust among survivors, Singer, obviously the focal point of the play, seems to divert our attention away from the Shoah. Singer's goal is to forget the trauma, and, as he does so, the audience follows with him. Singer deigns to ignore his former suffering and, as the immigration officer suggested, forge ahead with a new life in England. He is similar to many survivors who, as I have already discussed, attempted to assuage the trauma by "tricking" the mind to focus exclusively on work. Constantly hammered in Auschwitz with the idea that he was worthless, Singer tries to remake himself in England as a respectable person with business acumen. Furthermore, as Lifton mentioned, one characteristic of all survivors is their search for meaning in the trauma – a quest to overcome the death anxiety, guilt, and psychic numbing with which they are plagued; without a family, Singer becomes married to his work. Aaron Hass explains a survivor mentality that makes up for loss with intended profit and gain: "Yet, they are often more accomplished at experiencing joy in response to what they *have* than at attaining any inner contentment."[27] Singer's notion of citizenship amounts merely to acquiring goods that he was unable to attain in the camp; his talent for "organizing" allows him to climb the ranks of British society.

Singer begins his second life as a wisecracking con artist operating an office out of a phone booth in Bayswater. As he buys more property, he becomes notorious as a slum landlord who exploits his tenants. With similarities to the sarcastic Groucho Marx, Singer, a fast-talking shyster, views the world as his stage. Singer takes advantage of minority immigrants by renting them dilapidated apartments. He explains to Manik that since the two of them are no longer starving and no one is beating them, they have a reprieve from their former deaths in life, so "nothing *matters*" (16). Singer's attitude toward his employees is heartless, dismissing them at will for trivialities, such as dropping a spoon (44) or failing to clean a speck of dirt on a plate (45). At his party to announce his British citizenship, Singer tells Manik to crack down on uninvited guests: "And remember: if they show no invitation, you show no mercy. Out on their arses" (47). The journalist, Shallcross, sensing that Singer is ripe material for the tabloids, envisions the first sentence of his exposé on the slum landlord: "'With his vicious side-kick, half animal, half man, he terrorised defenceless people showing no pity when they begged for mercy" (34). Singer demonstrates the psychic numbness that Lifton mentioned served survivors well during their camp experience but became maladaptive after the Holocaust. Laub and Auerhahn stated that this emotional bankruptcy led survivors to avoid close ties with anyone lest such alliances would go awry as they inevitably did in the camps.[28] Thus, Singer's crass behavior makes perfect sense if one understands survivor mentality.

Critics have misconstrued the play as primarily an attack on modern British society because in Singer's second life as a ruthless businessman, he undercuts British culture at every opportunity. Although "nothing matters" to a fellow like Singer who has survived Auschwitz, language does matter to those who base their values on civilized decorum. Singer, the Polish refugee, cannot understand the mores of British society, yet he values British citizenship and its reward of providing him with a new identity as a human being. Singer boasts, "I'm British. I'm British! I'm not a stateless person anymore! I have a home!" (41). Yet Singer demeans the very culture that he hopes to adopt. For example, he encourages Stefan to paint English landscapes: "What about scenes of English life? The Changing of the Guard. The Lord Mayor's Show. The Notting Hill Race Riot" (38). At his party to celebrate his citizenship, Singer insults the royalty attending by besmirching their sordid genealogies. He then flaunts his crudity by asserting, "And if in the distant future I was ever to receive by some act of mindless generosity on the part of people up whose shoelaces I'm not worthy of doing, say a knighthood or maybe a humble CBE for starters, then I would truly know that I had arrived" (52). Singer even had the gall to attempt to quote Shakespeare as an indication of his assimilation, telling Manik, "Screw your courage to the sticky point" (28).

Singer's rapacious behavior, coupled with the well-known fact that Flannery wrote the play after reading Shirley Green's 1979 biography of Peter Rachman, allowed British critics to label the play a vicious satire of British culture. Singer and Rachman are comparable in several ways. Rachman was also a slum landlord in the Notting Hill area of London in the 1950s and early 1960s. Like Singer, Rachman was born in Lvov, was Jewish, became a British citizen after the War, exploited tenants, and was a compulsive womanizer. Thus, the stereotype of the Jew as Shylock led some critics to accuse Flannery of latent anti-Semitic caricature. However, the main difference between the two men is that Rachman was never interned in a concentration camp.[29] British critics failed to focus on the Holocaust as the prime motivator for Singer's behavior, but, as Glenda Abramson has noted, in Israel, when the play was staged at Beer Sheva in 1992, theater critics saw the play differently and lauded it as the portrayal of a survivor who parlayed his survival skills into success after the War.[30]

Singer moves into the third stage of his reformulation of his life when he has an epiphany that reminds him that he represents the spectre of the Holocaust, and his identity as a British citizen is merely a façade. His constant reminder of his past is the tattooed number on his arm, which he refused to have removed. Singer's refrain, "It's cold. So cold. So cold" (56), at night on a heath in Hampstead, leads him into the cold waters, partly as a suicide wish but mainly as a baptism. Singer, repeating the words he used to identify himself in Auschwitz, recognizes who he really is beneath the mask of British citizenship: "I'm worthless. Worthless. I am nothing" (56).

Singer's third stage of reformulation, of attempting to find meaning in the trauma, is to seek revenge on former Ukrainian guard Mirchuk. Eight years after his "baptism," Singer reemerges as an art dealer befriending Ruby Mirchuk, an artist and the daughter of the notorious Auschwitz guard. Mirchuk has become a recluse in a wheelchair who feels guilty about living through the Holocaust when so many others died. When Mirchuk enters to meet Singer and Stefan, Mirchuk's presence is the stimulus for the reenactment of Auschwitz, as Singer mutters to himself, "Cold. Cold. Cold" (71). Singer confronts Mirchuk about the atrocities he committed, the order he gave to beat Manik nearly to death, and the children Stefan provided to satisfy his pleasures. Mirchuk claims that he cannot remember the offenses, but Singer says that forgetting is impossible since the Holocaust frames one's life forever: "Old? Yes, I'm old, but I was never young. I got on to a train a young man who had never seen anybody die and I got off five days later an old man with death sewn into the lining of my clothes" (75). As Lifton implied in characterizing the trauma endemic to all survivors, they try to find an answer about why the Holocaust occurred in a civilized world. Singer's cross-examination of Mirchuk serves to illuminate a purpose for his suffering. He explains to Mirchuk, "My name was Pyotr Zinger. Oh yes, Peter Singer. I was a human being. You turned me into nothing. I was solid, I was real. I demand to know the reason why. *Why* was that done to me?" (76). Mirchuk swears to tell the truth in front of his daughter. He claims that he remembers Stefan but has no clue who Singer was, no memory of him being in the camp.

The confrontation with Mirchuk serves as a catharsis for Singer, who resurrects himself again in a fourth stage of reformulation. For the next twenty years, Singer performs charity work, serving bread and soup to the homeless. His noble intentions have become so famous that he is known in London as Saint Peter of the South Bank. Singer is even invited to have lunch with the prime minister at Ten Downing Street. At the luncheon, government bureaucrats convince Singer that the 1980s will be a time of renewed profit and a chance for free enterprise to flourish. They hope that the old Peter Singer, the ruthless slumlord, will provide insight for young Thatcherites to thrive in the cutthroat markets of the 1980s.

Singer is eager to adjust to the new political climate in England. He tells Stefan, "It's like the '50s again out there, but with the gloves off this time. A country looking to the future at last, not obsessed anymore with the past. My God, I have such a good feeling again!" (88). The budding entrepreneurs motivate Singer to lead their consortium because he was the original pioneer of the profitable scheme of buying up cheap properties, dividing them up, and then selling them to make a huge profit. When Stefan questions why a man who gave his life to the homeless for twenty years would prostitute himself, Singer replies that the world is nothing but lies. Stefan argues that Singer was a cultured man in Lvov, a respected mentor to him, and a person with a taste for life. Singer responds that his life before Auschwitz has been snuffed out: "It doesn't exist anymore, Stefco. There is no time before. I, Peter Singer was born in the camp" (93). However, when Singer learns that homeless mental invalids are going to live in "camps" and those not conforming to the strict regulations will be beaten, Singer morphs into Pyotr Zinger of Auschwitz.[31] He states, "I feel cold. Cold. Cold" (95). The play thus becomes circular: the last scene mirrors the first; Auschwitz is viewed as an everlasting state of mind. Singer has attempted to reformulate himself through different personae, but in the denouement, he realizes that his life in Auschwitz has resonated eternally, ghostlike, always underneath the surface. In his book, *And We Are Not Saved*, Holocaust survivor David Wdowinski explains why Singer's quest to reformulate life again can never assuage the spectre of the *lager*: "Why rake up old ashes, I am constantly asked. Forget and start life over again. It seems they will never understand that *we* cannot forget, that we must not forget. Thus, those of us who have survived are condemned unto death to an incomprehensible loneliness."[32] After the War, survivors, like Singer, attempted to distract themselves from the traumata by remaking their lives or finding a cause they could support to create meaning in their lives; these pursuits were essentially attempts to mask the psychopathology. After Stefan's suicide, Singer realizes that, although he has led several lives, there is only one that has permanent resonance: "I'm going back to the first of all. The one I thought I'd left behind in a railway car. You were right, Stefan. It wasn't a mistake to remember. The mistake was not remembering enough" (97). Although there has been a paucity of international productions of *Singer*, Flannery's well-nuanced and meticulously crafted play provides one of the more thought-provoking portraits of the complex psychopathology of Holocaust survivors.

In their studies of trauma, Kleber and Brom corroborate what was classified in the DSM-III-R as one of the major symptoms of post-traumatic stress disorder: increased arousal that often leads to irritability, hypervigilance, and outbursts of anger.[33] American playwright Richard Atkins's 2013 play, *DelikateSSen*, best reflects the lingering effects of anger and hostility prevalent in Holocaust survivors years after the trauma. Atkins, who was Guy Lombardo's pianist in the late 1970s, is a composer, lyricist, actor, and director. He operates a small theater between Sante Fe and Albuquerque, New Mexico, where he lives. Atkins's serio-comic play *The Men of Mah Jongg* is currently being adapted for film. *DelikateSSen* premiered 3 April 2015 at the Adobe Theatre in Albuquerque, New Mexico. James Franco's company Rabbit Bandini Productions is considering the play for adaptation into a film with Franco playing the lead role of David Shapiro.[34]

DelikateSSen in performance runs approximately two hours and is composed of twelve scenes in two acts. Fourteen projections, often accompanied by classical music, are interspersed throughout the play. The original purpose of the projections, which are typically located at the end of each scene, was to keep the audience stimulated while the stage crew changed scenery.[35] However, with the positive reaction to this stage device during the readings of the play, Atkins expanded the projections to include Nazi quotations, as well as quotations from survivors. This "ying-yang" balance coincided with the highs and lows of the play: when events get dire, we hear Nazi projections, and when the mood is more sanguine, we hear positive messages. These projections include quotations from journalist Fern Schumer Chapman, American prisoner of war Oliver Omanson, Primo Levi, Elie Wiesel, Isaac Bashevis Singer, Heinrich Himmler, Winston Churchill, poet Barbara Sonek, Anne Frank, Hitler, Hermann Goering, Joseph Goebbels, Tadeusz Borowski, Rudolf Höss, Viktor Frankl, Adolf Eichmann, and Rabbi Joseph Weiss.

Upon the suggestion of Mark Medoff, the author of *Children of a Lesser God* who served as Atkins's dramaturge, Atkins set *DelikateSSen* in October 1972. Thus, the play takes place near the close of the Summer Olympics in Munich, when eleven Israeli athletes and coaches had been killed while they were taken hostage by Palestinians belonging to the Black September organization. The event brought back emotions of hostility and anger among many Holocaust survivors and in the play served to rekindle David Shapiro's overtly aggressive feelings toward Nazis.

David and his younger brother Yossi Shapiro are both survivors of Buchenwald and Auschwitz who operate a Jewish delicatessen in Manhattan. Yossi is described in the stage directions as *"level headed, sympathetic, the voice of reason,"* while David is *"high strung, easily agitated, bitter."*[36] Yossi and David are both married and also have families to support. Their delicatessen is in dire financial straits to the point where David and Yossi find it difficult to pay their business's rent each month. They have a few loyal customers, such as Maria Schneider and Franz Becker, but overall their business has declined over the years.

David represents the extreme example of the hypervigilant Holocaust survivor who directs his hatred against all Germans. When Atkins was growing up in the largely Jewish neighborhood of Pikesville in Baltimore, he heard his father many times echo the sentiment that the only good German is a dead one;[37] this line is quoted by David Shapiro in the play and, because of the Holocaust, it colors his opinion of all Germans. The Munich Olympics tragedy becomes the catalyst for David's hypervigilance. When Yossi notes Rabbi Weiss's recent sermon on forgiveness, David disagrees, stating that Nazi murderers still roam the streets and cites Himmler's daughter operating a Munich asylum for Nazis as evidence that the cycle of terror is ongoing.

David is haunted by the spectre of the Holocaust and his experience in Auschwitz. His mother contracted typhus in Auschwitz and died shortly afterwards. He watched helplessly when his father came down with fever and thus was sent to the gas chamber. He even recalls the Nazis forcing a Jewish violinist to serenade the victims waiting in line to go to their deaths: "Some knew, others would guess soon enough. Germans just laughed it up . . . monsters" (5). Now violins act as a trigger to stimulate bad memories for him. David reminds Yossi that an SS officer who lost his balance when a woman threw herself on him begging for mercy, causing him to trip in the mud, became so enraged that he shot her and her baby as well. David lost sixteen family members in the Shoah, and when Rabbi Weiss offers condolences, David states, "The horror lives within me like a cancer" (25). David also feels guilty about how he prostituted himself in Auschwitz. Assuming the job of polishing an SS colonel's boots, David was compromised when he was asked to save his crippled brother's life by performing oral sex on the officer. Yossi, who had been accidentally shot days earlier, was a candidate for extermination. David saved his brother from death by providing fellatio to the Camp Commander on a routine basis.[38]

With Shapiro's delicatessen business floundering, tensions escalate when a German delicatessen-biergarten opens across the street from David's restaurant. David immediately frames the competition in terms of Jewish-German relations and tells Rabbi Weiss, "If they still want a fight, that's what they'll get" (27). David's first impression is that the Germans are again trying to evict Jews – this time running them out of their New York City neighborhood. The new deli provides entertainment as well, so when the customers gravitate toward the novelty, the German business begins to prosper. The owner, Klaus Reinhardt, who decides to become acquainted with his neighbors across the street, pays them a visit. Although Klaus is polite, friendly, and deferential, David treats him with suspicion and disrespect. Klaus asks, "Why are you so angry, Herr Shapiro?" (50). David cannot be placated and can only assume that anti-Semitism is the underlying reason why a German business would open across the street from a Jewish delicatessen. David makes false accusations and then asks his competitor to leave: "You break in, you threaten and lie to me and then ask to be my friend? Get the fu –" (51). Upon departing, Klaus offers to shake hands with David, but the latter refuses to do so.

During the remainder of the play, the audience watches as the Shapiro family completely unravels because of David's psychopathology that induces paranoia and obsessive hypervigilance, prompting his violent and irrational behavior. Although his failing business has nothing to do with the Holocaust, David puts the blame squarely on the Germans. He tells Yossi, "Face it! We're screwed because of this stinking German" (60). The red neon lights of Reinhardt's business trigger for David an unusually hypervigilant reaction, and he screams, "TURN THAT LIGHT OFF BEFORE I SHOVE IT DOWN YOUR NAZI THROAT" (65). Both Yossi and David have been consistently plagued with nightmares about the Holocaust, but David now has a new bad dream; in it, Klaus, in the guise of an SS colonel, visits the deli and forces Yossi to sing, dance, and become subordinate. Klaus demeans Yossi by calling him Jewish scum and Jew bastard and then, at gunpoint, puts him in a noose for hanging. Before Yossi dies, David wakes up in terror as the red neon light continues to flash – this time in Yossi's face. David realizes that the dream sequence reflects his former latent anxiety about Yossi's fate at the hands of the Nazis but also reveals the concomitant shame that he had to endure to save his brother's life. While weeping, David confesses, "I'm sorry, Yossi! I had no choice. I simply –" (74).

David hires Nazi hunter Yaakov Zeiman to spy on Klaus, but by doing so, he complicates his life. Yossi claims that he was mysteriously followed home one evening and swiped a guardrail to evade his pursuers. Although Zeiman's initial investigation discovered no Nazi ties to Klaus, David urges him to dig further and find information on Klaus's wife, cousins, or uncles. After Zeiman pursues other avenues, he learns that Franz Becker appears to be Ernst Richter, the notorious Butcher of Buchenwald, and Klaus Reinhardt is actually his son Hans.

As the fury with the Nazis continues for David, his family life deteriorates. David suffers from high blood pressure and heart problems, and when his health worsens over the anxiety, his wife Sarah and son Michael become alarmed. Like many Holocaust survivors who shield their offspring from the horrors of the Shoah, David has told Michael nothing about his internship in Birkenau. Michael learns about the Holocaust by watching a film in school, and when David hears that an Irishman is teaching the subject, he becomes irate. David rolls up his sleeve to reveal his tattooed number and then admits to the ghastly fate of Michael's grandparents. Having overheard David's conversations with his wife and with Klaus about Germans, Michael, upon learning about his father's history, now begins to understand the ramifications of those previous discussions. The Holocaust begins adversely affecting Michael's behavior. At school, he becomes prone to get into fights, the violence all the while being encouraged by David. Sarah is at her wit's end, complaining, "I can't take much more of this, David. I really can't" (97).

David's family life starts to disintegrate quickly. Zeiman suspects he is being followed by Nazi sympathizers, so David, paranoid about Michael's safety, refuses to allow his son to walk home alone. Some anonymous visitor to the deli seems to have thrown a rock through the window. David sees the signs of the Shoah returning, telling Sarah, "They're trying to obliterate us again" (99). Sarah, however, views her husband's psychopathology as abnormal, questioning his unusual case of paranoia: "I can't be looking over my shoulder every two seconds! Worried about Michael at school; Michael walking home? This is a free country, David. You're not in the concentration camp anymore!" (99). The second generation is also adversely affected by the Survivor Syndrome, as Michael claims that he is losing his mind over the family in-fighting. When David inculcates his son with the idea that the outside world is dangerous, Michael responds, "Then *you* made it that way" (100). Meanwhile Yossi, after comprehending the newly revealed revelation that his brother prostituted himself in Auschwitz, botches a suicide attempt and winds up seeing a psychiatrist.

Michael, deciding to put an end to a seemingly interminable situation and fearing that his father's weak heart would eventually falter, plants a bomb at Reinhardt's delicatessen, hoping to destroy the source of the family problem. However, his best laid plans go awry, and instead of destroying the restaurant, the explosion takes the life of his mother. Michael himself winds up in prison at Rikers Island. When David visits his son in prison, Michael seems to put the blame on his father's symptoms accrued from the trauma, explaining to him, "How can I show respect for someone who just couldn't put the past behind" (123). David's psychopathology has led his son to become a murderer. David feels downtrodden that his son, given every chance in life to be successful, unlike the Jews of Europe during the Holocaust who had their futures destroyed, has now been turned into a felon. Thus, near the end of the play, David's wife is dead, his brother is committed to a mental health facility, his business is ruined, his son is in prison for twenty-five years, and he himself is a broken man, physically and mentally – all because of traumatic symptoms that could never be alleviated and an obsession that could never be abated.

The last scene of the play occurs in Central Park five years later when David inadvertently runs into Klaus Reinhardt sitting on a park bench. David has aged considerably, walking now with a cane, sporting a gray beard, and recovering from quadruple bypass surgery. Klaus explains that his life was ruined as well after the explosion. David tries to justify his actions to Klaus: ". . . Sixteen of them . . . We had to live with that . . . Our time in the camp . . . years just to function . . . your whole life changed . . . Forever" (126). Essentially, David is inferring that the Holocaust persona that he was forced to live with was beyond his control. We also learn that Zeiman, dragged into David's neurotic fantasies through no fault of his own, has mysteriously disappeared from the public. David, frail and now looking years beyond his age, is still plagued by the trauma. He admits to Klaus, "I am too weak to fight anymore . . . Yet, have the rage of ten men inside me" (127).

The tale ends on a note of conciliation, which was Atkins's original intention for writing the play. The voice of reason, Rabbi Joseph Weiss, states in a sermon given at the Park Avenue Synagogue, "If we as Jews, continue to hate the German people for what their grandfathers and fathers did, it can only lead us down an even darker road. We must remember . . . we must reflect . . . we must forgive, but never . . . forget . . . For in the end, hate would kill us all" (128). The stage directions tell us that David Shapiro, at the relatively young age of fifty-eight, died of congestive heart failure one month after his rendezvous with Klaus Reinhardt in Central Park. Faced with severe symptoms of the Survivor Syndrome manifested through hypervigilance and pent-up anger and hostility, David was forced to realize that the effects of the trauma took its toll on him. The rabbi, by profession a peaceful man of Scripture, cannot speak for the traumatized. Those who survived the Holocaust are spectres, ghosts of their former selves, unable to slough off the past. Atkins has written a play that demonstrates the devastating effects of Holocaust trauma on the minds of the victims, who may be able to assimilate to a new culture, but as Delbo suggests, can never adapt to a new skin.

Notes

1 For example, see Paul Chodoff, "Late Effects of the Concentration Camp Syndrome," *Archives of General Psychiatry* 8, no. 4 (1963): 324–325.
2 Robert J. Lifton, "Understanding the Traumatized Self: Imagery, Symbolization, and Transformation," in *Human Adaptation to Extreme Stress: From the Holocaust to Vietnam*, eds. John P. Wilson, Zev Harel, and Boaz Kahana (New York and London: Plenum Press, 1988), 19.
3 There is a paucity of information on Morris Freed. I am indebted to Joel Berkowitz, professor of foreign languages and literature at the University of Wisconsin at Milwaukee and an expert on Yiddish theater, for this information. Joel Berkowitz, email message to author, 23 June 2014.
4 Morris Freed, *"Coupled by Fate,"* in *The Survivors: Six One-act Dramas*, trans. A.D. Mankoff (Cambridge: Sci-Art Publishers, 1956), 43. All subsequent citations from the play are from this edition and will be included within parentheses in the text.
5 Morris Freed, *"Sparks,"* in *The Survivors: Six One-act Dramas*, trans. A.D. Mankoff (Cambridge: Sci-Art Publishers, 1956), 54. All subsequent citations from the play are from this edition and will be included within parentheses in the text.
6 Freed mistakenly notes in the play that the Americans liberated Treblinka (61). Treblinka was dismantled on Himmler's orders in October 1943 after the revolt in the camp on 2 August 1943. The Russian forces arrived at Treblinka on 16 August 1944.
7 For more biographical information on Amichai, see Glenda Abramson, *The Writing of Yehuda Amichai: A Thematic Approach* (Albany: State University of New York Press, 1989); and "Amichai, Yehuda," in *Current Biography Yearbook*, ed. Elizabeth A. Schick (New York and Dublin: H.W. Wilson, 1988), 19–22.
8 Critics have ignored the fact that *Bells and Trains* takes place in a fictional city and write about the play as if the locale was in Germany. There is a Siegburg in Westphalia but no place known as Singburg.
9 Yehuda Amichai, *Bells and Trains*, trans. Aubrey Hodes, *Midstream: A Monthly Jewish Review* 12, no. 8 (1966): 56. All subsequent citations from the play are from this edition and will be included within parentheses in the text.

10 Judith Lewis Herman, *Trauma and Recovery* (New York: Basic Books, 1992), 91.
11 Henry Krystal, *Massive Psychic Trauma* (New York: International Universities Press, 1968), 68.
12 Ibid., 78.
13 For example, see Paul Chodoff, "Psychiatric Aspects of the Nazi Persecution," in *American Handbook of Psychiatry, New Psychiatric Frontiers*, vol. 6, 2nd ed., eds. David A. Hamburg and H. Keith Brodie (New York: Basic Books, 1975), 940; Rolf J. Kleber and Danny Brom, *Coping With Trauma: Theory, Prevention and Treatment* (Amsterdam: Swets & Zeitlinger, 1992), 25–26; and Patricia Benner, Ethel Roskies, and Richard S. Lazarus, "Stress and Coping Under Extreme Conditions," in *Survivors, Victims, and Perpetrators: Essays on the Nazi Holocaust*, ed. Joel E. Dimsdale (Washington, DC and New York: Hemisphere Publishing, 1980), 243.
14 Alvin Goldfarb, "Inadequate Memories: The Survivor in Plays By Mann, Kesselman, Lebow and Baitz," in *Staging the Holocaust: The Shoah in Drama and Performance*, ed. Claude Schumacher (Cambridge: Cambridge University Press, 1998), 129.
15 Edward R. Isser, *Stages of Annihilation: Theatrical Representations of the Holocaust* (Madison: Fairleigh Dickinson University Press, 1997), 118.
16 Aaron Hass, *The Aftermath: Living With the Holocaust* (Cambridge: Cambridge University Press, 1995), 55.
17 Herman, *Trauma and Recovery*, 91.
18 Chodoff, "Late Effects of the Concentration Camp Syndrome," 325. Also see Chodoff, "Psychiatric Aspects of the Nazi Persecution," 940. Krystal cites the same survivor symptoms described by Chodoff, Trautman, and Matussek. Krystal writes, "The depressive component makes itself visible in the complete withdrawal, apathy, brooding seclusion, state of depression, and especially the permanent feeling of loss and sadness in these people." See Krystal, *Massive Psychic Trauma*, 68.
19 Hass, *The Aftermath: Living With the Holocaust*, 4.
20 Gilles Ségal, *The Puppetmaster of Lodz*, trans. Sara O'Connor (New York: Samuel French, 1989), 8. All subsequent citations from the play are from this edition and will be included within parentheses in the text.
21 Aharon Appelfeld, "The Awakening," in *Holocaust Remembrance: The Shapes of Memory*, ed. Geoffrey H. Hartman (Oxford: Blackwell, 1994), 150.
22 Charlotte Delbo, *Auschwitz and After*, trans. Rosette C. Lamont (New Haven and London: Yale University Press, 1995), 267.
23 Saul Friedlander, *Memory, History, and the Extermination of the Jews of Europe* (Bloomington and Indianapolis: Indiana University Press, 1993), 126.
24 William B. Helmreich, *Against All Odds: Holocaust Survivors and the Successful Lives They Made in America* (New Brunswick: Transaction Publishers, 1996), 149.
25 For more biographical information about Flannery and productions of his plays, see Margaret Llewellyn-Jones, "Peter Flannery," in *British and Irish Dramatists Since World War II*, second series, ed. John Bull (Detroit: Gale Group, 2001), 120–127.
26 Peter Flannery, *Singer* (London: Nick Hern, 1992), 2. All subsequent citations from the play are from this edition and will be included within parentheses in the text.
27 Hass, *The Aftermath: Living With the Holocaust*, 75.
28 Dori Laub and Nanette C. Auerhahn, "Failed Empathy – A Central Theme in the Survivor's Holocaust Experience," *Psychoanalytic Psychology* 6, no. 4 (1989): 377–400.
29 Rachman was in a Soviet labor camp but never in a concentration camp. During the War, he fought with the Allied forces in the Middle East and Italy.
30 Glenda Abramson, "Anglicizing the Holocaust," *Journal of Theatre and Drama* 7/8 (2001–2002): 116. Abramson, who does recognize that the significance of being a Holocaust survivor has a sustaining effect on Singer's mentality, also argues that the play is anti-Semitic: "This is not only because the character of Singer is a nasty stereotype of a Jew, but because he is seen to bring the filth of the Holocaust into British genteel society, like a disease, and to corrupt it" (114).
31 The British critics complained about this segment of the play. In the last scene, the parallels between National Socialism and the policies of the Thatcher administration were deemed to be hyperbole, certainly crude and in poor taste. The attack on Thatcher's

government diverted the attention away from the Holocaust and onto contemporary politics. For example, Abramson writes, "Flannery's purpose is to demonstrate graphically how Rachmann [*sic*], who was pilloried in his time as the worst incarnation of rampant capitalism, would not only be accepted, but glorified under Mrs. Thatcher's government" (114).

32 David Wdowinski, *And We Are Not Saved* (New York: Philosophical Library, 1963), 18.

33 Kleber and Brom, *Coping With Trauma: Theory, Prevention and Treatment*, 25–26.

34 The biographical information on Atkins and the production history of the play were provided to me by the playwright. Richard Atkins, email message to author, 26 June 2014.

35 Richard Atkins, email message to author, 26 June 2014.

36 Richard Atkins, *DelikateSSen* (Sandia Park, NM: Photocopy, 2013), unpaginated cast list. All subsequent citations from the play are from this edition and will be included within parentheses in the text.

37 Richard Atkins, email message to author, 26 June 2014.

38 Atkins did considerable research before writing the play. With regard to sexual perversions in Auschwitz, it has been well documented that the Nazis used the Children's Block for their sexual pleasures (this was even known to Flannery, who mentioned it in *Singer*), and there was a bordello in the camp as well. Through his research, Atkins learned that several Nazi guards had inmates perform oral sex on them in attempts to fulfill their homoerotic fantasies. Atkins's research also consisted of examining films such as *Schindler's List* and *The Pianist*, as well as spending six months studying the design of German uniforms and the nuances of German dialects. He was particularly impressed with Marion Schreiber's *The Twentieth Train: The True Story of the Ambush of the Death Train to Auschwitz*, an account of the efforts of resistance fighter Youra Livchitz and his two friends who raided a German deportation train to free seventeen men and women. Atkins also interviewed Simon Gronowski, who survived that deportation as a child when his mother tossed him out of the train.

3

DRAMATIZING SURVIVOR GUILT

As mentioned in Chapter 1, in their studies of Holocaust survivors, Paul Chodoff, Henry Krystal, Guenther Emil Winkler, and William G. Niederland included guilt as one of the distinctive symptoms. The DSM-IV corroborated that guilt was part of the trauma. Robert Jay Lifton also mentions death guilt as one of five characteristics of survivor trauma. This chapter will explore survivor guilt as manifested in five representative plays: Ron Elisha's *Two*, Gabriel Dagan's *The Reunion*, Enzo Cormann's *Toujours l'Orage*, Robert Caisley's *Letters to an Alien*, and Ben-Zion Tomer's *Children of the Shadows*.

Survivor guilt is predominantly related to loss and typically is the result of the fact that the victim survived while one's relatives or friends perished. Niederland views this burden of guilt as twofold: first, the extermination of loved ones initiates grief, and second, the conscious or unconscious dread of punishment for having survived the Holocaust while the loved ones succumbed increases the depression.[1] Elie Wiesel testifies to this burden with which the Holocaust survivor must confront: "I am alive, therefore I am guilty. If I am still here, it is because a friend, a comrade, a stranger, died in my place."[2] William B. Helmreich states that guilt is a normal emotion felt by most people, but Holocaust survivor guilt takes on a special meaning since the victims feel guilty about being unable to save their loved ones.[3] They ponder the question of why they survived when others, certainly just as worthy and perhaps more generous, did not. Survivors may rationalize that their friends or family members were better human beings than they were and thus were the ones who should have been saved. Ernest A. Rappaport mentions that Holocaust survivors often feel as if by having been spared they abandoned their loved ones that they should have, out of loyalty, followed into the gas chambers.[4] Charlotte Delbo, writing about the deaths of her colleagues in Auschwitz, laments, "Despite knowing I'm not at fault, I feel guilty. I cheated our dead and betrayed my own self, my ambitions, my fits of enthusiasm."[5] For example, during the selections in the extermination camps, quotas were established for the mandatory numbers of *Häftlinge* that had to be gassed. Of course, prisoners were relieved when someone else was selected for gassing. Wiesel writes that this joy later turned into guilt: "*I am happy to have escaped death* becomes equivalent to admitting: *I am glad that someone else went in my place.*"[6]

The passivity in the face of the Holocaust was often devastating for survivors. Most survivors felt guilty about their inability to save their loved ones from death and thus blame themselves for their cowardice and powerlessness. One could reasonably argue that intervention was meaningless in the camps and would have resulted in one's own threat to survival. Judith Lewis Herman states that this argument does not console survivors, who feel completely humiliated by their helplessness in the camps.[7] At times, these feelings of guilt were related to particular episodes when the victim felt that adopting a different behavior might have saved someone's life. Moreover, the survivor may feel guilty about allowing family members to board the trains and thus going to their deaths without doing enough to resist their fates. As Henry Krystal has commented, "One feels anger, guilt, or shame whenever one is unable (refuses) to accept the necessity and unavoidability of what happened."[8] For example, Olga Lengyel, in the first sentence of her book about survival in Auschwitz, refers to the overwhelming burden of responsibility for deaths of loved ones shared by the majority of survivors:

> *Mea culpa*, my fault, *mea maxima culpa!* I cannot acquit myself of the charge that I am, in part, responsible for the destruction of my parents and of my two young sons. The world understands that I could not have known, but in my heart the terrible feeling persists that I could have, I might have, saved them.[9]

In *The Drowned and the Saved*, Primo Levi discusses the guilt engendered when the victims watched the Nazis commit crimes against humanity with impunity. He describes the downtrodden feeling of the victim whose will was proven nonexistent, feeble, or incapable of putting up a viable defense. Furthermore, Levi argues, guilt increased when the victims committed crimes against their colleagues in the camps, such as stealing from them in order to survive.[10] Levi claims that survivors tend to block from memory their transgressions against fellow inmates. However, a much worse offense was one's failure at collegiality, which made all victims feel guilty. Levi notes, "The demand for solidarity, for a human word, advice, even just a listening ear, was permanent and universal but rarely satisfied."[11] Survivors tend to feel guilty that they had no patience, strength, or time for their colleagues; instead, their selfish desire to survive dominated any virtues with which they were endowed. They may also feel wonderment about the vastness of the human tragedy in which they were forced to participate. Finally, as Herman has suggested, the sense of shame among survivors is not only related to the failure to intercede, but also comes from the realization that the perpetrators had usurped the inner lives of their victims, virtually destroying the will and spirit of the individual.[12]

On the conscious level, survivor guilt typically resulted in depression, deeply rooted *angoisse*, apathy, or a feeling of being persecuted and despised.[13] Guilt also served as a commemorative role in displaying fidelity to the dead. Paul Chodoff mentions that although survivors were tortured by persistent memories of the dead that led to anger and despair, they had an obligation to bear witness and sought to remember their relatives despite the psychological disadvantages of doing so.[14] Many survivors understood that trying to purge themselves of guilt by forgetting their dead relatives was an act of disloyalty. Moreover, since the dead never received the appropriate burial rites that might have ameliorated some of the guilt among the survivors, the latter often felt that their suffering was more than warranted. Dominick LaCapra even observed that survivors frequently demonstrated anxiety about building a new life for fear that it would signify a betrayal of loved ones who died during the Shoah.[15]

Survival guilt is also prevalent on an unconscious psychopathological level. Since survivor guilt imposes such an intolerable burden on the psyche, it is often repressed for as long as possible. Chodoff has stated that the feelings of guilt may be unconsciously related to a need to suffer to bear witness to the atrocities rather than to heal, thus forgiving the persecutors but betraying their murdered friends and relatives.[16] This is the psychopathology of masochism, a version of self-punishment based upon the need to take revenge on the parents for not protecting the child from the persecution. However, the most common form of unconscious guilt occurs in daydreams or nightmares that reenact the feeling of being responsible for what one has not done. The survivor intuits that if he or she had died instead of one of their friends or relatives, that person would have lived. Thus, they feel that their resumption of vitality in the absence of formerly taking responsibility during the incarceration is wrong. Robert Jay Lifton explains this unconscious mentality of the survivor: "Death guilt ultimately stems from a sense that until some such enactment is achieved, one has no right to be alive."[17] Since these images associated with guilt and self-condemnation are static, the traumatized victim is debilitated, often to the point of neurosis.[18]

Australian playwright Ron Elisha was born in Jerusalem in 1951 and came with his family to Melbourne in 1953. In 1975, he graduated with a medical degree from the University of Melbourne and has practiced medicine there since completing his residency requirements in Sydney in 1977. His first play, *Duty Bound* (1978), began his exploration of Jewish issues; the play focused on a young Jewish doctor whose family opposed his marriage to a gentile woman. His most famous play, *Einstein* (1981), which won an Australian Writers' Guild Award (Awgie) for best stage play, was taken on a tour of the United States by the Melbourne Theatre Company in 1982. Elisha has written twenty plays, a telemovie script (*Death Duties*, 1991), two children's books, and several newspaper articles. His plays have been performed throughout Australia and the United States, as well as in New Zealand, Canada, Poland, France, Israel, and the United Kingdom.

Two, a two-act play written in 1982, premiered at the Hole in the Wall Theatre in Perth on 3 August 1983 under direction by Pippa Williamson. The cast included

Rod Hall as Chaim and Denise Kirby as Anna. The next production was at the Marian Street Theatre in Sydney, where it received the 1984 Awgie award for best stage play. The American premiere of the play was on 9 September 1987 at the Northlight Theatre in Evanston, Illinois (adjacent to the well-populated Jewish community in Skokie). This production was directed by Barbara Damashek and starred Mike Nussbaum as Chaim and Barbara E. Robertson as Anna. In 2011, Daniela Flynn adapted Anna's long monologue in act 2 into an eight-minute film titled *Two* in which Flynn directs herself playing Anna. Produced by Robert Henry of Carriage House Media, the film was shown at the 2011 Hollywood Film Festival and at the Santa Fe Film Festival.

In his preface to the play, Elisha makes it clear that his starting point in writing the drama was an exploration of the philosophical notion of good versus evil. Although he does not cite Hannah Arendt by name, Elisha adopts Arendt's concept of the banality of evil. Arendt, attending Adolf Eichmann's trial in Jerusalem in 1962, studied the mentality of the *Obersturmbannführer* and concluded that he showed no guilt and insisted that he was merely conscientiously following orders in sending Jews to the deaths. As a Nazi bureaucrat, Eichmann acted like so many thousands of other citizens of Europe who were responsible for the genocide. Arendt concluded, "The trouble with Eichmann was precisely that so many were like him, and that the many were neither perverted nor sadistic, that they were, and still are, terribly and terrifyingly normal."[19] Elisha comes to the same conclusion about the nature of evil: "My own instinct told me that no problem existed; that the source of evil was as obvious as that of good; that both entities were created in the same breath."[20] Thus, the title of the play indicates the spirit of reconciliation between what would otherwise be two opposite systems of polarity: the Judaism of Rabbi Chaim Levi and the SS stewardship of Anna.

Two is set in an unspecified German town in 1948, where Rabbi Chaim Levi, a man in his sixties, resides in a stark cellar sparsely furnished with only basic accoutrements. He is visited by Anna, a Jewish woman in her thirties, who offers to pay the rabbi to teach her Hebrew so she can speak the language when she immigrates to Palestine. Levi is skeptical, jaded, and cynical, but he finds Anna to be intelligent and seems to enjoy sparring verbally with her, so he reluctantly agrees to the Hebrew lessons. The rabbi plays the piano, and Anna, although she has not touched a musical instrument in years, dabbles at the violin; the rabbi wants musical accompaniment, so Anna fulfills that purpose for him and both share a mutual interest in chess – a game that requires a partner. At first, Anna acknowledges that she survived the camps because of her ability to speak five languages; she hopes that by learning Hebrew, she will create a function for herself in Palestine.

Tension erupts when Chaim notices that Anna does not have a tattooed number on her forearm. Anna admits that she wants to become a Jew and feels as if a knowledge of Hebrew would help her achieve that goal. Rabbi Levi agrees to teach Anna what it means to be a Jew: he rolls up his sleeve to reveal the tattooed number 175834. The rabbi frames Jewish identity solely in terms of the suffering victim. He says to Anna, "You really believe in a land of the Jews? The Jews have no land.

They never will have. There will always be someone there to take it from them"
(26). The rabbi tells her that the Hebrew language is without vowels, and, as such,
is a skeleton of a language: "This language of skeletons. The language of the dead"
(27). Anna, however, having had enough of the rabbi's nihilism, slips up and calls
him a *Muselman*. When the rabbi realizes that only a concentration camp inmate
could ever know the meaning of that word, Anna reveals that she was in Auschwitz
as a member of the SS.

Part of Anna's responsibility in Auschwitz was to provide chocolates to the children before they were gassed – one of Eichmann's ideas to calm fears and thus make
the genocide appear to be orderly. Now the authorities are searching for Anna, the
war criminal. Anna's mother was a Jewess, but being ashamed of her religion, Anna
passed herself off as a gentile, which she could do since her father was Christian.
Anna considered Judaism to be "a horrible, lurking shadow" (36), so she joined
the SS, an organization determined to eradicate the shadow from the face of the
earth. Furthermore, Anna's father persecuted his wife, coerced her to convert, and
when Hitler came to power, he treated her like a third-class citizen. He beat her,
cursed her, spat on her, broke her bones, and eventually turned his wife into a pitiful,
groveling animal. Anna, forced to hate her own mother, joined the SS as a means to
eradicate the image of the groveling victim, admitting to Chaim, "I wanted to kill. I
ached to kill" (47). Anna, however, does not need psychotherapy, for she understands
the source of her frustration. She realizes that instead of despising her parents, she
hated herself as a Jew, and now she plans to travel to Palestine to add value to the
fledgling Jewish nation. She does not feel guilty about the Holocaust and provides
the moral lesson that Elisha wants to convey to his audience: good and evil are
embedded in everyone. Before leaving for *aliyah*, she tells Chaim, "Rav Chaim
Levi – there *are* no 'others'! Jew and Arab. Victim and executioner. Saint and Devil.
They are us. All of them us" (53).

Anna's optimistic attitude of beginning life anew in Palestine cannot be compared with the rabbi's depression because Anna does not suffer from survivor guilt
since she was a perpetrator, not a victim, in Auschwitz. Unfortunately, Chaim Levi
spent two and a half years in Auschwitz and feels guilty about his impotence during the incarceration. Chaim entered Auschwitz with his younger brother Mendel
and helplessly watched him waste away. Three months before the liberation, Mendel, who had the will to endure, was close to death. Chaim, unable to see his
brother suffer any longer, prayed for his death. Two days later, Chaim's prayers were
answered when the other prisoners beat the *Muselman* to death to steal his meager
possessions. Chaim also feels guilty about lending his musical skills to the camp
orchestra in which he was forced to play the violin as accompaniment for those in
line for gassing. Moreover, his guilt has been exacerbated by his immoral actions in
the camp. A pregnant woman in Auschwitz typically suffered a horrible fate: upon
the birth of her child, the two of them would be thrown into the crematorium
alive. To prevent such a fate, Chaim participated in an abortion attempt that went
awry: by knocking the woman unconscious and then watching her fellow inmates
thrusting a bent piece of metal in between her wasted thighs, he murdered both the

child and its mother. Yet the image of the camps that had the most damaging effect on Chaim was the lingering memory of a legless, mute child nicknamed Absalom, who had entered the camp at age three. When Chaim was chosen for selection, the camp's Jewish hierarchy decided that his contacts with the underground were too valuable to have him gassed, so Absalom was sent to his death in Chaim's place. The death guilt that Lifton mentions as part of the Survivor Syndrome is clearly personified in Chaim, who explains to Anna, "And yet, some four and a half years later, that smoldering ember still burns within me. Still reproaches every beat of my heart . . . Oh God, if only I had died, instead of him" (39). In Auschwitz, being spared meant someone else had to die in your place; thus, Chaim feels guilty that he survived while Absalom, a child with his whole life ahead of him, perished. Chaim also suffers from collective guilt after having witnessed the crimes committed in the camp. He confesses to Anna, "There is such a thing as corporate guilt – metaphysical guilt. The guilt we bear for the sins of others. For men must answer for that which men do" (44). Thus, when Anna confesses that after a war, a modicum of guilt is expected, Chaim insists, "Some of us have managed to 'acquire' a little more than others" (22).

Guilt is merely one of the many symptoms of the Survivor Syndrome from which Chaim suffers. The guilt complex has led to his depression, a state of mind that is antithetical to most spiritual leaders. Coinciding with the fact that his Jewish congregation has become depleted because of the Holocaust is the rabbi's loss of faith in God. Chaim asserts that he is now an atheist since God died during the Holocaust; in short, a rabbi without faith in God is a man without a vocation. For Chaim, then, he is a ghost of his former self. When Anna asks Chaim how a rabbi could become an atheist, he responds that God granted his death wish for his brother in Auschwitz: "How could I possibly believe in a God who would answer such a prayer?" (37). He has also lost faith in humanity after witnessing man's inhumanity during the Shoah. While explaining to Anna the concept of the *Lamed-vav*, the Talmudic notion of the Thirty-six Just Men who bear humanity's suffering on their shoulders, he infers that such biblical lore no longer applies to post-Holocaust culture. He admits to Anna, "There are no more . . . righteous men" (8).

After the War, Chaim, like many survivors who vent their anger as a reaction to the trauma, became a violent person. After Anna admits that she participated in crimes as a member of the SS, Chaim smacks her in the face, lands heavy blows to her neck, and once she collapses, he continues to pound her with his fists until his hands are bloody. Later he explains to her that he acquired the cellar through violence. When he was accused by a beggar of usurping the tramp's living quarters soon after the War, Chaim beat up the vagrant. When a young Aryan claimed that he owned the cellar before entering into his army service, Chaim pulled a knife on the man and told him he had five seconds to leave.

Chaim's survivor guilt has resulted in masochism: the audience witnesses his continual effort to debase himself while he relishes in suffering. He defines his Jewish identity in terms of suffering, explaining to Anna, "You want to know what a Jew is? A Jew is what he happens to be suffering at the time the question is asked!" (28).

Chaim alleges that the Star of David, originally a coat of arms emblazoned on King David's shield, has morphed into the tattooed number on his forearm. He states, "We, we Jews, we took a shield – a symbol of strength, and of pride and of security – and turned it into the cross of our suffering, the symbol of our abject humiliation, the face of death itself" (25).

Anna herself recognizes Chaim's masochistic tendencies, diagnosing his condition as "clinically dead" (32) and comparing him to a *Muselman* who has surrendered his humanity and now accepts a life of eternal suffering as a person "[f]ull of self-pity and death and decay" (32). One does not have to be a psychiatrist to understand that a former spiritual healer who confines himself to a secluded life in a sparsely furnished, desolate cellar while drinking whisky all day has masochistic tendencies. The masochism of survivors is almost always linked, consciously or unconsciously, to Holocaust guilt. The camp environment still colors Chaim's everyday actions; for example, after purchasing sugar, Chaim frames the activity in the language of the *lager*, telling Anna, "I organized some sugar this morning" (40). Certainly the most obvious representation of this deeply embedded masochism is his insistence on living near a train route. As we have seen in *Bells and Trains*, the sound of trains has become a metonym for the Holocaust experience. As in Amichai's play, Elisha inundates us with the sounds of roaring trains throughout the play. Anna asks Chaim how he tolerates the constant infernal noise of the trains, and he replies that at night, it is quite soporific. In essence, the noise of the trains clanging on the tracks is self-inflicted suffering, a type of masochistic humiliation for the responsibilities he did not assume in Auschwitz.

At one point during the Hebrew lessons, when Anna compares the Hebrew letter Aleph to a winged bird, Chaim states, "I might remind you that this is a Hebrew lesson – not a psychiatric consultation" (7). He is partially correct: Anna, the perpetrator in the camps, does not need psychiatric help, but Chaim, the traumatized victim, clearly requires therapy. If there is a weakness to the play, it revolves around how Chaim seems to succumb readily to Anna's attempt at psychotherapy. Anna accuses Chaim of reneging on responsibility, becoming so personally absorbed in his guilt that he has become a negation of all things living. She puts the blame squarely on Chaim for not being more proactive:

> One by one, you've shed all your responsibilities. To your congregation, as a rabbi; to those whom you might have permitted to come close to you, as a husband and father; to yourself, as a human being; to your God, as a Jew; and to the Jews, as a Zionist.
>
> *(50)*

Chaim, aware of Anna's nurturing abilities, even tells her that, in Hebrew, the name "Anna" means "[f]ull of grace, mercy and prayer" (9). After leaving for Palestine, Anna's legacy apparently has had a profound effect on Chaim's psyche. He comes to realize that over the course of the many Hebrew lessons he gave her, he was able to form a bond with another human being – remarkably, even a former member of the SS. The play ends with a letter that Chaim writes to Anna in Palestine, thanking her for reawakening his soul, his sense of humanity previously buried by survivor guilt. In the letter, Chaim writes, "You might remember that I once asked you how one knows whether or not a language is dead. For me, a language is alive for as long as it still has meaning. The same is true of human beings. My life here, in this cellar, has no such meaning, and I find that I must move on" (55). Elisha's sugar-coated ending suggesting that this type of disguised psychotherapy can produce a catharsis in those traumatized and plagued with survivor guilt may be wishful thinking but will invariably make modern audiences feel comfortable.

Israeli playwright Gabriel Dagan was born in Czechoslovakia in 1922. A Holocaust survivor, he spent three years in Theresienstadt and Auschwitz. After the liberation, he studied theater and psychology in Prague. In 1949, he immigrated to Israel, where he found work as a stage manager and playwright for various theater companies. He later wrote scripts for film and radio while doing social psychology work in a kibbutz. He was the primary screenwriter for the 1960 Israeli film *Hem Hayu Asareh (They Were Ten)*, produced by Orav Films, and for *Af Milah L'Morgenstein (Not a Word to Morgenstein)*, a 1963 eighty-minute Hebrew-language movie. Dagan was also the co-author of *The Death March*, a documentary that provided testimonies of three survivors who participated in the death march from Auschwitz to Germany in 1945. Dagan passed away in Tel Aviv in 2008.

Dagan's play *The Reunion* had its debut at Tsavata, an experimental theater in Tel Aviv, on the eve of Holocaust Day in 1972. Although the play was translated into English and published in 1973, there has been a dearth of productions since its premiere. With a receptive audience from a large Jewish population in Miami, Florida, *The Reunion* received its next production at Miami's Temple Beth Am in June 1975. The play was also performed at the Staatstheater in Darmstadt, Germany, in November 1990.

The Reunion takes place in a hotel room in an unnamed Central European city in 1970.[21] Peter Stone, née Stein, is a Jewish survivor of Auschwitz now turned New York-based playwright. Peter and Martha Stein, his cousin, were the only survivors in the family. Peter, who lost both of his parents in the camp, vividly remembers watching the smoke of the crematorium filter through the air after his father had been gassed and then burned. Peter reminds his former fellow comrade and best friend in the camp, Eddie Runzig, who is now a psychiatrist in Berlin, that after his father went up in flames, he said to him, "'A strange way to attend my father's funeral.'"[22] Martha had no friends in the camp, and after her mother, father, and aunt (Peter's mother) perished there, she was forced to fend for herself. Martha was particularly traumatized because she was only twelve years old at the time of her incarceration and was forced to witness her mother lined up for her death in the gas chamber. After the liberation, Peter and Martha immigrated to the United States, and this is their first time returning to Europe in twenty-five years.

Peter, Martha, and Eddie form a triumvirate for the purpose of staging a Holocaust psychodrama that they hope will work as psychotherapy to assuage their survivor guilt. For their audience, they have invited Peter's uncle Arthur, who has not seen Peter since September 1945 and accepts the invitation to what he understands is to be a family reunion. Although Arthur lost two brothers in Auschwitz, he did not participate in the Holocaust, and, for the past twenty-five years, he has been mystified about how six million Jews could go to the slaughterhouse like sheep. Peter, in particular, immersed in guilt accrued from his inability to save his loved ones, finds his uncle's attitude to be offensive and misguided. Peter would like to expiate the guilt, but as a playwright, he does not feel that he can write about Auschwitz. Peter, like most Holocaust survivors, is torn between a life of unbearable memories and the compelling need to bear witness for the dead. He describes his plight to Eddie, hinting that writing a play about Auschwitz would be inadequate: "That death in life – that life in death. No words . . . No words . . . But memories . . . Memories . . ." (8). Like most survivors, Peter and Martha suffer from nightmares as well. Martha and Peter unsuccessfully attempt to forget the past, while Eddie has learned to live with his nightmares. Peter is trying to solve the dilemma of being unable to write about the trauma, so he concocts the notion of a psychodrama that will serve as a catharsis for the triumvirate, as well as for a teaching lesson for Arthur, the Holocaust dilettante. Martha goes along with the charade, believing that she can amend the helplessness that she experienced during the horror of her father's death as Arthur replaces her dead father; of course, in this scenario, the daughter will see her father live through the disaster. In his comments that precede the published text of the play, Baruch Hochman adeptly explains the goal set by Peter, Eddie, and Martha: "For various reasons they all crave another chance. They would like somehow to have the irrecoverable chance to act against their tormentors, or to assuage the guilt of both having failed to act and failed to die" (4).

Dagan does a wonderful job of setting the audience up for the shock of the play-within-the play that stages the Holocaust. Act one is written as a benign domestic drama in which the audience is provided exposition and is introduced to the characters in Peter's hotel room – an innocuous setting. When Dutch journalist Jan De Vries arrives to interview the American playwright for a newspaper article, Peter recruits him to participate in the charade. Another comrade from Auschwitz that Peter has not seen since the liberation, Karl Schulz, now a professional actor in Vienna, has agreed to participate in order to do whatever is necessary to help these former colleagues who provided him with moral support in the extermination camp.

In act 2, the pleasantries of act 1 continue as Arthur and his wife engage in after-dinner small talk with Peter and Eddie. Suddenly, the conversation is interrupted by a moaning voice coming from the adjoining room in the hotel. As the lights go out, we hear shots, German commands, and shouts of terror that Arthur and aunt Helen are unaware are coming from Peter's tape recorder. Karl enters in a Nazi uniform, salutes "Heil Hitler," and presents himself as Obersturmbandfuehrer Hans Schnitzer of the SS. Insisting that he is not there to answer questions, Karl barks orders to Arthur and Helen while Peter and Eddie play along with the scenario. In essence, this psychodrama becomes a reenactment of the trauma of Jewish persecution. Arthur is told that he is not allowed to leave, and when he makes a motion to depart, Karl reminds him that his men in the corridor can be trigger happy. Karl demands that Arthur produce his identity papers (his passport), asks if he is Jewish, and then forces him to put his hands up and face the wall. All the while, Arthur and Helen are terrified and thus willingly comply with orders, even calling Karl "sir" in the process. Arthur is then forced to empty his pockets, turn all of his possessions over to Karl, and then strip off his clothing to don a tunic emblazoned with a big yellow Jewish star. When Arthur complains that the pants are too large and have no belt, Karl sarcastically retorts, "We will have a tailor make a pair for you at Auschwitz – custom made" (22). Karl tells Arthur to take off his cap, put it back on, and take it off – a parody of the inane "hats on-hats off" routine that humiliated the prisoners in the camps. Arthur and Helen are also given numbers, and Karl begins to refer to them as numbers rather than by name. Meanwhile, Karl hurls insults at the couple, scaring them to death: "Don't sit on a chair, you Jewish ass! Don't you dare sit on a chair! They are for human beings – not for you" (22). Karl informs Arthur and Helen that the moaning that they hear in the adjoining room comes from a Jewess who had to be beaten to make her comply during her arrest. Arthur and Helen learn that their fate is to be sent in a consignment of forty individuals delivered for deportation. When Karl demands that Arthur agree to consign his property to the German government, Arthur signs the papers immediately without question.

The hoax seems to work perfectly, as Arthur is soon begging for his life. He tries to convince Karl that he is capable of hard work so as to avoid the gas chamber, but when Arthur is forced to hold out his hands, Karl refuses to believe that he is a laborer. To humiliate the Jew, Karl orders him to do thirty-nine squats for ten repetitions. As Karl leaves Arthur and Helen momentarily, he tells them that they have five minutes before they will be separated for life. Alone in the room, Arthur and his wife react as if the terror is palpable, wondering whether they will be able to barter Helen's diamond ring to "organize" food in Auschwitz. Without salvation, devoid of help from others, Arthur and Helen reenact the terror that Jews endured while waiting for their deportations.

Suddenly, Martha, disguised as a beaten Jew, stumbles into the room and falls onto the floor. She is barefoot, wears a tunic with the Jewish star, has her head shaved, and is covered in blood. Martha, moaning on the floor, claims that Arthur looks like her father. Martha abreacts in this psychodrama as she recalls the gassing of her parents in Auschwitz, lamenting to Arthur and Helen how helpless she was to prevent their deaths. Martha mentions that her father gave her a departing glance before the whip of the SS officer lashed his face. The psychodrama is too much for Martha to bear, too close to reality, so she breaks down in torment. Recognizing that the scenario is too close to reality, Martha, now substituting Arthur for her father doomed to die, cannot allow history to repeat itself. She pleads with Peter to end the charade, stammering incoherently and in confusion, "So I ran away, because his face . . . Because your face . . . Because father . . . I can't, uncle Arthur, I can't Peter, I can't . . . I can't . . . ." (28).

After the "reunion" ends and Arthur realizes that he has been a participant in this imposture, he is furious and inconsolable. The ruse has been effective in getting Arthur to understand why the Jews boarded the trains, and Arthur is allowed to keep as a memento the contract that he signed, turning his property over to the Nazis. Peter has definitely lost an uncle, but it was more important to him to attempt to exorcise the demons of Auschwitz from his psyche. Eddie explains to De Vries what it means to feel guilty about losing one's relatives and then having to face yourself for the rest of your life: "You see, Mr. De Vries; Karl, Peter, Martha and myself – we were in Auschwitz. In Auschwitz! – we survived – yes – but the nightmares are still with us" (31). Peter's hoax may have been able to mitigate the guilt temporarily, but Eddie, the psychiatrist, tells him to forget about trying to get Auschwitz out of his system. Indeed, at the end of the play, Peter fixates on Karl's boots, a visceral reminder of Nazis trampling over the victims. Peter aims a revolver at the boots, and in growing anxiety, recites the last words of the play: "They are still marching . . . My god, they are still marching! . . ." (32). The implication is that even noble attempts by survivors to bear witness in psychodrama as psychotherapy cannot assuage their guilt.

French playwright Enzo Cormann is director of the department of Dramatic Writing at the École Normale Supérieure des Arts et Techniques du Spectacle in Lyon. Born in Sos, France, in 1953, his early education was in philosophy, but since 1980, he has devoted himself to acting, directing, and writing for the theater. He has written nearly thirty plays and texts for music, including *Credo, Sade, Concert d'enfers, Diktat, Cairn, Corps perdus, La Révolte des anges, Sang et eau,* and *L'Autre.* His plays have been translated into German, English, Italian, Spanish, Greek, and Polish. Cormann has also recorded several radio dramas for France Culture and has written a triptych of prose fiction: *Testament de Vénus* (2006), *Surface sensibles* (2007), and *Vita Nova Jazz* (2011). He has worked on musical productions, such as the mini-opera *Diverses Blessures,* and regularly performs jazz on stage.

Cormann's *Toujours l'Orage*, published in 1997 by Minuit, was first produced under direction by Henri Bornstein at the Théâtre de la Tempête in Toulouse, France, from 25 November to 21 December 1997. The next major production was directed by Ghislain Filion in October 2003 at Théâtre Prospero in Montreal. The National Jewish Theater Foundation commissioned the first English translation of the play (*Storms Still*) for production at the Lark Play Development Center in New York City in 2012.

The Never-ending Storm consists of thirteen episodes that occur over a three-day period of conversations between seventy-six-year-old Theodor Steiner and forty-year-old Nathan Goldring. Each episode is introduced by a quotation from *King Lear*, excluding episode 2, which begins with "All is but toys" from *Macbeth. Storms Still,* an alternative title for the English translation, is a recurring theme in *King Lear,* especially when Lear rages madly during the storm on the heath. Cormann's play also occurs in a desolate, stormy wasteland where Steiner lives and is visited by Goldring. As the conversation between Steiner and Goldring becomes more heated inside, the weather outside becomes more inclement; when their passions subside, the weather outside becomes calmer.

Steiner, a well-known actor, has spent the last twenty-five years as a recluse in a rural farmhouse in the Morvan. He abandoned the theater exactly a quarter of a century ago after performing Macbeth four times at the Burgtheater in Vienna. Goldring, fifteen years old at the time, witnessed one of those four performances and was so enamored with Steiner's rendition of Macbeth, that he has sought him out to play King Lear in a production that Goldring will direct. Recently named director of the Neue Bühne theater in Berlin, Goldring is determined to convince Steiner that, at his advanced age, he would be the perfect choice to play Lear. Goldring's offer not only is unflattering to Steiner, it is contemptible as well. Steiner, the curmudgeon, is at ease living as a hermit, painting landscapes as a source of refuge, without need of public recognition. He tells Goldring that he is worthless as a human being, "cantankerous, unjust, arrogant, a harpie, conceited."[23]

Steiner would evict Goldring from the premises if it were not for the fact that he finds the younger man to be a worthy sparring partner. Steiner is the seasoned intellectual, cynical and jaded, and seems to be intrigued by the youthful exuberance of Goldring, who is obviously brilliant enough to be chosen as the director of such a prestigious theater as the Neue Bühne and was courted to direct plays in Vienna, London, and Paris. Steiner also seems to relish a subliminal type of ecstasy in which an actor has a chance to match wits with a talented director. As they verbally spar throughout the play and even engage in a game of chess, which requires a type of intellectual warfare mentality, Steiner learns that he shares with Goldring more than just an interest in the theater. Goldring, like Steiner, is Jewish, and both men were adversely affected by the Holocaust. Goldring, although not a practicing Jew, remembers that his father hid in Sweden from the Nazis, but his mother died in Bergen-Belsen when Nathan was only twelve years old. Steiner, at age twenty-two, was sent to Terezin (Theresienstadt) with his parents in September 1942 and remained there until the camp's liberation in May 1945.[24] Nearly ninety thousand Jews in Terezin were deported to the death camps in the east, most of them sent to Auschwitz; Steiner was one of the few who survived.

Although Goldring was indirectly affected by the Holocaust, Steiner was fully immersed in it. Many of the inmates of Terezin had formerly been artists, musicians, actors, or directors. The Nazis promulgated cultural events in Terezin that often consisted of concerts or theater performances. Steiner even had a chance to play Edgar in a 1944 production of *King Lear* staged at Theresienstadt. The camp commandant, Carl Rahm, a lover of the arts, greatly admired Steiner's rendition of the role. On 16 October 1944, Rahm was prepared to sign a list of deportees destined for Auschwitz, when he told Steiner that there was one name too many on the list that included Steiner and his parents. Rahm gave Steiner a pen to cross one name off the list. In an attempt to save the lives of his parents, Steiner asked if he could cross three names off the list. When told that the only option he had was to cross out one name, Steiner crossed out his own, thus sending his parents to their deaths. Steiner made the choice of survival at the cost of his parents' lives, thus initiating for him a lifelong lineage of trauma as a result of survivor guilt. Steiner's misery is exacerbated by the fact that he snuffed out the life of a man who was a world-renowned virtuoso pianist and a woman who dreamed of seeing her beloved son, an architect, design sets for the theater. In short, like many Holocaust survivors who had to make choices with regard to the loss of loved ones in the camps, Steiner's single stroke of a pen has forever affected him psychoanalytically.

Goldring believes that because of his age and his theatrical expertise, Steiner is the ideal candidate to play Lear. Besides, Goldring assumes that Steiner's demeanor is also suited for the character of Lear, a "wasted chief" (16). Steiner tells Goldring about the last time that he acted on stage, which was in the 1971 production of *Macbeth* at the Burgtheater. At the conclusion of the fourth show, Carl Rahm, after having served fifteen years in prison, came to Steiner's dressing room to praise his performance. He then asked Steiner to sign the program for him with his fountain pen. Explaining to Steiner that, at age eighty-six, he would die soon, Rahm convinced Steiner to do the honors. After signing, Steiner immediately felt remorse: "I closed my eyes. When I reopened them, I was alone again. I remained like that for a long time, contemplating the pen in my right hand and forcing myself to suppress the absurd and weak thank you which came to my lips" (29). The connection between the pen and the theater placed Steiner back in Terezin. With the pen, he signed his parents' death certificate; the theater was the vehicle that allowed him to survive. At that moment in Vienna in 1971, Steiner associated the pen and the theater with survivor guilt. Moreover, as Jean-Paul Pilorget has noted, playing Macbeth, the murderous king, only served to unearth the deeply rooted trauma that Steiner suffered from as a result of his responsibility for the murders of his own parents.[25]

That night, Steiner left the theater and never returned to acting again. He confides to Goldring, "For me, theater was at the time synonymous with absence, of loss and solitude – I haven't really evolved on this point, but that's another story" (11). He became a recluse, avoiding the public at all costs and abandoning the theater, which he equated to a form of opiate for the masses that allowed the genocide to flourish. Steiner explains to Goldring the correlation between Rahm and the German masses attending his performance as Macbeth:

> And what do you think I saw, that evening, when I saw this old man in my dressing room, this Nazi officer who made me the executioner of Heydrich, Müller, Kaltenbrüner, and Eichmann, by making me ratify with a pen line the death of my parents? I saw the public, the public as the people, the people as the executioner, a cowardly public, pleading its ignorance, and yet draped in a convenient and vague feeling of guilt; and, among this public, these real guilty people, denying their guilt by evoking their impeccable sense of duty.
>
> *(30)*

For Steiner, the thought of attempting to play Lear is much too close to reality and will only reinforce the trauma. He quotes Shakespeare to Goldring: "THAT WAY MADNESS LIES, LET ME SHUN THAT; NO MORE OF THAT" (7). He mentions thoughts of suicide (8) and admits that he was in psychoanalysis years earlier (11). Playing Lear has a two-fold meaning for Steiner: in Terezin, the role of Edgar in Lear saved his life but ultimately meant the unbearable burden of guilt for surviving at the expense of his parents' lives. Goldring even admits that Lear is a tale about loss, and "The product of loss is nothingness. Or chaos" (18). Lear ranting on the heath about a corrupt world is much too close to Steiner's loss of faith in humanity after the Holocaust. With a tempest raging outside Steiner's residence, the parallels between Steiner's suffering in the storm and Lear ranting in agony on the heath are foreboding to the former actor. Goldring's request for Steiner to play Lear is indeed pushing Steiner further into the chaos of madness. Steiner even makes a suicide attempt by hanging himself, but Goldring intervenes in time to save his life.

The title of the play suggests that, for Steiner, the Holocaust survivor, the tempest endures forever. Despite their mutual interests and common ties, Goldring and Steiner are two totally different individuals because of the Holocaust. Goldring is only tangentially affected by the Holocaust, but Steiner is fully immersed in the trauma. Goldring's game of forcing Steiner into a catharsis to purge his madness will not work. Goldring may think that Steiner is the ideal person to play Lear, but for Steiner, theater is not a game; instead, it was the source of guilt that can never be assuaged.

American playwright Robert Caisley was born in Rotherham, England, in 1968. He is professor of Theater and Film and chair of the Dramatic Writing Program at the University of Idaho. From fall 2001 to fall 2005, he served as artistic director for the Idaho Repertory Theatre. He has been successful in getting most of his major plays produced on stage, including *Kite's Book* (1995), *Bad Manners* (1996), *The Lake* (2001), *FRONT* (2002), *Good Clean Fun* (2003), *The 22-Day Adagio* (2004), *Santa Fe* (2005), *Kissing* (2007), and *Happy* (2011). *Happy* was a finalist for the Woodward/Newman Award for Drama and has been nominated for a Bay Area Critics Circle Award for Best Original Script. From 1990–2005, he performed as an actor in two dozen roles, many of them in plays by Shakespeare. Since 2002, he has directed more than twenty-five productions, including plays by Shakespeare, Molière, Richard Brinsley Sheridan, Neil Simon, Rebecca Gilman, Timberlake Wertenbaker, and Christopher Hampton.

Letters to an Alien, a one-act play in four scenes, was commissioned for the Idaho Theatre for Youth's 1994–1995 touring season.[26] Caisley proposed several ideas to the artistic director, and they mutually agreed on the subject of the Holocaust. Caisley's interest in the Shoah began when he was an undergraduate at Rockford College, where guest speaker Elie Wiesel said to the audience that the responsibility to teach about the Holocaust does not rest merely with survivors; Caisley informed me that that idea resonated with him for years.[27] When Caisley was in graduate school at Illinois State University, he had the opportunity to enroll in a course on the theater of the Holocaust with Holocaust drama scholar Alvin Goldfarb, who became a major influence on Caisley's education. The production of *Letters to an Alien* in 1994 in Boise, Idaho, starred Dan Peterson as Pops and Anna Lisa Maldonado as Hannah, under direction by Michael Baltzell. In 1996, *Letters to an Alien* was produced by the Mad Horse Theatre Company in Portland, Maine. The play has since been staged by the Jewish Centre Theatre, in Pittsburgh, Pennsylvania (1998); by the Young Actors' Company at the Saskatchewan Regional Drama Festival and on tour in Saskatoon, Canada (2005); at Greenville College in Greenville, Illinois (2006); and by the Gretna Players Drama Club in Gretna, Virginia (2008).

In *Letters to an Alien*, Hannah Stern, a young Jewish girl, is sent to her grandfather's house to learn more about her Jewish heritage. Her grandfather Eli, called Pops by Hannah, gets more accustomed to his granddaughter by having her sit still while he paints her portrait. Hannah's attention span is short, and she is much more interested in playing with her Game Boy video game than she is in being mentored. Hannah is a typically rebellious teenager who hates her own self-image, her parents for making her visit, and her grandfather for appearing to be strange to her.[28] Hannah wants to fit in at school, and being Jewish is not the way to do that. With regard to her grandfather, Hannah states, "I don't understand him, he's so different. He's the kind of Jew everyone makes fun of. He doesn't . . . blend in. I don't want to be like him. I don't want to be part of his world."[29] She notices that her grandfather, wearing a prayer shawl and a yarmulke, recites the Kaddish, which Hannah can only associate with "a stupid song" without "a catchy tune," something "depressing" that is incompatible with a lively tune needed for dancing (14).

While playing with her Game Boy, Hannah's imagination channels up two space aliens who look exactly like the blue creatures on her screen. These Philostians, named Kayak and Kroevnik, have come to Earth to study human beings in an attempt to learn about new civilizations. They have the ability to activate a hologram to transport Hannah and Eli through different historical time periods. Hannah has heard about the Holocaust in school, but to her, the subject is meaningless, just another boring history lesson. Eli prefers silence, refusing to talk about the Holocaust even with his relatives. The aliens provide an interesting mechanism to bridge the gap between Hannah and her grandfather as they access information from Eli's historical past in Poland during 1943.[30]

Letters to an Alien focuses around the term "aliens," a word that is repeated throughout the play. Hannah feels alienated from her grandfather and vice versa. Pops calls his granddaughter "an intruder," "An Alien Invader" (9) while Hannah, with her overwhelming need to fit in with her peers, states, "I don't wanna be an alien" (18). Hannah tells her grandfather, "We are aliens . . . to each other" (23). Hannah, who is preparing a presentation for her classmates at school, fears embarrassing herself in front of the other students who might mistake her for "some kind of alien" (26). When Pops slaps his granddaughter after she accuses him of hating his Jewishness, Hannah concludes, "I was wrong, we're not aliens, we're exactly the same, you and I. Forwards and backwards. Inside and out. We both hate so much what we are" (32). It is thus fitting that Kayak and Kroevnik, who know what it actually means to be aliens, bring these two aliens together.

Kayak and Kroevnik take us back to 1943 in the Polish home of Eli and his older sister Hannah, who is an aspiring artist. We hear the sounds of breaking glass, people screaming, and Nazi soldiers shouting orders. As the Nazis evict Eli and Hannah from their home, they destroy Hannah's paintings. Hannah spits in the face of one of the Nazis and then slaps him. Eli, a young boy, defends his sister as best he can, ripping his Star of David off his sleeve in defiance of Nazi laws but almost gets shot in the process. Hannah and Eli are deported to a concentration camp, where they are put to work sorting the belongings of the deportees. The guard threatens them:

"Get to work! If you're caught stealing anything, you'll be shot" (29). Alone, forced to fend for themselves without their parents, Eli and Hannah, at such a young age, live in fear for their lives. Even more traumatic for them is the fact that while sorting the clothing of the soon-to-be-deceased inmates, Hannah and Eli discover their father's silk handkerchief with his monogrammed initials.

Eli lost his parents in the camp and his sister as well. Before she was taken to be gassed, Hannah painted a portrait of Eli carrying the last flower growing in the camp. She explains to her brother her reasons for doing artwork that saps strength needed for camp labor: "I'm painting so I never forget this place. I'm painting you so I can remember how you looked at this very moment. If anything happens to me, these paintings will help people understand what happened here. The past will become the present, and that becomes the future" (34). Hannah then asks Eli to confirm that he will never forget what happened to the Jews in the camps and that he will promise to teach others about the Holocaust. As it turns out, Eli was the only member of his family to survive.

Letters to an Alien is essentially about survivor guilt and the survivor's need to bear witness to the atrocities of the Holocaust.[31] Many Holocaust survivors named their sons or daughters after a relative who perished during the Shoah; thus, Eli's granddaughter is named after his dead sister. Like Stefan in *Singer*, who painted so as never to forget the horrors of Auschwitz, Eli paints portraits of the camp to keep his promise to his sister to bear witness. Hannah misconstrues what she perceives to be her grandfather's hatred of his religion, but she senses his burden of survivor guilt and accuses him of it: "Because you hate yourself, you hate feeling guilty because you didn't die, because you really hate being a Jew" (32). To Hannah, Eli's tattooed number indicates that he is an alien – something that she herself dreads being associated with as a teenager who seeks peer approval. Yet the survivor guilt is palpable and particularly overwrought as Eli, at times crying, repeats the Kaddish several times. Prayers for the dead are expected during the anniversaries of the deceased; to say the Kaddish daily is abnormal. Eli is further conflicted by his need to bear witness and his inability to speak of the Holocaust. As we have seen, silence is typical for survivors who have difficulty explaining the trauma to outsiders, but it is also an unhealthy attitude to adopt. Kayak tries to explain the dilemma to Kroevnik: "They possess the same fears and dreams, not unlike ourselves, but they do not share their ideas. Perhaps they feel it is dangerous to share their feelings. It is a very . . . interesting phenomenon" (33).

Letters to an Alien is a poignant play that was written for an audience of adolescents to help them understand the Holocaust. Working with the fundamental principle that survivor guilt is endemic to the atrocity, Caisley has written a play that brings together these diverse aliens. Hannah, once ashamed of her grandfather as an alien, has come to understand his trauma, and even discusses it with her peers in class. Eli, once silent about the Holocaust, speaks to Hannah's class to keep his promise to his sister to bear witness to the Shoah by mentioning his dead relatives; he also brings his sister's paintings to show to the class. Eli describes the genocide to the class, putting it in terms of how the Jews were considered to be aliens: "During the war, the Germans took us to the camps. They were terrible places, many people died there. We were Jewish and we were different and they wanted us gone" (37). Finally, the aliens, in learning about the Holocaust by studying life on our planet, leave us with vital lessons about humanity. They remind the class that six million Jews were murdered and that the human species is violent. The comment, "it is very unusual for a species to want to destroy itself" (26), is a lesson about how aberrant the Holocaust really was. The play ends with Eli and the aliens reciting the Kaddish in front of Hannah's class in one final gesture to the dead.

Israeli playwright Ben-Zion Tomer was born in 1928 in the small Polish town of Bilgoraj. Upon the outbreak of World War II, the family fled to Russia, where they were expelled to Krasnoyarsk in Siberia. In 1943, during the Nazi invasion of Russia, Tomer was among the "Tehran" children who were allowed to immigrate to Palestine. From 1943 to 1945, he lived in the Mishmar Haemek kibbutz. During the War of Independence, Tomer served as an officer in the Palmach and was captured by the Jordanians, who placed him in a prisoner of war camp for eleven months. Following the war, Tomer studied philosophy and literature at the Hebrew University in Jerusalem, where he also began translating Russian and Polish texts. Tomer became the editor of the literary magazine *Masa* and taught literature at various kibbutzim and teachers' colleges. From 1966 to 1968, he was Israel's cultural attaché in Brazil and then took a post as the advisor to the Ministry of Culture and Education from 1969 to 1977. His writing output includes two collections of poetry and one novel titled *Derekh Hamelach* (*Salt Road*). *Yaldei ha-Tzel* (*Children of the Shadows*), written in eleven scenes spread over two acts, premiered at the Habimah, Israel's national theater, in Tel Aviv during 1962. Although the play has not been widely performed internationally, it has been translated into English, German, Spanish, and French. Tomer passed away in 1998.

Children of the Shadows, which occurs in Israel in 1955, contrasts two types of guilt as a result of Holocaust survival. Yoram Eyal, twenty-eight years old, emigrated from a small town in Poland as one of the Tehran children to arrive in Palestine in 1941 at the age of fourteen. He is a Diasporic Jew who has spent exactly half of his life in the Old World and half in Israel but is clearly defined by his European roots and his inability to adapt to a new culture. Yoram feels guilty about abandoning his relatives, who perished during the Shoah. On the other hand, Yoram's brother-in-law, Dr. Sigmund Rabinowitz, was fully immersed in his native European culture during the Holocaust. Unlike Yoram, accused of being "here" (in Israel) rather than "there" (in Europe), Sigmund has no such guilt in betraying his loved ones. Instead, he feels guilty about being a member of the Judenrat (Jewish Council), which aided and abetted the Nazi plans for Jewish genocide.

Upon entering Palestine, Yoram tried his best to remake himself to conform to native Israeli (Sabra) culture. He joined a kibbutz, changed his name from Yossele to Yoram, and even denied any knowledge of Yiddish. Yoram abandoned his native Polish vocabulary and tried to learn Hebrew. He began to model himself on his friend Dubi, a Sabra Jew who was a good tractor driver, captain of the soccer team, an excellent speaker, the best dancer in the kibbutz, and attractive to women. Yoram tells his friend Nurit about his transformation to an assimilated Israeli through his emulation of Dubi: "And Naomi was his girl. Inside me, I began to murder Yossele. Yossele is dead! Long live Yoram! A year later, I was king. Naomi was in my arms. I learned to dance the polka. I learned the ropes."[32]

Yoram, who would like to marry native-Israeli Nurit, initially refuses to commit to marriage because of his guilt-ridden past. However, when his parents announce their visitation to Israel, Yoram confesses the truth to Nurit. He admits to being born in Goray, a dirty little Polish town in which he lived in poverty with his sister Esther and supported his family by stealing food from the market. Yoram tells Nurit, "And when I came to this land and it fed me from the tree of forgetfulness, I burned my lice-infested clothes along with myself. Along with Yossele. And Esther. And my parents" (155).

The Sabra Jews in the play appear jovial; they can celebrate a festive occasion such as Independence Day, but the Diaspora Jews are depicted as guilt-ridden and constantly sulking, incapable of salvation. Yoram is disturbed by the visit of his brother Yanek and his wife Helenka because their presence becomes a reminder of his inability to act while his family suffered in Europe during the Shoah. Yoram tells Nurit that Yanek and Helenka will activate his deeply rooted guilt, and thus they cannot stay with them even temporarily: "Because . . . So as not to have to see Helenka's eyes every day, as if I'd stolen something from her, as if it were my fault that I didn't go through what she went through, my fault that I came to Israel before she did, that I'm here!" (162). Yoram intuitively understands that Yanek and Helenka make him feel guilty about himself, even though he did nothing in particular to be ashamed of. Yoram confides to Nurit, "Their tales of horror make me the guilty one. Guilty without having done anything" (168). Indeed, when Yanek confronts his brother, the tone is accusatory, as Yanek implies the latent references of "here" versus "there": "It's easy for you to talk, you were never there" (165). Yoram survived, but his parents, two sisters, and brother suffered the agony of the concentration camps, where his sister Esther died. Yoram lived in the safety of modern Israel but suffered from nightmares about the hunger and typhus he remembers from his native Lvov, as well as the death of his own sister. Yanek participated in the Warsaw Ghetto Uprising while Yoram was sipping beverages comfortably in an Israeli café and then treated himself to a movie. Yoram guiltily recalls what he was doing when his brother was fighting for his life: "I had two free hours. . . . I sat down and enjoyed the sun. It was a lovely day" (178). Thus, when the rest of the world asked the question about why the Jews went to the slaughter willingly, Yoram was left out of the discussion. When Yanek mentions that the Diaspora Jews asked that same question, Yoram angrily responds, "You had the right to! I didn't" (179). This guilt about the past has segregated Yoram from an Israeli society that looks to the future and feels at home in the Promised Land. Yoram views life in Israel with a chip on his shoulder, a burden that only serves to increase his self-immolation.

Following Yoram as his shadow is Dr. Sigmund Rabinowitz, a fellow comrade from Lvov, who serves as a lingering reminder of the fate of the Diaspora Jews under Hitler: they are both "children of the shadows." When Yoram denies that he was ever "there," Sigmund blows smoke straight upward from his cigarette – a visceral reminder of families who literally went up in smoke in Poland.

Sigmund was born as Benjamin Apfelbaum in Vilna. He studied at Heidelberg to become a doctor of philosophy and then assumed a position as a professor of Renaissance art at the university in Lvov. During the Nazi Occupation, Sigmund, a respected member of the community and a graduate of a distinguished German university, was hand-picked by the Nazis to join the Judenrat. As such, he selected Jews for deportation to the camps, two of which included his wife Esther and their son. Apparently, Sigmund himself survived a concentration camp since he refers to himself as 155370, the number that is tattooed on his arm. After arriving in Palestine in 1947, he was later put on trial by the Israelis for collaborating with the Nazis.

Sigmund suffers interminably from survivor guilt, which has destroyed his psyche. As a former humanist, he cannot fathom that he took part in the destruction of his fellow Jews, admitting to Yoram, "I want you to understand that I was a human being, and the most terrible thing of all was that they were human, too" (184). Unlike Yoram, who would like to forget the past and assimilate with the Sabras, Sigmund's survivor guilt is masochistic. Michael Taub corroborates this view of Sigmund: "Therefore, he feels like an accomplice, a traitor who must pay the price by inflicting on himself a sort of eternal self-flagellation."[33] Once a former distinguished professor of the humanities, Sigmund in Israel demeans himself as a vagabond living underneath a bench on the seaside boardwalk. He adopts different personae and disguises, hoping to remain underneath the radar in a society that puts collaborators on trial and cannot come to grips with why the Jews did not do more to resist the Nazis. Sigmund mumbles to himself about being a medusa, a spineless jellyfish. He writes poetry that masochistically reminds him of his role in the Holocaust, including such lines as these: "And always in that moment of recall/ I hear the sound of railcars/ Emptied of their children as of coal./ Their warm, sweet smell./ A ragdoll left behind" (157). He refers to himself as a type of traitor, a "rat" (171), and glorifies in his misery, even when talking to himself: "I have to be judged by someone, I have to be" (173). At one point in the play, he faces the audience and virtually convicts himself, saying, "Shameless mortal, sinful one,/ Take a pound and I'll be gone" (173). Sigmund also suffers from nightmares in which Esther exhorts him to resign from the Judenrat and join the revolt. Even in his dreams, Sigmund is found guilty and pleads with his wife to free him from eternal shame: "Remove your eyes from me! I'm not to blame. Be gone!" (154). Sigmund's madness is the only quality that he has to cling to, for he refers to himself as "a ghost" (175), "the equivalent of a corpse" (175), a member of the walking dead. He refuses suicide in order to wallow masochistically in self-pity, explaining to Yoram, "To die, to sleep, no more . . . is to forgive . . . There must be no forgiveness! None!" (185).

When one examines survivor mentality, guilt typically is a part of the neurosis. Although survivor guilt is endemic to the Survivor Syndrome, the five plays discussed in this chapter have been paired together because they focus almost exclusively on that guilt. We have seen that survivor guilt comes in myriad forms, typically accrued from what one could have or should have done to prevent loss of human life. The result for the traumatized victim is often self-immolation or the death wish of not wanting to be alive when someone more worthy has perished instead. Most civilized people have an intrinsic desire to live a moral life defined by a mutually agreed upon code of conduct. Viewing these plays, audiences come to understand that the Holocaust eroded civilized values, making individuals feel guilty at their loss of human willpower during times of extreme duress.

Notes

1 William G. Niederland, "The Problem of the Survivor," *Journal of the Hillside Hospital* 10 (1961): 238.
2 Elie Wiesel, *Legends of Our Time* (New York: Holt, Rinehart and Winston, 1968), 171.
3 William B. Helmreich, *Against All Odds: Holocaust Survivors and the Successful Lives They Made in America* (New Brunswick: Transaction Publishers, 1996), 224.
4 Ernest A. Rappaport, "Survivor Guilt," *Midstream* 17, no. 7 (1971): 44.
5 Charlotte Delbo, *Auschwitz and After*, trans. Rosette C. Lamont (New Haven and London: Yale University Press, 1995), 263.
6 Wiesel, *Legends of Our Time*, 172.
7 Judith Lewis Herman, *Trauma and Recovery* (New York: Basic Books, 1992), 84.
8 Henry Krystal, "Trauma and Aging: A Thirty-Year Follow-Up," in *Trauma: Explorations and Memory*, ed. Cathy Caruth (Baltimore and London: Johns Hopkins University Press, 1995), 87.
9 Olga Lengyel, *Five Chimneys: The Story of Auschwitz* (Chicago and New York: Ziff-Davis, 1947), 1.
10 Primo Levi, *The Drowned and the Saved*, trans. Raymond Rosenthal (New York: Summit Books, 1986), 75.
11 Ibid., 78.
12 Herman, *Trauma and Recovery*, 84.
13 Niederland, "The Problem of the Survivor," 241.
14 Paul Chodoff, "Depression and Guilt Among Concentration Camp Survivors," *International Forum for Existential Psychiatry* 7 (Summer–Fall 1969): 24.
15 Dominick LaCapra, *Representing the Holocaust* (Ithaca and London: Cornell University Press, 1994), 200.
16 Paul Chodoff, "Late Effects of the Concentration Camp Syndrome," *Archives of General Psychiatry* 8, no. 4 (1963): 332.
17 Robert Jay Lifton, *The Broken Connection: On Death and the Continuity of Life* (New York: Simon and Schuster, 1979), 171.
18 Virtually all of the studies on survivor guilt point to its debilitating effects on the victims. However, for a counterargument, see H.Z. Winnick, "Psychiatric Disturbances of Holocaust ('Shoa') Survivors," *Israel Annals of Psychiatry and Related Disciplines* 5 (1967): 99. Winnick contends that guilt feelings can affirm meaning in one's life. Winnick writes, "He who believes in his own guilt and responsibility, establishes or reinstates his active involvement and part in life and endows it with purpose, thus repudiating his spiritual annihilation" (99).
19 Hannah Arendt, *Eichmann in Jerusalem* (New York: Viking Press, 1964), 276.
20 Ron Elisha, *Two* (Sydney: Currency Press, 1985), viii. All subsequent citations from the play are from this edition and will be included within parentheses in the text.
21 In the brief preface to the play, Israeli theater critic Baruch Hochman specifies that the locale is Amsterdam. There is no evidence in the play to suggest that Amsterdam is the setting. The hotel address is 29 Zuyder Strast, so Zuyder would suggest a Dutch location, but Strast is of Czech origin. Dagan probably created a fictional address.
22 Gabriel Dagan, *The Reunion*, in *Midstream: A Monthly Jewish Review* 19, no. 4 (1973): 9. All subsequent citations from the play are from this edition and will be included within parentheses in the text.

23 Enzo Cormann, *The Never-ending Storm*, trans. Guila Clara Kessous, 6, Photocopy. Holocaust Theater Archive. I am indebted to Arnold Mittelman, founder of the National Jewish Theater Foundation, for granting me permission to quote from this text photocopied from the Holocaust Theater Archive. All subsequent citations from the play are from this edition and will be included within parentheses in the text.

24 Cormann's research on Terezin came from two sources: Joza Karas's *Music in Terezin* and H.G. Adler's *Theresienstadt 1941–1945*.

25 Jean-Paul Pilorget, "Un théâtre pavé d'horreur et de folie: *Toujours l'orage* de Enzo Cormann," in *Témoignages de l'après-Auschwitz dans la littérature juive-française d'aujourd'hui*, ed. Annelise Schulte Nordholt (Amsterdam and New York: Rodopi, 2008), 222.

26 The title of the play was derived from a summer program in London, sponsored by the Royal Court Theatre, that Caisley was invited to attend in 1993. During one of the workshops with various well-known British playwrights and directors that Caisley attended, he was asked to write a letter to aliens visiting our planet and explain to them the best and the worst that our world had to offer. This assignment ultimately led to the title of the play. Robert Caisley, email message to author, 25 July 2014.

27 The play was written for a youth audience. Caisley told me that he wrote the play as a coming-of-age story that would have a rapport with teenagers, who, like Hannah, were trying to find their own identity and fit in with their peers. Robert Caisley, email message to author, 25 July 2014.

28 Robert Caisley, email message to author, 25 July 2014.

29 Robert Caisley, *Letters to an Alien* (Woodstock, IL: Dramatic Publishing, 1996), 9–10. All subsequent citations from the play are from this edition and will be included within parentheses in the text.

30 Explicating the Holocaust through space aliens not only is novel, but also appears to be apropos of the Shoah as a historical event that seems alien to humanity. These aliens assist us in providing a perspective of an outsider, reinforcing the idea of how absurd and unimaginable the Holocaust might appear to be to someone looking at history from a fresh perspective. The aliens also provide humor in an otherwise serious play. Caisley explained to me why the concept of aliens worked so well in the play: "I knew I was writing for a young audience. And I knew I was treating potentially troubling and difficult subject matter. So I was looking for a way to really engage the imagination of my intended audience. The aliens seemed like the perfect dramatic vehicle to take both these considerations into account. The aliens in the play possess an intellectual curiosity about something they know nothing about – they are hungry for knowledge. So they are proxy for the audience. I get to have them ask 'dumb' questions about an incredibly complex and troubling part of our history, without it seeming overtly clunky or expositional." Robert Caisley, email message to author, 25 July 2014.

31 During my correspondence with Caisley, he wrote that at the University of Idaho, he taught a course on Representations of the Shoah in Theatre and Film in which he discussed the concept of survivor guilt. He added, "When I wrote LETTERS, I was interested in how people respond to surviving atrocity." Robert Caisley, email message to author, 25 July 2014.

32 Ben-Zion Tomer, "*Children of the Shadows*," trans. Hillel Halkin, in *Israeli Holocaust Drama*, ed. Michael Taub (Syracuse: Syracuse University Press, 1996), 40. All subsequent citations from the play are from this edition and will be included within parentheses in the text.

33 Michael Taub, "Ben Zion Tomer," in *Holocaust Literature: An Encyclopedia of Writers and Their Work*, vol. 2, ed. S. Lillian Kremer (New York and London: Routledge, 2003), 1267.

4

DRAMATIZING CHILDHOOD SURVIVOR TRAUMA

The Nazis murdered approximately 1.5 million children during the Holocaust.[1] Children who entered the extermination camps were gassed immediately; adolescents who were old enough to work were spared. Teenagers who were interned in concentration camps, labor camps, or extermination camps suffered the same traumata as adults, but the separation from parents and family members exacerbated their psychiatric problems. J. Tas, a psychiatrist who was interned at Bergen-Belsen in 1944, describes the children there as behaving "psychopathically" because of the desocializing nature of the camp.[2] Even children who had parents interned in the camp found that because parents were engaged in work all day, the lack of supervision led to children wandering aimlessly, eventually becoming wanton. Tas noted that children interned in concentration camps displayed unusual symptoms of irritability, fits of rage and aggression, phobias and nocturnal anxieties, and frequent bouts of enuresis.[3]

Other children survived as nomads hiding with partisan groups in the forests. These children, orphaned and abandoned by their parents, suffered from hunger and cold. They were also subject to anti-Semitic cruelty from peasants who mingled with the partisans. Many other children lived incognito with Christian families or in safe havens, such as convents. Moskovitz and Krell report that children who were in hiding during the Holocaust recall constantly living in fear.[4] They remember fear of starvation, fear of being discovered or betrayed, or fear of abandonment if they did not please their guardians.[5] Moreover, these children in hiding understood that being able to be quiet and subdued meant survival, thus inhibiting the child's natural proclivity to run, explore, and express their emotions freely. Psychiatrist Hillel Klein argues that because the parents who initially had protected the child were now absent, the child in hiding developed feelings of guilt, deprivation, and abandonment.[6] Often, the child's religious beliefs were also undermined by Christian families who were uncomfortable with regard to the spiritual needs of Jewish children.

Another category of traumatized children includes those who were forced to emigrate from Europe without their parents soon after Kristallnacht. Realizing that the fate of Jewish children was abysmal after the violence against Jews during Kristallnacht, parents who had the ability to obtain visas for their children sent them to safety in England or the United States. These children, confused about being sent by their formerly nurturing parents to live with strangers in a foreign county, now felt that they were abandoned by their mothers and fathers. As a result of the genocide, many of these children were never able to see their parents again. The psychological problems that accrued from such childhood trauma will be discussed in detail in this chapter.

The level of trauma varied according to the age of the child. In their research on child survivors, Moskovitz and Krell learned that older survivors, including adults and adolescents who remembered a normal prewar life, had a bulwark of stability that was absent in the younger child survivors.[7] Survivors who were traumatized as young children did not have a normal childhood and have only fragmented memories of normalcy before the War. The youngest among them may not recall their parents, family members, or even their native language. Krell acknowledges that the loss of parents that the children may not have ever known leads to the loss of the nucleus of one's own identity.[8] Some survivors who were children at the time of the trauma may remember how their cries were stifled by parents who feared that the wails would give away a hiding place; others recall a father figure who was removed from the family and then incarcerated by the Nazis. The dominant impression that many of these child survivors have is that of family instability and an inhospitable environment of hunger, cold, and fear. Mazor et al. discovered that somewhat older children who could remember their parents were faced with their inability to mourn their deaths appropriately because they were consumed with the struggle for their own survival.[9] On the whole, the lack of a normal childhood precludes child survivors having a relatively stable psychological presence. Psychiatrists typically agree that child survivors, no matter what their age, are different from adult survivors because they were forced to endure formidable stressors without the benefit of adult coping mechanisms.[10]

At the end of the War, the psychological scars were evident among most child survivors. Deaths in a family are normal occurrences, but genocide is not. Krell states, "Seldom does a child lose all his or her parents, brothers, sisters, aunts, uncles, grandparents and cousins, as occurred during the Holocaust."[11] After the liberation, when the news of finding lost relatives was hopeless, children had to realize that they were orphaned and without a home. They had been ostracized, degraded, and threatened with death, thus forcing them to lose trust in authority figures. Bereavement was made difficult without a gravesite and without an official date or record of death. Child survivors were often distraught at the lack of opportunity to bid their parents farewell. The children also frequently felt guilty about their inability to save their parents from their deaths, despite the imminent pre-Holocaust signs of foreboding. Sarah Moskovitz interviewed adults who, as children, were interned in Theresienstadt and Auschwitz or were in hiding during the Holocaust and were ultimately sent to the Lingfield Orphanage in England during spring and summer 1945. Moskovitz notes, "Intertwined with the problem of loss and recurrent mourning is a haunting anxiety about belonging."[12] Kestenberg and Kestenberg reported that, in a desperate sense to belong and not feel excluded, children separated from their mothers during the Holocaust attached themselves to transitional objects, such as scarves or combs, that belonged to both mother and child.[13] Even children that were placed in foster homes shortly after liberation struggled with issues about security. Many of the children expressed fears of being outsiders who were uprooted, persecuted, and exiled by a regime that saw fit to murder their family members. Child survivors thus often considered themselves to be of a different breed and concomitantly felt shame to be "a child of the Holocaust."[14] This typically translated into feelings of humiliation and lack of self-esteem. Moskovitz also concluded that the Lingfield children, feeling alienated as outsiders unsure of their worth, had difficulties with intimacy.[15] Increasing the children's state of depression was the ubiquitous mourning for the loss of the more ideal world they experienced before the Nazi genocide. The children mourned the self that, under normal conditions, would have been educated in the school system, would have achieved more with loving parents, and would have prospered in an otherwise healthy environment. What is mourned is a lost world and lost opportunities that can never be recaptured.

Memory wreaks havoc on child survivors of the Holocaust. On the one hand, the children feel an obligation to remember nurturing parents who raised them in a somewhat idyllic, pristine pre-Holocaust environment. On the other hand, the child, instead of blaming the persecutors, feels abandoned by parents who could not protect the children from catastrophe; as Moskovitz and Krell infer, the child becomes the bearer of a shameful secret too terrible to discuss even with their foster parents.[16] Thus, child survivors are often conflicted between keeping silent and having an entrusted mission to bear witness. Children who survived through hiding and remaining unobtrusive during the War are typically even more conflicted about the dialectic. Furthermore, many children who were sent to foster homes by their parents were told time and again that if they did not keep quiet and behave, their new guardians would reject them. The importance of not speaking out – remaining silent – was firmly cemented among child survivors. This conflict between fear of speaking about the trauma and a desire to remember, combined with unresolved grief and incomplete mourning, increases guilt, thus preventing the child's total reintegration into a normal life.[17] In his extensive research on child survivors, Hillel Klein further acknowledges that the older child or adolescent suffered from more intense guilt accrued from the knowledge of his or her survival while others had perished.[18] Judith Kestenberg also adds that when the child recalls the pain and suffering of the parents during the Holocaust, guilt feelings are reinforced.[19]

Psychological studies of child survivors corroborate diagnoses of post-traumatic stress disorder. In the earliest recorded study of child survivors, Paul Friedman, who observed subjects detained on Cyprus in 1946, noted their unusual shallowness of emotions, an "affective anesthesia"; this condition plagued all of the child survivors, whether they were in labor camps, in concentration camps, or in hiding.[20] The first major study of child survivors was conducted by Shalom Robinson, who collected data on 106 patients at Talbieh Psychiatric Hospital in Jerusalem between 1966 and 1975; all of these children were under the age of seventeen during the Holocaust. Robinson diagnosed half of these child survivors as psychotic.[21] Fifty-eight of the 106 patients were found to suffer from persecutory thoughts, paranoia, and depression, while forty-four percent were plagued with anxiety or phobias.[22] Comparing a control group to the child survivors, Robinson concluded, "The high incidence of paranoid symptoms and aggressiveness must be ascribed to the Holocaust experiences."[23] Shortly after Robinson's research was published in 1979, Sarah Moskovitz's study of the Lingfield children (1983) reiterated that "continuing anxiety over possible persecution" was a common legacy of the child survivors she interviewed.[24]

Working with Judith Hemmendinger, Robinson pursued his research on child survivors in the early 1980s. After sending out questionnaires and interviewing fourteen male survivors of Buchenwald, Robinson and Hemmendinger found that they suffered from post-traumatic symptoms of guilt, depression, insomnia, and nightmares about the past.[25] During 1986–1987, A. Mazor, Y. Gampel, R.D. Enright, and R. Orenstein interviewed ten male and five female child survivors who immigrated to Israel after the Holocaust. The team discovered that shortly after the liberation, the children survived psychologically through what Lifton had described as psychic numbing to defend against the trauma.[26] After the early years, the victims tried to cope by occupying themselves with establishing families, finding employment, or contributing productively to the state of Israel – all of which took their minds off the traumata. Mazor et al. inferred, "In this sense, while these people concentrated upon building their lives through certain tasks, emotionally the trauma continued to linger and influence their lives."[27]

In 1992, Shalom Robinson, M. Rapaport-Bar-Sever, and J. Rapaport interviewed 103 Holocaust survivors who were under the age of thirteen when the Nazi persecution began. They discovered that fifty years after the outbreak of World War II, child survivors were still suffering from symptoms of the Survivor Syndrome.[28] The most common symptom was hypermnesia concerning the Holocaust (seventy-three percent), followed by nervousness (sixty-two percent), fatigue (fifty-nine percent), insomnia (fifty-five percent), and "emotional instability" (fifty percent); more than one-third of the population of child survivors suffered from nightmares with Holocaust content, headaches, psychosomatic complaints, depression, chronic anxiety, and anhedonia.[29] The other noteworthy finding was that there was no clear correlation between the age of the child during the persecution and the extent of psychological suffering experienced when they were adults.[30] In another landmark study conducted by Rachel Lev-Wiesel and Marianne Amir, 170 Holocaust child survivors completed questionnaires about post-traumatic stress. The survivors were divided into four categories, depending upon the setting of their survival during the Holocaust: in Catholic institutions, in Christian homes, in concentration camps, or in hiding with partisans. Wiesel and Amir found that there was no difference in the levels of post-traumatic stress disorders among child survivors in any of these categories.[31]

Similar to adult survivors of the Holocaust, child survivors adopted coping mechanisms to assuage their traumatic symptoms. Robinson, Rapaport-Bar-Sever, and Rapaport reported that child survivors showed high ability in coping and adjustment in order to provide meaning in their lives.[32] Child survivors want to believe that they belong in society, and thus, as a whole, they strive to cope with their psychological problems. Many child survivors view coping and prospering as a means to combat a ruthless Nazi regime that was determined to destroy them. Children who were abandoned by their parents to be sent elsewhere to escape the Nazi menace were found to have an unusual desire for independence that translated into pulling themselves up by their own bootstraps.[33] Older children remembered their nurturing parents and attempted to emulate positive family values that they had experienced before the Holocaust by raising children and making sure their children's lives were much better than their own.[34] For child survivors, having children overcame Nazi genocide and offered subliminal satisfaction in triumphing over Hitler, as well as symbolically replacing their own family that had been destroyed or splintered during the Shoah. Giving their children the security of a home provided child survivors with the ability to restore their own lost childhoods that were largely spent homeless or in institutions of foster care. Child survivors even frequently named their own children after dead parents, thus constituting a symbolic resurrection. Another measure of adopting a family that they were denied during their childhood was to unite with similar refugees who had been in orphanages after the War. Other child survivors went to Israel and joined a kibbutz; such a communal institution alleviated their feelings of exclusion.[35]

Despite suffering from symptoms of trauma, child survivors found altruistic mechanisms to alleviate their *angoisse* while concomitantly recreating a sense of belonging for themselves. Child survivors may want to keep alive the spiritual values of their dead family members or may view their survival as having some spiritual significance, as if God had spared them for some special purpose in life.[36] Other child survivors may remember the parting words of their parents, exhorting them to do well in their new lives with foster parents and not cause problems for anyone. Kestenberg and Kestenberg mention that caring wards became models of altruism for these children, ultimately leading them to careers as rescuers.[37] Still others feel the need to become saviors, thus filling the void that existed in their own early lives. Many child survivors thus took jobs in the healing professions, worked in orphanages or with agencies that were devoted to child care, or were employed in organizations devoted to the improvement of humanity (thus, subliminally rejecting the death instinct).

There is a paucity of drama reflecting the traumata of children who survived the Shoah and virtually no plays written about children who were in hiding, living with the partisans, or in concentration camps or labor camps. The remainder of this chapter will focus on the traumata experienced by child survivors who were abandoned by parents who tried to shield their children from the horrors of the genocide; two plays that represent such traumata are Diane Samuels's *Kindertransport* and Wendy Graf's *Leipzig*.

British playwright Diane Samuels was born into a Jewish family in Liverpool in 1960. She studied history at Sidney Sussex College in Cambridge and later read drama at the University of London. Samuels taught drama in London secondary schools for five years and then worked as a children's education officer at the Unicorn Theatre. Her first two plays, *Frankie's Monster* and *Chalk Circle*, were selected in 1991 by *Time Out* magazine as best plays for children. Her other plays include *The True Life Fiction of Mata Hari, Cinderella's Daughter, Salt of the Earth*, and *3 Sisters on Hope Street* (co-written with Tracy-Ann Oberman). Samuels has also written several plays for children, including *The Bonekeeper, One Hundred Million Footsteps*, and *How to Beat a Giant*. Moreover, she has penned various radio plays aired by the British Broadcasting Company, such as *Swine, Doctor Y, Watch Out for Mister Stork, Hen Party*, and *Tiger Wings*. Finally, Samuels has dabbled in musical theater, writing the book and lyrics for *Persephone* and the book for *The A-Z of Mrs P*.

Kindertransport premiered at the Cockpit Theatre in London on 13 April 1993, in a production staged by the Soho Theatre Company and directed by Abigail Morris. The play won the Meyer Whitworth Award in 1993 and was co-winner of the Verity Bargate Award for new writing. The American debut of the play was at the Manhattan Theater Club in New York City in May 1994, in a production once more directed by Abigail Morris. After its closing in June 1996 at the Palace Theatre in Watford, the play transferred to the Vaudeville Theatre in the West End. In 2007, *Kindertransport* went on a national tour of the United Kingdom in a production directed by Polly Teale of Shared Experience Theatre Company. Another tour of the play, with performances directed by Andrew Hall, occurred in the United Kingdom during 2013/2014. Productions of the play have been mounted in Sweden, Germany, Austria, Australia, New Zealand, Japan, Switzerland, Israel, Canada, South Africa, and the United States. *Kindertransport* is now studied at Cambridge International's AS and A levels in Great Britain and is part of the curriculum in English Literature for the General Certificate in Secondary Education (GCSE) in schools in England, Wales, and Northern Ireland.

The idea for *Kindertransport* began in 1989, during the fiftieth anniversary of the kindertransports, when Samuels first learned of the emigration of the children from Germany and Austria.[38] Through Rena Gamsa, a friend of her husband, who was the son of German-Jewish refugees, Samuels met Bertha Leverton, who was organizing a reunion of former survivors of the kindertransports. After Bertha introduced Samuels to other child survivors, the British playwright was intrigued upon hearing their stories. Samuels also watched a television documentary about the ordeals that the children endured and their subsequent adjustment to life in England after their emigration. Serious writing began on the play during 1990, when Samuels's second child was born. Living now in a family of three males, Samuels had a need "to dream up some kind of feminine environment."[39] The result was the all-female world of *Kindertransport* (minus the mythical male character of the Ratcatcher). The idea of writing a play about childhood trauma derived from Samuels's employment as an education officer at the Unicorn Theatre, where she was working to mount productions for children.

The need for Jewish parents to send their children to safety to avoid Nazi persecution began after Kristallnacht (9 November 1938). Before Kristallnacht, most Jews considered Nazi persecution to be merely another round in a long history of German anti-Semitism that ebbed and flowed. Intelligent Jews and Germans saw Hitler as a raving lunatic whose ideas would never be seriously accepted in an educated society such as Germany. Besides, Jews had been fully assimilated into German society for generations. Although Jews felt Nazi persecution acutely in the early and mid-1930s, even to the extent of losing citizenship due to the Nuremberg Laws, they fully accepted the fact that they were born and raised in Germany, educated in German institutions, spoke the German language (more fluently than Hitler did in speaking sud-Deutsch), and were well represented in the professions there, thus seeing no need to emigrate. Many Jews even told jokes to their comrades about Hitler, Goering, Himmler, or Goebbels. However, after the well-orchestrated terror of Kristallnacht, everything changed for the Jews. During 9 and 10 November, Jews were harassed, beaten, and murdered; their bank accounts were purged, their property was destroyed, and their homes and synagogues were ravaged. Moreover, the Nazis typically rounded up the male heads of households and sent them to concentration camps. When these father figures returned weeks or even months later, they were hardly recognizable to their family members. They had been starved, beaten, and worked to exhaustion in the cold winter of 1938/1939. Parents then realized the frantic need for their families to leave Germany.

On 21 November 1938, the House of Commons agreed to allow Jewish refugees to enter Great Britain. Since Europe was recovering from the Depression and the British economy remained stagnant, adult refugees who would compete for scarce jobs were discouraged from immigrating there. Christian and national organizations, with the help of charitable Christian individuals, such as the Quakers, galvanized to save Jewish children from Nazi persecution. Vast sums of money were raised to help defray the costs of transporting and housing these children. Between 2 December 1938 and the beginning of the War on 1 September 1939, when all transports ceased, nearly ten thousand children from Germany, Austria, and Czechoslovakia went unaccompanied on trains and by ship to England. The ages of the children ranged from three months to seventeen. The children were temporarily housed in reception centers before they were claimed by assigned guardians, relatives, or citizens hoping to become foster parents. Many of these children were eventually housed in hostels or private homes in some Jewish, but mostly non-Jewish, households.

Child survivors of the kindertransports recall the various incidents of their long ordeals that eventually led to their traumatization. Edward Mendelsohn, one of the Kinder who survived, wrote, "The Kindertransport was at the center of many episodes, which all together added up to one huge destabilizing, alienating and ongoing trauma."[40] Even before Kristallnacht, Jewish child survivors recall their parents being harassed or beaten in the streets. In school, these children were ostracized and teased by their Aryan schoolmates; eventually, their religion precluded their attendance, so they were expelled from school, thus contributing to their feelings of exclusion. Many of these children witnessed the horrors of Kristallnacht and afterwards felt insecure and afraid when their fathers were sent to a concentration camp. They began living a life of terror and suffering with the ultimate threat of themselves being marched away constantly looming in the background.

With the imminent need to send their offspring on the kindertransports in order to save their lives, the children grew increasingly apprehensive. Several of the adolescents were anticipating the adventure of a new experience and relished the opportunity to flee from their persecutors. However, the younger children were distraught at being abandoned by their parents. In her accounts of anonymous child survivor remembrances of the kindertransports, Karen Gershon cites one such *Kind* whose voice seems to speak for many without a voice: "I remember crying bitterly and saying: 'Please, Mummy, please don't send me away.' I was eleven years old at the time."[41] Many of these children were also concerned about whether they would be accepted by their new surrogate guardians; their need to belong was paramount.

The seeds of the traumatic experience were cultivated when parents bade farewell to their children at the train stations. Child survivor Shulamit Amir vividly remembers the harrowing scene: "The scene at the railway station before our departure will remain in my memory for ever [*sic*]. Most of the children were crying at the prospect of being parted from their parents, and the parents were trying to put on a brave face."[42] Amid panic, fear, and confusion among the children, the Nazi guards herded them into the train compartments. Ruth Kagan recalls the deeply rooted despair that was forever etched in her mind at the departure:

> On the platform, mothers and fathers were holding each other, weeping as the train swept their beloved children away, into the unknown. I was gripped by feelings of panic. A part of me wanted to jump out through the train window, but my feet were frozen and all I could do was press my face against the dirty pane of glass for that last longing look at my parents as the train crept out of the station.[43]

The train ride through Germany exacerbated the terror. Without fully imagining that the extent of the Nazi genocide would result in the deaths of their parents, many of the children during the train ride gradually began to realize that they might never see their family members again. Many of the younger children, entrusted to the care of the adolescents, cried throughout the journey. En route, the German guards unpacked the children's suitcases, looking for valuables to steal. They confiscated any money or jewelry they could find, leaving the children penniless. The children were even stripped and searched in the private parts of their anatomy. One child survivor recalls the passing of the train out of Germany to Belgium: "Fear was in all of us, until the moment the whistle blew, the Nazis left and the train passed over the frontier."[44]

The fear briefly subsided as the youngsters passed through Holland and across the English Channel, knowing they could speak with impunity once they were free of the Nazi yoke. However, once on British soil, their feelings of exclusion began to reemerge. Most of the children were alienated because they did not speak English, yet the British authorities knew no German. The children, fatigued, unwashed, hungry, and benumbed, were stranded in a foreign country without friends or relatives and unable to communicate with the strangers who were questioning them. Herbert Holden recalls his first day in England: "I was trying desperately hard to be as brave as a thirteen year old boy was expected to be, and I spent most of that day in and out of the toilet so that no one would see the tears which were running down my cheeks."[45] Some of the children had foster parents coming to meet them at the reception centers. Vera Reichman remembers the unnerving experience: "On arrival in England, I vaguely recall standing in a room full of people. My name was called and when I came forward, someone handed me over to a lady who led me away. It was a traumatic moment."[46] Other children who did not have guardians were sent to refugee camps until they could be claimed by charitable residents. One anonymous child survivor described to Karen Gershon how the selection process led to a loss of individuality among the refugees: "Prospective foster-parents were usually shown round at mealtimes, when we sat, boys and girls separately, according to age. The people walked down the rows of children, picking out this one or that, rather like a cattle market."[47]

Jewish child refugees living in England during the War desperately tried to belong by becoming quickly acculturated to their new environment. They learned English fairly easily and adapted well to most British customs and mores. Although foster parents typically provided for the children's food, clothing, and shelter, they could not always offer the same loving environment that the refugees experienced in their native countries. If the foster parents had children of their own, the refugees often felt they were outsiders to the family. Jewish children were also alienated because of their religion; many of them were encouraged to go to church with their foster parents, although indoctrination into Christianity was not the norm. Nevertheless, Jewish children felt conflicted, and religion was often the source for their exclusion. The child survivors were also terribly homesick for their parents and soon began writing letters back home, at times almost incessantly. One child survivor explains the rationale for the letter writing: "I used to boast during my first years here [in England] that I never suffered from homesickness. I now realise that this frantic letter-writing was just that."[48] Meanwhile, the children feared for the safety of their parents in Nazi Germany and wondered if they would ever be able to see them again.

These child survivors also felt excluded at school since they were frequently the only Jewish refugees in the class. Once the War began and British homes were soon bombed by the Germans, refugees were considered to be "enemy aliens," which further ostracized them. One such child survivor recalls what it meant to be a refugee and an enemy of the state: "In a boy of eight years, all these feelings were exaggerated and added up to one overriding emotion: bewilderment."[49] As the War progressed, letters from parents ceased abruptly when they were deported to their deaths. Children thus lost contact with their relatives; approximately eighty percent of the Kinder never saw their parents again.[50] This doubt about the safety and whereabouts of their parents augmented the anxiety that they felt in being alone and excluded.

After the Holocaust, almost all child survivors in England felt immense gratitude to the British for saving their lives.[51] Although they were fully acculturated into British society, the children were typically tainted souls whose wounds rarely healed as a result of their loss. Renate Buchthal recalls how guilt plagued many child survivors like her after the War: "There is still the guilt – that I was saved when so many children were not."[52] Gershon cites another such child survivor who admitted, "This hate, and hate it is, is bound up with a tremendous feeling of guilt, both in taking the atrocities as if they were my own, and inversely, for having got away so lightly."[53]

The overwhelming desire to slough off their Holocaust past and begin life anew in a society in which acculturation made child survivors feel as if they belonged and were no longer excluded as vermin or *Untermenschen* ultimately produced two selves: the traumatized victim of the past and the rejuvenated British citizen of the future. In Chapter 1, I discussed how Charlotte Delbo, after surviving Auschwitz, mentioned that she consisted of two divided selves: her shameful Holocaust persona, which, after shedding her skin like a snake, morphed into a post-Holocaust self that again became acculturated. No matter how many shades of veneer can be plastered onto the civilized self, the traumatized self was always omnipresent for Delbo. In an interview with Cathy Caruth, Robert Jay Lifton explained psychoanalytically what Delbo was trying to convey. Lifton argued that extreme trauma creates a second self as a form of doubling in the traumatized person, and recovery is impossible until the traumatized self is integrated. Lifton concludes, "So the struggle in the post-traumatic experience is to reconstitute the self into the single self, reintegrate itself."[54]

Most child survivors experienced the two selves that plagued Delbo. Like Delbo, they wanted nothing to do with a shameful, tainted past. One former child survivor acknowledged, "I renounced my background; I was ashamed of it. I wanted to forget everything. If I was asked where I came from it was tantamount to being accused of a crime. To be reminded that I was Austrian, or worse still, Jewish, and a refugee child, was an insult."[55] These child survivors did not have a need to return to their native countries and instead were determined to slough off their old personae and, in an effort to belong, acculturated themselves into British society. Once they had the ability to speak English, they denounced their native German language to the point of even forgetting how to speak it. Many former child survivors surrendered their birth names and adopted an Anglicized name instead. Some insisted on being baptized and even became members of the Church of England. Others married British spouses and were determined to raise families in the country that saved their lives. All of them showed allegiance to the country that helped to defeat Germany. However, as Delbo lamented, the trauma of the Holocaust always trumped any attempt by the psyche to acculturate to psychological peace. For example, Erika Shotland, a child refugee originally from Kirel, Vienna, who settled in Manchester, revealed that after living her life as a British citizen, she still can never fully assimilate: "After fifty years in England, being happily married, bringing up lovely daughters and now being a grandmother myself, a feeling of loss still persists."[56] To cite another example, Elfriede Colman, a survivor from Vienna who married and raised two children in England, describes how the childhood trauma affected her relationship with her family: "My deficient childhood made me incapable of giving the unstinting love they all deserved, and it wasn't until my late thirties that an extended period of psychotherapy turned me into a reasonably adequate human being."[57]

Kindertransport explores the symptoms of ever-lingering trauma that was endemic to child survivors of the Holocaust. Diane Samuels discussed her purpose for writing *Kindertransport*: "Most of all, my focus when writing the play was to probe the inner life where memory is shaped by trauma, history meets story, in order to gain psychological and emotional insight into how a damaged psyche can survive, possibly recover, and whether there might ever be an opportunity to thrive."[58]

The setting of the play is an attic in England during the mid-1980s, where Evelyn's daughter Faith is going through her mother's belongings and relics. Faith, in her twenties, is leaving the nest, so Evelyn is hoping that some of her kitchen utensils can be of use in her daughter's new household. An attic is typically a place of hidden treasures, secrets, and old relics; the play focuses on Evelyn's trauma, her deeply rooted secret that is gradually revealed as Faith explores with Evelyn these "old relics" from Evelyn's past. Polly Teale, who directed *Kindertransport*, discussed the importance of the attic as a symbolic setting for the play: "There's also an opportunity to create a metaphorical attic, that's about this locked room inside Evelyn."[59] All of the remaining scenes in the play are essentially flashbacks from the conversations that Evelyn and Faith have in this attic. As the audience witnesses Evelyn's trauma unfold through the flashbacks, the attic, not the closet, becomes the place that unlocks the skeletons of her past.

During the first flashback, nine-year-old Eva[60] Schlesinger is in Hamburg, Germany, with her mother Helga, who is teaching her child to sew on buttons as a step toward learning how to take care of herself. They are reading from a fairy tale titled *Der Rattenfänger* (*The Ratcatcher*), which, throughout the play, develops into stimuli for the onset of the trauma with which Eva will be plagued. Eva asks a pertinent question about the children's story: "What's an abyss, Mutti?" Helga replies, "An abyss is a deep and terrible chasm" (1). These first two lines of the play indicate the abyss that Eva falls into – a split personality, as Delbo indicated, in which the traumatized self ultimately refuses to identify with her own mother who personifies the Holocaust persona.

The episode in which Helga prepares her daughter for the train transport reflects Eva's confusion about leaving her family. Eva wonders why her parents cannot protect her and why they would abandon her to live with strangers in a foreign country. Helga makes promises that Eva will later remember as being lies: "We will not let you leave us behind for very long. Do you think we would really let you go if we thought that we would never see you again?" (7). Helga promises to visit Eva in England when the permits arrive.

During the train ride in 1939, Eva is inundated with the cries of whimpering children who are frightened to death of traveling into the abyss without their parents. A Nazi officer, branding Eva with a number and labeling her luggage with the Star of David, reminds her of her Jewish origins. Eva is terrified as she watches the Nazi officer trash her belongings and confiscate her money. At the reception center in Harwich, Eva is met by the English Organizer, who tries to convey to her that her foster mother has been delayed by a late train. The nine-year-old girl is distraught since she knows no English and is totally confused by her plight. Eva speaks in German, but the British magistrate cannot understand her. Eva, terrified at being left alone in a strange land, begins crying uncontrollably while at the same time, speaking in German, blames her mother for her plight: "But my mother said that I had a family here. She said it had been arranged" (25). When Lil Miller[61] arrives, her friendly nature temporarily assuages Eva's fears. Lil points to the Star of David on the suitcase, and Eva responds, "Ach, das ist blöd" ("that's stupid"), an early indication that her Jewishness is intricately related to her traumatic experiences.

Eva eventually settled in Manchester with loving foster parents and gradually began to learn English. The culture was often difficult to adapt to, especially the cuisine, which featured nonkosher food such as ham. Eva was homesick at first and petitioned the local authorities to provide her parents with permits to obtain work in England. At that point in her life, Eva explained to Lil that she was "Nicht Englisch! Deutsch! Ich bin Deutsche" (41). After having learned from Lil that immigrants can only work as domestic servants in England, Eva canvasses wealthy people to embolden them to hire her parents as butlers or housekeepers. Like most children who were exhorted by their parents to behave in their new households, Eva feels guilty when Lil explains that knocking on doors is shameful behavior. Eva wonders if Lil will send her back to Germany and abandon her like her parents did, but Lil's magnanimous attitude assuages the youngster's fears.

During the War, when England was being bombed, children were evacuated; Lil also agrees that Eva should be in a safe haven. Lil's protective measure appears subliminally to Eva to be a reinforcement of Helga abandoning her in Germany. Eva tells Lil that she is hesitant to leave because she saw some vague spectre on the train platform "waiting in the shadows" for her (62). Eva claims that she would rather risk dying with Lil than being abandoned. As the train pulls out of the station, Eva, choking with paranoia, exclaims, "We've got to stop! He'll take us over the edge. Got to get away from him" (63). Assuming that she has landed in the abyss and has been cornered by the Ratcatcher, Eva, in terror, leaps off the train. Lil, realizing her transgression, provides solace for her foster child and subsequently reconsiders her decision to send Eva away even temporarily.

When the War breaks out and Eva comprehends that her parents have no viable way out of Germany, she fears that she will never see them again. Eva removes her jewelry and her Star of David as if to sever her past – a life that became traumatic because of German anti-Semitism. Lil, however, agrees to keep these possessions stored away in the attic.

The recurrence of Eva's trauma throughout the play is embodied in the shadowy, threatening figure of the Ratcatcher.[62] In Hamburg, Helga had read the story of the Ratcatcher to Eva, cementing in her mind the tale of the mythical person who took naughty children away, promising them, "I will take the heart of your happiness away" (17), leading them into the abyss. The Ratcatcher personifies all of Eva's childhood fears, demons, traumata, and nightmares. The Ratcatcher hovers over the play, reinforcing Eva's abandonment, her sense of loss, her fears of being excluded, the threat of imminent danger or death, and the shame of her past life as a Jew. He represents authority figures similar to Nazis who interrogated Jews like Eva and made them feel unwanted and uncomfortable. Moreover, the Ratcatcher traps his prey, and Eva, intuitively understanding the German concept that Jews were trapped animals, has been reminded of the threat by her mother's storytelling. Samuels also notes, "There is an element of mystery and unpredictability about him. He is a fairytale character. That actually makes him feel more scary because he is unpredictable. He can't be defined."[63]

The Ratcatcher is always depicted as a male since most Nazi authority figures that we envision terrorizing Jews in uniforms were male. When the Ratcatcher is mentioned during Eva's train trip, he morphs into the Nazi officer who accosts Eva by stealing her money. He then appears as the English Organizer who is the first person to interrogate her once on British soil. He is later represented by the Postman, who perceives Eva to be an enemy alien that smells like all Germans, thus reiterating to Eva that she is excluded from civilized British society. Finally, the Ratcatcher appears in the form of a Station Guard who cross-examines Eva about her country of origin while Lil is preoccupied in the cloakroom. At the end of the play, during Evelyn's encounter with her mother, she reveals that she also associates Helga with the Ratcatcher because she blames Helga for precipitating the trauma when she abandoned her to an unknown fate.

Much like Delbo who tried to shed the mortal coil of her Auschwitz past and assimilate herself back into cultured life, Eva attempts to assuage her traumatic past as a German-Jewish refugee by remaking her life into a respected British citizen. Eric J. Sterling remarks, "Knowing that many people hate her and even wish her dead because she is Jewish, Eva wonders whether she deserves to be punished, whether she is in fact inadequate because of her ethnicity, as Nazi propaganda affirms. She therefore wishes to dissolve her bonds with her Jewish parents and heritage."[64] Eva, like so many other child survivors who Anglicized their names, became Evelyn. Sterling astutely comments on the conversion: "The fact that she changes her name is telling because Eva is the name of her great-grandmother and thus part of her heritage – a heritage that she clearly wishes to disown."[65] The caring, nurturing Lil Miller, a surrogate mother, now replaces Helga as Evelyn's mother. At the age of sixteen, Evelyn even changed her birthday to the day Lil met her at the station. Evelyn gladly loses the ability to speak German; as a matter of fact, her English, without a trace of foreign accent, is highly polished and sophisticated. Upon first meeting Lil and seeing her smoking a cigarette, Eva told her that only common people smoke; however, over time, Evelyn picks up her foster mother's habit and eventually relishes it. The jewelry that Helga entrusted Eva with becomes worthless to her, for she chooses never to wear it. Evelyn admits to Lil that even as an heirloom to be passed down to her daughter, the jewelry is nothing more than a tainted memory of her past, stating, "I'd rather hand down things I feel happy about" (79). When Faith asks Evelyn about the copy of *Der Rattenfänger* and the Passover Haggadah that she found in the attic, Evelyn reduces these gifts that Helga graciously sent to her during the War as nothing more than bad memories from a tainted heritage: "One is a storybook and the other is for some Jewish festival" (92). The mouth organ that Eva so cherished as a child and had such difficulty passing through the Nazi security protocols becomes nothing more to Evelyn than a useless trinket. Furthermore, Evelyn has given up her Jewish heritage and tells Faith that when she was baptized at eighteen, "I was cleansed that day. Purified" (91). When Evelyn got married and had a family, she named her daughter Faith, a distinctly non-Jewish name. Faith was raised as a Christian and was baptized as well. Evelyn explains to her daughter the need she had to shed herself of her old German-Jewish skin and acculturate herself as a reborn person who belonged in a country that accepted her as a British citizen:

> Germany spat me out. England took me in. I love this place: the language, the food, the countryside, the buildings. I danced and sang when I got my first British passport. I was so proud of it. My certificate of belonging. You can't imagine what it was like.
>
> *(91)*

The final, and most difficult, act of sloughing off her Holocaust-tainted skin is Evelyn's rejection of her own mother. Although Evelyn's father perished in Auschwitz, Helga survived the Holocaust. When Evelyn was seventeen years old in 1947, she met her mother again, utterly transformed and wizened from her suffering. Of course, Helga calls her Eva, who insists on being referred to as Evelyn. Instead of speaking in her native German tongue, Evelyn ensures that the conversation is in English. The encounter between mother and daughter is cold and impersonal. Helga has plans to bring Evelyn to live with their uncle in New York City, but Evelyn, claiming that her family is in England, refuses to go. Eva Fogelman explains that child survivors have an emotional attachment to their rescuers that they fear will be undone by any natural parents who may have survived the War.[66] Thus, as Eric J. Sterling mentions, if Evelyn agrees to leave England with Helga, she would feel as if she deserted her rescuer and concomitantly would be abandoning her foster mother in the same way that Helga abandoned her.[67]

After being with her mother for one week, Evelyn bids her goodbye at quayside in Liverpool. Evelyn is literally sick over the departure, having been vomiting in the lavatory. Evelyn understands that if she were to leave with her mother, she would have to surrender her persona as Evelyn and thus shed her skin once again to return to her former self as victim of the Holocaust. Helga wonders why her daughter acts so coldly to her. After suffering through the Holocaust, Helga explains to Evelyn that she did not lose herself and wonders why her daughter lost *her* identity. Evelyn then exclaims that Helga represents the Ratcatcher and thus wishes that her mother had died during the War. Evelyn views Helga's decision to send her away in 1939, not as a life-saving gesture, but as an abandonment. She confides to Helga the source of her deeply rooted angst:

> You should have hung on to me and never let me go. Why did you send me away when you were in danger? No one made you! You chose to do it. Didn't it ever occur to you that I might have wanted to die with you? Because I did. I never wanted to live without you and you made me! What is more cruel than that?
>
> *(96)*

Helga, employing the same imagery that Delbo used to emphasize her totally different persona after Auschwitz, rebukes Evelyn for trying to remake herself: "Snake! Slithering out of yourself like it was an unwanted skin. Skinless snake. Worm!" (96).[68] This is the last time Evelyn saw her mother, who died in 1969; Evelyn refused to introduce Faith to her grandmother.

The rational part of the self would have the individual believe that parents sent their children away after Kristallnacht to save their lives. However, the deeply embedded unconscious self that affects memory can alter that perception, leaving the adult to believe that the parents abandoned their children. Most children at the time of their abandonment would probably have preferred to remain with the parents even at the risk of dying with them rather than embark on a new life with strangers in a country with a foreign culture, a different religion, and a new language. In their study of child survivors who were later placed in foster homes after the War, Lev-Wiesel and Amir cite one such example of a child who wonders why her parents abandoned her when she had done nothing wrong: "Rationally I know I should forgive my parents. No, no, understand them for their courageous deed; but inside, I am so angry. They should have let me die with them."[69] Child survivors experienced their traumata within the framework of the family. Krell writes, "The child was rarely capable of discerning the broader events which determined their parents' action or inaction. Hence the child blamed the parent for his or her abandonment, inadequate nourishment and other hardships."[70] Psychotherapist Judith S. Kestenberg contends that child survivors with guilt feelings leading to anger had a tendency to blame their surviving parents, rather than the Nazis, for the anxiety subsequently created in their lives.[71] Kestenberg's husband Milton, who, along with his wife, interviewed many child survivors, concluded, "Quite a few child survivors whose mothers survived also bear a grudge against their mother, making them responsible for what happened to them, blaming them in lieu of blaming their persecutors. They put great stress on their abandonment."[72]

For most of her life, Evelyn has tried to assimilate into British culture to slough off her former persona as a Holocaust victim. However, during conversations with her inquisitive, probing daughter in the attic, the secrets about her traumata surface. Evelyn's assimilation has protected her from the abyss, but the wounds of the trauma still remain. Samuels discusses Evelyn's dual selves that compete for psychological balance in her adult life; Samuels poses these questions about the nature of whether the trauma can ever be resolved: "Are you who you appear to be on the outside, or are you what you inherit from your culture and 'ancestors', much of which is concealed? Are you one person or two – someone who is 'out' and someone else who is 'in'?"[73]

Faith brings to the surface her mother's trauma that she has tried to hide for so many years. Evelyn seems obsessed with cleaning windows and polishing glasses, creating an orderly household. There is no place in her home for imperfection, so chipped glasses have to be discarded. Susanne Greenhalgh has written about the psychology behind Evelyn's obsession with cleanliness: "Rather it can be read as a sign of her internalization of the Nazi doctrine of the Jews as pollution, from which her baptism as a Christian has 'cleansed' and 'purified' her."[74] Evelyn was considered vermin in Germany, so she must constantly clean to leave her tainted self behind in England. Psychotherapist Judith S. Kestenberg explains the psychological ramifications for Jewish child survivors in Germany: "Children who grew up in German culture are especially prone to thinking that they can never become as good as the Germans and that they are destined to be inferior. This, in turn, engenders a fear of being abandoned, left alone because of their badness."[75] Evelyn thus has refused to recognize her Jewish origins, which is also a rejection of her mother, who urged Eva to mingle with Jews once she found refuge in England lest she lose her religious heritage. Faith's probing about her mother's origins is therefore psychologically damaging to Evelyn, for it unearths her former, hidden self. Evelyn tries to convey to Lil that this invasion of her privacy is returning her to the abyss: "The whitewash has been stripped away and underneath is pure filth" (60).

There is much evidence to suggest that Evelyn's Holocaust past can never be kept hidden, despite her most noble efforts to assimilate and to avoid discussing the past with her daughter. Before leaving Germany, Helga reminded Eva of the Passover story told through the Haggadah, as well as the story of the Ratcatcher. Both tales are latent reminders of the persecution Jews endured when they were about to be faced with the abyss. Helga sent Evelyn a copy of *Der Rattenfänger* and a Haggadah, which she made a conscious decision to save among her other valuable possessions. Eric J. Sterling remarks, "Her [Evelyn's] refusal to throw away documents, despite being compulsively neat, suggests that unconsciously she realizes that she can never completely disassociate herself from her Jewish past."[76] When Evelyn resorts to tearing up documents to attempt to cover up her past, her efforts become futile.

The true indicators that Evelyn can never fully belong in any society no matter how acculturated she becomes are the symptoms of her trauma. Evelyn, like Delbo, is forced to face the fact that she can never shed her former skin, no matter how many documents from her past she attempts to shred. Moskovitz and Krell write, "There are those who make a conscious decision not to remember, to live as if the Holocaust never happened, and who choose a non-Jewish identity as part of their denial. . . . The unwanted reminder may appear unexpectedly, at any time. The fragments of memory, triggered by endless stimuli, must be warded off with a great expenditure of psychic energy."[77] Evelyn displays many of the symptoms of post-traumatic stress disorder discussed in Chapters 1 and 2, and those are much more significant than her incessant need to clean and polish. In her nonclinical diagnosis, Faith assesses her mother's obsession with cleanliness as "paranoid" (46). She then mentions Evelyn's panic attacks replete with "shaking and gulping like you're going to die" (47). Faith also cites the stimuli that activate Evelyn's anxiety about the Holocaust: "You can't go on a train without hyperventilating. You cross the road if you see a policeman or traffic warden" (47). Child survivors of the kindertransports have reported similar traumatic reactions to such stimuli. For example, Helga Samuel, who was originally from Leipzig and eventually settled in Middlesex, recalls, "I remember my fears of men in uniform and for many years after coming to England, I was afraid of policemen."[78]

Decades after the Holocaust, Evelyn is still affected by the trauma, as evidenced by her relationship with Faith. Samuels chose Faith as a non-Jewish name that Evelyn would adopt for her daughter since it embeds her choice of Christianity and her rejection of her Jewish roots.[79] Throughout the mother-daughter relationship, Evelyn has been disingenuous with Faith, refusing to reveal anything about her Jewish origins. This coincides with Helga lying to Eva by telling her that her emigration would be temporary and that she would soon be reunited with her parents. Although Helga saved Eva's life, Evelyn's overriding memory of a mother that abandoned her paints her as a cold, impersonal woman. Evelyn thus tries to be the exact opposite of Helga, extending her cooperation to Faith and being patient with her when she pries into her mother's past. The crux of their current relationship centers on whether Faith will remain at home or will move out to share living quarters with her friends. Evelyn gives Faith material possessions to take with her, just as Helga did in 1939. However, the major dilemma for Evelyn concerns whether she will allow her daughter to leave, thus abandoning her in the same manner that she believes her own mother did to her in 1939. Evelyn allows Faith to make the choice of staying with her parent or being abandoned, wishing that Helga had allowed her the opportunity to make that choice herself. When Faith asks her mother if she should go, Evelyn responds, "What I want is irrelevant. It is your life, Faith" (8). Later in the play, Evelyn confesses to Lil, "I don't want her [Faith] to be like me" (75).

Although the play occurs in the mid-1980s, child survivor trauma still exists as the subliminal force that determines the relationship of Evelyn and Faith. The setting of every flashback is the attic, where Evelyn's hidden secrets unfold. The doppelganger that is ever-present in the attic is the abyss of Holocaust trauma, consistently represented by the Ratcatcher. The play opens with Eva reading *Der Rattenfänger* and ends with this stage direction: "*The shadow of the Ratcatcher covers the stage*" (98). *Kindertransport* visibly demonstrates that nearly forty-five years after the trauma occurred, the wounds of the Holocaust still linger among most of the victims.

Wendy Graf is a Los Angeles-based playwright whose full-length plays include *The Book of Esther, Lessons, Behind the Gates, Closely Related Keys*, and *No Word in Guyanese for Me*. Several of her one-act plays have won awards, including *Bethany Bakol, Ashes to Ashes, Lester and Schloss, A Hollywood Fable*, and *Reports of My Death Have Been Greatly Exaggerated*. *Leipzig* opened in Los Angeles on 20 October 2006 at the Marilyn Monroe Theater of the Lee Strasberg Institute. The production was directed by Deborah Lavine and featured a cast that included Salome Jens, Mimi Kennedy, and Mitchell Ryan. The play was nominated for Best New Play by the Los Angeles Drama Critics and won the Backstage West Garland Award for Best Play.

The genesis of the play began when Graf, who was asked to speak before a women's group about being a Jewish playwright, met a woman who had accompanied her mother on a two-week trip to Leipzig, Germany. The woman's mother, Eva Weisborg, had fled Germany in 1938, after Kristallnacht, and was invited to return to her homeland as part of a German government program that brought Jewish refugees back to their birthplaces. Fascinated by the subject, Graf interviewed the refugee and then went on to talk to many others who had escaped from Europe during the Holocaust. After researching and investigating the topic for more than one year, Graf was having difficulty putting all the information together to form a play. When Graf's mother-in-law began to show signs of Alzheimer's disease, she complained that she could not remember recent events but could recall incidents that occurred long ago. Graf explained to me how she put together the Alzheimer's with her research on the Survivor Syndrome to generate the idea for the play: "A light went off in my head. The refugees, the Kindertransport children, the hidden survivors . . . What if someone had a secret they tried their whole life to forget, and now they were desperate to remember, before it was too late? Thus the birth of *Leipzig.*"[80]

Eva Weisborg, who shares, ironically enough, the same first name of the protagonist in *Kindertransport*, fled Leipzig at age nine or ten on a ship bound for the United States.[81] Most of the play is set in Boston in 2007, where Eva Kelly, married to George, is suffering from Alzheimer's. Eva and George, both in their late seventies, have one daughter, Helen, who is in her forties and works as a journalist. Eva came to the United States to live with her guardians, Bridget and Robert. Years later, she married George Kelly, a Christian; they raised their daughter as a Catholic. Helen is unaware of Eva's Holocaust past and the fact that her mother was Jewish. Very much like *Kindertransport*, where Faith tried to unravel the secrets of her mother's trauma during the Holocaust, *Leipzig* is concerned with Helen's journalistic-type probing to disentangle the truth of her mother's tainted past.

Eva has lived a life full of secrets, denying her former childhood identity in Germany and refusing to reveal anything about it to her daughter. Eva Fogelman and Flora Hogman explain the denial of identity as a common reaction among child survivors: "These child survivors have coped with the trauma of massive persecution and multiple losses in a variety of ways. Some have used denial and repression as defenses and avoided talking about their pasts with spouses, children, and friends."[82] This psychic numbing, combined with the subliminal use of defense mechanisms such as negation, denial, and repression, provided child survivors such as Eva with the ability to adapt during postwar life. Diane Samuels commented on Ruth Barnett, a Kindertransport survivor who spent much of her life in denial about her childhood past. Barnett observed that when survivors aged, they could no longer keep their lives a secret because the memories came out through flashbacks, nightmares, or daydreams: "It takes a lot of mental energy to keep a trauma repressed, and when your mind gets weaker, if you're old and you have an illness, then you can't any longer keep it repressed and it all comes out."[83] This layman's view of the reappearance of the repressed memories of the trauma in later life is corroborated by the research of A. Mazor et al. Mazor et al. wrote, "At present 13 individuals (who are about 50 years old), stated that throughout the last few years they have found that they are able to remember a lot of the experiences that they had avoided thinking of in the past."[84] According to Graf, Eva's Alzheimer's disease, which is typically a product of aging, is the impetus that allows Helen to penetrate her mother's repressed memories of a traumatic childhood. Graf stated to me, "Plus in my experience with Alzheimer's I think it unlocks the trauma and the neurosis that made Eva try to suppress her memories for so long."[85]

As a result of the Alzheimer's, Eva cannot remember simple facts about her present life. She asks Helen if her son-in-law Arthur is arriving soon, but Helen reminds her that she has divorced Arthur. Eva queries her daughter about school, but Helen responds, "I graduated a long time ago, Mom. I'm a journalist now, remember?"[86] Eva wonders why Helen has not brought their dog Nikki into the house, and George responds, "Eva, Nikki's been dead a long time now, remember?" (52). The Alzheimer's is getting worse, and Eva has to be hospitalized when she gets burned upon putting wet towels into the oven, erroneously thinking that it was the dryer.

Helen becomes suspicious when Eva begins to speak in German – a language she has not used at home – and say prayers in Hebrew. George is protective of his wife and believes that the unraveling of Eva's secrets will only unleash the repressed feelings within her. Like Faith in *Kindertransport* who wants to understand her ancestry, Helen, the investigative journalist, persists in her attempts to unlock the family secrets. She says to her father, "You should have told me! I had the right to have a life that wasn't completely built on lies! I had the right to know who I really was!" (13). Helen reveals that she suspected something was not right when she was growing up, for she recalls that her mother tiptoed out of Mass before Communion and later in life realized that it was unusual for a Catholic family to have only one child.

In Helen's attempt to come to grips with her secret past and learn more about the Jewish religion, she enlists the help of Jesus Christ. Graf's decision to have Jesus explain Judaism to a Catholic creates levity in a play that is otherwise solemn. For example, Helen complains to Jesus, "I don't know who I am! All my life I thought I was one thing and now I just found out I'm this completely different person!" (20). After a brief pause, Helen continues with these amusing lines: "I don't know what to do. What would Jesus do?" (20). Jesus tries to talk Helen "off the ledge," explaining to her that her relationships have failed because she has a penchant for "cold, withholding men with secrets" (19). Helen, stunned by the revelation that she is Jewish, is aided by Jesus, who points to himself, saying, "Some of your best friends are Jewish" (19). Helen attends synagogue services to learn about the religion; Jesus appears and tells her which page the congregation is reading the Hebrew from, explaining that Hebrew is read back to front. When Helen is confused by the elaborate rituals, the *davening*, and the prayer shawls, Jesus confides, "You picked an orthodox synagogue. For my first taste of Judaism, I would have gone with reform"

(37). The humor provided in these exchanges is perhaps the one element that differentiates *Leipzig* from the more sober *Kindertransport*.

Eva, like her counterpart in *Kindertransport*, tried to assimilate after the War. Living in the United States, she surrendered her German culture to adopt an American way of life. She also gave up her language and her religion while living with Bridget and Robert. Once she married George, they agreed never to speak of her past, essentially remaining silent about the Holocaust. This psychic numbing is merely a defense mechanism against the trauma. Many psychotherapists have agreed that repressed memory is not therapeutic for child survivors. For example, Krell notes, "Not to have memories deprives one of a connection to all those who loved and nurtured you as an infant and child."[87] However, once the Alzheimer's disease alters the functioning of Eva's brain, repressed memories of her former life begin to surface.

Eva's trauma is expressed in two forms: she mourns for her idyllic existence in Leipzig before the Holocaust and suffers from loss, producing symptoms of guilt, as a result of what occurred during the Shoah. Sarah Moskovitz describes the tendency of child survivors who mourn for the loss of their pre-Holocaust existence: "Many mourn for the loss of the more ideal, accomplished self that might have been: the self that might have, under normal conditions, learned better in schools, behaved more appropriately, achieved more."[88]

Eva's remembrance of Leipzig in her old age is essentially a mourning for the ideal world of Germany before the Holocaust. Eva recalls her nurturing, loving mother Helena married to Herr Doktor Weisborg, an eminent physician and a member of a prominent Zionist fraternity. The couple would entertain important German citizens, such as Martin Buber, who visited the household frequently. Eva received a good education from some of the best German schools. Leipzig itself was considered to be a world-renowned cultural center, having been the headquarters of the German book publishing industry since 1825. Eva describes the idyllic Leipzig to Helen: "It was a wonderful place, where famous men like Goethe and Bach and Mendelssohn lived. There was beautiful architecture, nice houses, green parks . . ." (44). In her happiest moments, Eva recalls visiting the park on Sundays, with the orchestra playing on the bandstand and children frolicking. She has especially fond memories of feeding the swans and having tea in the pavilion at the park with her older brother Erich. In essence, Eva's assimilation has masked the memories of her former idyllic life, but once the daydreams persist as a result of the Alzheimer's, she attempts to merge with a lost past, telling Helen, "I must go back to Leipzig. Something that's mine. I want you to know them. I want you to know who I am" (44).

Eva is conflicted by memory, for she daydreams about the idyllic world in Leipzig before the Shoah but is simultaneously plagued by memory of the reality of the Nazi terror after Kristallnacht. Eva tells Helen, "I just want to remember the happy things" (32), but, of course, memory does not function that way. Eva remembers the shattering of glass, dogs barking, Nazis pounding at the door, bricks coming through the window, and Helena clapping her hands over her daughter's mouth to silence the crying girl – images that reverberate as stimuli for the onset of her fright. She recalls the indignation of German Jews who had to wear the yellow star in the

1930s, as well as how Jews were forbidden to go to the botanical gardens, where she loved watching the swans. Coming from a well-educated family, Eva recollects how her education was halted when the Nazis forbade Jews to attend schools. She also has nightmares about how the Nazis terrorized Erich, who came home during Kristallnacht beaten and bloodied.

Similar to Samuels's protagonist who felt abandoned by a mother that put her on a train, never to see her daughter again, Graf's Eva has gone through much the same harrowing experience that haunts her for life. Eva's parents sent her on a ship to the United States to spare her life, but Eva resents them for doing so. Helena tells Eva that the family will be reunited once the temporary pogroms are over, but this is no solace for the youngster, who eventually incorporates her mother's words as lies. Eva begged her parents to let her stay with them. In response to her mother's request for daily letters, Eva implored her mother for answers: "Why are you sending me away, Mutti? Don't you love me anymore?" (55). Eva, the Alzheimer's patient, recalls the day the ship sailed, and, while crying, she made one last plea to avoid being abandoned: "Please don't go! . . . *Bitte!* . . . Don't leave me alone . . . !" (58). Eva does not view her voyage to America as life saving; instead, she insists it was an abandonment: "How could they have done it? How could they have sent me away?" (59). She muses, "They sent me all alone, across the world, to live with *strangers* —" (59). Even the advice that her parents gave her to adapt to a new life in America proved fallacious to Eva: "'Work hard. Learn the language. Adapt!' It was so cruel . . . *(beat; angry)* They never thought about what it would be like for me! Without them!" (60). Eva views the abandonment as nothing more than loss, and her parents' encouragement proved to be lies: "We pretended, but we all knew. We knew we'd never see each other again" (59). Eva even believes that her parents sent her away primarily to spite Hitler: "It was selfish! They did it for themselves! They wanted to show Hitler, insure their name was carried on!" (59). The assimilation process also proved to be an alienating experience for Eva, for she admits, "Bridget had her own children. She cared for me, yes, but it was never really my own home" (43).

The major symptom accrued from Eva's pre-Holocaust trauma is guilt. Eva feels a double sense of guilt. On the one hand, she feels guilty about deserting her family when their lives were at stake. In her hallucinations about the past, she mutters seemingly to her parents, "I would have saved you! I would have saved you and gotten you out!" (56). On the other hand, the abandonment is seen as an evasion of her family that resulted in her survival while her loved ones perished. Like many survivors, Eva feels guilty about being the only family member to be spared, so her daydreams of her parents focus primarily on how the abandonment always unconsciously relates to loss: "If only you'd have listened! If only you would have left when I did!" (56). When Helen reminds her mother that if she had stayed with her parents in Leipzig, she would have died, Eva responds, "I wanted to" (59); like her counterpart in *Kindertransport*, Eva would have preferred staying with her parents rather than living the rest of her life plagued by guilt.

After Helen writes to Yad Vashem, the Holocaust archive in Jerusalem, to discover the destiny of Eva's family during the Holocaust, her reasons for her mother's post-Holocaust traumata are revealed. Although the family was evacuated from their home by the Nazis and Eva's brother Erich pleaded with his parents to emigrate, they stubbornly believed that the persecution would be temporary and thus made a token gesture to obtain passports. As a result, Eva's parents and most of her mother's family were exterminated in Treblinka during 1943; other family members, such as Eva's grandparents, cousins, and aunts, were murdered in Leipzig, Treblinka, or Auschwitz. Their deaths were reported to Eva in 1958, but because she tried to keep her Holocaust past a secret, she never told her husband about the tragedies. Eva is particularly traumatized by the death of her beloved older brother Erich, who rebelled against the Nazis. Erich had dreams to study architecture at Harvard University, but his aspirations were cut short by the Nazis. Refusing to wear the yellow star and viewed as an enemy of the state, Erich was sent to Sachsenhausen concentration camp in 1942. Erich became part of the resistance movement in Sachsenhausen, where he managed to smuggle many prisoners out and thus saved their lives. He was eventually shot by the Nazis after organizing a mass breakout from the camp. Eva feels burdened with the irony that her brother wanted to leave Germany while she desired to remain there with her family. In her fantasies, Eva expresses her guilt that she should have died in place of her brother, who had such an aspiring life ahead of him: "You were everything to me . . . You were going to be a great architect, a great artist. You were the best of us! It should have been me" (82). Feeling guilty that she was safe in America while her brother suffered in a concentration camp, Eva, in deeply rooted anguish, hallucinates to her sibling, "I should have done more. I should have tried harder to make them [her parents] listen. If only I'd refused to go, they would have sent you. I could have saved you" (83). In essence, as is typical of most traumata, the source of the neurosis almost always centers around loss. Sarah Moskovitz, who wrote about the loss of the idyllic life before the Shoah, states, "Add this to mourning for a lost sister, brother, or the parent-that-might-have-been had that parent survived at all, or survived unharmed, and we see that what is mourned is no less than a lost world."[89]

Holocaust survivors who suffered from devastating losses and who tried to become inured to the trauma frequently lost empathy with their family members during assimilation. While she was growing up, Helen acutely felt this lack of empathy with her mother. Helen admits, "All my life she was unreachable to me. Maybe she couldn't deal with having a daughter because she never dealt with losing her mother" (45). Eva clearly relates this lack of empathy for her daughter to her unconscious grief in being abandoned by her parents. Eva apologizes to Helen for behavior that she could not consciously control: "I wanted to be a good mother, Helen. I knew what it was like not to feel loved completely. I had been . . . and then . . . I tried to reach you. I just . . . couldn't" (43). Helen, becoming aware that her mother defined herself by what she had lost, complains to Jesus: ". . . a loss, incidentally, that became an enormous wedge between us, causing her complete and total emotional unavailability to me my entire life" (19). Helen is clearly resentful that Hitler's ideology not only produced a non-empathetic mother, but also affected the lives of the second generation as well. She complains to Jesus, "His legacy lived on, didn't it? It colored my mother's entire life and then mine" (29).

Eva's assimilation provided a mask for her Holocaust traumatization. Growing up, however, Helen sensed that something was wrong with her mother, especially when she saw Eva sobbing in the bathroom for hours. Helen states to her father, "Ever since I was a little girl, I felt this *grief*" (14). George defends the assimilation and the notion of keeping Eva's Holocaust past secret as a means to maintain his wife's health and sanity. George describes the symptoms of the trauma to his daughter: "Any reminder and she'd fall into a horrible depression, isolate herself . . . And the nightmares . . . Hell, she'd have nightmares for days, screaming out God knows what. You can't imagine how painful it was –" (14).

The Alzheimer's disease is the impetus for the resurgence of the traumatized self that Eva kept suppressed as she assimilated into a new Christian life in a foreign country where her Holocaust past, including her religion, the root cause of the paranoia, had been kept hidden. Now, near the end of her life, Eva's trauma reemerges full blown as she spends her days crying, talking to herself, and suffering nightmares. Eva begins praying in Hebrew and increasingly falls into the native German of her origins. Much of the play focuses on her consistently frightening hallucinations in which, while speaking to her daughter, she imagines herself back in Leipzig carrying on conversations with her parents. These simultaneous exchanges indicate the dire straits of the neurosis. Helen speaks to Eva, but Eva believes she is talking to her parents in Germany. In one particular frightening conversation, Eva speaks to her father, who exhorts his daughter to speak in English, for she is in the United States now. Eva responds, "And you are, too. You, and Mutti, and Erich. . . . We're all together again. Just like it never happened" (76). George regrets the change in his wife's persona because for years he helped her to forget the past. Helen responds, "Yeah, well, funny thing. Now it's all she remembers" (71).

Eva Weisborg from Leipzig, like Eva Schlesinger from Hamburg, tried to assimilate in order to forget the trauma. Eva Weisborg is terribly conflicted: she would like to remember her idyllic pre-Holocaust Jewish life in Leipzig. As a matter of fact, her mother sewed a gold and pearl Jewish star into the hem of her dress upon leaving Germany so Eva would not forget about her Jewish origins. However, memory, which can never be selective, also prompts the trauma of the Shoah. Assimilation does not trump the neurosis. Eva contends, "All my life everyone told me to forget. I tried to push it down, bury it, rub it out, but it was always there, every day . . . always with me . . ." (16). Helen confirms her mother's assessment: "What I see is that you can push it away and push it away, but it ultimately comes to get you" (70). Samuels and Graf demonstrate that child survivors of the Holocaust come to realize that the trauma rarely abates. The Ratcatcher typically prevails, and the wounds ominously linger.

Notes

1 Robert Krell, "Child Survivors of the Holocaust: 40 Years Later," *Journal of the American Academy of Child Psychiatry* 24, no. 4 (1985): 378.
2 J. Tas, "Psychical Disorders Among Inmates of Concentration Camps and Repatriates," *Psychiatric Quarterly* 25, no. 4 (1951): 680.

3 Ibid., 682.
4 Sarah Moskovitz and Robert Krell, "Child Survivors of the Holocaust: Psychological Adaptations to Survival," *Israel Journal of Psychiatry and Related Sciences* 27, no. 2 (1990): 82.
5 Ibid.
6 Hillel Klein, "Child Victims of the Holocaust," *Journal of Clinical Child and Adolescent Psychology* 2 (1974): 45.
7 Moskovitz and Krell, "Child Survivors of the Holocaust: Psychological Adaptations to Survival," 83.
8 Krell, "Child Survivors of the Holocaust: 40 Years Later," 379.
9 A. Mazor et al., "Holocaust Survivors: Coping With Post-Traumatic Memories in Childhood and 40 Years Later," *Journal of Traumatic Stress* 3, no. 1 (1990): 2.
10 See Rachel Lev-Wiesel and Marianne Amir, "Growing Out of Ashes: Posttraumatic Growth Among Holocaust Child Survivors – Is It Possible?" in *Handbook of Posttraumatic Growth: Research and Practice*, eds. Lawrence G. Calhoun and Richard G. Tedeschi (Mahwah, NJ: Lawrence Erlbaum, 2006), 250.
11 Robert Krell, "Child Survivors of the Holocaust – Strategies of Adaptation," *Canadian Journal of Psychiatry* 38 (August 1993): 386.
12 Sarah Moskovitz, *Love Despite Hate: Child Survivors of the Holocaust and Their Adult Lives* (New York: Schocken Books, 1983), 227.
13 Milton Kestenberg and Judith S. Kestenberg, "The Sense of Belonging and Altruism in Children Who Survived the Holocaust," *Psychoanalytic Review* 75, no. 4 (1988): 538.
14 Ibid., 229.
15 Ibid., 230.
16 Moskovitz and Krell, "Child Survivors of the Holocaust: Psychological Adaptations to Survival," 84.
17 Ibid., 89.
18 Klein, "Child Victims of the Holocaust," 46.
19 Judith Kestenberg, "Child Survivors of the Holocaust – 40 Years Later: Reflections and Commentary," *Journal of the American Academy of Child Psychiatry* 24, no. 4 (1985): 410.
20 Krell, "Child Survivors of the Holocaust – Strategies of Adaptation," 384. The term "affective anesthesia" was used by Eugène Minkowsky in his research on trauma, also published in 1946 while Friedman was studying child survivors on Cyprus.
21 S. Robinson, "Late Effects of Persecution in Persons Who – As Children or Young Adolescents – Survived Nazi Occupation in Europe," *Israel Annals of Psychiatry and Related Disciplines* 17 (1979): 210.
22 Ibid., 211–212.
23 Ibid., 213.
24 Moskovitz, *Love Despite Hate: Child Survivors of the Holocaust and Their Adult Lives*, 231.
25 Shalom Robinson and Judith Hemmendinger, "Psychosocial Adjustment 30 Years Later of People Who Were in Nazi Concentration Camps as Children," in *Stress and Anxiety*, vol. 8, eds. Charles D. Spielberger and Irwin G. Sarason (Washington and New York: Hemisphere, 1982), 398–399.
26 Mazor et al., "Holocaust Survivors: Coping With Post-Traumatic Memories in Childhood and 40 Years Later," 6.
27 Ibid.
28 S. Robinson, M. Rapaport-Bar-Sever, and J. Rapaport, "The Present State of People Who Survived the Holocaust as Children," *Acta Psychiatrica Scandinavica* 89 (1994): 243.
29 Ibid.
30 Ibid., 244.
31 Rachel Lev-Wiesel and Marianne Amir, "Posttraumatic Stress Disorder Symptoms, Psychological Distress, Personal Resources, and Quality of Life in Four Groups of Holocaust Child Survivors," *Family Process* 39, no. 4 (2000): 453.
32 Robinson, Rapaport-Bar-Sever, and Rapaport, "The Present State of People Who Survived the Holocaust as Children," 244.

33 Moskovitz, *Love Despite Hate: Child Survivors of the Holocaust and Their Adult Lives*, 232.

34 Of course, child survivors who became parents wanted their children to succeed. However, this does not necessarily indicate that they were loving parents. In Chapter 1, I mentioned the study conducted by Dori Laub and Nanette C. Auerhahn that discussed failed empathy among survivors who had divorced themselves of human feelings while incarcerated in the camps. Other survivors who had hardened themselves while hiding or had lived in cold and hunger with the partisans had difficulty getting close to anyone after the War. Although they supported their offspring in their attempts to assimilate, these parents often found that providing love and nurturing to their children was psychologically impossible.

35 See Judith S. Kestenberg, "Overview of the Effect of Psychological Research Interviews on Child Survivors," in *Children During the Nazi Reign: Psychological Perspectives on the Interview Process*, eds. Judith S. Kestenberg and Eva Fogelman (Westport: Praeger, 1994), 30.

36 See Moskovitz and Krell, "Child Survivors of the Holocaust: Psychological Adaptations to Survival," 85.

37 Kestenberg and Kestenberg, "The Sense of Belonging and Altruism in Children Who Survived the Holocaust," 549.

38 Diane Samuels, *Diane Samuels' Kindertransport: The Author's Guide to the Play* (London: Nick Hern, 2014), 10.

39 Ibid., 17.

40 Diane Samuels, "Personal Accounts of the Kindertransport," in *Kindertransport*, ed. Diane Samuels (New York: Plume, 1995), xv. All subsequent citations from the play are from this edition and will be included within parentheses in the text.

41 Karen Gershon, ed., *We Came as Children: A Collective Autobiography* (New York: Harcourt, Brace & World, 1966), 19.

42 Bertha Leverton and Shmuel Lowensohn, eds., *I Came Alone: The Stories of the Kindertransports* (Sussex, UK: The Book Guild, 1990), 15.

43 Ibid., 162.

44 Gershon, ed., *We Came as Children: A Collective Autobiography*, 27.

45 Leverton and Lowensohn, eds., *I Came Alone: The Stories of the Kindertransports*, 149.

46 Ibid., 253.

47 Gershon, ed., *We Came as Children: A Collective Autobiography*, 39–40.

48 Ibid., 38.

49 Ibid., 60.

50 See Janet E. Rubin, *Voices: Plays for Studying the Holocaust* (Lanham, MD: Scarecrow, 1999), 98.

51 In the biographical statements cited by Leverton and Lowensohn, so many of these child survivors wrote that, despite the psychological traumata they experienced during the War, they recognized that the British were responsible for offering them a second chance at life. For example, see Leverton and Lowensohn, eds., *I Came Alone: The Stories of the Kindertransports*, 13, 28, 33, 96, 117, and 335.

52 Leverton and Lowensohn, eds., *I Came Alone: The Stories of the Kindertransports*, 51.

53 Gershon, ed., *We Came as Children: A Collective Autobiography*, 140.

54 Cathy Caruth, ed., *Listening to Trauma: Conversations With Leaders in the Theory and Treatment of Catastrophic Experience* (Baltimore: Johns Hopkins University Press, 2014), 12.

55 Gershon, ed., *We Came as Children: A Collective Autobiography*, 140, 87–88.

56 Leverton and Lowensohn, eds., *I Came Alone: The Stories of the Kindertransports*, 314.

57 Ibid., 60.

58 Samuels, *Diane Samuels' Kindertransport: The Author's Guide to the Play*, 12.

59 Ibid., 138.

60 Samuels chose Eva from the name of her ex-husband's aunt who had fled Germany soon after Hitler came to power in 1933.

61 Lil is named after Samuels's grandmother Lily – both from the same generation.

62 The original source for the Ratcatcher was the Grimms' tale of the Pied Piper of Hamelin. The tale was popularized in England during the nineteenth century in Robert Browning's poem "The Pied Piper of Hamelin: A Child's Story." Ulrike Behlau and Beate Neumeier have noted that Samuels has changed the story to reflect a sense of guilt and punishment in which naughty children have been taken away from home by the Ratcatcher, who leads them into an abyss. See Ulrike Behlau, "Remembering the Holocaust in British-Jewish Drama of the 1990s: Diane Samuels, Julia Pascal, and Harold Pinter," in *Staging Displacement, Exile and Diaspora*, eds. Christoph Houswitschka and Anja Miller (Trier: Wissenschaftlicher Verlag, 2005), 202; Beate Neumeier, "*Kindertransport*: Memory, Identity and the British-Jewish Diaspora," in *Diaspora and Multiculturalism: Common Traditions and New Developments*, ed. Monika Fludernik (Amsterdam and New York: Rodopi, 2003), 109; and Beate Neumeier, "Kindertransport: Childhood Trauma and Diaspora Experience," in *Jewish Women's Writing of the 1990s and Beyond in Great Britain and the United States*, eds. Ulrike Behlau and Bernhard Reitz (Trier: Wissenschaftlicher Verlag, 2004), 67.

63 Samuels, *Diane Samuels' Kindertransport: The Author's Guide to the Play*, 65.

64 Eric J. Sterling, "Rescue and Trauma: Jewish Children and the Kindertransports During the Holocaust," in *Children and War: A Historical Anthology*, ed. James Marten (New York and London: New York University Press, 2002), 65–66.

65 Ibid., 71.

66 Eva Fogelman, "Effects of Interviews With Rescued Child Survivors," in *Children During the Nazi Reign: Psychological Perspectives on the Interview Process*, eds. Judith S. Kestenberg and Eva Fogelman (Westport: Praeger, 1994), 81, 85.

67 Sterling, "Rescue and Trauma: Jewish Children and the Kindertransports During the Holocaust," 71.

68 I asked Samuels if she knew of Delbo, and she responded, "I have not come across Charlotte Delbo or her writings so the snake shedding its skin reference is entirely coincidental, although this is a common metaphor to describe transformation from one stage of life or being to another." Diane Samuels, email message to author, 3 January 2015.

69 Lev-Wiesel and Amir, "Posttraumatic Stress Disorder Symptoms, Psychological Distress, Personal Resources, and Quality of Life in Four Groups of Holocaust Child Survivors," 456.

70 Krell, "Child Survivors of the Holocaust – Strategies of Adaptation," 386.

71 Kestenberg, "Overview of the Effect of Psychological Research Interviews on Child Survivors," 13.

72 Milton Kestenberg, "The Effects of Interviews on Child Survivors," in *Children During the Nazi Reign: Psychological Perspectives on the Interview Process*, eds. Judith S. Kestenberg and Eva Fogelman (Westport: Praeger, 1994), 60.

73 Samuels, *Diane Samuels' Kindertransport: The Author's Guide to the Play*, 16.

74 Susanne Greenhalgh, "Stages of Memory: Imagining Identities in the Holocaust Drama of Deborah Levy, Julia Pascal, and Diane Samuels," in *"In the Open": Jewish Women Writers and British Culture*, ed. Claire M. Tylee (Newark: University of Delaware Press, 2006), 216.

75 Kestenberg, "Overview of the Effect of Psychological Research Interviews on Child Survivors," 14.

76 Sterling, "Rescue and Trauma: Jewish Children and the Kindertransports During the Holocaust," 68.

77 Moskovitz and Krell, "Child Survivors of the Holocaust: Psychological Adaptations to Survival," 90.

78 Leverton and Lowensohn, eds., *I Came Alone: The Stories of the Kindertransports*, 286.

79 Samuels, *Diane Samuels' Kindertransport: The Author's Guide to the Play*, 109.

80 Wendy Graf, email message to author, 22 December 2014.

81 Graf based her protagonist's name after the real-life Eva Weisborg. When I asked her if she knew of Samuels's use of the same name, she told me that she had not read nor seen *Kindertransport* when she wrote *Leipzig*. Eva's age at the time of Kristallnacht is

undetermined in the play, but Graf confided that she was nine or ten upon leaving Germany. Wendy Graf, email message to author, 22 December 2014.

82 Eva Fogelman and Flora Hogman, "A Follow-up Study: Child Survivors of the Nazi Holocaust Reflect on Being Interviewed," in *Children During the Nazi Reign: Psychological Perspectives on the Interview Process*, eds. Judith S. Kestenberg and Eva Fogelman (Westport: Praeger, 1994), 74.

83 Samuels, *Diane Samuels' Kindertransport: The Author's Guide to the Play*, 188.

84 Mazor et al., "Holocaust Survivors: Coping With Post-Traumatic Memories in Childhood and 40 Years Later," 6.

85 Wendy Graf, email message to author, 22 December 2014.

86 Wendy Graf, *Leipzig*, photocopy, 2010, 39. I am indebted to Arnold Mittelman, founder of the National Jewish Theater Foundation, for granting me permission to quote from this text photocopied from the Holocaust Theater Archive. All subsequent citations from the play are from this edition and will be included within parentheses in the text.

87 Krell, "Child Survivors of the Holocaust – Strategies of Adaptation," 386.

88 Moskovitz, *Love Despite Hate: Child Survivors of the Holocaust and Their Adult Lives*, 228.

89 Ibid.

5

SYMPTOMS OF PSYCHOLOGICAL PROBLEMS AMONG CHILDREN OF SURVIVORS

At the conclusion of the Holocaust, survivors who had lost everything and were suffering from deeply rooted despair often decided that marriage was a means to counter their misery. In most cultures, family and friends provide support for mourners of the dead. However, Holocaust survivors frequently lacked a support system and had no community to which they could return. Males and females who had nothing in common except the Holocaust married to assuage the pain and suffering they had mutually experienced and to reenter into the cultural experience. Nearly eighty percent of survivors married other survivors, not out of love, but out of mutual understanding and the desire to face the abyss together rather than alone.[1] Yael Danieli notes, "Recreating a family was a concrete act to compensate for their losses, to counter the massive disruption in the order and continuity of life, and to undo the dehumanization and loneliness they had experienced."[2] Moreover, survivors also subliminally wanted to become better parents than their own mothers and fathers, who were unable to protect their offspring from the Nazis, and, as we have seen in *Kindertransport*, were often perceived as having abandoned their children.[3]

The children of Holocaust survivors soon became precious symbols as counters to Hitler's goal to exterminate Jews. Children were often named after relatives who had perished during the Shoah and thus became constant reminders of the losses experienced by the parents. Designating these children as "memorial candles," Dina Wardi asserts, "These little children were given the role of lifesavers for the confused souls of their parents. But the parents saw the children not only as lifesavers, but also as new content for their lives."[4] The parents perceived of their offspring as the continuing generation that defied Hitler's wish to prevent the Jews from reproducing, therefore filling their enormous emotional void. The child also functioned as a link to the survivor parents' own parents and siblings who were exterminated by the Nazis, thereby acting as a therapeutic object to rehabilitate their identities that had been obliterated.[5] The children thus have a dual function: preserving the memory of lost relatives and strengthening the denial of the loss that the parents were unable to mourn during their more pressing attempts at survival. The children are viewed as blessings or miracles, symbols of victories over the Nazis and therefore emblematic of the future.

After having endured near-death experiences related to suffering, fatigue, anxiety, and starvation, Holocaust survivor parents made sure that their offspring were exempt from extinction and therefore tended to overprotect them.[6] Paranoia derived from the Holocaust led to parents' fears that external forces would harm the child, thus resulting in overprotective behavior. However, although the children sensed their parents' overprotectiveness, they were unsure of the source of that anxiety because of their parents' silence about the trauma. Survivors were reluctant to discuss the Holocaust because they were at a loss for words that could communicate the vast extent of the trauma to their children. In their new societies, immigrants were perceived as going to the slaughter like sheep, so they had difficulty explaining circumstances to others. Furthermore, discussing the Holocaust with their children typically only led to exacerbation of guilt feelings about the loss of loved ones and the loss of morality concomitant with the need to survive. In short, parents never sat down with their children to tell them the full story of their Holocaust pasts. Instead, the children were immersed in the Holocaust as a deep secret that threatened the well-being of their parents; the story was revealed to the offspring only in bits and pieces, hints, innuendoes, and snippets of information. The children often grew up in painful bewilderment but always were aware that the psychological presence of the Holocaust dominated family life.[7] Unlike their parents, the children feel the presence of an absence that permeated their lives.

Despite the fact that the parents overprotected their children against external influences, the family atmosphere was typically devoid of empathy. As I discussed earlier in this book, survivors were able to cope during the Holocaust by divesting themselves of any emotional involvement, inuring themselves against empathy with others. This hardening of the soul was virtually impossible to slough off in the post-Holocaust environment of marriage and the nurturing of children.[8] In a study of children of survivors, Fran Klein-Parker reported that her subjects considered their parents to be emotionally detached from them because of the lingering aftereffects of the Holocaust.[9] Parents were often cold and unemotional with their children, even in the formative years. Parents were overly consumed with their own emotional problems and thus had difficulty attending to the psychological needs of their children. Children rationalized that their parents had dulled their emotions in order to survive; this stoicism eventually became a major part of the child's persona.[10] Since emotional problems translated into weakness and concomitantly Hitler's triumph over his victims, parents were unwilling to acknowledge that their beloved offspring could have any emotional problems of their own. Parents more readily understood physical problems among their children.[11] The parents' lack of emotional attachment to their children typically made family life into a pathogenic environment. As a result of their emotional depletion, parents were frequently unable to enjoy family events with their children and isolated the family socially from others.[12]

During the late 1960s and 1970s, psychiatrists became alarmed at the increasing number of children of Holocaust survivors who were seeking counseling and psychological assistance.[13] Vivian Rakoff, a psychiatrist at the Jewish General Hospital in Montreal, was the first to acknowledge that the children of Holocaust survivors displayed "severe psychiatric symptomatology."[14] Early studies conducted in Israel and Canada by Shamai Davidson and Bernard Trossman, respectively, corroborated Rakoff's findings.[15] In the first major study of children of survivors of Nazi persecution, J.J. Sigal et al. reported that from the 144 survivor families they studied, adolescents had more behavioral problems and more feelings of anomia and alienation than subjects in the control group.[16] At first, psychiatrists such as Harvey A. Barocas argued that children of concentration camp survivors exhibited psychiatric features similar to the Survivor Syndrome.[17] After dozens of studies were conducted, psychiatrists tempered their conclusions, arguing that the psychological effects of the Holocaust on children of survivors tended to be complex and often were severe, but such aftereffects did not imply the more daunting psychopathology of mental illness that affected their parents.[18] Psychiatrists and psychologists noted that several variables among the parents affected the severity of the psychological effects on their children, including pre-Holocaust personalities, the harshness and duration of the trauma, the age when the traumatization occurred, their country of origin, and their abilities to cope with stress.[19] Obviously, the most significant variable was the type of conditions survivors endured during the Holocaust.[20]

Many of the psychological problems shared by children of Holocaust survivors stem from the parents' need to live vicariously through their children, their raison d'être; thus, from the grief of the Holocaust comes the resurrection. Often the child, particularly the first born, was named after the parents' father, mother, or sibling and, as hope for the future (or restitution), replaces the parents' sense of loss during the trauma. The child is thus tasked with the responsibility of mitigating the past, changing it to effect a different outcome, restoring a positive identity for the parents who feel guilty and lack self-esteem, and providing meaning in their parents' lives. Several Holocaust survivor parents reported that they relived their own lost childhood through their offspring or even identified their children with their own deceased parents.[21] Judith S. Kestenberg has written about the messianic role that children of survivors typically play: "The children seemed to sense that they must go back in time, become part of the parents' experience of the past, and resolve the unresolvable."[22] The child often becomes the parents' protector and shield, thus parenting the parents – trying to heal a mother and father who were unable to heal themselves. Nanette C. Auerhahn and Ernst Prelinger argue that the children try to assimilate the trauma experienced by the parents in order to heal them and are consequently fraught with emotional baggage.[23] However, the child experiences the Holocaust in bits and pieces of anecdotal information without fully understanding the trauma. The result is that the children are fully rooted in the pain of their parents without understanding the historical antecedents of the anguish.

The problem with overprotectiveness and parents' need to live vicariously through their children is that children of survivors were taught primarily to serve their parents' psychological needs rather than to develop their own identities. Holocaust survivor parents often became obsessed with controlling the lives of their children.[24] Children who tried to be independent were considered to be betraying their parents.[25] Harvey A. Barocas and Carol B. Barocas contend that in families of Holocaust survivors, parents go to great lengths to prevent the breaking of the symbiotic bond with their children, and autonomous strivings of their offspring are discouraged. Barocas and Barocas conclude, "The individuation process of the children appears to reactivate the lifelong mourning of the survivors, and the additional threat of yet another object loss."[26] Children thus become objects – extensions of their parents' wishes rather than distinct personalities. Because the children are objects that gratify their parents' wish fulfillment or replace the parents' original families, their autonomous growth is inhibited. Psychotherapist Dina Wardi, who treated dozens of sons and daughters of Holocaust survivors, claims that due to the need to fulfill their parents' unsatisfied wishes and drives, such "memorial candles" are unable to occupy themselves with the satisfaction of their own personal needs – a condition that retards their individuation.[27] Psychoanalyst Judith S. Kestenberg agrees, stating, "Resolving the problems of a parent's individual past can become a hindrance in the development of autonomy, of one's own sense of reality and actuality, and of one's values and aspirations."[28] Survivor parents often are single-mindedly concerned with the child's conformity to their needs at the expense of the child's own wishes.

Children of survivors consistently allege that the Holocaust past of the parents taints their own lives.[29] Auerhahn and Laub mention that even at an early age, such children are allowed to play freely but are taught to be constantly vigilant about a world that is life threatening. In their desire to overprotect their children, survivors inculcate their offspring with distrust of outsiders, especially authority figures, and thus with a need to symbiotically cling to the family.[30] In one of the earliest studies of adolescent children of concentration camp survivors, Bernard Trossman noted that the overprotectiveness of parents coupled with frequent warnings of impending danger caused many offspring to become moderately paranoid.[31] Survivors who view outsiders as potential persecutors also manifest fears of duplicity, deceit, and betrayal in their children.[32] Although the tales are never completely revealed to the children and references to the traumata are frequently indirect, the offspring understand that their parents suffer from profound grief, uninterrupted mourning, depression, and anxiety, typically transmitting such gloom, pain, insecurity, and suffering to the next generation.[33] These symptoms, combined with failed empathy from their parents, led children to adopt self images of degradation, low self-esteem, paranoia, and even depression.[34] Psychologists Arnold Wilson and Erika Fromm report than in many Holocaust survivor families, children recall that their households were pervaded by an ambience of gloom, as if the Shoah was on a cycle of eternal return;[35] joy was perceived as nothing more than frivolity. The overall feeling among many children of survivors is that they cannot be happy because their parents are continually distressed, often having breakdowns that frightened the children; many offspring even have nightmares about what they imagine happened to their parents.[36]

Studies have indicated that many children of survivors suffer from much of the same type of guilt that afflicts their parents. Kestenberg notes that the degradation survivors endured and their guilt accrued from their inability to rescue friends and relatives is transmitted to the child.[37] Fran Klein-Parker stated that among the children of survivors, "Guilt was intensified when the parent suffered silently or was difficult to please. Guilt was also intensified when the adult children did not live up to their parents' expectations and when they became aware of how much better their lives were than their parents."[38] In other words, children of survivors often felt guilty over what their parents had endured and were indebted to them, constantly trying to please the survivors in order to assuage their anxieties. As Yael Danieli acknowledges, such guilt causes depression because it is a no-win situation for the children, who are helpless to undo the trauma suffered by their parents.[39] Children of survivors frequently felt guilty about being entitled to happiness as a result of their parents' efforts to raise them and wondered why they should enjoy themselves when so many others, perhaps more deserving, had been deprived of that opportunity.[40] Psychologists have reported that children who inflicted pain on their parents in the normal course of their individuation felt guilty because they feared that they, too, acted like Nazis;[41] in short, children who misbehaved or disobeyed the parent felt more guilt than children in normal families. Parents thus employed Holocaust guilt as a means to control their children; when the children acted out, parents often made such comments as "You're acting like a little Hitler," "I was spared from the Nazis for this?" or "Better that I had died in the camp than to experience this misery from my children." Moreover, in his intensive study of nine child survivors, Samuel Slipp concluded, "All reported a great deal of difficulty separating from their parents; they felt guilty leaving their parents."[42]

Survivor parents frequently raised their children to be overachievers and to excel in life so as to counter the Nazi notion that Jews were *Untermenschen* unworthy of citizenship. Kestenberg writes that survivor children are tasked with the expectation that they will redeem their parents' low self-esteem, degraded identity, and lost opportunities through their successful academic and professional achievements; children therefore are destined to heal the family, and many ultimately went into the healing professions or travelled to Israel to fight for the nation in its early years.[43] Sigal and Weinfeld state that the clinical literature supports the view that survivor parents pressured their children to achieve goals that did not typically match the wishes or the abilities of the offspring.[44] Thus, one of the major laments of second-generation children is that they feel compromised as objects unable to establish their own identity. In her extensive study of children of survivors, Ilse Grubrich-Simitis reported, "One of the most frequent complaints of second-generation patients is that they can only function mechanically, that they are unable to experience themselves as being alive."[45] Yael Danieli also notes that survivor parents refused to tolerate weakness or failure in their children, and even illness that temporarily halted motivation was faced only when it became a crisis; relaxation and pleasure were considered to be superfluous.[46] Children learn that overachievement leads to security, which becomes the only goal worth striving for; aspirations such as happiness and self-expression are perceived in the family as worthless luxuries.[47]

Survivor parents were proud of their children's successes, but because of their lack of empathy derived from their ability to divest themselves of emotions during the Holocaust, they were often unable to express praise for their children's accomplishments. Moreover, because the Holocaust deprived them of good role models for parenting (parents could not protect them from the Nazis), survivors had no skill sets from which to learn. Bar-On et al. noted that in their quest for perfection, survivor parents refrained from lauding their children's achievements but instead spent more time criticizing them lavishly.[48] Thus, the child is torn between his or her own ego ideal and the wishes of parents who demand overachievement but refuse to acknowledge it when it is ultimately attained in adolescence and adulthood. The result is that children may react aggressively toward their mothers and fathers or rebel against the tight strictures imposed on them by their parents. This aggressive psychopathology, which is complex and comes in myriad forms, warrants in-depth examination in a separate chapter; the subject will therefore be explored in Chapter 6.[49]

The remainder of this chapter will focus on the psychopathology of children of Holocaust survivors as expressed in Faye Sholiton's *The Interview*, Ronald John Vierling's *Adam's Daughter*, and Ari Roth's *Andy and the Shadows*.

Playwright Faye Sholiton holds an M.A. in French language and literature; she has spent years working as a journalist for local, regional, and national publications. She was the founding artistic director of Interplay Jewish Theatre in Cleveland, Ohio, and developed her work in the Cleveland Play House Playwrights Unit from 1996–2011. Her plays include *The Good Times, A Form of Hope, V-E Day, Telling Lives, All Things Being Equal, U.S. v. Howard Mechanic, The Last Prisoner of the Vietnam War, The Lake Effect, Panama, Last Call, In His Own Words: Aubrey's World*, and *A Brief History of Mah Jongg*. Her full-length plays have been read or produced in more than four dozen venues worldwide and have garnered more than twenty national honors, including winning the Individual Excellence Award four times from the Ohio Arts Council.

Sholiton's background well qualifies her to write a play about the children of Holocaust survivors. As a volunteer who helped organize historical exhibits and in her role as a journalist for the *Cleveland Jewish News*, she interviewed dozens of Holocaust survivors for years before taking testimony for the Shoah Foundation in 1995. She also spoke with therapists who worked with survivor families. As a journalist, she won the Smolar Award for Excellence in North American Jewish Journalism (Council of Jewish Federations) for her research. In addition, she co-chaired the 2004 touring exhibit "Image and Reality: Jewish Life in Terezin," trained docents for exhibits on Anne Frank and on Auschwitz, and has been guest speaker at gatherings of Holocaust survivors and educators.

Sholiton penned the first draft of *The Interview* in 1995; the premiere of the play, directed by Jennifer Lockwood, was staged at the Dayton Playhouse on July 26, 1997. The first Equity production was at the Jewish Community Center's Halle Theatre in Cleveland in March 2002. The play has had more than three dozen

staged readings and productions throughout the United States, including perfor-
mances at the Raven Theatre in Chicago (April 30 to June 6, 2005), the Chester
Theatre Company in Chester, Massachusetts (July 2007), and two productions by
the Women's Theatre Project (Ft. Lauderdale, April to May 2009 and Boca Raton,
January 2013). *The Interview* has won three national new play contests: FutureFest
(Dayton, Ohio), Midwest Theatre Network (Rochester, Minnesota), and Charlotte
Rep (Charlotte, North Carolina).

The Interview, consisting of two acts, each with three scenes, occurs in 1995 at
the home of sixty-nine-year-old Holocaust survivor Bracha Weissman in Beach-
wood, Ohio. Bracha has reluctantly agreed to be interviewed about her Holocaust
experiences by Ann Meshenberg, the forty-eight-year-old daughter of Holocaust
survivors who works for the Western Reserve Oral History Project. Bracha's information is obtained in various stages, with Ann gathering preliminary information
before she brings in a videographer to tape the final interview.

At the time of the interview, Bracha is observing the annual ritual of remembrance for her husband who passed away twelve years earlier. She commemorates
his death through a yahrtzeit (memorial) candle that glows throughout the play to
remind audiences of the spectre of death that haunts Bracha's memories.

Bracha Lebowicz was born in 1925 into a well-to-do family that owned a saw-
mill in Lodz, Poland. She had four older siblings, including a sister named Rifka.
During the early war years, she spent four years living in the horrendously squalid
conditions of the Lodz ghetto. In 1944, she and her parents were deported to Auschwitz, where she remained for four months. Then she was sent to labor camps, where
she was plagued with more starvation and misery, including roll calls that lasted for
hours early in the mornings. Upon liberation, Bracha, then nineteen years old, was
rescued on the road by an American soldier while she was wandering alone. Virtually a skeleton, she was then taken to Belsen to recover from typhus. Later she was
sent to displaced persons camps, where she met Max, who had survived hard labor
at Dora and had witnessed the massacres at Gardelegen. After marriage, Max and
Bracha left for the United States in 1947. From eighty-six family members, only
one, a cousin, survived the Shoah.

Bracha and Max adapted well to American life. Max built his own home repair
business while his wife worked thirty years in cosmetics for the May Company.
Their firstborn, Manny, was named after his grandparents and uncle – typical of
the need for survivors to name their offspring after their relatives who had perished
during the Holocaust. Bracha's daughter, Rifka Leah, was named after Bracha's sister.

Bracha may lack self-pity as she recalls the traumatic events of her life, but she
suffers from the major symptoms of the Survivor Syndrome. When Ann mentions
that the interview will reawaken a lot of memories, Bracha states, "They were never
asleep."[50] Bracha's old photographs have been stored away in the closet as if she
has tried to erase past memories. However, her constant nightmares rekindle her
traumata. Bracha's story has been documented in a manuscript titled *Mama's War*,
Rifka's second-hand account of the devastation – with similarities to Hitler's *Mein
Kampf*. Ann reads from Rifka's text:

My war never ends. It sticks to me like a second skin and gnaws away at me, body and soul. Yes, I survived the war; but each battle left me wounded, and every wound chipped away a piece of me, leaving eyes that would never weep again, a heart filled with poison, and a tongue with no words to describe what I saw. I walked through hell in my bare feet, leaving behind everyone I ever loved. Why, God, did I live? Why didn't I die?

(29)

Bracha's text recalls Delbo's vision after Auschwitz – a snake shedding its skin to begin life anew but always remaining encapsulated in an older skin of tainted memories. Bracha's statement, with its tacit understanding of surviving while more deserving relatives perished, has all the earmarks of survivor guilt. During the interview, Bracha has resurrected her old family photos from the closet because, as she reveals to Ann, "I needed to see my family whole again. I got their images burned in my brain and a lot of them aren't so pleasant" (31). The most unpleasant of those images, and certainly the event that makes Bracha feel the most guilty, is the death of her sister Rifka. While Rifka was working, the Nazis took her daughter when young Bracha was at home supposedly protecting the toddler. After Rifka returned to find her daughter kidnapped, she ran to the deportation center looking for her, which ultimately led to her death. Bracha assumes responsibility for her sister's death, telling Ann, "I killed her" (33). Now Bracha spends her life in isolation, constantly evoking a dead, estranged sister.

When Manny was born, Bracha, like many Holocaust mothers, became over-protective of her son. Bracha remembers, "When I was carrying him, every day and night I pray to God, make him safe!" (33). Max told Bracha, "You can't protect him" (33) and exhorted his wife to make him strong, in contrast to the European Jews who had little control over their fates. Thus, Bracha, adhering to the psychopathology of survivor parents, makes her son overachieve. Manny wins all the awards at school, graduates early, and takes the state's wrestling title: he becomes strong physically and academically. Although Manny receives scholarships to attend college, he abandons the offers. Instead, like many children of survivors who are attracted to Jewish life in Israel like a moth gravitates to the light, Manny enlists in the Israeli Army. He ended up dead in the 1967 War, his fate being latently but inexorably linked to his mother's Holocaust-driven persona.

Rifka is even more closely defined by her mother's Holocaust past, but she has lived longer than her brother and thus has had more time to react adversely to her tainted environment. In the cast of characters, Rifka is described as Bracha's "estranged daughter" (4). Like most survivor parents who refused to sit down with their children to tell their complete horror stories, Rifka learned of her mother's past in bits and pieces of information. As Bracha explains her Holocaust past through Ann's inquisition, Rifka comments, "I've never heard you tell that from start to finish" (17). Silence was the norm in the family. Bracha responds, "I never heard you ask" (17). Most offspring of Holocaust survivors intuitively understand that asking their parents to speak of their Holocaust past only serves to exacerbate their parents' pain and suffering. Refusing to inflict more pain on parents who have already suffered greatly only serves to embed the mystique of secrets into the infrastructure of the family. Sholiton explained this tacit conspiracy of silence to me: "Parents and children avoided naming the Monster, but for all of them, he was still under the bed every night. They developed elaborate coping mechanisms to *keep* him in the dark, making unrealistic demands on themselves and their loved ones."[51]

Bracha's frightening experiences during the Holocaust have been transmitted to her daughter in the form of paranoia. Sholiton explained this estrangement thusly: "Past suffering is a poison that runs through generations."[52] Rifka admits that as a child she was frightened "Of everything" (19). During civil defense drills in grade school designed during the Cold War as preventative measures against a Russian attack, Rifka recalls what those training exercises meant to her atavistically: "The Nazis had found me at Roxboro Elementary School!" (19). When Bracha explains to Rifka that she never knew what it meant to have a gun to her head, Rifka responds, "But I knew from fear. Wasn't that bad enough?" (24). During their deportation to Auschwitz, Bracha's mother made her daughter swear to remember a Yiddish prayer about waking up whole again after the misery; Bracha insists that Rifka recite the same poem nightly. Rifka reflects about how this spectre of the Holocaust – a mandatory reminder of the devastation – influenced her life: "The very words frightened me, but still I said them every night" (43).

Bracha's parents could not protect their children from the trauma, so Bracha is determined to be a much better parent to her own children. Bracha's attempt to overprotect her daughter led to Rifka's overachievement. Like her brother, Rifka won trophies and medals. Rifka learned to play the piano, her mother's favorite instrument, before she was four years old. Bracha relates that accomplishment to the Nazi terror: "Her little feet wouldn't touch the floor, but she had to know the piano so if it happens again, maybe they will let her live" (34). Bracha reminds Rifka, "There was nothing in the world you couldn't do! Tops in your class! Pitching for the *boys'* baseball team. And your beautiful music!" (24). Bracha even embellishes Rifka's accomplishments when she recalls that her daughter, merely reciting a poem in school, won a poetry contest that never existed.

Since Rifka is seen onstage only through Bracha's troubled conscience, the audience understands that the household was toxic for Rifka, and Bracha virtually admits as much. Holocaust guilt was transmitted from mother to daughter. Rifka was proud of her mother's survival skills but appears guilty about never being able to discuss the subject with her. Rifka admits to Bracha, "We [Rifka and Manny] spent our lives trying to live up to your example, and when we failed, you sure let us know about it; served up every night at the dinner table" (25). Rifka mentions that Bracha kept the children in line by referring to any misbehavior with a reference to the Holocaust: "I'd like a dime for every time you said, 'I survived the camps for *this*?' What guilt you gave us, Mother!" (25). Holocaust survivors frequently admonish their offspring to toe the line rather than whine because their children's lives are devoid of pain and suffering. Rifka recalls how such admonishment exacerbated her feelings of guilt: "Nothing I did ever counted for you! When I wanted to talk about making cheerleaders or shaving my legs, or my rotten social life, you had one reply: 'You have it too good'" (25).

Recognizing the burden of carrying the name of a dead person, engrossed in fear and paranoia, guilty about not being able to confront her mother about her past, faced with a household dominated by pain and sorrow, and unable to understand Bracha's lack of empathy (Rifka claims her mother never even asked her about her intimate feelings), Rifka rebels. Growing up, Rifka threatened to throw herself out of a window. After her father passed away, Rifka threw out all of the mementoes of her "overachieving childhood" (30) and left the toxic household. Rifka explains that the move was necessary "because I think Hitler's claimed enough victims. He's not going to get me and he sure as hell isn't going to get my kids" (30). Thus, when Rifka gives birth to twins, she names them Kirk and Kyle, distinctly non-Jewish names that she hopes will be "without baggage" (16). In an email message to me, Sholiton explained, "Rifka leaves town not only to protect herself; she probably believes she is also protecting her mother. Rifka knows that Bracha removed the physical reminders of painful memories (the piano, dining room table, photographs). In an act she must see as kindness, Rifka removes herself from view."[53] Rifka lives in Los Angeles and never sees or speaks with her mother, even though Bracha would like to get to know her grandchildren. Rifka states to her mother, "Do you finally understand why I couldn't be your living *yahrtzeit* candle? I was unwilling to make your memories the most important events in my life" (39). Bracha, with her daughter's best intentions in mind, understood and even encouraged her daughter to leave the tainted environment. She admits to Ann that Rifka "never had a moment's peace under my roof" (34).

The Interview provides audiences with a double dose of the psychological effects of Holocaust trauma transmitted to the second generation since Ann, the forty-eight-year-old interviewer, suffers from many of the same symptoms that plagued Rifka. Although Ann is an intelligent, extremely focused professional whose job it is to interview a Holocaust survivor, Bracha's comments about Rifka become cathartic for her; in other words, the interview morphs into much-needed psychotherapy for Ann.

Ann has volunteered to interview Holocaust survivors because the subject is endemic to her psychological well-being. Like Bracha, Ann's mother, Rose Lieber, was in the Lodz ghetto before she was deported to Auschwitz; her father survived Dachau and Buchenwald. When Ann comments that her parents met in a barn after the liberation, Bracha quips, "That Hitler was some matchmaker" (18). Even after the liberation, Ann's mother spent considerable time looking for lost relatives. Ann states to Bracha, "My mother could never go to another city without looking for Liebers in the phone book" (28). Like Rifka, who was named after Bracha's sister, Ann's name was derived from her mother's sister Anna and thus becomes another memorial candle for the family.

Ann's mother, like Bracha, maintained the silent treatment about the Holocaust, providing her daughter with nothing more than snippets of information. Ann states that her mother "talked around it" (8), creating a void that Ann could not penetrate. Ann became frustrated in her attempt to find the source of her mother's *angoisse*, lamenting to Bracha, "I mean, I have no idea what happened to her in Auschwitz. What she *did* there" (12). When Bracha asks Ann what she wants to gain from the interview, Ann responds, "What my parents wouldn't tell me! They kept telling me to remember all the time, but they never told me what I was supposed to be remembering" (32). To make some sense of the Holocaust experience, Ann even visited Auschwitz ten years ago, but Bracha, mocking her, states, "Not the same thing, is it?" (35). When Rose passed away, her secrets went with her to the grave. Ann also notes that her father "kept a lifetime of secrets and then lost [his] memory!" (35).

Ann's dilemma, like that of Rifka, becomes paradoxical: she wonders how she could have penetrated her mother's silence without inflicting pain on a woman whose life was defined by suffering. Ann remembers that her mother "always had so much panic in her" (18). She recalls her mother's persona: "She almost never smiled. I used to ask Daddy to make me a magic wand so we could make her happy" (19).

Despite this desire to parent the parents, as we have seen, Holocaust survivor parents tried to overprotect their offspring so they could thrive as memorial candles and resurrect the spirit of the dead. Rose remembers that the last thing she ever did for her sister Anna was to pack her suitcase, ostensibly for the deportation. When Ann was invited to sleep over at a friend's house, she had to pack for the overnight excursion. She recalls, "The worst thing for Mama was separation . . ." (20). Apparently, such an innocuous event as her daughter's adolescent bonding experience became a nightmare for Rose. Ann tells Bracha, "Suddenly she went absolutely stone-faced on me and then she started weeping and couldn't talk" (20).

Like most children of survivors, the spectre of the Holocaust has imbued Ann with fear, depression, and paranoia. Ann admits that as a child, she was always frightened of an unknown dread lurking through the resonances of the Nazi terror: "Thunder, lightning, the dark. It's strange. I knew the worst had already happened, but I lived in fear that they'd come back for the rest of us . . ." (19). Like Rifka, who panicked during civil defense drills in elementary school, Ann recalls that other children thought of it as a game, yet she became so "hysterical" that she had to be sent home (19). She remembers that even when she felt comfortable at home eating snacks with her mother, afterwards, "we'd get up, move on and wait for the next crisis" (20). Although Ann claims to have loved her mother and refuses to hurt a woman who suffered so much, she also begins to realize through the catharsis with Bracha that she must, as a memorial candle, never forget that the Holocaust is essentially about loss. Rose forced Ann to repeat the same Yiddish prayer that Rifka recited every evening as a reminder of the losses and the hope that "I may wake up again whole" (42). Ann comments that the prayer she memorized was said not out of love, but fear.

Ann's life has been miserable because of the spectre of the Holocaust in her family's past, calling her family "dysfunctional" (20). When Ann inquires about the reason to forgive her parents, Rifka responds, "For screwing you up" (20). Ann is undergoing psychotherapy for her psychological problems; when the psychotherapist is unavailable, she resorts to cigarettes to calm her nerves. Bracha makes Ann realize that she is very angry, not just at her parents for a lifetime of secrets, but at the whole legacy of a Holocaust that has engendered loss. She even feels guilty about a past that disallowed her to have a normal childhood with loving grandparents (35). In particular, she blames her mother who "drummed it into her [Ann] that everything you love can disappear!" (35). Ann cannot evade what she refers to as "this endless loop of flashbacks to places I've never been" (36), the most pervasive image being the recurrent dream of her mother crawling out of a pile of bones. Even Ann's daughter, seven-year-old Rosie, named after Ann's mother, is adversely affected by the intergenerational effects of the Holocaust on her mother. When her second grade class performed a theatrical version of *Hansel and Gretel*, Rosie began screaming when the children opened the oven door. Confiding in Bracha, who understands Ann's angst, Ann confesses that the interview has been therapeutic, admitting, "I hate the Nazis for all the shit in my life!" (36).

American playwright Ronald John Vierling was born in Des Moines, Iowa, in 1938. After serving in the army, he received a bachelor of fine arts degree in English and art at Drake University. He then began a forty-year career teaching at five independent preparatory schools; while doing so, he earned an M.A. degree in English at the University of Wyoming in 1973. He has written a collection of poems, *The Prairie Rider Cantos*, and a trilogy of novels (*Clementine Camille*) that trace the lives of a teenaged African-American woman married to a young Caucasian American who together survive for generations with dignity amidst a racist American society. He has also written six plays: *Adam's Daughter, Common Ground, Seder, The Attic Room, The Tower*, and *The Children of Moses Davar*; only *The Tower* and *The Children of Moses Davar* are not directly related to the Holocaust. His interest in the Holocaust stemmed from his 1989 study at Yad Vashem Institute in Jerusalem.[54] His plays were written when he later became writer in residence at the Holocaust Resource and Education Center of Central Florida. In 2000, *Common Ground* won the Florida New Play of the Year Contest.

Adam's Daughter, originally written and staged in 1990, was eventually published in 1996, and then was slightly revised for publication in 2010. Vierling directed the premiere at Trinity Preparatory School, in Winter Park, Florida, where he was the senior English instructor.

The play takes place in 1987 in Chicago, where Natalie, the daughter of a Holocaust survivor named Adam,[55] tries to find her own identity free from her father's traumatic experiences during the Shoah. The title of the play clearly indicates that the focus of the drama is on the daughter rather than on the survivor himself; in short, Vierling's major concern in the play is the psychological aftereffects of the Holocaust on the second generation. In a letter that Vierling wrote to me, he confirmed the focal point of his play: "Survivor guilt is obviously at the heart of *Adam's Daughter*, in concert with identity issues that sometimes plague the children of survivors. (I have even seen the issue visited on third and fourth generation grandchildren of survivors.)"[56]

Adam grew up in a small Polish village, where he was raised by supportive parents. His mother Tessa was a caring parent who taught him the importance of a kind heart. His father Aaron was an intellect who loved reading books, studying, and discussing great ideas with his colleagues. As a youngster, Adam riled the village elders by writing stories about Polish life that were not in the Torah. The elders believed that talented youths with potential should study at the Yeshivah instead of wasting their time writing fiction. Aaron tells his comrades, "Adam wants to know more than just the history of us Jews. He wants to know about the whole world."[57] Adam thus went to the University of Warsaw, where he excelled as a student of poetry.

After the Nazis arrived in Poland, Tessa urges her children, who can pass as Aryans, to leave the country. However, the Nazis acted swiftly, and Adam wound up with the rest of his family in Auschwitz. After the liberation, Adam was the only surviving member of his family; the dead included his parents, his sister Stella, his uncle Solomon, and his aunt Rose.

As a result of Adam's reputation as an Ashkenazi poet, influential American Jews brought him to the United States. In 1947, Adam participated in an arranged marriage with a young Jewish American woman with a distinctly European background. Soon afterwards, Eva and Adam have a child that they name Nathan, who perishes upon birth. In 1962, Natalie is born, but her mother dies during childbirth. Meanwhile, Adam develops a distinguished reputation as a professor of poetry at the University of Chicago. Students there are enamored with his clarity, his ability to explicate poetry, and his love for the humanities. Jews in particular would travel great distances to hear Adam's lectures.

Yet, like most Holocaust survivors, Adam's life is imbued with a sense of loss. Adam, once the endowed humanist, follows Adorno's dictum of the death of art after the Holocaust: he refuses to write poetry any longer. Natalie explains to the audience, "I think that mostly he was just bewildered by what happened. He lost so much happiness. (*Slowly*) Does that make sense? It wasn't the sorrow that he suffered that made him cry. It was the happiness that he lost that made him cry" (22). Influential Jews brought Adam to America to preserve "something that had been lost" (30); the irony is that, as Natalie understands, "But my father lost his voice at Auschwitz" (30). Natalie recalls growing up with her father's angst always hovering over his persona: "Sometimes, when I watched him teach, when I heard students, I almost forgot about the pain I knew he carried with him every day . . . the beautiful life he'd known in Poland. The life the Jews had made in Poland. The life they lost. The life *he* lost" (17). Confessing to his wife, Adam confirms what Natalie has observed about her father: "I will tell you a truth, Eva. There is pain in me. I try to hide it every day. Perhaps that is why I am hesitant. But there is pain in my heart" (29).

Natalie becomes the child that Adam needs to assuage the pain and the losses that he suffered in Poland; in short, Natalie functions as a memorial candle to resurrect the dead. Natalie is named after her brother Nathan, the son who was lost. In essence, Natalie takes the place of the firstborn son, as well as dead relatives. When she asks Adam who she is supposed to be, her father says, "All of them, Natalie. You are all of them!" (30). Natalie represents the next generation of Jews to continue a legacy that Hitler could not destroy. Moreover, since her mother died during child-birth, Natalie assumes the role of yet another survivor. Adam provides his daughter with fatherly wisdom, a university education, and the ability to think for herself. On his death bed at the end of the play, he admits to Natalie how proud he has been of her.

While Natalie provides an identity for her father, at age twenty-five, she struggles to find her own identity like most children of survivors. Natalie does not understand her role as a memorial candle because of Adam's silence about his Holocaust past. Her first words of the play are the same words that end the play. She laments to the audience, "I walk among ghosts every day . . . my father's memories. I keep waiting for them to talk to me, but they don't. They talk to each other, but they don't talk to me" (15). She tells Sam Blake, her comrade in the theater, "Even my father doesn't talk about it [the Holocaust] . . . not very often at least" (37). Instead, she claims that her father talks in circles, riddles, or vague hints; like most offspring of survivors, Natalie receives her knowledge of the Holocaust in bits and pieces without ever hearing the full story. The dark secret that Adam shares with other survivors keeps her from ever understanding her father's anguish. Natalie comments, "And so I grew up always at his side, always warmed by his touch, his tenderness, but always outside" (31). Of course, like most of the second generation who intuitively sense that their parents suffer in pain, Natalie perceives that her father has been "to hell and come back" (53), which is perhaps why she has never broached the subject with him. Thus, as Vierling stated to me, "Natalie suffers from a conflict of needs: the need to get it all said versus the need to keep it all secret."[58]

Natalie rebels against the concept that she represents "all of them" and candidly asserts to her father that she seeks her own identity: "No! I am not all of them! I am me, Papa! Me! Just me!" (30). After graduating from college, Natalie decides to pursue an acting career. She states, "It was as if I'd been shown a secret" (34). In becoming an actress, Natalie is emulating her father, who hides secrets in his daily life. I asked Vierling to discuss why Natalie chose the stage for her profession. Vierling wrote, "Acting requires performers become someone else, explore the someone else they find inside themselves. Acting is all about finding secrets then carefully allowing an audience to know only what the actor wishes to reveal."[59] Natalie has secrets that she has to live with, just like her father. She was born because of a dual dilemma that haunts her psyche: she replaced the firstborn, and her mother died giving birth to her. Actors and actresses always know more about the characters they portray on stage than they can ever reveal to audiences; they must keep the secrets to themselves. Natalie's decision to become an actress allows her to adopt various personae, thus embodying other characters; she reveals to the audience, "I suppose I must have thought I could escape" (34). Vierling also explained to me Natalie's major motivation for an acting career: "Learn how to keep characterization secrets so you can also learn how to keep your own painful secrets."[60] Choosing a career as an actress allowed Natalie to hide behind secrets, much like her father did for most of his post-Holocaust life.

Natalie had a paucity of opportunities to act in New York. One of the most germane was her role of Thea in *Hedda Gabler*, which Adam remembers as a play riddled with "Lots of suppression. Psychological self-suppression" (60). Yet when director Sam Blake asks her to play Tevye's daughter in *Fiddler on the Roof*, Natalie declines. Although she has played Fanny Brice, an American Jew in *Funny Girl*, Natalie argues that she cannot possibly play a Russian Jew because the role is about loss. Natalie argues, "It's about a village, It's about good people, good Jews, living in a village . . . who were forced to leave. So for my father . . . for me . . . it's about what *was*. What *once* was . . . but isn't anymore" (38). The comment is apropos of Natalie's psychological problem as the offspring of a survivor: she is intricately linked to her father's psychopathology and cannot divorce herself from a life haunted by past ghosts. Sam even picks up on this mental illness and latently exhorts Natalie to get professional help: "Natalie, I'm not a shrink so don't ask me to be one. But you know what I mean better than I do. You're smart enough to understand everything you need to understand. I'm just disappointed you aren't brave enough to do something about it" (39).

One evening, when Natalie is out with her African-American stage cohort Maggie, they are raped by four hoodlums. Both Natalie and Maggie end up hospitalized and then talk to a crisis counselor. Maggie has been traumatized by the rape, and the result is that she has insomnia and consistently relives the harrowing ordeal. Natalie, on the other hand, is less affected by the actual rape and is more concerned with the fact that one of the rapists referred to the victims as "a nigger and a kike" before committing the crime. The counselor finds this unusual: "Maggie's reaction is to try to pull up her jeans so she can't be hurt again. You keep remembering the man called you a kike" (45). The counselor reveals that Natalie appears to want psychotherapy because she voluntarily keeps coming back for more sessions. When the counselor suggests that the problem runs deeper, Natalie responds as if she is speaking again to Sam Blake: "I've played every part you ever asked me to play" (46). The counselor then retorts, "You're a survivor, Natalie. A survivor. But you can't decide what you've survived. (*Moving away into the darkness*) You can't come to terms with being raped, Natalie, until you come to terms with the other parts" (47). The counselor is referring to Natalie as a survivor of rape, which Natalie readily accepts but refuses to acknowledge "the other parts" (her legacy as a second-generation Holocaust survivor). Furthermore, Natalie recognizes that Maggie has been emotionally traumatized with wounds that are nearly impossible to heal – much like her father's condition. The counselor tells Natalie, "I can't help you come to terms with what happened until you know who you are" (47). After reiterating to the counselor that her identity is that of a survivor, specifically "Adam's daughter," Natalie understands that her identity has been established for her long before she was alive; she therefore seeks to find herself through group therapy with other children of survivors.

Natalie's attendance at group therapy sessions with the second-generation survivors is the first step to answering questions about her identity. Before Natalie can determine who she is, she must first resolve the issue of why her father survived when millions of others, including all of his family members, did not. In other words, Natalie's existence was precarious because if her father had perished, as was the norm for Jews during the Holocaust, she would not be alive.

At first, Natalie is reticent about the psychotherapy and claims to be "just a regular young Jewish woman" (50). The children of survivors understand her psychological dilemma and make her realize that as "Adam's daughter," she is an exception, and there is nothing "regular" about her psychopathology. She is asked to decide from three choices about why she exists as a result of her father's survival: her life is either a quirk of fate, an act of God, or the result of the failure of the Nazis to carry out the Final Solution. However, since Adam never discussed exactly what happened to him in Auschwitz, Natalie cannot answer the question. Natalie readily accepts the notion that her father's survival at the expense of the rest of his family could not be an act of fate. Besides, providence means that there were no choices available; Natalie agrees that the Germans certainly made their own choices. If she accepts the idea that God saved Adam, then she must also accept the premise that the Nazis were actors in God's plans. The conclusion she derives, and concomitantly the lesson she must learn, is that the Nazis ran out of time to murder all of Europe's Jews. In other words, Natalie begins to understand that there is no philosophical or theological meaning of the Holocaust; her existence is based upon sheer accident. Once she realizes that her existence is an accident, she can come to grips with her identity. There is no moral reason for her existence. As one of the second-generation survivors tells her, "It also means that you can't let the trauma get you" (57). Without the realization of the fact that there is no moral reason for the accident, one becomes a denier, like Natalie. However, since Natalie wants to be a "normal" person without any hint of transmission of any psychopathology, she questions the use of the word "denier." One of the group therapy participants explains that a denier is "Someone who denies any of it happened. Not historically but personally . . . psychologically. Someone who refuses to come to grips with it" (57). Natalie now has the answer to her plight. However, as Vierling confided to me, "'Why me' becomes the question the child must either answer or simply stop asking. Natalie cannot stop asking."[61]

Natalie has the chance to unlock the secrets of her father's past when she visits Adam dying in the hospital due to the effects of the pneumonia he contracted in Auschwitz. Adam explains to his daughter why language and art could never convey the inexplicable horror of what happened during the Holocaust. Adam expresses the trauma in terms of loss and guilt: "The truth is lost, Natalie. It was lost even when we were living it" (62). Natalie tells her father that she needs to know the secrets that have been withheld from her all of her life. Adam reveals that he was charged in Auschwitz with preparing the lists for selection. When his own father's name appeared on the list, he skipped over it, thus allowing another prisoner to die in his father's place. Adam managed to keep his father's name off of four lists before Aaron died in his sleep. Adam feels guilty about being unable to save any of his relatives from the gas chambers. He insists that God has chastised him for his behavior: "That is why God has punished me. He took away my voice! He took away my voice, Natalie! He took away my Eva!" (64). Adam's guilt is ostensibly the reason why he kept these secrets from Natalie. Remembering his behavior in Auschwitz would have meant that he was anything but a humanist. He thus stopped writing poetry and refused to talk of the unspeakable. He explains to Natalie, "we tried to forget every day even when it was going on" (62).

In the denouement, Natalie once again says that she is waiting for her father's ghosts to speak to her. As sanguine as she appears to be, Natalie's quest for answers as a child of survivors is tenuous. She states, "They [the ghosts] talk to each other, but they do not talk to me" (69). She has heard her father's confessions on his death bed (ostensibly unraveling some of his secrets), has undergone group therapy, and has used the theater as a hiding place in which she adopted different personalities. She even acted (perhaps therapeutically) in Ibsen's *Ghosts*, a play about how the past affects the present – which is essentially Natalie's dilemma. Natalie's role in life is to make her father's existence as a survivor have significance. However, never having experienced the Shoah directly, she will never be able to unravel those secrets and thus the burden will always be with her.

Ari Roth, the son of German-born refugees of the Holocaust, was born in Chicago on January 10, 1961. After studying playwriting at the University of Michigan, Roth taught there as a lecturer in the English and Theater departments from 1988 to 1997. He has taught dramatic literature and theater at Brandeis University, New York University, Carnegie Mellon University, and George Washington University. In 1989, he was commissioned by Arena Stage to write a play based on Austrian journalist Peter Sichrovsky's *Schuldig Geboren* – a book of interviews with children and grandchildren of Nazis. The result was the play *Born Guilty*, which premiered in 1991 at Arena Stage in Washington, D.C. in a production directed by Zelda Fichandler. *Born Guilty* was subsequently directed by Jack Gelber off-Broadway in 1993 at the American Jewish Theater and has had forty different productions throughout the United States in such venues as Atlanta, Dallas, San Francisco, and Boston. The sequel to *Born Guilty*, *The Wolf in Peter*, which is about Sichrovsky's political partnership with anti-Semitic Jorg Haider, leader of the Austrian Freedom Party, premiered in 2002 at Theater J in Washington, D.C. Roth's other plays include *Life in Refusal* (1988), *Oh, The Innocents* (1990), *Goodnight Irene* (1996), and a collection of four one-act plays titled *Love and Yearning in the Not-for-Profits and Other Marital Distractions* (2001). From 1997 to 2014, Roth served as artistic director of Theater J, where he produced nearly 130 plays, including 44 world premieres, and 150 staged workshops and readings. He is currently the artistic director of the Mosaic Theater Company in Washington, D.C.

Andy and the Shadows is a prequel – the first part of what Roth refers to as "The *Born Guilty* Cycle" or his "trilogy on post-war remembrance." The original 1987 draft of the play, titled *Giant Shadows*, won the first Helen Eisner Award for Young Playwrights, made possible by the Streisand Center for Jewish Culture. After several staged readings, a revised version of the play debuted in 2011 as the third part of the trilogy, staged at the Theatre Lab in Washington, D.C. The final version, *Andy and the Shadows*, was mounted at Theater J during April and May 2013 in a production directed by Daniella Topol and featuring Alexander Strain as Andy.

The title of Roth's two-act drama denotes that Andy Glickstein, the twenty-five-year-old protagonist of the play, is plagued by shadows that represent the spectre of the Holocaust looming over his life. The play is somewhat autobiographical since Roth's parents were survivors from Germany, yet his mother and father each experienced the Holocaust differently.[62] Like most children of survivors, Andy experiences the Holocaust tangentially without ever hearing the full horror story from his parents. To determine his own identity, Andy attempts to unravel the secrets his parents have kept from him.

Andy and the Shadows occurs in Chicago in 1985, with occasional flashbacks to Andy's youth in 1971 and 1978, as well as glimpses of the Holocaust in 1944. Andy's parents, Raya and Nate, like many Holocaust survivors who were "born again" after the Shoah, have made successful lives adapting well in the United States. Andy's mother, who speaks seven languages and has a Ph.D., presumably in psychology, works in a ghetto clinic attending to drug addicts and other impoverished persons. Nate is a lawyer who retreats from the real world through his history books and relaxes by making various sorts of fruited jams in his quiet basement. Andy's parents complement each other: Raya is highly strung and competitive while her husband is mellow yet resilient. Raya even mocks Nate for failing to rise to senior partner in his law firm; ironically, Nate is the one with heart palpitations.

Raya and Nate never quite reveal their full secrets about the Holocaust to their offspring; instead, Andy and his two siblings Amy and Tammy hear the stories in bits and pieces. For eight years, Raya has been writing her memoirs, tentatively titled *Mysteries of Resilience: Triumph in the Face of Trauma* but can never seem to venture past the first paragraph of the book. She admits to Andy, "Why bother? 'Triumph In The Face of Trauma?' Who the hell triumphs in the face of trauma? You think *I* have?"[63]

Like most Holocaust survivors who are embarrassed by their sordid pasts, Raya and Nate never tell their children their full stories; consequently, the audience must also glean the narratives haphazardly in bits and pieces. Raya, who is more glib than Nate, seems to have suffered more directly from the Holocaust. Her father, a rabbi, was a political prisoner in Sachsenhausen, where he perished before the war began. Raya recalls that her mother and sister tried to evacuate by boat with British soldiers at Dunkirk, but young Raya, having premonitions of disaster, refused to get onboard. In a stroke of luck, the family managed to board a truck to safety after a German bomber sank the ship, killing three hundred soldiers. The family fled to Vichy France, where young Raya reveals the fear she suffered while in hiding during those war years: "No one has been able to catch us YET! There's about four different countries all on the look-out for us, but my Mom just shows 'em some fake papers or gives 'em a piece of jewelry and we walk right by those border guards" (29). Covered in lice, destitute, and ill, Raya's mother took a husband for support. In a harrowing incident, the Nazis took young Raya and her family to the Central Police Station in Nice, but Raya cried so much that the guards released her. Before her release, Raya disowned her stepfather and saved her own life by denying her Jewish origins. Her stepfather was transported to Auschwitz but was shot en route when he attempted to jump from the train. Like so many beleaguered survivors who lived due to sheer luck while others perished in their places, Raya suffers from Holocaust guilt. Pressed by Andy to tell the tale she adamantly has refused to share, Raya begrudgingly admits the source of her guilty conscience: ". . . Why I lived, and he jumped. Why I ate lamb chops, and he was shot. Why I walked home, and he bled. Bled to death in the snow? Because I 'disowned'? Is this what you wanted to hear?" (76). In 1944, Raya hid as a Catholic in an Italian convent to avoid Nazi persecution. After the War, Raya, her sister, and her mother fled to Palestine to build anew and replace what had been lost during the Shoah.

Nate's Holocaust past is related indirectly much more so than his wife's history because he understands that to dwell on misery will only aggravate his heart condition. Nate is fatigued, and unlike his passionate wife, his attitude toward the past is one of resignation. However, when Nate has a nearly fatal heart attack and lands in the hospital, Andy makes a plea for Nate to reveal his angst before his possible death.[64] Andy brings up his grandmother's death when Nate was not yet five years old in Germany. Nate suffered under the Nuremberg Laws, having been expelled from school and having his farm animals killed. Andy explicates his father's suffering in terms of loss, pleading with Nate for some meaning for his father's silence: "I mean, your Mom dies when you're four, right? Your cow dies when you're eight. You lose your friends. You lose your house. You lose your land. You lose your memory −" (92). Nate explains to Andy that silence became his friend and functioned as a shield from outsiders who could never understand the Holocaust experience; after the War, Nate and Raya shared a strong bond, so, as was true of many Holocaust refugees, they married. Nate apparently shared an appreciation for the fact that Israel harbored refugees like his wife, for after law school, he spent a year doing hard labor on a kibbutz there.

As is true of most Holocaust survivors who overprotect their offspring and exhort them to be overachievers to compensate as memorial candles for the dead, Nate and Raya become models for successful acculturation. At the age of ten, Andy was reminded by his mother, "You are The Healer in this family. It is a *wounded* family, and you are its Healer" (25). Raya views Andy as a Savior − one who is shown a world of "Purpose and Hope" (77) without being lost or wounded as are his parents. She envisions her son's future as a judge, obviously following in his father's legal profession. Even as a ten-year-old, Andy was castigated by his mother for bringing home a D+ in Library Period. However, Andy's sisters have adapted better than Andy to their roles as high achievers. Andy's older sibling Amy suffered the plague of the First Born. Her thoughts as a child gravitated to the gruesome − obviously enhanced by her parents' harrowing pasts. Tammy recalls, "In Arts and Crafts, she would draw the most beautiful ballerinas, and there would be these long, dangling scars on their cheeks" (36). Andy explains the burden on Amy: "Talk about a sister who has overcome major afflictions. Being the eldest, we can assume a proximity to parental pain that's been all but rooted out with each subsequent offspring −" (35). Tammy claims that her older sister considered herself to be a witch because "Whenever she looked in the mirror, she would see scars"

(36). Amy emigrated to become a soldier, medic, and peace activist in Israel, thus following in her mother's footsteps. Israel became a place for Amy to help Jews; the country represented for her Jewish survival rather than the Jewish victimization she was more accustomed to in her family life. Tammy rationalizes her sister's motivation to emigrate: "I guess Amy's found a place where there's something more important than just the 'I.' A place where she can focus her energies outward, and not search so hard for *scars* where there aren't any" (37). Moreover, Amy's role as medic is to heal a divided territory by applying "salves to blistering Arab-Israeli wounds" (38). In effect, Amy is subliminally acting as an overachiever to heal the wounds of the past. Like Amy, Tammy is also a sort of healer. In her adolescence, she participated in youth group hunger strikes. As an adult, Tammy works in Thailand helping homeless refugees being turned away at the border. Tammy's Life Force apparently is centered around her parents' traumata. She even understands her own subliminal motivations, explaining to Andy, "That's kind of what it's like with me and Thailand, I guess. There are plenty of Holocausts around now" (37). Finally, with their aversion to murder and their adopted roles as healers, Amy and Tammy have both become vegetarians, not for a healthier lifestyle, but, as Andy notes, "for moral reasons" (29).

Whereas Andy's sisters have abandoned the family nest, Andy cannot escape the immediate impact that the Holocaust has on his life. Andy's relationship with his parents is based upon love-hate: although, like most offspring of Holocaust survivors, Andy admires his parents for the suffering they endured, he is also plagued by the shroud of secrecy that engulfs his life. Inquisitive Andy asks his parents, "What's my tragedy?" (9); rather than dredging up ghosts without understanding their origins, Andy wants answers that his parents will not provide. Andy remarks, "It is a Sad House. It has always been a Sad House. And *I* have A Room In It" (17). Raya and Nate have provided Andy with material comforts, yet they refuse to have any deep, meaningful conversations with him about the Holocaust. Andy implores his mother to explain why she left Israel to return to Europe: "So? Europe sucked! You should'a stayed. What kinda guilt were you holding onto? What kinda crap are you passing on? What's wrong with us?" (43). Andy feels that his parents' Holocaust pasts have created a barrier preventing him from ever knowing the source of their suffering. Andy views the secrecy as debilitating, exclaiming, "We have been Pumped Full of Hot Air, and Big Distortions and Locked Out Of The Reality of your lives . . ." (49). Frustrated that his parents are unwilling to share their heroic stories with him, Andy at least urges his mother to finish the book about the Holocaust, pleading, "I am trying to SAVE this family's MEMORY!" (43). Andy is reminded never to forget the trauma suffered by his parents (54) but remains conflicted because what he is supposed to remember relates to ghosts and secrets held from him. When Andy probes about specific incidents and people involved, Raya either refuses to discuss the past or simply states that her son is asking about "Someone you don't know" (73). Andy responds, "I *know* it's 'someone I don't know.' That's the point: I *need* to know" (73). In her desire to overprotect her offspring, Raya mentions that she refuses to reveal the intricate details about her Holocaust past to free Andy from pain and suffering. Furthermore, Raya understands that words could never match the actual experience, and so it would be futile to explain the Shoah to others; after all, she cannot get past the first paragraph of her book. When Andy persists in interrogating his mother about her past, Raya shouts, *"You will never understand, young man, and don't you ever forget it!"* (27). This sentence is terribly ambiguous, for Andy is asked never to forget something he has never fully grasped.

Andy's quest for his own identity is quixotic and is often enigmatic. As a budding filmmaker, Andy's search for identity is often framed by nebulous images of freedom in such films as *Brian's Song, Sounder,* or Stanley Kramer's *The Defiant Ones.* At the core of Andy's supposed liberation is Garcia Lorca's concept of *duende,* which Andy associates with an aesthetics of soul. Andy even confirms to his fiancée Sarah Liebman the reason he hesitates to cement plans for their engagement: "Because I am 100% across-the-board *incapable* of coming up with the sufficient '*Duende*' to provide the *grist* your gift demands" (10). When Sarah threatens to remove Andy's copy of the Portable Ernest Hemingway, Andy doubts whether he has any "soul" of his own: "Give that! 'A Life-Force.' That's what he [Hemingway] calls it. Bullfighters have it. Flamenco dancers have it. Did I project an 'Ecstatic Life-Force' to you in my thesis film? Do I embody the Tragic? Do I have ANY '*Duende?*'" (10–11). As is true of the majority of children of survivors, their search for *duende* is frustrating because, like Andy, they are haunted by ghosts of the past they can never fully comprehend.

Andy's impending engagement to Sarah ostensibly would be a means to assuage his fixation on the Holocaust. Sarah, a doctoral student in Soviet studies, seems to be an intellect, an overachiever like Andy, and certainly loves the filmmaker. Sarah, whose family life is disjointed, yearns for an intact family and reminds Andy how wonderful his life is because of the close contact the family members have with each other: "You sing songs after supper. You pick each other up at airports. You bake cakes, and support each other's travel ambitions – Not rip each other to shreds because of them – And I want to be a part of that future!" (34). Yet Andy, who has "Moral Responsibility fixations" (1), cannot commit to an engagement. He cautions Sarah, "But do a little digging, and there is a deep, dark something –" (12). Andy warns his potential fiancée that the family she is about to enter is not the pillar of stability she envisions: "This family is not in a stable position, as you have just seen. We wake up with these Ghosts; we go to work with these Shadows, I'm tellin' ya, they're 100 feet high!" (45). Andy realizes he cannot aspire to greatness because of the yoke of suffering embedded in his family history. He reiterates to Sarah, "We are going to Move the Earth just like in FOR WHOM THE BELL TOLLS, but first We Gotta Blow Up The Bridge!" (13). Sarah understands that her relationship with Andy is forever co-mingled with the ghosts that haunt Andy's parents. She exclaims, "Because you're still doing it! Intertwining our lives and your parents'. Our courtship and theirs. Our *love* and theirs! It's kinda weird" (67). Andy admits to Sarah that the engagement cannot be consummated because of his personal problems as the child of survivors: "*I'm* not dissatisfied with you; I'm dissatisfied with *me!*" (44). Roth explained to me why the engagement will not work:

"Sarah sees that Andy's got a lot of unfinished business with his mother – with his father too. He insufficiently understands his parents, and those deficits have become sink-holes into which he plunges, and in the process, he disrespects or invalidates the integrity of the new life he's trying to carve out with Sarah."[65] Thus, Andy, with family members reuniting from far-away places to attend a twenty-table engagement party, bails out on Sarah at the last moment. Sarah tries to justify Andy's motivations, wondering "Are you really *that miserable*?" (33). Andy later explains to his sisters the reason for his defection: "Sarah would still be here if we weren't so screwed up!" (43).

Andy attempts to exorcise his demons by making a documentary film that will rewrite his family's Holocaust history and therefore heal him so he can find his *duende*. He has had practice with this genre since his previous film was about children of the civil rights movement. This low-budget film, made in one day on the parking lot of a synagogue, is aptly titled *Cast a Giant Shadow* based on the previous Hollywood war epic with the same title; in effect, the documentary is primarily concerned with the shadows that haunt Andy. The film takes place in Jerusalem where Colonel Mickey Marcus, a hero with the American infantry, saves Jews from an Arab ambush, several of which have caused the Jewish nation to starve to death. Andy has no trouble casting his mother as Magda, a young pioneer in Israel, for he views her as an angel, an icon of heroism who defied the Nazis and prevailed despite overwhelming odds.[66] In his version of revisionist history, Andy casts his meek father as American hero Marcus who saves Jerusalem. Although his parents met at the University of Chicago, Andy's film has his father as a Jewish savior who wins the hand of young Raya, who is enamored with Nate's heroism. Furthermore, as Roth told me, the docudrama reinforces Andy's delusion that his parents would have had a more heroic life living in Israel rather than in "the more quotidian survivor's context" in the United States, where they were "surrounded by the trappings of American materialism."[67] Andy seems relieved that the film is an exorcism and pleads, "I get this over and done with for good, and then All Of Us are Free Forever!" (65). Sarah disagrees, claiming that the film in which Andy shoots his doppelgangers is an ineffective way of relating to the Holocaust:

> You've put them on a pedestal – only to shoot them off – *again* – as you've been doing your whole life! Your Mother's 'This Great War Hero'; all you've ever wanted is your Father to be the same! And now it sounds like you've actually gone and Made An Entire Cinematic Fiasco Around That Very Premise!
>
> *(67)*

Sarah is correct in her assessment, for Andy's attempt at healing results in a jail sentence for the crime of assemblage without a permit. His sisters have to bail him out of jail, and his mother, who expects her son to be a high achiever instead of a felon, expresses her disappointment with her wry comment, "And did you have a *nice time in jail, Andrew*?" (85). Even Andy himself recognizes the futility of the attempt to rewrite his family's past, admitting, "I have been walking around with a Box in front of my face and – it's true – It *is* a 'toy.' Movies are just an elaborate mechanism for disengaging from pain, and commitment –" (68).

Andy and the Shadows begins and ends twenty-five years later as Andy finally weds his sweetheart. Andy, like his parents, has adapted to living with his demons. The wedding ceremony is consummated as Andy stomps on a light bulb, which traditionally commemorates the destruction of the Second Temple in A.D. 70 Yet the stage directions indicate that the stomping on the glass also suggests Kristallnacht, the Night of Broken Glass, which typically is understood as the beginning of the Shoah: "*As a Thunderous Crash of Breaking Glass Echoes Through the Theater and the wedding party is tussled about*" (97). Sarah's comment about the breaking of the glass is particularly relevant about how this festive occasion is co-mingled with memories of the Holocaust for Andy's family: "Wherein a happy celebration shares the stage with a guilt-ridden memory. Which *is* The Jewish Way" (97). This earth-shaking moment literally becomes Andy's *duende*: his bliss is forever intertwined with a legacy he can never escape.

The three plays discussed in this chapter were included because they best represent the dilemma that the second generation is plagued with: how to find an identity free from the legacy of the Holocaust with which they are burdened. Such a quest becomes quite problematic. The children must protect or heal their parents from their traumata, but unlike psychotherapists, the second generation can never get their parents to abreact. The offspring often grow up bewildered, mistrustful, and paranoid, confined by the needs of their parents that adversely affect their own abilities to mature as distinct personalities.

Notes

1 William B. Helmreich, *Against All Odds: Holocaust Survivors and the Successful Lives They Made in America* (New Brunswick: Transaction Publishers, 1996), 121.
2 Yael Danieli, "Families of Survivors of the Nazi Holocaust: Some Short- and Long-term Effects," in *Stress and Anxiety*, vol. 8, eds. Charles D. Spielberger and Irwin G. Sarason (Washington and New York: Hemisphere, 1982), 406.
3 Judith S. Kestenberg and Milton Kestenberg, "Psychoanalyses of Children of Survivors From the Nazi Persecution: The Continuing Struggle of Survivor Parents," *Victimology: An International Journal* 5, nos. 2–4 (1980): 371.
4 Dina Wardi, *Memorial Candles: Children of the Holocaust*, trans. Naomi Goldblum (London and New York: Tavistock/Routledge, 1992), 27.
5 Ibid., 38.
6 For example, see Hillel Klein, "Children of the Holocaust: Mourning and Bereavement," in *The Child in His Family: The Impact of Disease and Death*, vol. 2, eds. James Anthony and Cyrille Koupernik (New York: John Wiley, 1973), 404.
7 See Danieli, "Families of Survivors of the Nazi Holocaust: Some Short- and Long-term Effects," 408; and Yael Danieli, "Differing Adaptational Styles in Families of Survivors of the Nazi Holocaust," *Children Today* 10, no. 5 (1981): 7.
8 Ilse Grubrich-Simitis discusses several factors that interfered with an optimal cathexis for mothers and their babies after the Holocaust. She mentions increased narcissism provoked by the constant threat of death, the mother's need for nurturing, her pent-up aggressive hostilities, and possible reservations of attachment to new objects after suffering great loss during the traumata. See Ilse Grubrich-Simitis, "Extreme Traumatization as Cumulative Trauma," *The Psychoanalytic Study of the Child* 36 (1981): 432–433.

9 Fran Klein-Parker, "Dominant Attitudes of Adult Children of Holocaust Survivors Toward Their Parents," in *Human Adaptation to Extreme Stress: From the Holocaust to Vietnam*, eds. John P. Wilson, Zev Harel, and Boaz Kahana (London: Plenum Press, 1988), 202.

10 Ibid., 203.

11 Danieli, "Families of Survivors of the Nazi Holocaust: Some Short- and Long-term Effects," 409.

12 Shamai Davidson, "The Clinical Effects of Massive Psychic Trauma in Families of Holocaust Survivors," *Journal of Marital and Family Therapy* 6 (January 1980): 13.

13 For example, see Harvey A. Barocas, "Children of Purgatory: Reflections on the Concentration Camp Survival Syndrome," *International Journal of Social Psychiatry* 21, no. 1 (1975–1976): 87; and Harvey A. Barocas and Carol B. Barocas, "Wounds of the Fathers: The Next Generation of Holocaust Victims," *International Review of Psycho-Analysis* 6 (1979): 331.

14 We must keep in mind that Rakoff's assessments were of children whose parents recognized the need for psychiatric help. Many other children who never sought psychological treatment also suffered from symptomatology. See Rakoff, "Long-term Effects of the Concentration Camp Experience," *Viewpoints* 1 (1966): 19.

15 See Davidson, "The Clinical Effects of Massive Psychic Trauma in Families of Holocaust Survivors," 11–21; and Bernard Trossman, "Adolescent Children of Concentration Camp Survivors," *Canadian Psychiatric Association Journal* 13, no. 2 (1968): 121–123.

16 J.J. Sigal et al., "Some Second-Generation Effects of Survival of the Nazi Persecution," *American Journal of Orthopsychiatry* 43, no. 3 (1973): 320–327.

17 Barocas, "Children of Purgatory: Reflections on the Concentration Camp Survival Syndrome," 87.

18 For example, see Judith S. Kestenberg, "Psychoanalyses of Children of Survivors From the Holocaust: Case Presentations and Assessment," *Journal of the American Psychoanalytic Association* 28 (1980): 776; and Arnold Wilson and Erika Fromm, "Aftermath of the Concentration Camp: The Second Generation," *Journal of the American Academy of Psychoanalysis* 10, no. 2 (1982): 290.

19 See Kestenberg, "Psychoanalyses of Children of Survivors From the Holocaust: Case Presentations and Assessment," 776; and Jack Nusan Porter, "Social-Psychological Aspects of the Holocaust," in *Encountering the Holocaust: An Interdisciplinary Survey*, eds. Byron L. Sherwin and Susan G. Ament (Chicago: Impact Press, 1979), 206–208.

20 As a result of her work with approximately 300 children of survivors, Yael Danieli characterized four major types of survivor families: victim families, families of fighters, numb families (parents who were the sole survivors in their families), and "those who made it" (parents who tended to deny the long-term effects of the Holocaust). In each category, the rearing of children differed, and thus the psychological effects on the children varied. See Yael Danieli, "Families of Survivors of the Nazi Holocaust: Some Short- and Long-term Effects," 405–421; Yael Danieli, "Differing Adaptational Styles in Families of Survivors of the Nazi Holocaust," 6–10, 34–35; and Yael Danieli, "The Treatment and Prevention of Long-term Effects and Intergenerational Transmission of Victimization: A Lesson From Holocaust Survivors and Their Children," in *Trauma and Its Wake: The Study and Treatment of Post-Traumatic Stress Disorder*, ed. Charles R. Figley (New York: Brunner/Mazel, 1985), 295–313.

21 Judith S. Kestenberg and Milton Kestenberg, "The Experience of Survivor-Parents," in *Generations of the Holocaust*, eds. Martin S. Bergmann and Milton E. Jucovy (New York: Basic Books, 1982), 48.

22 Kestenberg, "Psychoanalyses of Children of Survivors From the Holocaust: Case Presentations and Assessment," 781.

23 Nanette C. Auerhahn and Ernst Prelinger, "Repetition in the Concentration Camp Survivor and Her Child," *International Review of Psycho-analysis* 10, no. 31 (1983): 37.

24 In his study of Ashkenazi soldiers whose parents were Holocaust survivors, Israeli psychotherapist Theo de Graaf delved into an explanation of the need of Holocaust survivor parents to control their offspring. He concluded that the immanent separation of the

child from the parents reactivated the parents' conflicts about separating from their own parents and/or siblings during the Shoah. See Theo de Graaf, "Pathological Patterns of Identification in Families of Survivors of the Holocaust," *Israel Annals of Psychiatry and Related Disciplines* 13 (1975): 348.

25 Danieli, "Differing Adaptational Styles in Families of Survivors of the Nazi Holocaust," 8.

26 Barocas and Barocas, "Wounds of the Fathers: The Next Generation of Holocaust Victims," 334.

27 Wardi, *Memorial Candles: Children of the Holocaust*, 154.

28 Judith S. Kestenberg, "Survivor-Parents and Their Children," in *Generations of the Holocaust*, eds. Martin S. Bergmann and Milton E. Jucovy (New York: Basic Books, 1982), 100.

29 Nanette C. Auerhahn and Dori Laub, "Play and Playfulness in Holocaust Survivors," *Psychoanalytic Study of the Child* 42 (1987): 56.

30 Yael Danieli has written that this mistrust is particularly true of "victim families." See Danieli, "The Treatment and Prevention of Long-term Effects and Intergenerational Transmission of Victimization: A Lesson From Holocaust Survivors and Their Children," 299.

31 Trossman, "Adolescent Children of Concentration Camp Survivors," 121.

32 See Nanette C. Auerhahn, Dori Laub, and Harvey Peskin, "Psychotherapy With Holocaust Survivors," *Psychotherapy: Theory, Research & Practice* 30, no. 3 (1993): 439.

33 Robert Krell, a psychiatrist at the University of British Columbia, made this conclusion after years of observation of children of Holocaust survivors. See Krell, "Holocaust Families: The Survivors and Their Children," *Comprehensive Psychiatry* 20 (1979): 564.

34 In their study of children of Holocaust survivors in thirty-two families who were brought to the Psychiatric Outpatient Department of the Jewish General Hospital in Montreal, John J. Sigal and Vivian Rakoff noted more depressive features in the sample population when compared to the control group. See John J. Sigal and Vivian Rakoff, "Concentration Camp Survival: A Pilot Study of Effects on the Second Generation," *Canadian Journal of Psychiatry* 16 (1971): 395. These findings were reproduced by Helen Lichtman, who examined sixty-four Jewish children of survivors and determined that guilt-inducing communication by the parents resulted in paranoia and low ego strength in their offspring. See Lichtman, "Parental Communication of Holocaust Experiences and Personality Characteristics Among Second-Generation Survivors," *Journal of Clinical Psychology* 40, no. 4 (1984): 917, 920.

35 Wilson and Fromm, "Aftermath of the Concentration Camp: The Second Generation," 301.

36 Barocas and Barocas, "Wounds of the Fathers: The Next Generation of Holocaust Victims," 331, 336.

37 Kestenberg, "Survivor-Parents and Their Children," 98.

38 Klein-Parker, "Dominant Attitudes of Adult Children of Holocaust Survivors Toward Their Parents," 206.

39 Danieli, "Differing Adaptational Styles in Families of Survivors of the Nazi Holocaust," 9.

40 See Dan Bar-On et al., "Multigenerational Perspectives on Coping With Holocaust Experience: An Attachment Perspective for Understanding the Developmental Sequelae of Trauma Across Generations," *International Journal of Behavioral Development* 22, no. 2 (1998): 324.

41 Harvey Peskin, Nanette C. Auerhahn, and Dori Laub, "The Second Holocaust: Therapeutic Rescue When Life Threatens," *Journal of Personal and Interpersonal Loss* 2 (1997): 16.

42 Samuel Slipp, "The Children of Survivors of Nazi Concentration Camps: A Pilot Study of the Intergenerational Transmission of Psychic Trauma," in *Group Therapy 1979: An Overview*, eds. Lewis R. Wolberg and Marvin L. Aronson (New York: Stratton Intercontinental Medical Book Corp., 1979), 202.

43 Judith S. Kestenberg, "Psychoanalytic Contributions to the Problem of Children of Survivors From Nazi Persecution," *Israel Annals of Psychiatry and Related Disciplines* 10, no. 4 (1972): 321.

44 John J. Sigal and Morton Weinfeld, *Trauma and Rebirth: Intergenerational Effects of the Holocaust* (New York and Westport: Praeger, 1989), 97.

45 Grubrich-Simitis, "Extreme Traumatization as Cumulative Trauma," 433.

46 Danieli, "The Treatment and Prevention of Long-term Effects and Intergenerational Transmission of Victimization: A Lesson From Holocaust Survivors and Their Children," 302.
47 See Wardi, *Memorial Candles: Children of the Holocaust*, 122.
48 Bar-On et al., "Multigenerational Perspectives on Coping With Holocaust Experience: An Attachment Perspective for Understanding the Developmental Sequelae of Trauma Across Generations," 326.
49 To provide fairness and credence to the subject of psychopathology among the second generation, I must address the opposing views. Studies in the latter part of the twentieth century have provided evidence to suggest that psychopathology among children of survivors is not consistently verifiable. For example, in chronological order, see Gloria R. Leon et al., "Survivors of the Holocaust and Their Children: Current Status and Adjustment," *Journal of Personality and Social Psychology* 41, no. 3 (1981): 503–516; Susan L. Rose and John Garske, "Family Environment, Adjustment, and Coping Among Children of Holocaust Survivors: A Comparative Investigation," *American Journal of Orthopsychiatry* 57, no. 3 (1987): 332–344; Sigal and Weinfeld, *Trauma and Rebirth: Intergenerational Effects of the Holocaust*; Norman Solkoff, "Children of Survivors of the Nazi Holocaust: A Critical Review of the Literature," *American Journal of Orthopsychiatry* 62, no. 3 (1992): 342–358; Miriam Rieck, "The Psychological State of Holocaust Survivors' Offspring: An Epidemiological and Psychodiagnostic Study," *International Journal of Behavioral Development* 17, no. 4 (1994): 649–667; and Bar-On et al., "Multigenerational Perspectives on Coping With Holocaust Experience: An Attachment Perspective for Understanding the Developmental Sequelae of Trauma Across Generations," 315–338. Leon et al. compared fifty-two survivors of World War II to a control group of twenty-nine persons of similar European and religious backgrounds and found that the children of survivors did not manifest serious psychological impairment (514). However, they provided the caveat that subjects volunteered to participate in the study and "may be different on a variety of parameters from persons who do not agree to participate" (514). Rose and Garske divided their seventy-three subjects into four groups: children of Holocaust survivors, children of Eastern European immigrants, Jewish controls, and non-Jewish controls; they found that children of survivors adjusted well and displayed no higher incidence of psychopathology than the members of the control groups (340). Rose and Garske note that the results are limited to the population assessed, which was self-selected individuals recruited from organizational mailing lists. In their study of survivors and their children living in Montreal in 1978 and 1981, Sigal and Weinfeld recognized that children of survivors had problems with anxiety, depression, aggression, and self-esteem, but they did not feel psychologically disturbed and have coped well (170). Rieck agreed with these findings; in her 1993 study of offspring aged five to sixteen, she concluded that the clinical impression of psychopathology was not pervasive among the second-generation (662). These findings were corroborated by Solkoff in 1992 (356) and Bar-On et al. in 1998 (318). The conclusions made by these psychologists do not negate studies conducted by psychotherapists in the earlier years. Since these clinical studies were conducted independently and derived the same conclusions, we can probably argue that there are definite psychological problems in the second generation but no clearly defined psychopathology. Like their parents, most children of survivors were adept at coping in adverse situations. They were also less likely to consider themselves to be psychologically impaired, and thus many would never volunteer to participate in a clinical study of the population, but they would go to psychotherapy if their parents had asked them to do so. In short, psychotherapists would have seen a different subset of individuals than the ones the psychologists surveyed while conducting their clinical studies later in the century.
50 Faye Sholiton, *The Interview* (New York: Speert Publishing, 2012), 23. All subsequent citations from the play are from this edition and will be included within parentheses in the text.
51 Faye Sholiton, email message to author, May 20, 2015.
52 Ibid.
53 Faye Sholiton, email message to author, June 2, 2015.

54 In an email he sent to me, Vierling mentioned that he based the character of Natalie on two real-life persons: a talented acting student named Reba Rosenberg that he taught in the drama program at Trinity Preparatory School and a twenty-year-old Yale student named Leah Strigler that he met in Israel; her father was a Holocaust survivor and a New York-based writer. Ronald John Vierling, email message to author, June 8, 2015.

55 Vierling assured me that Natalie and Adam were not given last names purposefully. Adam and Eva, of course, represent the first couple. Adam signifies the first man for the Hebrews, the first man to fall according to Christians. Natalie is the biblical author of the histories of David and King Solomon. In short, the names were chosen carefully by Vierling. Ronald John Vierling, email message to author, June 8, 2015.

56 Ronald John Vierling, letter to author, May 22, 2015.

57 Ronald John Vierling, "*Adam's Daughter*," in *Rising From the Ashes, Vol. 1: Beyond the Abyss* (n.p.: Xlibris Corporation, 2010), 21. All subsequent citations from the play are from this edition and will be included within parentheses in the text.

58 Ronald John Vierling, email message to author, June 8, 2015.

59 Ibid.

60 Ibid.

61 Ibid.

62 Ari Roth, email message to author, July 11, 2015.

63 Ari Roth, *Andy and the Shadows* (New York: The Barbara Hogenson Agency, 2013), 77. All subsequent citations from the play are from this edition and will be included within parentheses in the text.

64 The scene is eerily similar to the confessional scene in *Adam's Daughter*. Both scenes occur in a hospital, where offspring try to allow parents to unearth the secrets of their Holocaust pasts before they pass away from potentially life-threatening illnesses. Both parents attempt a confessional and certainly entertain the only serious discussion about the Holocaust that they ever had with their offspring, although admittedly Adam talks more freely than Nate.

65 Ari Roth, email message to author, July 11, 2015.

66 In an email message to me, Roth explained that the concept of Andy's mother having angel wings was autobiographical. Roth's mother told Ari that she graduated from an Italian convent in 1944 at the head of her class. In reality, his mother was only in the convent for three months. In Roth's imagination, his mother was a favorite among the nuns – one who, in hiding as a Catholic girl, demonstrated "mastery of a new culture and religion." Ari Roth, email message to author, July 11, 2015.

67 Ari Roth, email message to author, July 11, 2015.

6

AGGRESSIVE BEHAVIOR AMONG OFFSPRING OF HOLOCAUST SURVIVORS

Typically, survivors, particularly those who had been interned in concentration camps, tended to curb their offspring's aggressive behavior as a means to facilitate their survival in a hostile universe.[1] Such survivors, who readily understood that their own survival depended upon submission to Nazi authority, transmitted those values to their children. Moreover, any aggressive tendencies among offspring were perceived by survivor parents as being potentially destructive, for they threatened the parents' defenses against bottled-up hate and revenge impulses dating from the period of persecution.[2] As was noted in Chapter 5, parents who viewed aggressive tendencies or disruptive behavior in their children often responded by comparing them to "little Hitlers" or Nazis, thus stifling such behavior as counterproductive to the growth of the family. Furthermore, such children intuitively understood that their parents live vicariously through them and that they suffered greatly during the Holocaust; thus, many such offspring felt too guilty to openly rebel through aggression.[3]

When the offspring entered adolescence, they often defied such high standards that their parents had set for them as overachievers. As early as 1968, Bernard Trossman reported that adolescents frequently rebelled against parents who maintained a hostile attitude toward the world, yet, well aware of their parents' past sufferings, they internalized the aggression, often becoming mistrustful and even paranoid.[4] Aggression, which is typically part of the maturation process among adolescents, now becomes suppressed as pent-up anger against their parents. For Holocaust survivors, their offspring's adolescence caused more problems than typical teenagers, for the parents had a highly abnormal adolescence manifested by separation and loss of their own family members. Trossman also mentions specific instances in which the rebellion was prominently displayed in dating non-Jewish partners or by one angry young girl who failed all of her academic subjects except German in order to spite her parents.[5] In a study of children of survivors, Nadler, Kav-Venaki, and Gleitman discovered that descendants of survivors typically do not externalize their aggression but admit their own guilt and internalize aggressive tendencies; aggression is present but is often repressed for fear of protecting vulnerable parents.[6] In another study of thirty-six survivor families, Russell found that parents who seemed guilty about over-indulging their children typically produced adolescents who were "spoiled and aggressive."[7] Parents who forced their children to be overachievers often caused adolescents to prove their worthiness or to rebel and thus give up the quest.[8] Such adolescents, who could not display their anger toward their parents, either displaced their aggression onto siblings or reacted masochistically with self-punishing behavior.[9]

Martin S. Bergmann noted that it is not uncommon for children of survivors to rebel against the task of being the vehicle to undo the trauma of their parents.[10] The strain of fulfilling unreasonable ideals set by the parents often leads offspring toward external acts that are either destructive or self-destructive. Many such children rebelled against their parents' intrusiveness on their lifestyle. Jack Nusan Porter writes, "Because they are unable to cope with the continuous anxious responses of their parents to their behavior, the children either go out of control themselves or respond by withdrawal, either into fantasy at best or into an affectless state at worst."[11] Barocas and Barocas also noted that survivor parents imbued the children with the notion of being grateful for what they had rather than whining or complaining, which would cause retribution by hostile authorities; such constant admonishment to suppress aggressive behavior promoted a masochistic lifestyle.[12]

Aggression among offspring of survivors can be accrued in various other ways as well. Children of survivors have been found to be disruptive as a result of overly taxed, traumatized parents who could not provide adequate and appropriate feedback.[13] Studies have also shown that parental superego defects induced during the Shoah translate into superego defects in offspring that can result in delinquency.[14] Furthermore, survivor parents can encourage in their children aggressive tendencies that they were forced to mask during their internment and cannot express because of their burden of guilt, thereby freeing their sons and daughters to express themselves without the repression that they themselves were forced to endure.[15] The survivors, previously trained to repress their aggressive tendencies, may transmit subtle cues for the children to act aggressively, thus vicariously gratifying the parents' latent wishes.[16] Such aggression becomes full-blown when the children reach adolescence and beyond. Offspring can also resent their parents for providing a pervasive atmosphere of pessimism and hopelessness, and since they cannot overtly react to parents whose lives were embedded with misery through no control of their own, their anger and resentment are internalized masochistically. Finally, the tendency for parents to compare their children to Nazis when they misbehaved often created hostile, destructive reactions directed against the parents or against their surrogates, such as the Jewish community or culture.[17]

Many survivors detest the notion that they abandoned their relatives to their deaths and feel guilty about having done so. Consequently, many survivors raise their children to be aggressive toward a world proven to be hostile and menacing. In these households, there was a ubiquitous suspicion of a world that allowed the

Holocaust to flourish, and children were tasked with the responsibility that a second Holocaust would not occur.[18] There have been examples in which the offspring of survivors identified so strongly with their parents' past suffering that they engaged in a second version of the Holocaust to prevent any future persecution.[19] Such parents indoctrinated their children to mistrust others and to avoid speaking with anyone outside the safe family circle about issues that might be intimate.[20] This atmosphere of mistrust caused many adolescents to avoid forming intimate relations or even to venture out of the safe family unit to marry.

In Chapter 5, I mentioned the four categories of survivor families studied by Yael Danieli. In her last designated type of family, which she defined as "families of fighters," we see aggression and violence full blown among offspring. Parents in these families often survived the Holocaust by either fighting with the partisans or resistance leaders or hiding from Nazi persecution. Parents in fighter families did not allow their offspring to indulge in self-pity but instead encouraged them to take a proactive stance in resolving problems.[21] The goal was to build and achieve through pride and strength of character. Although physical illness was somewhat acceptable, behavior that might signify psychological weakness or victimization was not tolerated. Parents in families of fighters displayed mistrust of outside authorities and encouraged aggression against what they perceived were their enemies.[22] Offspring were primarily motivated to ensure that another Holocaust would never occur again. Relaxation and pleasurable activities were superfluous to the goals of this type of survivor family, making it more difficult for adolescents to form peer relationships or even to marry.

The remainder of this chapter will focus on the plays that best demonstrate two major types of aggressive reactions among offspring of Holocaust survivors: internalized/masochistic aggression toward parents, represented in Donald Margulies's *The Model Apartment*, and overt aggression in fighter families, best depicted in Marsha Lee Sheiness's *Second Hand Smoke*.

Born in Brooklyn, New York, on 2 September 1954, Donald Margulies was raised in lower-middle-class apartments in Sheepshead Bay and later in Trump Village, a Coney Island high-rise ghetto built by Donald Trump's father. Margulies studied art and literature at the State University of New York at Purchase, where he graduated with a bachelor of fine arts degree in visual arts. While working as a graphic artist after his college graduation, Margulies wrote several short stories and monologues. His first play, the one-act *Luna Park*, was staged at the Jewish Repertory Theater in 1982, followed by his first full-length drama, *Gifted Children*, staged by the Jewish Repertory Theater in 1983. In 1984, Joseph Papp produced Margulies's *Found a Peanut* at the New York Shakespeare Festival. Margulies's career received a big boost in 1992 when *Sight Unseen* won an Obie Award for Best New American Play, as well as the Dramatists Guild/Hull-Warriner Award, and was nominated for the Pulitzer Prize. His other major plays include *What's Wrong With This Picture* (1985), *Zimmer* (1988), *The Loman Family Picnic* (1989), *Pitching to the Star* (1990), *July 7, 1994* (1995), *Collected Stories* (1996; later nominated for the Pulitzer Prize), *God of Vengeance* (2000), *Brooklyn Boy* (2003), *Shipwrecked! An Entertainment*

(2007), *Time Stands Still* (2010), *Coney Island Christmas* (2012), and *The Country House* (2014). His most successful play, *Dinner With Friends* (1998), won the Pulitzer Prize in 2000. He has also written pilots and various episodes for television shows. Margulies has received playwriting fellowships from the New York Foundation for the Arts, as well as grants from the National Endowment for the Arts and the prestigious John Simon Guggenheim Memorial Foundation. He currently lives with his wife in New Haven, Connecticut, where he teaches courses in theater and playwriting at Yale University.

Margulies wrote *The Model Apartment* in 1986, and soon afterwards, Joseph Papp optioned the play. However, *The Model Apartment* was apparently too controversial for the Eugene O'Neill Theater Center and the Circle Repertory Company – two production companies that demonstrated an early interest in staging the play. Thus, *The Model Apartment* languished for two years before its premiere at the Los Angeles Theatre Center in November 1988 under direction by Roberta Levitow. Seven years later, in October 1995, *The Model Apartment* had its first New York staging at the Off-Broadway Primary Stages Company in a production directed by Lisa Peterson. Margulies later won the Obie Award for playwriting as a result of the production at Primary Stages. In its revival during October 2013 at Primary Stages' 59E59 Theaters in New York City, directed by Evan Cabnet, *The Model Apartment* was nominated for two Drama Desk Awards, including Outstanding Revival of a Play, and two Lucille Lortel Awards.[23]

Margulies's interest in the Holocaust stems from his early years in Brooklyn, where many survivors were living. Margulies told me that he spent a lot of time at age ten, in 1964, with his friend Steven Reisner, who was a child of survivors.[24] At the time of the Eichmann trial, Margulies's interest in the Holocaust was piqued by black-and-white newsreel photos of liberated concentration camp survivors shown on the Huntley-Brinkley nightly news. Before writing *The Model Apartment*, Margulies read Helen Epstein's *Children of the Holocaust* and attended second-generation survivor meetings with Reisner. Margulies stated, "I've always been attracted to stories about families, and the legacies parents instill in their children. By making the parents in a play Holocaust survivors, with an enormous legacy, I felt that stakes were higher than in a more conventionally burdened family (like mine)."[25] In addition, to portray Debby's mental condition accurately on stage, Margulies read Susan Sheehan's indelible portrait of a mentally ill woman in New York, *Is There No Place on Earth for Me?* The other impetus for the play derived from a 1970 Diane Arbus photo titled "Jewish Giant at Home with His Parents." This juxtaposition of a grotesque monster living in a middle-class Jewish family formed the genesis of the outline for the play.

The Model Apartment runs approximately one hour and twenty minutes and is composed of fifteen scenes that are not divided in acts. Margulies knew that the play was controversial, so he claims that he did not include an intermission because "I think people wouldn't come back."[26] *The Model Apartment* is difficult for critics to discern; the play is definitely not naturalistic but instead is much closer to black comedy. Robert Skloot characterizes the play as "an adult cartoon" – a "*shtik*-filled aria," amusing, yet producing "a profound sadness."[27] For some inflexible critics, this sort of combination of black comedy juxtaposed with the serious nature of the subject matter may be repugnant.

The Model Apartment occurs in an unnamed city in Florida, where Lola and Max, both Holocaust survivors now in their sixties, have come to retire after living for years in Brooklyn. Unfortunately, their condominium is not quite ready for habitation, so the couple are asked to spend one or two nights in a one-bedroom "model apartment" until they can move into their permanent residence. Since the model apartment is only for show, everything in this living space is artificial. The plants are plastic, and objects such as ashtrays and candlesticks, which function solely as decoration, are glued to surfaces. The television, stereo, and appliances are hollow fixtures. Max, the survivor, puts the couple's dilemma in terms of eternal victimization: "Who else has to go through this? Everybody else's condo is done. Painted, carpeted. Just us. The story of my life."[28] Just like in the concentration camps, there is not even a shred of toilet paper in the model apartment. Lola and Max are forced to suffer through the night, but the Holocaust has made them tolerant about such misery.

Lola's Holocaust experiences include internment at Bergen-Belsen, where she mentored Anne Frank. Lola was only eighteen years old at that time but already had witnessed the deaths of her parents and her sisters. Alone in Belsen, Lola befriended Anne Frank as the two of them helped each other survive the daily tortures. Anne supposedly kept a second diary of her daily life in the concentration camp and was encouraged by Lola to keep writing it in order to invigorate her spirits. Lola is particularly disturbed that her mother refused to evacuate her beautiful home and her furniture, thus allowing her daughter to become Nazi prey. Like most survivors, Lola has nightmares about the past, admitting that sleep ". . . tricks me. It's no friend to *me*" (162). Lola suffers from Holocaust guilt as a result of being unable to save her mother from death. This guilt is particularly omnipresent in her recurring nightmare about refusing to acknowledge her mother's presence while she was chosen for execution. Lola recalls, "I didn't look. She called me, her voice was torn up from screaming, but I walked, I kept on walking. I didn't look back. *Lights, and Lola's voice, begin to fade.* Like my own mother was a stranger. I didn't look . . . I didn't look . . ." (169). Lola acted cowardly without any humanity, justifying her reaction as a life-saving device: "They'd've made the connection. They'd've sent me *with* her . . ." (168). Max, fully understanding the concentration camp mentality of lack of empathy, nods approvingly and responds, "You don't want to call attention to yourself" (168).

Max, hoping to put his miserable existence behind him, wants nothing better than to live a comfortable life in retirement in sunny Florida. However, when asleep, Max has nightmares about his first-born daughter Deborah and his first wife. Max had been hiding from the Nazis in the woods, but when he emerged after the War, his wife and Deborah were dead. Max's approach to the trauma is silence. Max feels guilty about his inability to mourn the dead in the Jewish ritualistic ceremony called "sitting shiva." He asks Deborah for forgiveness: "This ache . . . it doesn't go away . . . it gets worse with time. Not better, worse. Tell me, sweetheart . . . tell me.

When does it end?" (183). In the last scene of the play, Deborah appears in Max's dreams to remind him of happier times, particularly when the Jewish holiday of Passover was celebrated before the War when the family was intact. The nightmares only serve to reinforce the notion that the halcyon days no longer exist for Max, despite his aspirations to live in peace near a beach.

Once Debby arrives on the scene, the audience soon realizes that the focus of the play is clearly on the children of survivors, not on the survivors *per se*. As was typical for children of survivors, Debby is named after a relative who perished during the Holocaust: her half-sister Deborah, who died in infancy. However, Debby, the outspoken rebel of the family, is the antithesis of the emblematic "memorial candle." Most memorial candles were groomed to be overachievers; Debby, on the other hand, cannot even take care of herself. In his dreams, Max envisions Deborah as respectful (164); Debby, in contrast, mocks her parents and even tortures them (184). Typically, memorial candles gravitated to the healing vocations as if to subliminally respond to their roles as healers for parents who had suffered unbearably. Debby is far from a healer; instead she is "mentally disturbed" (142) and thus incapable of even healing herself.

Like most memorial candles, Debby's persona has been established by her parents' history, thus making her search for her own identity problematic; however, the difference between Debby and the typical memorial candle is that Debby resents the fact that she is a child of survivors. Having heard her parents' Holocaust bedtime stories many times previously, Debby, unlike most children of survivors who listen to the tales without griping, chooses to mock her parents' suffering by applying the genocide to banal life in America. After eating at Howard Johnson's restaurant, Debby claims, "It's a front for the Nazis" (155). Debby states that one of the patrons at the restaurant was a Nazi who "was gonna sterilize me" (156). When her parents reiterate that they lack room for her in the apartment, Debby says, "I'll sleep on the floor, I don't care. I like sleeping on the floor. Like in the camps" (159). Debby relates her parents' move to Florida as an evasion from the Nazis:

> Boy. On the road again you two. Always on the road. Always running away from *some*thing. Load up the car, fill the tank, turn the key. Keep an eye on the rearview mirror, Daddy. You never know when that VW van'll turn on its siren and come and get you. Run, Daddy. Go. Get on the road at four in the morning, before the sun comes up. Make up a name when you check in at Howard Johnson's. You're on the road. You can be anybody on the road. Who knows a Jew from a goy on the road in West Virginia?
>
> *(161)*

Debby's comment about the lack of bathroom tissue in the apartment becomes a sarcastic latent reference to its absence in the camps: "You need toilet paper. Never hurts to have extra, right? No such thing as too much toilet paper. Stock up. You never know" (164–5). Moreover, Debby's comparison of the concentration camp to a bungalow colony, where ovens refer to cooking instead of extermination, is a dream in extremely bad taste, as she obviously attempts to hurt her parents: "They put chintzy drapes on the barbed wire. Raisin cookies were in the ovens. The food, Mommy! Such portions! I was stuffed! None of that stale bread and soup shit. All the salad bar you could eat! Shrimp! Like at Beefsteak Charlie's" (165). Debby's dream relates the extermination camp to summer camp, where the Nazis, in Bermuda shorts and T-shirts, were depicted as "Jewish fathers with numbers on their arms" (166). In her distorted dream vision of the camps, Debby morphs into a pool's lifeguard saving children from their deaths; she glows in her life-saving role, bragging, "The Nazis thought I had spunk" (166). Debby compares the extermination camp to an idyllic time when she won awards, such as an "adorable handbag made of Jewish hair" (166) and bonded together with friends "singing by the flames" (167). The culmination of this dream represents Debby's subliminal view that her parents are to blame for her psychopathology as she directly accuses her mother of figuratively murdering her: "I took off my pants, and my shirt, and my shoes. And I looked at myself in the mirror only it was *your* face and you told me to get ready for the gas chamber" (167).

Debby resents being defined by her parents' Holocaust pasts. Margulies provided this portrait of Debby: "She's also a metaphor for dreams and aspirations for the future – and the receptacle of all the parents' past suffering. Now, in her madness, she's living the nightmare her parents escaped from."[29] In an email message that he sent to me, Margulies was quick to note that he was much more interested in portraying Debby's madness as a metaphor than he was in portraying schizophrenia.[30] Margulies acknowledges that *The Model Apartment* is not meant to be a realistic play nor documentary theater, which is perhaps a comment implying that without a background in psychology, he did not intend to plumb the depths of Debby's psychopathology. Interestingly enough, in the same email interview that he conducted with me, Margulies admitted, "Playwrights may not be the best source of enlightenment about their work."[31] In short, whether portrayed consciously or inadvertently, Debby's psychopathology, documented earlier in this chapter by various psychotherapists, is not uncommon among children of Holocaust survivors.

Debby has also reacted negatively to her parents' attempts to stifle any hostility she may have toward them by relating her aggressive behavior to the torture the Nazis inflicted upon them. Debby laments to her father, "You never let me have fun. Such a killjoy. Such a poop" (186). Max reacts to his daughter's behavior by comparing the torture to what the persecutors did to him: "I walked out of the woods. For what? So I could come to America?" (191). Max also complains to Debby, "What Hitler didn't do to me, you are doing . . . !" (189). The implication is that Debby is exacerbating the suffering that the Nazis initiated in his life, and thus she shares part of the blame for Max's guilty conscience.

Debby's dilemma is that she cannot establish an identity for herself free from the Holocaust. Debby emphatically complains to her parents that the focal point of the family is on the Holocaust and on her identity as an object of memorial rather than on her unique qualities as an individual: "What you went through! Always what you went through! What about me?! What about what *I* went through?!" (159).

Debby explains that she is the product of a programmed identity created for her by Max, Auschwitz surgeon Dr. Mengele, and Frankenstein: "All the brain surgery you did on me! Night after night! Anne Frank was in the next bed. You rewired my brain! Took out my memory! That's why my head always aches!" (189). In essence, Debby can never be herself because the spectre of the Holocaust has created an identity for her. She laments to her parents, "They're all inside me. All of them. Anne Frank. The Six Million. Bubbie and Zaydie and Hitler and Deborah. When my stomach talks, it's *them* talking. Telling me they're hungry. I eat for them so they won't be hungry. Sometimes I don't know what I'm saying 'cause it's *them* talking . . ." (189). Debby even believes that she has a split personality comprised of her own unique identity and her Holocaust self created for her by her parents. She admits that this schizophrenia is counterproductive: "It's so crowded and noisy in here, I can't hear myself *think* anymore! This is not my heart. My heart never sounded like *this*. Where is *me*? What happened to *me*?" (190).

Debby is particularly troubled by the fact that she cannot live up to the legacy of her namesake. Debby confronts her father with the notion that she was supposed to personify the ideal that her half-sister represented for the future. Debby wonders if she could ever be svelte enough or pretty enough to please her father, whose image of his firstborn has always been nothing more than a fantasy. Yet because Deborah shared the vestiges of Holocaust suffering with her parents, she will always occupy a special place in their hearts. Debby acknowledges that she can never become like her suffering sibling: "Starve myself to death? Would that make you happy? Huh? How could I possibly be as pretty as Deborah? Skin and bones" (189). Debby rebels against the legacy of her sister that has determined an identity for her:

> Deborah talks to me. She tells me to do things. It all started with her, you know. You thought it was me. It's her fault. She was the life of the party but the party died before I got here. I can sing! I can pass out pigs in the blanket! I can be a lampshade! I'M ALIVE! I CAN'T HELP IT I WASN'T EXTERMINATED!
>
> *(189)*

Lola and Max fully understand that Debby is not like their fantasy of what Deborah might have been. Instead, the reality is that Debby mocks the Holocaust – the one event that defined their lives. Debby has abandoned the family legacy; in turn, Max and Lola abandon her. They leave her in Brooklyn, retiring on the sly to Florida at 4:00 a.m. without even saying goodbye to their daughter. Max explains the departure thusly: "She doesn't need us. She needs to *torture* us" (184).

Debby has rebelled against any effort to prove her worthiness to her survivor parents. Instead, her pent-up anger toward her parents (overtly expressed near the end of the play in her attempt to strangle her father) is typically manifested masochistically, especially since she has no living siblings with whom she can become aggressive. Debby's self-punishing behavior has resulted in her obesity and her unkempt appearance. Robert Skloot aptly summarizes Debby's masochism: "And

Debby's profoundly unhappy life as the inadequate inheritor of Deborah's name and nature produces a grossly overweight, crippled woman whose self-loathing transforms her desperate need for love into an unquenchable need for sex."[32]

Debby's need for love and her search for identity leads her to Neil, a fifteen-year-old mildly retarded African-American who lives on the streets of Manhattan. Debby's subliminal need to protect her parents as a child of survivors is displaced onto Neil who, as a street person, is a sort of refugee. More importantly, Neil provides Debby with an identity that she lacked when living with her parents. Debby states that Neil loves her, makes her feel attractive, and provides her with a much-needed social life as they go movie hopping in Times Square. Moreover, unlike Max, who perceives all outside threats to be Nazis and thus creates a household of paranoia, Neil, a weightlifter and a black belt in kung fu, provides Debby with much-needed security.

Despite the fact that Max and Lola may have sympathy for Neil as a homeless refugee from their old neighborhood in Brooklyn and who, like them, is a person who has lost close relatives, Neil represents the antithesis of what children of survivors typically seek in a mate. He is not Jewish, comes from a different class, and has a dysfunctional family life. At fifteen years of age, he is "jail bait," and sex with Debby thus becomes felonious activity. Furthermore, if children of survivors are required to overachieve, Debby's relationship with Neil, an unemployed bum, represents a child of survivors accepting the worst case of underachievement. Even more appalling, Neil is a criminal who casually steals a car off the street for Debby; by doing so, Neil makes Debby an accessory to criminal activity – the ultimate rejection of her parents' credo of working hard so as to prosper in America. In addition, Max and Lola, whose native language is Yiddish but have assimilated to the extent that English, their second language, is fluent, probably intuitively understand that Neil's black English is a dialect that further alienates him from acculturated Jews. Neil's only recognition of Jewish culture is the pathetic gift that he gives Debby's parents: a package of Sara Lee Bagels. When Neil and Debby have intercourse while Lola and Max look on aghast, it becomes clear that Debby's *chutzpah* degenerates into a rejection of her role as a memorial candle for the family.

Not only is Neil ignorant of Jewish culture, but also, even more significantly, he is clueless with regard to the Holocaust. When Lola inadvertently reveals her concentration camp number that is tattooed on her forearm, Neil, ignorant about its meaning, callously compares his tattooed arm with hers. As Lola tells the tale of losing all of her family members during the Holocaust, Neil, not understanding the meaning of such deeply rooted loss associated with trauma, nonchalantly compares Lola's suffering with his. Neil, without comprehending anything about the Holocaust, listens to Lola's tale about Anne Frank's harrowing last days at Belsen. Lola's reminiscences, no matter how incredulous or embellished the stories seem to be, would appear to even the most casual listener to be fascinating. Neil's lack of knowledge of Anne Frank, whose diary has been a metonym for the Holocaust, represents Debby's total rebellion against her survivor parents and everything they lived for after the liberation.[33]

Raised in a middle-class Jewish family, Debby, whose desire to take a retarded black teenager who is homeless and a criminal for a lover, displays a masochistic reaction to her role as a memorial candle. The play's title indicates breakdown: everything in the model apartment is dysfunctional. Debby, in her late thirties and no longer in need of parental nurture, left New York to reunite with her parents in Florida. Yet, from her first appearance in the play, she harasses her parents, and when Neil enters, her masochistic persona becomes understood as the underlying motive for Debby's attempt to "break down" her role as a memorial candle. The play is far removed from a domestic drama since Debbie's goal as a free spirit is to dispel, at every opportunity, her parents' paranoia about the Holocaust.

Marsha Lee Sheiness's *Second Hand Smoke* was adapted from Thane Rosenbaum's 1999 novel with the same title. Rosenbaum was born in New York City in 1960. His parents, both Holocaust survivors, moved to Miami Beach, where they raised their only son. The influence of the Holocaust on Thane's life was palpable and later became the focal point for much of his writing.[34] Thane graduated with a B.A. from the University of Florida in 1981, where he was class valedictorian. He earned an M.P.A. degree from Columbia University's School of Public Policy and Administration and then graduated from the University of Miami in 1986 with a degree in law. He later moved to New York to work as an attorney at the law firm of Debevoise & Plimpton. From 1992 to 2014, he taught courses on human rights, as well as law and literature, at the Fordham Law School in New York. His novel *Elijah Visible* won the Edward Lewis Wallant Book Award in 1996 for the best book of Jewish-American fiction. Rosenbaum is the literary editor of *Tikkun* magazine and has written reviews and essays for several periodicals, including *Newsday*, *Wall Street Journal*, *New York Times*, *Washington Post*, and *Miami Herald*. As the moderator of The Talk Show With Thane Rosenbaum at the 92Y, he has interviewed well-known public personalities, including many artists and politicians.

Marsha Lee Sheiness was born in 1940 and began her professional career as an actress in Los Angeles after receiving her B.A. degree in Speech and Drama. She later moved to New York City, where she acted in productions during tours with the National Repertory Theatre. Sheiness has written a dozen plays, the most noteworthy of which is *Monkey Monkey Bottle of Beer, How Many Monkeys Have We Here?* (1975), which aired on Public Television's "Theater in America" series. Her other plays include *Becoming Eleanor, Bernie and the Beast, Best All 'Round, Dealers' Choice, Eleanor of Acquitaine, Lipstick Politics, Lost and Found, Music to My Ears, Professor George, Reception,* and *The Spelling Bee*. She has also written four adaptations, including *Second Hand Smoke*, and five musical adaptations. Her plays have been produced in Japan, Canada, England, and the United States. In addition, she has directed more than thirty productions, including performances of such notable plays as *Bus Stop, The Miracle Worker,* and *Little Shop of Horrors*.

Second Hand Smoke, a two-act play that runs approximately one hour and forty-five minutes, was written in 2006. Sheiness told me that director Robert Kalfin had read Rosenbaum's novel and asked her to adapt it for the stage.[35] Rosenbaum met Sheiness and gave his consent for the project. Sheiness was particularly enamored with Mila Katz, the hardened Holocaust survivor who raises her son to be her avenger. After writing the first draft of the play, Sheiness gave it to Kalfin and Rosenbaum for their review; she then took any of their suggestions that she thought would improve the play and revised the script accordingly. The first reading was at the Lark Theatre, where Kalfin, Rosenbaum, and Sheiness heard the play for the first time; afterwards, Sheiness made some further revisions. After a staged reading at Richmond Shepard Theatre, the play was performed at the Jewish Community Center in Manhattan during November 2010. This production, directed by Robert Kalfin, featured television star Dylan McDermott as Duncan Katz and Marilyn Chris as Mila.

Mila Lewinstein, Auschwitz survivor from Warsaw with the number 101682 tattooed on her left arm, had been in the camp for two years – since she was fifteen.[36] She learned to be a highly skilled poker player in the displaced persons camps after the War. Mila considered herself dead after Auschwitz and after losing her parents in the Treblinka extermination center; she was unable to resurrect herself after the trauma and became cynical about life. As a child, Mila was proficient at the piano, but after the Shoah, she claims that the music stopped for her. As the only surviving member of her family, Mila the orphan became adept at fending for herself. Shortly after her liberation, Mila had a son named Isaac out of wedlock with Keller Borowski, a Polish jeweler also interned in the camps. In 1947, Mila, who realized that communist Poland presented for her the same sort of dangers that the Nazis imposed, tried to flee the country. Mila understood that her emigration would be more difficult by traveling with her six-month-old son, so she abandoned him with Keller. However, before she left, she obtained the Nazis' imprinting machine that they used to mark the *Häftlinge* with tattoos, which had been earlier pilfered by Keller as his "reparation right" from the camp. Mila used the machine to imprint her Auschwitz number onto Isaac's arm, ostensibly so she could find him in later years. However, the numbers actually served as Mila's imprint on her son to remind him of her Holocaust past because Isaac eventually grew up believing that, as a result of his tattooed forearm, he survived Auschwitz as a child. Although Mila was hardened from life in the camp and rarely showed any empathy, she admits to feeling Holocaust guilt about abandoning her son and branding him for eternity.

Mila went to Germany, where she met Yankee Katz, a survivor of Bergen-Belsen. They married and immigrated to Miami, where Mila became ensconced in the Jewish Mafia. Mila was admired as a tough survivor, a card shark, and a smart gambler. Morty the Mohel, one of the mobsters, remembers Mila's tenacity: "The lady had balls – a real street fighter. Nothing scared her. And she knew something about odds. Knew when to bet – Knew when to fold."[37] Mila did not want another child, yet when she became pregnant, Yankee convinced her not to have an abortion.

Mila named her son Duncan – an unlikely Jewish name – so he could assimilate more easily. Duncan is raised in what Yael Danieli has called a "fighter family," where children of survivors are trained to mistrust authority and outsiders. Duncan becomes an object in this fighter family – trained solely to avenge Mila for her death-in-life and prevent a future Holocaust from occurring. Sheiness explained to me that Mila "taught Duncan vengeance, so that what happened to her could never happen to him."[38] Mila's favorite piano piece was "Someone to Watch Over Them," which ultimately becomes the epitaph on her gravestone. Mila raises Duncan as the family guardian, a protector, someone who would "watch over them." Mila admits that she never loved Duncan and refused to breast-feed him during infancy, telling her nurse Louise, "Duncan had to be strong. I didn't want him to need a mother" (56). Mila is an indurated survivor who understood that empathy in the concentration camp led to death. Therefore, she shows no empathy for Duncan and raises him to be stoical about life. In the novel *Second Hand Smoke*, Rosenbaum explains Mila's intentions for her child in the very first words that begin the book: "He was a child of trauma. Not of love, or happiness, or exceptional wealth. Just trauma. And nightmare, too."[39] Mila is determined to control her son and turn him into a robot whose purpose is to defend the family from outside threats; Duncan is an extreme version of a memorial candle with no identity of his own other than the one Mila has created for him.

As a child, Duncan was raised to withstand pain and to avoid being one of the victims, or what Mila refers to as "sissies." At Duncan's bris, Mila refuses to give her eight-day-old son a drop of wine to assuage the pain of circumcision, admitting to her Mafia cohorts, "I want him to feel it" (12). Mila disallows Duncan to have toys or play the violin, since she insists that those activities are for "sissies" (87). In her attempt to create a Jewish golem out of Duncan, Mila forces the child to do pushups, lift weights, and practice karate. Mila says to Duncan, "No more watching the Honeymooners. You'll end up like Jackie Gleason – fat and afraid of your boss at the bus company. Better you should watch Tarzan. (*She fills her lungs, pounds her chest and lets out the familiar Tarzan yell*)" (15). In contrast to the Jews who forcibly had their heads shaven in the camps, Mila keeps Duncan's hair long. She claims that by shaving the Jews' heads, the Nazis' goal was to remove them of their pride. Mila argues that long hair symbolizes strength to fight the Nazis, telling Louise, "All the strong men had long hair – Samson, Tarzan, Hercules –" (55). Beginning in junior high school, Mila insists that Duncan play football as a linebacker, a position in which he will "hunt the players down and smash them" (19). As a result of his physical training, Duncan becomes a muscular hulk designed to avenge victims from their persecutors.

However, in high school, Mila's creation shows signs of early breakdown. Duncan starts to have stomach problems, so Mila takes him to a physician. When the doctor wonders whether the source of Duncan's ailment could be stress in his family environment, Mila, like many survivors who refuse to accept psychological problems among their offspring, becomes defensive. She tells the doctor, "You're not a psychiatrist, and even if you were, you're out of your league. You'll never understand who we are and where we came from; so don't waste your time. Just find out what's wrong with his stomach and send me the bill!" (20). During his high school years, Duncan also leads student protestors against the Vietnam War. Duncan even chants, "Make love, not war!" (22). When Mila arrives, she puts an end to the protests, grabbing the bullhorn from the school principal and then forcing the adolescents back to class. She tells the protestors, "This country liberated the world over twenty-five years ago. To fight a dictator is an honor. Sometimes war is good – and necessary and right" (22).

Duncan weds a Methodist from North Carolina, and they have a daughter named Milan after one year of marriage. Upon graduation from law school, Duncan becomes a law professor (like Thane Rosenbaum) and then begins a new job prosecuting former Nazi war criminals for the Justice Department's Office of Special Investigations (OSI). To obtain the job, Duncan asserts to his future boss Bernard Ross, "I was built to prosecute Nazi war criminals, Mr. Ross. It's in my genes" (23). When Duncan is hired, he states, "Mr. Ross, you've just made Mila Katz a very happy holocaust survivor" (28). In short, Duncan, without his own individuality, places his joy at being hired in his mother's persona.

Duncan's mistrust of others coupled with his obsession in his role as a golem defending Jews from Nazis ruins his social life. At home, Duncan, like Mila, suffers from nightmares about Nazis torturing and tattooing Jews. Eventually, his wife Sharon realizes that she is living with her own Frankenstein experiment and asks for a separation since Duncan's obsession threatens to destroy the family and adversely affect their daughter Milan. Although Sharon confesses to loving her husband, she cannot perform psychotherapy on the black hole inside Duncan. She admits, "But this house is polluted with smoke imported from those German ovens. We need some air to breathe" (36). Sharon rightly points to Mila as the source of the family's dysfunction, telling Duncan, "It's not your fault. The war did it to your parents and your parents did it to you. It's a vicious cycle. It's unfair to everybody" (36). During this segment of the novel, Rosenbaum editorializes in a long statement that Sheiness saw no need to incorporate in the play as Duncan and Sharon discuss the reason for their impending divorce:

> It was as though Duncan and his kind had all somehow been resettled on Earth from Planet Auschwitz, a universe unknown to astronomers and beyond the sight of telescopes or NASA's curiosity. Often these children of survivors looked and acted very much like everyone else. But in their most private and desperate moments, their eyes would become vacant, their heads shaven, their skin reduced to mere bone wrappings, their cavities suddenly unfilled and goldless. They breathed in the rarefied, choking vapors of an atmosphere known only to their parents. What had killed the survivors had somehow become oxygen for their children.
>
> (82–3)

Moreover, Mila's creation has even made Duncan an inept Nazi chaser, causing him to lose his ideal position as an OSI Nazi prosecutor. Duncan has been relentless to implicate Feodor Malyshko, a former ruthless Ukrainian guard in the Maidanek extermination camp who is currently living in New York under the name of Fred Maloney. To get a confession out of Malyshko, Duncan enters his apartment disguised as a member of a neo-Nazi organization in Montana that he believes Malyshko would support in their mutual condemnation of the threat of worldwide Jewry. Maloney claims that he was not a Nazi but was at the time an unwilling Ukrainian servant of the SS in the concentration camp. The result of Duncan's harassment of Maloney is that he loses his job at OSI for entrapment, stalking, and illegally taping his conversation with Maloney. Because of his obsessive behavior, Duncan inadvertently, and ironically, allows the Butcher of Maidanek to escape prosecution.

Duncan's excessive automatonlike behavior as a Nazi vilifier and as a German demonizer (he even tears apart a parked Mercedes) earns him a celebrity reputation. To boost her television ratings, Molly Rubin, hostess for a once-popular talk show, invites Duncan to a television debate. Duncan, who now works as a college professor teaching courses on the Holocaust, enters unshaven and wearing a motorcycle jacket, forcing Molly to deem him "the Jewish Terminator" (41). Duncan's debate opponent is Arthur Schweigert, a young leader of the Aryan Militia who wears a neo-Nazi uniform. After listening to Arthur rant about how Duncan persecuted Maloney, an innocent man who committed no crimes because the Holocaust was nothing but a vicious lie propagated by Jewish vermin, Duncan refuses to debate. Instead, he reacts emotionally, stating, "Shut the fuck up, Arthur – you ignorant moron! Romper Room is now officially over. Isn't there any public education in Nebraska? Where are your parents anyway? Why can't you just join a 4-H Club or Young Farmers of America, you putz?" (44). Duncan, programmed for violence, then lifts the table over his head and throws it at the cameraman.

Duncan, realizing the harmful influence that his mother's survivor past had on him, then refused to see his mother for ten years. He returned to Miami when Larry Breitbart, his godfather, told him that Mila was dying of pancreatic cancer. At Mila's funeral, Duncan tries to explain to the congregation how his mother stole his identity and treated him as an object for her wishes to avenge her Holocaust past: "Okay – I ran away from home and never came back. But I don't owe any of you an explanation. That's between Mila and me. You don't know the half of it. Mila gave new meaning to the term child abuse. Actually, I think she invented it" (13). Duncan, like Debby in *The Model Apartment*, rebels against his parents for inculcating him with a Holocaust past. Unlike Debby, who reacts masochistically to take revenge on her parents, Duncan's rage is overt. However, he apparently feels that because Mila has suffered so much in her lifetime, he cannot revolt against her until she is dead. At the funeral, Duncan has a catharsis that reveals his pent-up violence, explaining to the mourners that Mila's death is his liberation:

> You don't know what it was like in my house! Look at me – I'm her creation. Her creature. And I don't like myself one bit. You feel loss? Well, I feel freedom. Liberated. Today is not about mourning . . . it's about celebration. No sitting shivah – not for me. I don't want to remember her at all. Mila can go straight to hell!

(14)

Yet before Mila's death, her guilt was so burdensome that she forced Larry to reveal to Duncan that he has an older half-brother who lives in Warsaw. Duncan finds the news to be astounding and tells his godfather, "Impossible. She would never abandon a child – torture a child, yes – but abandon one – never" (51).

Having lost his job, his wife, and now his mother, Duncan travels to Poland to find his brother, Isaac Borowski. Duncan is cautious about going to an anti-Semitic country, especially one that was the antecedent for his mother's paranoia. Upon Duncan's arrival, Isaac confirms that he is a respected yoga teacher and caretaker at the Jewish cemetery in Warsaw.[40] In the novel, Rosenbaum explained that Isaac became known to the Poles as a mystic and spiritual healer because they mistakenly believed that he was the only baby to have survived the camps and thus became holy like "A Christ child" (243). With his ability to see inside souls, Isaac immediately detects that Duncan is ". . . blocked. Nothing is flowing inside" (63). Duncan is worried that he will not find a suitable gym or a decent health-food store in Poland. Isaac tells him, "On the outside, little brother, you're an Adonis – but on the inside you're a car wreck" (75). As Alan Berger has noted, Isaac "is the antithesis of Duncan, both physically, temperamentally, and spiritually."[41] Duncan is muscular; Isaac is short and overweight. Duncan is acerbic; Isaac prefers calm meditation. Duncan is not religious; Isaac is a holy man.

Indeed, Duncan has come to Poland not only to find a brother, but also to make amends for what his parents had lost during the Holocaust. Duncan appears serious when he tells Isaac that he is determined to reclaim the synagogue in which his great-grandfather had been chief rabbi and then repossess the house Mila once lived in before she was deported. He also proposes a messianic rebuilding of Poland in a reverse Aliyah that will make it safe for Jews to once again live in Poland. Of course, Duncan's approach is through violence and rebellion – two emotional reactions that have molded his life. Isaac disagrees, telling his brother, "I don't live with demons. I choose to surrender my rage – to live a life with inner peace. Fists and anger are not the way" (71). Isaac implores Duncan to seek a spiritual life rather than to be imprisoned by fear or anger, which he insists are nothing but distractions.

As might be expected, Duncan's trip to Poland provides him with the opportunity to visit Auschwitz with his brother. During the visit to Birkenau, Duncan faints from the sight of the source of his nightmares; while unconscious, he has a hallucination in which he believes neo-Nazis have taken repossession of the camp. In this dream sequence, the neo-Nazis attack Duncan and Isaac, knock them unconscious, and then imprison them in the barracks. Duncan and Isaac wake up in prisoners' tunics with their heads shaved; in essence, Duncan reenacts Mila's concentration camp experience. Meinthaler, the leader of the group and reminiscent to Duncan of neo-Nazi Arthur Schweigert, claims that the two brothers are about to die. Meinthaler's death threat evokes what should have happened to Mila, the card shark, when he says to Isaac and Duncan, "This is a Nazi death camp and you are Jews. We are not playing poker here" (95). Duncan panics, but Isaac's reaction to the situation is one of calm tranquility. The hallucination became an epiphany for Duncan. Upon awakening, Duncan seemed to grasp the cause of his demons. His hallucination cements the idea that his physical abilities proved useless, and under extreme stress, he had to be comforted by his seemingly weak brother. Both siblings were marked for life by the curse of the Holocaust: Mila branded her tattooed numbers on Isaac's forearm while she turned Duncan into a golem protecting Jewish lives. The difference is that while both sons were offspring of Holocaust survivors, Mila's influence on Duncan was immediate and direct, in contrast to the indirect authority that she had over Isaac. As in typical "fighter families," Mila encouraged mistrust and aggression. Isaac, who was not under Mila's supervision, has achieved his own transcendent peace and lives a lifestyle that Duncan comes to view as advantageous, even under extreme stress when one is threatened by neo-Nazis.

Duncan argues that his doctor told him that he has abandonment anxiety. Isaac counters that Duncan can heal himself only by exorcising his mother's spirit and concomitantly his mother's influence on him. Isaac explains, "Mourn your mother, Duncan. Let her go. You never sat shiva for her; you walked away, carrying all the grief with you" (96). Duncan convinces Isaac to return to the United States to guide him through this spiritual transition.

When Duncan and Isaac arrive in Miami, Louise explains to them that Mila, on her deathbed, revealed how sorry she was for what she did to her sons. Out of love for Mila, Louise has been saying the *kaddish* for her. According to Jewish custom, a relative typically recites the prayer for the dead, but until now, Duncan has refused to partake in the *kaddish*. Isaac, whose name derives from the biblical tale in which he was to be sacrificed as Abraham's offering to God yet was spared by the Lord's graces, has been miraculously spared from Mila's tutelage. Like most children of Holocaust survivors, Isaac is a healer by profession. Mila ensured that Duncan would be a destroyer, not a healer. Isaac has healed his brother, exorcising the demons of an aggressive, violent man relentlessly searching for Nazis. In the denouement of the play, Duncan accepts advice from his new mentor, his brother, and embraces saying the *kaddish* for Mila. In essence, as Alan Berger has mentioned, Isaac promotes the healing power of proper mourning, not just for Mila, but also for the murder of the Jews during the Holocaust.[42] Moreover, the concept of the *kaddish* has particular resonance in the Jewish religion, which seems to indicate that Duncan is now willing to accept his role as a Jew rather than merely as a Holocaust victim. Duncan's last words, which are the final ones to be spoken in the play, reveal that he has now sought peace with himself, and thus, as a person once deprived by his mother of partaking in playing any musical instrument, he asks his brother, "Do you think I'm too old to learn the violin?" (108).

The two plays discussed in this chapter seem to imply that aggressive behavior among children of survivors is often destructive – whether it is internalized masochistically or expressed overtly through violence. The difference between Margulies and Rosenbaum is that the former accepts that the influence of the Holocaust on the parents is too burdensome to combat, while Rosenbaum is more sanguine. Rosenbaum's somewhat sugar-coated notion that offspring of survivors can begin to heal by accepting Judaism provides some hope for those who attempt to explain the Holocaust philosophically. However, such a religious approach to the Shoah seems to conflict with the results obtained by psychologists and psychotherapists that indicate that the transgenerational effects of the Holocaust are more profound than any faith-based solution can provide.

Notes

1 Harvey A. Barocas and Carol B. Barocas, "Separation-Individuation Conflicts in Children of Holocaust Survivors," *Journal of Contemporary Psychotherapy* 11, no. 1 (1980): 10.

2 Ilse Grubrich-Simitis, "Extreme Traumatization as Cumulative Trauma," *The Psychoanalytic Study of the Child* 36 (1981): 435–436.

3 Lisa Newman, "Emotional Disturbance in Children of Holocaust Survivors," *Social Casework: The Journal of Contemporary Social Work* 60, no. 1 (1979): 48.

4 Bernard Trossman, "Adolescent Children of Concentration Camp Survivors," *Canadian Psychiatric Association Journal* 13, no. 2 (1968): 122.

5 Ibid.

6 This study comprised nineteen adolescents whose parents lived as Jews in Nazi-occupied Europe for at least two years, and the mother spent at least six months in a concentration camp. The control group in this study consisted of nineteen young adults whose parents were born in prewar Poland but fled to Palestine before 1939. See Arie Nadler, Sophie Kav-Venaki, and Beny Gleitman, "Transgenerational Effects of the Holocaust: Externalization of Aggression in Second Generation of Holocaust Survivors," *Journal of Counseling and Clinical Psychology* 53, no. 3 (1985): 368.

7 A. Russell, "Late Psychosocial Consequences in Concentration Camp Survivor Families," *American Journal of Orthopsychiatry* 44, no. 4 (1974): 615.

8 See Harvey A. Barocas and Carol B. Barocas, "Manifestations of Concentration Camp Effects on the Second Generation," *American Journal of Psychiatry* 130, no. 7 (1973): 821.

9 Shamai Davidson, "The Clinical Effects of Massive Psychic Trauma in Families of Holocaust Survivors," *Journal of Marital and Family Therapy* 6 (1980): 15.

10 Martin S. Bergmann, "Recurrent Problems in the Treatment of Survivors and Their Children," in *Generations of the Holocaust*, eds. Martin S. Bergmann and Milton E. Jucovy (New York: Basic Books, 1982), 265.

11 Jack Nusan Porter, "Social-Psychological Aspects of the Holocaust," in *Encountering the Holocaust: An Interdisciplinary Survey*, eds. Byron L. Sherwin and Susan G. Ament (Chicago: Impact Press, 1979), 206.

12 Harvey A. Barocas and Carol B. Barocas, "Wounds of the Fathers: The Next Generation of Holocaust Victims," *International Review of Psycho-analysis* 6 (1979): 335. Howard B. Levine also noted masochistic traits among survivor children that were seen in several studies of this population. See Levine, "Toward a Psychoanalytic Understanding of Children of Survivors of the Holocaust," *Psychoanalytic Quarterly* 51 (1982): 76–77.

13 Erica Wanderman, "Children and Families of Holocaust Survivors: A Psychological Overview," in *Living After the Holocaust: Reflections by the Post-War Generation*, eds. Lucy Y. Steinitz and David M. Szonyi (New York: Bloch, 1976), 120.

14 For example, see Stephen M. Sonnenberg, "Workshop Report: Children of Survivors," *Journal of the American Psychoanalytic Association* 22 (1974): 202.

15 Martin S. Bergmann and Milton E. Jucovy, "Prelude," in *Generations of the Holocaust*, eds. Martin S. Bergmann and Milton E. Jucovy (New York: Basic Books, 1982), 20.

16 Barocas and Barocas, "Manifestations of Concentration Camp Effects on the Second Generation," 820.

17 Levine, "Toward a Psychoanalytic Understanding of Children of Survivors of the Holocaust," 87.

18 See Arnold Wilson and Erika Fromm, "Aftermath of the Concentration Camp: The Second Generation," *Journal of the American Academy of Psychoanalysis* 10, no. 2 (1982): 307.

19 See Harvey Peskin, Nanette C. Auerhahn, and Dori Laub, "The Second Holocaust: Therapeutic Rescue When Life Threatens," *Journal of Personal and Interpersonal Loss* 2 (1997): 18.

20 Davidson, "The Clinical Effects of Massive Psychic Trauma in Families of Holocaust Survivors," 15.

21 See Yael Danieli, "Families of Survivors of the Nazi Holocaust: Some Short- and Long-term Effects," in *Stress and Anxiety*, vol. 8, eds. Charles D. Spielberger and Irwin G. Sarason (New York: Hemisphere, 1982), 416; Yael Danieli, "Differing Adaptational Styles in Families of Survivors of the Nazi Holocaust," *Children Today* 10, no. 5 (1981): 10; and Yael Danieli, "The Treatment and Prevention of Long-term Effects and Intergenerational Transmission of Victimization: A Lesson From Holocaust Survivors and Their Children," in *Trauma and Its Wake: The Study and Treatment of Post-traumatic Stress Disorder*, ed. Charles R. Figley (New York: Brunner/Mazel, 1985), 302.

22 Danieli, "Families of Survivors of the Nazi Holocaust: Some Short- and Long-term Effects," 416; and Danieli, "Differing Adaptational Styles in Families of Survivors of the Nazi Holocaust," 10.

23 For a thorough biographical précis about Margulies, see William C. Boles, "Donald Margulies," in *Dictionary of Literary Biography, Vol. 228: Twentieth-Century American Dramatists*, ed. Christopher J. Wheatley (Detroit: Gale, 2000), 193–203.

24 Donald Margulies, email message to author, July 12, 2015.

25 Ibid.

26 Stephanie Coen, "Donald Margulies: In His Family Plots, Nothing's Funnier Than Despair," *American Theatre* (July–August 1994): 47.

27 Robert Skloot, ed., *The Theatre of the Holocaust*, vol. 2 (Madison: University of Wisconsin Press, 1999), 26–27.

28 Donald Margulies, "The Model Apartment," in *'Sight Unseen' and Other Plays* (New York: Theatre Communications Group, 1992), 148. All subsequent citations from the play are from this edition and will be included within parentheses in the text.

29 Janice Arkatov, "Playwright Explores Emotional Legacies," *Los Angeles Times* (November 11, 1988), sec. 6, 24.

30 Donald Margulies, email message to author, July 12, 2015.

31 Ibid.

32 Skloot, ed., *The Theatre of the Holocaust*, 27.

33 In her research on children of survivors, Shamai Davidson noted an example of how one female tried to bond with her suffering parents by identifying with Anne Frank and insisted that the family should change their surname to Frank. Davidson concludes that the child was symbolically trying to include herself in her parents' suffering. See Davidson, "The Clinical Effects of Massive Psychic Trauma in Families of Holocaust Survivors," 18. In contrast, Neil's ignorance of Anne Frank, and Debby's choice of him as her partner, reflects her attempt to *disassociate* herself from her parents' suffering.

34 Rosenbaum wrote, ". . . I focus on the looming dark shadow of the Holocaust as a continuing, implacable event, how it is inexorably still with us, flashing its radioactive teeth, keeping us all on our toes, imprinting our memories with symbols of, and metaphors for, mass death." See Rosenbaum, "Art and Atrocity in a Post-9/11 World," in *Jewish American and Holocaust Literature*, eds. Alan L. Berger and Gloria L. Cronin (Albany: State University of New York Press, 2004), 125.

35 Marsha Lee Sheiness, email message to author, July 22, 2015.

36 Jennifer M. Lemberg has noted that Mila's name evokes the famous street in the Warsaw Ghetto, which was memorialized in Leon Uris's *Mila 18*. That street has come to epitomize resistance against the Nazis, which is, of course, Mila's raison d'être. See Jennifer M. Lemberg, "'Unfinished Business': Journeys to Eastern Europe in Thane Rosenbaum's *Second Hand Smoke* and Jonathan Safran Foer's *Everything Is Illuminated*," in *Unfinalized Moments: Essays in the Development of Contemporary Jewish American Narrative*, ed. Derek Parker Royal (West Lafayette, IN: Purdue University Press, 2011), 82.

37 Marsha Lee Sheiness, *Second Hand Smoke*, 7, Photocopy. Holocaust Theater Archive. I am indebted to Arnold Mittelman, founder of the National Jewish Theater Foundation, for granting me permission to quote from this text photocopied from the Holocaust Theater Archive. All subsequent citations from the play are from this edition and will be included within parentheses in the text.
38 Marsha Lee Sheiness, email message to author, July 22, 2015.
39 Thane Rosenbaum, *Second Hand Smoke* (New York: St. Martin's Press, 1999), 1. All subsequent citations from the novel are from this edition and will be included within parentheses in the text.
40 Andrew Furman has astutely noted that Rosenbaum's novel occurs in Miami Beach, New York, and Warsaw, which are three central milieus of the Jewish diaspora. See Furman, *Contemporary Jewish American Writers and the Multicultural Dilemma: The Return of the Exiled* (Syracuse: Syracuse University Press, 2000), 79.
41 Alan Berger, "Mourning, Rage and Redemption: Representing the Holocaust: The Work of Thane Rosenbaum," *Studies in American Jewish Literature* 19 (2000): 10.
42 Ibid., 12.

CODA

Once the Nazi plan for the genocide of European Jewry went awry, the world was left with skeletons who had to remake themselves physically, culturally, and psychologically. Many of the ailments would remain forever, but competent physicians could relieve patients of some bodily disorders. As a result of their ability to adapt to the most horrendous conditions imaginable during the Shoah, survivors often could *cope* with their new cultures. Healing themselves psychologically was much more difficult. Unlike typical trauma that is associated with a brief, yet palpably defining moment, Holocaust trauma occurred over several years. The victims survived via psychic numbing, thus removing themselves from all vestiges of empathy, ultimately becoming hollow spectres of their former selves. Coupled with loss and guilt endemic to the Holocaust experience, survivors were typically condemned to a life plagued by paranoia, anxiety, depression, and irritability. In particular, deeply embedded guilt about having acted like a nonhuman in order to survive the brutality of the camps made recovery to a civilized state of existence highly improbable. Moreover, since the trauma was never fully assimilated at the time of occurrence, it appeared in a latency stage, typically in dreams and in waking hours when certain stimuli activated what the brain was trying to repress. Finally, survivors who endured the traumata while they were children or adolescents faced loss during their formative years, thus forcing themselves to accept the reality of a life of lost opportunities.

With their early years having been stolen from them, survivors live those lost years vicariously through their children. The offspring of survivors become objects that exist primarily as memorial candles for their parents. These children are encouraged to overachieve and become successful, thus replacing lost loved ones that had no opportunity to achieve under Nazi reign. However, the parents, having had to surrender empathy and become emotionally detached during the Holocaust in order to survive, typically engage in a futile attempt to regain an affective persona in order to raise their children. Inculcated with mistrust of others and guilt about the suffering of their parents, children of survivors often became depressed and paranoid. The children, faced with such a legacy of parental emotional baggage, subliminally try to heal or protect the parents. This immense burden endemic to offspring of survivors ultimately retards their individual growth, inhibiting them from developing an identity of their own. There have been instances in which adolescents rebelled against the standards imposed on them. However, being unwilling to inflict pain on their parents who have suffered through no fault of their own, the children, instead of reacting directly against their parents, may internalize the aggression or overtly rage against their parents' Nazi persecutors.

This study can be problematic for Jewish scholars who want to find something of value in the Holocaust. In this manuscript, the psychopathology of survivors is associated with long-term negative effects; in truth, there is little that is positive about the study of the effects of the genocide on survivors. Holocaust survivors themselves might also find the results disturbing. Survivors endured the worst hardships known to humanity, so they do not necessarily consider themselves to be psychologically impaired. However, the studies of survivors that are cited in this manuscript were conducted by psychologists with Ph.D. degrees or psychiatrists with medical degrees; their findings were reported in the most distinguished journals in the field of psychology and psychiatry. Survivors would have difficulty refuting the findings. We must keep in mind that many survivors who were "liberated" in 1945 perished years later from the terrible burden of living daily with deteriorated bodies; others committed suicide. Scientists and social scientists never had the opportunity to interview them, but their tales would have corroborated the devastating extent of the traumata documented by psychologists who conducted their experiments. Finally, laymen, such as theater critics and literary scholars, who dispute such findings, arguing that depression, paranoia, anxiety, and other neuroses are endemic to modern society, are being disingenuous about the deeply rooted effects of the genocide. To make such an argument is actually insulting to many survivors.

During the twenty-first century, all Holocaust survivors and their offspring will die, and thus their first-hand accounts of the trauma will die with them. Of course, historical records can provide statistics about the traumatized victims, and published results of research conducted by psychologists and psychiatrists will document the effects of the trauma. However, statistics and data accrued from psychoanalytical studies cannot always fully convey the emotional impact of the trauma among survivors and their offspring. Theater, which is a visual art, can relate to audiences in a way that fiction or poetry cannot and can potentially reach more people worldwide than other literary forms. Holocaust drama can be an effective learning tool, thereby introducing the traumatic effects of the Shoah to audiences that might mistrust statistics or may not be conducive to reading texts or research essays that often appear inaccessible to laymen. Moreover, theater affects us emotionally in a direct way that other art forms cannot match. In short, theater can function as one of the most effective means of visually and viscerally conveying the long-term psychological effects of what happens when humans have survived extreme traumata.

BIBLIOGRAPHY

Abramson, Glenda. "Anglicizing the Holocaust." *Journal of Theatre and Drama* 7/8 (2001–2002): 105–23.

———. *The Writing of Yehuda Amichai: A Thematic Approach.* Albany: State University of New York Press, 1989.

Alexander, Jeffrey C. "Toward a Theory of Cultural Trauma." In *Cultural Trauma and Collective Identity*, edited by Jeffrey C. Alexander et al., 1–30. Berkeley: University of California Press, 2004.

American Psychiatric Association. *Diagnostic and Statistical Manual of Mental Disorders*, 4th ed. Washington, DC: American Psychiatric Association, 1994.

Amichai, Yehuda. "*Bells and Trains*". Translated by Aubrey Hodes. *Midstream: A Monthly Jewish Review* 12, no. 8 (1966): 55–66.

Antonovsky, A., et al. "Twenty-Five Years Later: A Limited Study of the Sequelae of the Concentration Camp Experience." *Social Psychiatry* 6, no. 4 (1971): 186–93.

Appelfeld, Aharon. "The Awakening." Translated by Jeffrey M. Green. In *Holocaust Remembrance: The Shapes of Memory*, edited by Geoffrey H. Hartman, 148–52. Oxford: Blackwell, 1994.

Arendt, Hannah. *Eichmann in Jerusalem.* New York: Viking Press, 1964.

Arkatov, Janice. "Playwright Explores Emotional Legacies." *Los Angeles Times*, November 11, 1988, Sec. 6, 24.

Atkins, Richard. *DelikateSSen.* Sandia Park, NM: Photocopy, 2013.

Auerhan, Nanette C., and Dori Laub. "Play and Playfulness in Holocaust Survivors." *Psychoanalytic Study of the Child* 42 (1987): 45–58.

Auerhahn, Nanette C., Dori Laub, and Harvey Peskin. "Psychotherapy With Holocaust Survivors." *Psychotherapy: Theory, Research & Practice* 30, no. 3 (1993): 434–42.

Auerhahn, Nanette C., and Ernst Prelinger. "Repetition in the Concentration Camp Survivor and Her Child." *International Review of Psycho-Analysis* 10, no. 31 (1983): 31–46.

Barocas, Harvey A. "Children of Purgatory: Reflections on the Concentration Camp Survival Syndrome." *International Journal of Social Psychiatry* 21, no. 1 (1975–1976): 87–92.

Barocas, Harvey A., and Carol B. Barocas. "Manifestations of Concentration Camp Effects on the Second Generation." *American Journal of Psychiatry* 130, no. 7 (1973): 820–1.

———. "Separation-Individuation Conflicts in Children of Holocaust Survivors." *Journal of Contemporary Psychotherapy* 11, no. 1 (1980): 6–14.

————. "Wounds of the Fathers: The Next Generation of Holocaust Victims." *International Review of Psycho-Analysis* 6 (1979): 331–41.

Bar-On, Dan et al. "Multigenerational Perspectives on Coping With the Holocaust Experience: An Attachment Perspective for Understanding the Developmental Sequelae of Trauma Across Generations." *International Journal of Behavioral Development* 22, no. 2 (1998): 315–38.

Behlau, Ulrike. "Remembering the Holocaust in British-Jewish Drama of the 1990s: Diane Samuels, Julia Pascal, and Harold Pinter." In *Staging Displacement, Exile and Diaspora*, edited by Christoph Houswitschka and Anja Müller, 193–210. Trier: Wissenschaftlicher Verlag, 2005.

Benner, Patricia, Ethel Roskies, and Richard S. Lazarus. "Stress and Coping Under Extreme Conditions." In *Survivors, Victims, and Perpetrators: Essays on the Nazi Holocaust*, edited by Joel E. Dimsdale, 219–58. Washington, DC: Hemisphere, 1980.

Berger, Alan. "Mourning, Rage and Redemption: Representing the Holocaust: The Work of Thane Rosenbaum." *Studies in American Jewish Literature* 19 (2000): 6–15.

Bergmann, Martin S. "Recurrent Problems in the Treatment of Survivors and Their Children." In *Generations of the Holocaust*, edited by Martin S. Bergmann and Milton E. Jucovy, 247–66. New York: Basic Books, 1982.

Bergmann, Martin S., and Milton E. Jucovy, eds. *Generations of the Holocaust*. New York: Basic Books, 1982.

Bettelheim, Bruno. *The Informed Heart*. Glencoe, IL: Free Press, 1960.

————. *Surviving and Other Essays*. New York: Alfred A. Knopf, 1979.

Boles, William C. "Donald Margulies." In *Dictionary of Literary Biography. Vol. 228: Twentieth-Century American Dramatists*. Second series, edited by Christopher J. Wheatley, 193–203. Detroit: Gale, 2000.

Braham, Randolph L., ed. *The Psychological Perspectives of the Holocaust and of Its Aftermath*. New York: Columbia University Press, 1988.

Caisley, Robert. *Letters to an Alien*. Woodstock, IL: Dramatic Publishing, 1996.

Caruth, Cathy. *Listening to Trauma: Conversations With Leaders in the Theory and Treatment of Catastrophic Experience*. Baltimore: Johns Hopkins University Press, 2014.

————, ed. *Trauma: Explorations in Memory*. Baltimore and London: Johns Hopkins University Press, 1995.

————. *Unclaimed Experience: Trauma, Narrative, History*. Baltimore and London: Johns Hopkins University Press, 1996.

Chodoff, Paul. "Depression and Guilt Among Concentration Camp Survivors." *International Forum for Existential Psychiatry* 7 (1970): 19–26.

————. "The German Concentration Camp as a Psychological Stress." *Archives of General Psychiatry* 22, no. 1 (1970): 78–87.

————. "Late Effects of the Concentration Camp Syndrome." *Archives of General Psychiatry* 8, no. 4 (1963): 323–33.

————. "Psychiatric Aspects of the Nazi Persecution." In *American Handbook of Psychiatry, New Psychiatric Frontiers*, 2nd ed., vol. 6, edited by David A. Hamburg and Keith H. Brodie, 932–46. New York: Basic Books, 1975.

Coen, Stephanie. "Donald Margulies." *American Theatre*, July/August 1994, 46–7.

Cohen, Elie A. *Human Behavior in the Concentration Camp*. Translated by M.H. Braaksma. New York: W.W. Norton, 1953.

Cormann, Enzo. *The Never-ending Storm*. Translated by Guila Clara Kessous. n.p. Photocopy. Holocaust Theater Archive.

Dagan, Gabriel. "The Reunion." *Midstream: A Monthly Jewish Review* 19, no. 4 (1973): 3–32.

Danieli, Yael. "Differing Adaptational Styles in Families of Survivors of the Nazi Holocaust." *Children Today* 10, no. 5 (1981): 6–10, 34–5.

———. "Families of Survivors of the Nazi Holocaust." In *Stress and Anxiety*, vol. 8, edited by Charles D. Spielberger and Irwin G. Sarason, 405–21. Washington and New York: Hemisphere, 1982.

———. "The Treatment and Prevention of Long-Term Effects and Intergenerational Transmission of Victimization: A Lesson From Holocaust Survivors and Their Children." In *Trauma and Its Wake: The Study and Treatment of Post-traumatic Stress Disorder*, edited by Charles R. Figley, 295–313. New York: Brunner/Mazel, 1985.

Davidson, Shamai. "The Clinical Effects of Massive Psychic Trauma in Families of Holocaust Survivors." *Journal of Marital and Family Therapy* 6 (1980): 11–21.

de Graaf, Theo. "Pathological Patterns of Identification in Families of Survivors of the Holocaust." *Israel Annals of Psychiatry and Related Disciplines* 13 (1975): 335–63.

Delbo, Charlotte. *Auschwitz and After*. Translated by Rosette C. Lamont. New Haven and London: Yale University Press, 1995.

Des Pres, Terrence. *The Survivor: An Anatomy of Life in the Death Camps*. New York: Oxford University Press, 1976.

Dimsdale, Joel. "The Coping Behavior of Nazi Concentration Camp Survivors." *American Journal of Psychiatry* 131, no. 7 (1974): 792–7.

———, ed. *Survivors, Victims, and Perpetrators: Essays on the Nazi Holocaust*. Washington, DC: Hemisphere, 1980.

Dinnerstein, Leonard. "Displaced Persons, Jewish." In *Encyclopedia of the Holocaust*, vol. 1, edited by Israel Gutman, 377–90. New York: Macmillan, 1990.

Dor-Shav, Netta Kohn. "On the Long-Range Effects of Concentration Camp Internment on Nazi Victims: 25 Years Later." *Journal of Counseling and Clinical Psychology* 46, no. 1 (1978): 1–11.

Eaton, William W., John J. Sigal, and Morton Weinfeld. "Impairment in Holocaust Survivors After 33 Years: Data From an Unbiased Community Sample." *American Journal of Psychiatry* 139, no. 6 (1982): 773–7.

Eitinger, Leo. "Auschwitz – A Psychological Perspective." In *Anatomy of the Auschwitz Death Camp*, edited by Yisrael Gutman and Michael Berenbaum, 469–82. Bloomington and Indianapolis: Indiana University Press, 1994.

———. *Concentration Camp Survivors in Norway and Israel*. London: Allen & Unwin, 1964.

———. "Concentration Camp Survivors in the Postwar World." *American Journal of Orthopsychiatry* 32, no. 3 (1962): 367–75.

———. "The Concentration Camp Syndrome: An Organic Brain Syndrome?" *Integrative Psychiatry* 3 (1985): 115–19.

———. "The Concentration Camp Syndrome and Its Late Sequelae." In *Survivors, Victims, and Perpetrators: Essays on the Nazi Holocaust*, edited by Joel E. Dimsdale, 127–62. Washington, DC: Hemisphere, 1980.

———. "Denial in Concentration Camps: Some Personal Observations on the Positive and Negative Functions of Denial in Extreme Life Situations." In *The Denial of Stress*, edited by Shlomo Breznitz, 199–212. New York: International Universities Press, 1983.

———. "Jewish Concentration Camp Survivors in the Post-War World." *Danish Medical Bulletin* 27 (1980): 232–5.

———. "Pathology of the Concentration Camp Syndrome." *Archives of General Psychiatry* 5, no. 4 (1961): 371–9.

Elisha, Ron. *Two*. Sydney: Currency Press, 1985.

Epstein, Helen. *Children of the Holocaust: Conversations With Sons and Daughters of Survivors*. New York: G.P. Putnam's Sons, 1979.

Farrell, Kirby. *Post-Traumatic Culture: Injury and Interpretation in the Nineties*. Baltimore and London: Johns Hopkins University Press, 1998.

Fenig, Shmuel and Itzhak Levav. "Demoralization and Social Supports Among Holocaust Survivors." *Journal of Nervous and Mental Disease* 179, no. 3 (1991): 167–72.

Flannery, Peter. *Singer*. London: Nick Hern, 1992.

Fogelman, Eva and Flora Hogman. "A Follow-up Study: Child Survivors of the Nazi Holocaust Reflect on Being Interviewed." In *Children During the Nazi Reign: Psychological Perspectives on the Interview Process*, edited by Judith Kestenberg and Eva Fogelman, 73–80. Westport, CT: Praeger, 1994.

Frankl, Viktor E. *Man's Search for Meaning*. New York: Simon & Schuster, 1984.

Freed, Morris. *The Survivors: Six One-act Dramas*. Translated by A.D. Mankoff. Cambridge: Sci-Art Publishers, 1956.

Freud, Sigmund. *Mourning and Melancholia*. Translated by Joan Riviere. In *Collected Papers*, vol. 4. New York: Basic Books, 1959.

———. *The Standard Edition of the Complete Psychological Works of Sigmund Freud*, vol. 2. Edited and translated by James Strachey. London: Hogarth Press, 1955.

———. *The Standard Edition of the Complete Psychological Works of Sigmund Freud*, vol. 18. Edited and translated by James Strachey. London: Hogarth Press, 1955.

———. *The Standard Edition of the Complete Psychological Works of Sigmund Freud*, vol. 20. Edited and translated by James Strachey. London: Hogarth Press, 1959.

Friedlander, Henry and Sybil Milton. "Surviving." In *Genocide: Critical Issues of the Holocaust*, edited by Alex Grobman and Daniel Landes, 233–5. Los Angeles: Simon Wiesenthal Center, 1983.

Friedlander, Saul. *Memory, History, and the Extermination of the Jews of Europe*. Bloomington and Indianapolis: Indiana University Press, 1993.

Friedman, Paul. "Some Aspects of Concentration Camp Psychology." *American Journal of Psychiatry* 105, no. 8 (1949): 601–5.

Furman, Andrew. *Contemporary Jewish American Writers and the Multicultural Dilemma: The Return of the Exiled*. Syracuse: Syracuse University Press, 2000.

Furman, Erna. "The Impact of the Nazi Concentration Camps on the Children of Survivors." In *The Child in His Family: The Impact of Disease and Death*, vol. 2, edited by E. James Anthony and Cyrille Koupernik, 379–84. New York: John Wiley, 1973.

Gershon, Karen, ed. *We Came as Children: A Collective Autobiography*. New York: Harcourt, Brace & World, 1966.

Goldenberg, Jennifer. "The Hows and Whys of Survival: Causal Attributions and the Search for Meaning." In *Transcending Trauma: Survival, Resilience, and Clinical Implications in Survivor Families*, edited by Bea Hollander-Goldfein, Nancy Isserman, and Jennifer Goldenberg, 85–109. New York and London: Routledge, 2012.

Goldenberg, Jennifer, Nancy Isserman, and Bea Hollander-Goldfein. "Introduction: The Transcending Trauma Project." In *Transcending Trauma: Survival, Resilience, and Clinical Implications in Survivor Families*, edited by Bea Hollander-Goldfein, Nancy Isserman, and Jennifer Goldenberg, 3–12. New York and London: Routledge, 2012.

Goldfarb, Alvin. "Inadequate Memories: The Survivor in Plays by Mann, Kesselman, Lebow, and Baitz." In *Staging the Holocaust: The Shoah in Drama and Performance*, edited by Claude Schumacher, 111–29. Cambridge: Cambridge University Press, 1998.

Goldhagen, Daniel Jonah. *Hitler's Willing Executioners: Ordinary Germans and the Holocaust*. New York: Alfred A. Knopf, 1996.

Graf, Wendy. *Leipzig*. n.p. Photocopy. Holocaust Theater Archives.

Grauer, H. "Psychodynamics of the Survivor Syndrome." *Canadian Psychiatric Association Journal* 14, no. 6 (1969): 617–22.

Greenhalgh, Susanne. "Stages of Memory: Imagining Identities in the Holocaust Drama of Deborah Levy, Julia Pascal, and Diane Samuels." In *'In the Open': Jewish Women Writers and British Culture*, edited by Claire M. Tylee, 210–28. Newark: University of Delaware Press, 2006.

Grobin, W. "Medical Assessment of Late Effects of National Socialist Persecution." *Canadian Medical Association Journal* 92, no. 17 (1965): 911–17.

Grubrich-Simitis, Ilse. "Extreme Traumatization as Cumulative Trauma." *The Psychoanalytic Study of the Child* 36 (1981): 415–50.

Harel, Zev, Boaz Kahana, and Eva Kahana. "Psychological Well-Being Among Holocaust Survivors and Immigrants in Israel." *Journal of Traumatic Stress* 1, no. 4 (1988): 413–29.

Harvey, John H. *Perspectives on Loss and Trauma: Assaults on the Self.* Thousand Oaks, CA: Sage Publications, 2002.

Hartman, Geoffrey, ed. *Holocaust Remembrance: The Shapes of Memory.* Oxford: Blackwell, 1994.

Hass, Aaron. *The Aftermath: Living With the Holocaust.* Cambridge: Cambridge University Press, 1995.

Helmreich, William B. *Against All Odds: Survivors and the Successful Lives They Made in America.* New Brunswick: Transaction Publishers, 1996.

Herman, Judith Lewis. *Trauma and Recovery.* New York: Basic Books, 1992.

Hollander-Goldfein, Bea, Nancy Isserman, and Jennifer Goldenberg, eds. *Transcending Trauma: Survival, Resilience, and Clinical Implications in Survivor Families.* New York and London: Routledge, 2012.

Hoppe, Klaus. "The Aftermath of Nazi Persecution Reflected in Recent Psychiatric Literature." *International Psychiatry Clinics* 8, no. 1 (1971): 169–204.

———. "The Psychodynamics of Concentration Camp Victims." *Psychoanalytic Forum* 1, no. 1 (1966): 76–85.

———. "Re-Somatization of Affects in Survivors of Persecution." *International Journal of Psycho-Analysis* 49, parts 2–3 (1968): 324–6.

Isser, Edward R. *Stages of Annihilation: Theatrical Representations of the Holocaust.* Madison, NJ: Fairleigh Dickinson University Press, 1997.

Jaffe, Ruth. "Dissociative Phenomena in Former Concentration Camp Inmates." *International Journal of Psycho-Analysis* 49, parts 2–3 (1968): 310–12.

Jucovy, Milton E. "The Effects of the Holocaust on the Second Generation: Psychoanalytic Studies." *American Journal of Social Psychiatry* 30, no. 1 (1983): 15–20.

Kahana, Boaz, Zev Harel, and Eva Kahana. "Predictors of Psychological Well-Being Among Survivors of the Holocaust." In *Human Adaptation to Extreme Stress: From the Holocaust to Vietnam,* edited by John P. Wilson, Zev Harel, and Boaz Kahana, 171–92. New York and London: Plenum Press, 1988.

Kestenberg, Judith. "Child Survivors of the Holocaust – 40 Years Later: Reflections and Commentary." *Journal of the American Academy of Child Psychiatry* 24, no. 4 (1985): 408–12.

———. "Overview of the Effects of Psychological Interviews on Child Survivors." In *Children During the Nazi Reign: Psychological Perspectives on the Interview Process,* edited by Judith Kestenberg and Eva Fogelman, 3–33. Westport, CT: Praeger, 1994.

———. "Psychoanalyses of Children of Survivors From the Holocaust: Case Presentations and Assessment." *Journal of the American Psychoanalytic Association* 28 (1980): 775–804.

———. "Psychoanalytic Contributions to the Problem of Children of Survivors From Nazi Persecution." *Israel Annals of Psychiatry and Related Disciplines* 10, no. 4 (1972): 311–25.

———. "Survivor-Parents and Their Children." In *Generations of the Holocaust,* edited by Martin S. Bergmann and Milton E. Jucovy, 83–102. New York: Basic Books, 1982.

Kestenberg, Judith and Eva Fogelman, eds. *Children During the Nazi Reign: Psychological Perspectives on the Interview Process.* Westport, CT: Praeger, 1994.

Kestenberg, Judith S., and Milton Kestenberg. "The Experience of Survivor-Parents." In *Generations of the Holocaust,* edited by Martin S. Bergmann and Milton E. Jucovy, 46–61. New York: Basic Books, 1982.

————. "Psychoanalyses of Children of Survivors From the Nazi Persecution: The Continuing Struggle of Survivor Parents." *Victimology: An International Journal* 5, no. 2–4 (1980): 368–73.

Kestenberg, Milton. "Discriminatory Aspects of the German Indemnification Policy: A Continuation of Persecution." In *Generations of the Holocaust*, edited by Martin S. Bergmann and Milton E. Jucovy, 62–79. New York: Basic Books, 1982.

————. "The Effects of Interviews on Child Survivors." In *Children During the Nazi Reign: Psychological Perspectives on the Interview Process*, edited by Judith Kestenberg and Eva Fogelman, 57–71. Westport, CT: Praeger, 1994.

Kestenberg, Milton and Judith S. Kestenberg. "The Sense of Belonging and Altruism in Children Who Survived the Holocaust." *Psychoanalytic Review* 75, no. 4 (1988): 533–60.

Kleber, Rolf J., and Danny Brom. *Coping With Trauma: Theory, Prevention and Treatment.* Amsterdam: Swets & Zeitlinger, 1992.

Klein, Hillel. "Children of the Holocaust: Mourning and Bereavement." In *The Child in His Family: The Impact of Disease and Death*, vol. 2, edited by E. James Anthony and Cyrille Koupernik, 393–409. New York: John Wiley, 1973.

————. "Child Victims of the Holocaust." *Journal of Clinical Child and Adolescent Psychology* 2 (1974): 44–7.

Klein, Hillel, Julius Zellermayer, and Joel Shanan. "Former Concentration Camp Inmates on a Psychiatric Ward." *Archives of General Psychiatry* 8, no. 4 (1963): 334–42.

Klein-Parker, Fran. "Dominant Attitudes of Adult Children of Holocaust Survivors Toward Their Parents." In *Human Adaptation to Extreme Stress: From the Holocaust to Vietnam*, edited by John P. Wilson, Zev Harel, and Boaz Kahana, 193–218. New York and London: Plenum Press, 1988.

Koenig, Werner. "Chronic or Persisting Identity Diffusion." *American Journal of Psychiatry* 120, no. 11 (1964): 1081–4.

Kogon, Eugen. *The Theory and Practice of Hell: The German Concentration Camps and the System Behind Them.* Translated by Heinz Norden. New York: Farrar, Straus and Giroux, 2006.

Koranyi, Erwin K. "Psychodynamic Theories of the 'Survivor Syndrome'." *Canadian Psychiatric Journal* 14 (April 1969): 165–74.

Krell, Robert. "Aspects of Psychological Trauma in Holocaust Survivors and Their Children." In *Genocide: Critical Issues of the Holocaust*, edited by Alex Grobman and Daniel Landes, 371–80. Los Angeles: Simon Wiesenthal Center, 1983.

————. "Child Survivors of the Holocaust: 40 Years Later." *Journal of the American Academy of Child Psychiatry* 24, no. 4 (1985): 378–80.

————. "Child Survivors of the Holocaust – Strategies of Adaptation." *Canadian Journal of Psychiatry* 38 (August 1993): 384–9.

————. "Holocaust Families: The Survivors and Their Children." *Comprehensive Psychiatry* 20 (1979): 560–8.

Krystal, Henry, ed. *Massive Psychic Trauma.* New York: International Universities Press, 1968.

————. "Trauma and Aging: A Thirty-Year Follow-Up." In *Trauma: Explorations in Memory*, edited by Cathy Caruth, 76–99. Baltimore and London: Johns Hopkins University Press, 1995.

Krystal, Henry and Yael Danieli. "Holocaust Survivor Studies in the Context of PTSD." *PTSD Research Quarterly* 5, no. 1 (1994): 1–5.

Kuch, Klaus and Brian J. Cox. "Symptoms of PTSD in 124 Survivors of the Holocaust." *American Journal of Psychiatry* 149, no. 3 (1992): 337–40.

LaCapra, Dominick. *History, Theory, Trauma: Representing the Holocaust.* Ithaca and London: Cornell University Press, 1994.

Lang, Berel, ed. *Writing and the Holocaust.* New York and London: Holmes & Meier, 1988.

Langer, Lawrence L. *The Holocaust and the Literary Imagination.* New Haven and London: Yale University Press, 1975.

———. *Holocaust Testimonies: The Ruins of Memory.* New Haven and London: Yale University Press, 1991.

———. *Versions of Survival: The Holocaust and the Human Spirit.* Albany: State University of New York Press, 1982.

Laub, Dori and Nanette C. Auerhahn. "Failed Empathy – A Central Theme in the Survivor's Holocaust Experience." *Psychoanalytic Psychology* 6, no. 4 (1989): 377–400.

Lavsky, Hagit. "Displaced Persons, Jewish." In *Encyclopedia of the Holocaust*, vol. 1, edited by Israel Gutman, 377–84. New York: Macmillan, 1990.

Lederer, Wolfgang. "Persecution and Compensation: Theoretical and Practical Implications of the 'Persecution Syndrome'." *Archives of General Psychiatry* 12, no. 4 (1965): 464–74.

Lemberg, Jennifer M. "'Unfinished Business': Journeys to Eastern Europe in Thane Rosenbaum's *Second Hand Smoke* and Jonathan Safran Foer's *Everything Is Illuminated.*" In *Unfinalized Moments: Essays in the Development of Contemporary Jewish American Narrative*, edited by Derek Parker Royal, 81–94. West Lafayette, IN: Purdue University Press, 2011.

Lengyel, Olga. *Five Chimneys: The Story of Auschwitz.* Chicago and New York: Ziff-Davis, 1947.

Leon, Gloria R., et al. "Survivors of the Holocaust and Their Children: Current Status and Adjustment." *Journal of Personality and Social Psychology* 41, no. 3 (1981): 503–16.

Leverton, Bertha and Shmuel Lowensohn, eds. *I Came Alone: The Stories of the Kindertransports.* Sussex, UK: The Book Guild, 1990.

Levi, Primo. *The Drowned and the Saved.* Translated by Raymond Rosenthal. New York: Summit Books, 1986.

Levine, Howard B. "Toward a Psychoanalytic Understanding of Children of Survivors of the Holocaust." *Psychoanalytic Quarterly* 51, no. 1 (1982): 70–92.

Lev-Wiesel, Rachel and Marianne Amir. "Growing Out of the Ashes: Posttraumatic Growth Among Holocaust Child Survivors – Is It Possible?" In *Handbook of Posttraumatic Growth: Research and Practice*, edited by Lawrence G. Calhoun and Richard G. Tedeschi, 248–63. Mahwah, NJ: Lawrence Erlbaum, 2006.

Lichtman, Helen. "Parental Communication of Holocaust Experiences and Personality Characteristics Among Second-Generation Survivors." *Journal of Clinical Psychology* 40, no. 4 (1984): 914–24.

———. "Posttraumatic Stress Disorder Symptoms, Psychological Distress, Personal Resources, and Quality of Life in Four Groups of Holocaust Child Survivors." *Family Process* 39, no. 4 (2000): 445–59.

Lifton, Robert Jay. *The Broken Connection: On Death and the Continuity of Life.* New York: Simon and Schuster, 1979.

———. "Understanding the Traumatized Self: Imagery, Symbolization, and Transformation." In *Human Adaptation to Extreme Stress: From the Holocaust to Vietnam*, edited by John P. Wilson, Zev Harel, and Boaz Kahana, 7–31. New York and London: Plenum Press, 1988.

Lingens-Reiner, Ella. *Prisoners of Fear.* London: Victor Gollancz, 1948.

Linney, Romulus. "Donald Margulies." *BOMB* 80 (Summer 2002): 68–73.

Llewellyn-Jones, Margaret. "Peter Flannery." In *British and Irish Dramatists Since World War II*, edited by John Bull, 120–27. Detroit: Gale Group, 2001.

Luchterhand, Elmer. "Early and Late Effects of Imprisonment in Nazi Concentration Camps." *Social Psychiatry* 5, no. 1 (1970): 102–10.

———. "Prisoner Behavior and Social System in the Nazi Concentration Camps." *International Journal of Social Psychiatry* 13, no. 4 (1967): 245–64.

Margulies, Donald. "Afterword." In *"Sight Unseen" and Other Plays*, 337–42. New York: Theatre Communications Group, 1992.

———. *"The Model Apartment."* In *"Sight Unseen" and Other Plays*, 141–95. New York: Theatre Communications Group, 1992.

Matussek, Paul. *Internment in Concentration Camps and Its Consequences*. New York: Springer-Verlag, 1975.

Mazor, A., et al. "Holocaust Survivors: Coping With Post-Traumatic Memories in Childhood and 40 Years Later." *Journal of Traumatic Stress* 3, no. 1 (1990): 1–14.

Meerloo, Joost A.M. "Neurologism and Denial in Psychic Trauma in Extermination Camp Survivors." *American Journal of Psychiatry* 120, no. 1 (1963): 65–6.

Moskovitz, Sarah. *Love Despite Hate: Child Survivors of the Holocaust and Their Adult Lives*. New York: Schocken Books, 1983.

Moskovitz, Sarah and Robert Krell. "Child Survivors of the Holocaust: Psychological Adaptations of Survival." *Israel Journal of Psychiatry and Related Disciplines* 27, no. 2 (1990): 81–91.

Nadler, Arie and Dan Ben-Shushan. "Forty Years Later: Long-Term Consequences of Massive Traumatization as Manifested by Holocaust Survivors From the City and the Kibbutz." *Journal of Counseling and Clinical Psychology* 57, no. 2 (1989): 287–93.

Nadler, Arie, Sophie Kav-Venaki, and Beny Gleitman. "Transgenerational Effects of the Holocaust: Externalization of Aggression in Second Generation of Holocaust Survivors." *Journal of Counseling and Clinical Psychology* 53, no. 3 (1985): 365–9.

Nathan, T.S., L. Eitinger, and H.Z. Winnik. "A Psychiatric Study of Survivors of the Nazi Holocaust: A Study in Hospitalized Patients." *Israel Annals of Psychiatry and Related Disciplines* 2, no. 1 (1964): 47–80.

Nelkin, Meyer. "Survivors of Nazi Concentration Camps: Psychopathology and Views of Psychopathology." *Canadian Journal of Psychiatric Nursing* 20, no. 6 (1979): 560–8.

Neumeier, Beate. "Kindertransport: Childhood Trauma and Diaspora Experience." In *Jewish Women's Writing of the 1990s and Beyond in Great Britain and the United States*, edited by Ulrike Behlau and Bernhard Reitz, 61–70. Trier: Wissenschaftlicher Verlag, 2004.

———. *"Kindertransport*: Memory, Identity and the British-Jewish Diaspora." In *Diaspora and Multiculturalism: Common Traditions and New Developments*, edited by Monika Fludernik, 83–112. Amsterdam and New York: Rodopi, 2003.

Newman, Lisa. "Emotional Disturbance in Children of Holocaust Survivors." *Social Casework: The Journal of Contemporary Social Work* 60, no. 1 (1979): 43–50.

Niederland, William G. "The Clinical Aftereffects of the Holocaust in Survivors and Their Offspring." In *The Psychological Perspectives of the Holocaust and of Its Aftermath*, edited by Randolph L. Braham, 45–52. New York: Columbia University Press, 1988.

———. "Clinical Observations on the 'Survivor Syndrome'." *International Journal of Psychoanalysis* 49, parts. 2 and 3 (1968): 313–15.

———. "The Problem of the Survivor." *Journal of the Hillside Hospital* 10 (1961): 233–47.

———. "Psychiatric Disorders Among Persecution Victims." *Journal of Nervous and Mental Disease* 139, no. 5 (1964): 458–74.

———. "The Survivor Syndrome: Further Observations and Dimensions." *Journal of the American Psychoanalytic Association* 29 (1981): 413–25.

Peskin, Harvey. "Observations on the First International Conference on Children of Holocaust Survivors." *Family Process* 20, no. 4 (1981): 391–4.

Peskin, Harvey, Nanette C. Auerhahn, and Dori Laub. "The Second Holocaust: Therapeutic Rescue When Life Threatens." *Journal of Personal and Interpersonal Loss* 2 (1997): 1–26.

Phillips, Russell E. "Impact of Nazi Holocaust on Children of Survivors." *American Journal of Psychotherapy* 32, no. 3 (1978): 370–8.

Pilorget, Jean-Paul. "Un théâtre pavé d'horreur et de folie. *Toujours l'orage* de Enzo Cormann." In *Témoignages de l'après-Auschwitz dans la littérature Juive-Française d'aujourd'hui*, edited by Annelise Schulte Nordholt, 219–30. Amsterdam and New York: Rodopi, 2008.

Plunka, Gene A. *Staging Holocaust Resistance*. New York: Palgrave Macmillan, 2012.

Porter, Jack Nusan. "Social-Psychological Aspects of the Holocaust." In *Encountering the Holocaust: An Interdisciplinary Survey*, edited by Byron L. Sherwin and Susan G. Ament, 189–222. Chicago: Impact Press, 1979.

Rakoff, Vivian. "Long-term Effects of the Concentration Camp Experience." *Viewpoints* 1 (1966): 17–22.

Rappaport, Ernest A. "Beyond Traumatic Neurosis: A Psychoanalytic Study of Late Reactions to the Concentration Camp Trauma." *International Journal of Psycho-Analysis* 49, part 4 (1968): 719–31.

———. "Survivor Guilt." *Midstream* 17, no. 7 (1971): 41–7.

Reuven, Ben Yosef. "'Bells and Trains' by Yehuda Amichai." *Hebrew Book Review*, Spring 1969, 36–41.

Rieck, Miriam. "The Psychological State of Holocaust Survivors' Offspring: An Epidemiological and Psychodiagnostic Study." *International Journal of Behavioral Development* 17, no. 4 (1994): 649–67.

Robbin, Sheryl. "Life in the Camps: The Psychological Dimension." In *Genocide: Critical Issues of The Holocaust*, edited by Alex Grobman and Daniel Landes, 236–42. Los Angeles: Simon Wiesenthal Center, 1983.

Robinson, Shalom. "Late Effects of Persecution in Persons Who – As Children or Young Adolescents – Survived Nazi Occupation in Europe." *Israel Annals of Psychiatry and Related Disciplines* 17 (1979): 209–14.

Robinson, Shalom et al. "The Late Effects of Nazi Persecution Among Elderly Holocaust Survivors." *Acta Psychiatrica Scandinavica* 82 (1991): 311–15.

Robinson, Shalom and Judith Hemmendinger. "Psychosocial Adjustment 30 Years Later of People Who Were in Nazi Concentration Camps as Children." In *Stress and Anxiety*, vol. 8, edited by Charles D. Spielberger and Irwin G. Sarason, 397–400. Washington and New York: Hemisphere, 1982.

Robinson, Shalom, M. Rapaport-Bar-Sever, and J. Rapaport. "The Present State of People Who Survived the Holocaust as Children." *Acta Psychiatrica Scandinavica* 89 (1994): 242–5.

Rose, Susan L., and John Garske. "Family Environment, Adjustment, and Coping Among Children of Holocaust Survivors: A Comparative Investigation." *American Journal of Orthopsychiatry* 57, no. 3 (1987): 332–44.

Rosen, Jules et al. "Sleep Disturbances in Survivors of the Nazi Holocaust." *American Journal of Psychiatry* 148, no. 1 (1991): 62–6.

Rosenbaum, Thane. "Art and Atrocity in a Post-9/11 World." In *Jewish American and Holocaust Literature*, edited by Alan L. Berger and Gloria L. Cronin, 125–36. Albany: State University of New York Press, 2004.

———. *Second Hand Smoke*. New York: St. Martin's Press, 1999.

Roth, Ari. *Andy and the Shadows*. New York: The Barbara Hogenson Agency, 2013.

Rubin, Janet E. *Voices: Plays for Studying the Holocaust*. Lanham, MD: Scarecrow, 1999.

Russell, Alex. "Late Psychosocial Consequences in Concentration Camp Survivor Families." *American Journal of Orthopsychiatry* 44, no. 4 (1974): 611–19.

———. "Late Psychosocial Consequences of the Holocaust Experience on Survivor Families: The Second Generation." *International Journal of Family Psychiatry* 3 (1982): 375–402.

Samuels, Diane. *Diane Samuels' Kindertransport: The Author's Guide to the Play*. London: Nick Hern, 2014.

————. *Kindertransport.* New York: Plume, 1995.

Schick, Elizabeth A., ed. "Amichai, Yehuda." In *Current Biography Yearbook.* New York and Dublin: H.W. Wilson, 1998.

Schmolling, Paul. "Human Reactions to the Nazi Concentration Camps: A Summing Up." *Journal of Human Stress* 10 (1984): 108–20.

Schumacher, Claude, ed. *Staging the Holocaust: The Shoah in Drama and Performance.* Cambridge: Cambridge University Press, 1998.

Ségal, Gilles. *The Puppetmaster of Lodz.* Translated by Sara O'Connor. New York: Samuel French, 1989.

Sheiness, Marsha Lee. *Second Hand Smoke.* n.p. Photocopy. Holocaust Theater Archive.

Sholiton, Faye. *The Interview.* New York: Speert Publishing, 2012.

Sigal, John J., et al. "Some Second-Generation Effects of Survival of the Nazi Persecution." *American Journal of Orthopsychiatry* 43, no. 3 (1973): 320–7.

Sigal, John J., and Vivian Rakoff. "Concentration Camp Survival: A Pilot Study of Effects on the Second Generation." *Canadian Journal of Psychiatry* 16 (1971): 393–7.

Sigal, John J., and Morton Weinfeld. *Trauma and Rebirth: Intergenerational Effects of the Holocaust.* New York and Westport, CT: Praeger, 1989.

Skloot, Robert, ed. *The Theatre of the Holocaust*, vol. 2. Madison: University of Wisconsin Press, 1999.

Slipp, Samuel. "The Children of Survivors of Nazi Concentration Camps: A Pilot Study of the Intergenerational Transmission of Psychic Trauma." In *Group Therapy 1979: An Overview*, edited by Lewis R. Wolberg and Marvin L. Aronson, 197–204. New York: Stratton Intercontinental Medical Book Corp., 1979.

Smelser, Neil J. "Psychological Trauma and Cultural Trauma." In *Cultural Trauma and Collective Identity*, edited by Jeffrey C. Alexander et al., 31–59. Berkeley: University of California Press, 2004.

Solkoff, Norman. "Children of Survivors of the Nazi Holocaust: A Critical Review of the Literature." *American Journal of Orthopsychiatry* 51, no. 1 (1981): 29–42.

————. "Children of Survivors of the Nazi Holocaust: A Critical Review of the Literature." *American Journal of Orthopsychiatry* 62, no. 3 (1992): 342–58.

Sonnenberg, Stephen M. "Workshop Report: Children of Survivors." *Journal of the American Psychoanalytic Association* 22 (1974): 200–4.

Sterling, Eric J. "Rescue and Trauma: Jewish Children and the Kindertransports During the Holocaust." In *Children and War: A Historical Anthology*, edited by James Marten, 63–74. New York and London: New York University Press, 2002.

Strauss, Hans. "Neuropsychiatric Disturbances After National-Socialist Persecution." *Proceedings: Virchow Medical Society* 16 (1957): 95–104.

Tas, J. "Psychical Disorders Among Inmates of Concentration Camps and Repatriates." *Psychiatric Quarterly* 25, no. 4 (1951): 679–90.

Taub, Michael. "Ben Zion Tomer." In *Holocaust Literature: An Encyclopedia of Writers and Their Work*, vol. 2, edited by S. Lillian Kremer, 1266–8. New York and London: Routledge, 2003.

Thygesen, Paul. "The Concentration Camp Syndrome." *Danish Medical Bulletin* 27, no. 5 (1980): 224–8.

Tomer, Ben-Zion. "*Children of the Shadows.*" Translated by Hillel Halkin. In *Israeli Holocaust Drama*, edited by Michael Taub, 127–85. Syracuse: Syracuse University Press, 1996.

Trautman, Edgar. "Psychiatric and Sociological Effects of Nazi Atrocities on Survivors of the Extermination Camps." *Journal of the American Association for Social Psychiatry* (September–December 1961): 118–22.

Trossman, Bernard. "Adolescent Children of Concentration Camp Survivors." *Canadian Psychiatric Association Journal* 13, no. 2 (1968): 121–3.

Valent, Paul. "Resilience in Child Survivors of the Holocaust: Toward the Concept of Resilience." *Psychoanalytic Review* 85, no. 4 (1998): 517–35.

van der Kolk, Bessel A. "The Psychological Consequences of Overwhelming Life Experiences." In *Psychological Trauma*, edited by Bessel A. van der Kolk, 1–30. Washington, DC: American Psychiatric Press, 1987.

Venzlaff, Ulrich. "Mental Disorders Resulting From Racial Persecution Outside of Concentration Camps." *International Journal of Social Psychiatry* 10, no. 3 (1964): 177–83.

Vierling, Ronald John. *"Adam's Daughter."* In *Rising From the Ashes. Vol. 1: Beyond the Abyss*, 7–69. n.p.: Xlibris Corporation, 2010.

Wanderman, Erica. "Children and Families of Holocaust Survivors: A Psychological Overview." In *Living After the Holocaust: Reflections by the Post-War Generation*, edited by Lucy Y. Steinitz and David M. Szonyi, 115–23. New York: Bloch, 1976.

Wardi, Dina. *Memorial Candles: Children of the Holocaust.* Translated by Naomi Goldblum. London and New York: Tavistock/Routledge, 1992.

Wdowinski, David. *And We Are Not Saved.* New York: Philosophical Library, 1963.

Weinfeld, Morton, John J. Sigal, and William W. Eaton. "Long-Term Effects of the Holocaust on Selected Social Attitudes and Behaviors of Survivors: A Cautionary Note." *Social Forces* 60, no. 1 (1981): 1–19.

Wiesel, Elie. *Legends of Our Time.* New York: Holt, Rinehart and Winston, 1968.

Wilson, Arnold and Erika Fromm. "Aftermath of the Concentration Camp: The Second Generation." *Journal of the American Academy of Psychoanalysis* 10, no. 2 (1982): 289–313.

Wilson, John P., Zev Harel, and Boaz Kahana, eds. *Human Adaptation to Extreme Stress: From the Holocaust to Vietnam.* New York and London: Plenum Press, 1988.

Winkler, Guenther Emil. "Neuropsychiatric Symptoms in Survivors of Concentration Camps." *Journal of Social Therapy* 5, no. 4 (1959): 281–90.

Winnik, H.Z. "Contribution to Symposium on Psychic Traumatization Through Social Catastrophe." *International Journal of Psycho-Analysis* 49, parts 2 and 3 (1968): 298–301.

———. "Further Comments Concerning Problems of Late Psychopathological Effects of Nazi-Persecution and Their Therapy." *Israel Annals of Psychiatry and Related Disciplines* 5, no. 1 (1967): 1–16.

———. "Psychiatric Disturbances of Holocaust ('Shoa') Survivors." *Israel Annals of Psychiatry and Related Disciplines* 5 (1967): 91–100.

Yehuda, Rachel et al. "Depressive Features in Holocaust Survivors With Post-Traumatic Stress Disorder." *Journal of Traumatic Stress* 7, no. 4 (1994): 699–704.

———. "Individual Differences in Posttraumatic Stress Disorder Symptom Profiles in Holocaust Survivors in Concentration Camps or in Hiding." *Journal of Traumatic Stress* 10, no. 3 (1997): 453–63.

INDEX